IF WE
HAD
KNOWN

IF WE HAD KNOWN

ELISE JUSKA

GRAND CENTRAL
PUBLISHING

NEW YORK   BOSTON

Copyright © 2018 by Elise Juska

Jacket design by Elizabeth Connor. Jacket photo © Adam Crowley/Blend Images. Cover copyright © 2018 by Hachette Book Group, Inc.

Grand Central Publishing

Hachette Book Group

1290 Avenue of the Americas, New York, NY 10104

grandcentralpublishing.com

twitter.com/grandcentralpub

First Edition: April 2018

Grand Central Publishing is a division of Hachette Book Group, Inc. The Grand Central Publishing name and logo is a trademark of Hachette Book Group, Inc.

The publisher is not responsible for websites (or their content) that are not owned by the publisher.

The Hachette Speakers Bureau provides a wide range of authors for speaking events. To find out more, go to www.hachettespeakersbureau.com or call (866) 376-6591.

Emoji icons supplied by EmojiOne

Library of Congress Cataloging-in-Publication Data has been applied for.

ISBNs: 978-1-4555-6177-3 (hardcover); 978-1-4555-6175-9 (ebook)

Printed in the United States of America

LSC-H

10 9 8 7 6 5 4 3 2 1

For Bill Hollenbach

Part One

One

It was an unseasonably hot late summer day in Maine when Maggie's daughter read about the shooting. The kind of hot you could sense just by looking: the sky that flat, empty blue. Along the back of Maggie's yard, the trees stood motionless and silent, thick green spruces and pale, thin-stemmed birches. The heat was like a haze, a filter through which the world appeared grayer, more obscure, like fog on glass.

It was just before noon, a Friday. In a little over a week, Maggie would be back to teaching, her life built around her classes and crowded with her students, but these final days of August were still long and shapeless, defined by the immediacy of Anna's leaving. Maggie looked up from where she knelt in her garden, pushed a lock of hair off her damp brow, and surveyed her property: a shaggy two acres strewn with rocks and wildflowers, an old red barn, woods on three sides. Later, looking back, the stillness of the trees that day would seem different—tense, knowing, braced for something—but in the moment, they appeared only sleepy in the heat.

Maggie tore a final handful of weeds from the garden, pushed herself to standing, closed and latched the fence gate, and headed for the back door. Inside, she let the screen flap shut behind her. The house was quiet. Anna was upstairs, packing. Maggie spied a few things—down comforter, windbreaker, old scuffed leather boots—in a pile by the front door. She had just turned on the faucet and was rinsing dirt from her hands when Anna shouted: "Mom?"

"Yes?" Maggie called back over the rush of water.

"Mom!"

Even from a floor below, Maggie could hear the telltale edge in her voice. "What?" she said, twisting the faucet off, and paused, leaning on the knob.

"Did you ever have Nathan Dugan?"

Right away Maggie recognized the name. She prided herself on her memory of her students—would argue she could summon up any one of them given ten seconds—and with this one she didn't miss a beat. "He was in my comp," Maggie said. She straightened and stood still, waiting, hands dripping over the sink. She heard movement in Anna's bedroom, footsteps hurrying down the hall. "Why?"

"So you knew him?" Anna said, louder as she ran downstairs.

"Of course," Maggie replied, calmly, but felt a kernel of worry. "He was my student." She pressed her wet palms to her jeans. "What is it, Anna?" she said as her daughter rushed into the room. She was still wearing the clothes she'd slept in—old T-shirt, plaid pajama bottoms—hair tied in a loose ponytail. But her expression was awake, alarmed: This was more than nerves, Maggie thought. Her eyes were wide, almost pleading, cheeks pale beneath her summer freckles. She carried her laptop under her arm. As she set it on the table, she kept her eyes on Maggie's face.

FATAL SHOOTING SPREE IN REED, ME MALL

AT LEAST THREE DEAD

SUSPECTED GUNMAN STUDENT AT CENTRAL MAINE STATE

"Oh my God," Maggie said. She could hear the stillness in her voice; she was conscious of the body's instinct to freeze, flatten and protect itself. "Oh my God," she repeated. It had happened again, happened here, just fifteen minutes down the road. As Anna scrolled down the screen, Maggie took in a photo of two teenagers standing outside the mall, hugging. A mother clutching her baby, her face such a raw mask of pain that Maggie felt indignant it had been put online. And suddenly: Nathan Dugan. *Alleged gunman takes own life*, the caption read. The picture was just his face. It was him, no question, though he looked considerably older—older than the number of years (four? five?) it had been since he was in her class. He was bigger now, heavier. His face seemed thicker. The buzz cut he'd worn as a freshman had grown past his ears. He had two faint lines of mustache, a cap with some kind of cartoon animal on it. His chin was raised, eyes angled down toward the camera, although his expression looked preoccupied, as if residing in his own private world. It was the thing that looked most the same about him. He'd worn that same look in class.

"Is that him?" Anna asked. She had folded herself into a kitchen chair, arms wrapped around her knees.

"That's him."

"Was he creepy?"

"Creepy," Maggie repeated. "I wouldn't say that."

Usually, this would have prompted a roll of the eyes—Maggie was a stickler for language, always looking for the best, the most accurate word—but her daughter had fallen quiet, reverent before the faint glow of the screen.

"What was he like?"

"He was—different." A simplistic word, and an obvious one. Her mind roamed, looking for a better way, the right way, to describe him. "He wasn't too engaged," she said. Other details were returning. The way, during class, Nathan always kept his eyes on the desktop, jiggling one shoe—heavy brown boots with thick, ridged soles—on the dusty tiles. The pair of headphones he'd kept around his neck and, the minute class was over, clamped back on his ears. He sometimes brought his dog to class—a chocolate Lab, who slept with its flank pressed against the radiator. To Maggie's recollection, Nathan never acknowledged the dog, and she didn't either.

"He didn't seem to care much about being there," she said. "He was restless."

"Restless how?" Anna asked. "Like anxious?"

"No, I don't think so," Maggie said, with a glance at her daughter's face. "More like—" She paused. "Distracted. Checked out."

She remembered how, if he spoke, which was rare, Nathan never raised his hand. He'd called her Mrs. Daley, even though she always told students to call her Maggie. She remembered his essays too—not the content so much as the look of them, long unbroken paragraphs and small, stifled font.

"He wasn't really a part of things," she said. "Part of the group." She thought again. "He was hard to get to know."

"Creepy, you mean."

She remembered his coat: a heavy olive-green parka with a hood trimmed in dirty, peppery gray fur. In winter, he'd never take it off. The coat would fill the small desk, the hood blocking Maggie's view of the students behind him and giving the permanent impression that class was about to end. With another student, she would have said, *Relax and stay awhile*, but with Nathan, she was certain she'd said nothing—his response would have been too literal, too humorless. And the coat, surely, would have stayed on, in so doing growing only more visible to the rest of them.

"Was he a good student?" Anna said, her eyes still on the laptop.

"In a way," Maggie said. "He was diligent, as I recall."

"Did he have friends?"

"Not that I knew of." She studied Nathan Dugan's face. His cheeks looked rougher, acne-scarred maybe, though it was hard to tell on the screen. "But I wouldn't have known, necessarily."

"Did you like him?"

Maggie did not think of her students in those terms, made a point of it, like parents with their children. But in fact: No, she hadn't liked him.

"I don't think of my students that way," she said.

From the living room, Anna's cell phone started ringing: the aftermath beginning. Outside, remarkably enough, the world looked as it had just moments before. The sky seemed muted, absent of everything: wind, colors, clouds. Against all that emptiness, the old red barn stood proud, near pristine, etched starkly against the pale afternoon.

Freshman Composition was a required course for all students at Central Maine State University, so it was one that most faculty resented teaching. It was invariably populated by freshmen who didn't want to be there— athletes, slackers, diligent but uninterested math and science majors—but Maggie didn't mind. She liked the challenge of convincing them to love a class they thought they didn't want to take. She prided herself on coaxing even the most passive among them to care about their writing. *Write about what matters*, she insisted. *Anything else is a waste of time.*

And they did—just last semester Tyler Barrington, a thickly bearded, 250-pound eighteen-year-old Forestry major and volunteer firefighter, produced lovely elegies to nature. Stacey Cole, who never spoke in class, wrote a moving description of silently building a campfire with her equally silent dad. After twenty-eight years, Maggie could rely on the arc of a semester: the way, in the beginning, the freshmen would be tentative, wary, fifteen variations on insecurity—the glibness, the shyness, the overwrought machismo; was there any teenage behavior without insecurity at the root?—but as the weeks passed, they gained confidence in their work. They came to care about their classmates' essays, respond to them with earnest nods and furrowed brows, script careful comments in the margins. Maggie took them seriously, so they took themselves seriously. (This, she maintained, was the key to being a good teacher: Care so much it's impossible for the students to not care back.)

At the end of fifteen weeks, her students' growth was palpable. On the last day, Maggie always delivered a speech. *I'm proud of what you've accomplished*, she told them, voice thick with feeling. *I will truly miss this class.* Often the students lingered, making promises to stay in touch, and Maggie smiled, knowing what they didn't: that despite all good intentions, the course was done. Fifteen weeks: a closed loop. The nostalgic fever of that final hour wouldn't last, and shouldn't; they would head back to their lives, remember the class fondly, and that was fine. The class would begin again. Still, Maggie sometimes felt a sharp sense of loss, almost like grief, driving home on the evening of the last class, final papers huddled in shopping bags on her backseat.

The irony was, outside the classroom, she was not a particularly emotional person. *Unshakable*—this was one of the more memorable words Tom had lobbed at her, out in the barn, where Anna wouldn't hear. He hadn't meant it kindly. *You're so closed off so rigid incapable of seeing things any other*—one subject bled into the next, spilling onto the old barn floor. Maggie had been stunned, gutted. Tom had always been easygoing, gentle—passive, even—but suddenly the muck that had been collecting silently inside him for seventeen years exploded like a burst pipe. There was another woman. Naturally. A social worker, from Portland. *She's helped me realize how unfulfilled I am*, he said, *how lonely*, and Maggie had not helped dispel these accusations by letting herself go empty, floating toward the ceiling, listening with a soothing sort of detachment, a faint humming sound in her ears.

With students, though, Maggie took comfort in knowing that things would never get so messy. She could state her feelings safely, framed by the contents of their essays, the language and the themes. They were the students and she the teacher—it could go only so far. Even when her marriage was collapsing, and the first true glints of Anna's anxiety were surfacing, and Maggie drove home down the dark wooded roads waiting for the evening when her husband's unhappiness solidified into something—suitcase standing by the door, Anna weeping on the porch—even then Maggie had relied on this structure: Whatever else was happening with her family, in the classroom she could maintain a certain pose, fervent and energetic, tough but affectionate, never breaking character, for ninety minutes focused on nothing but the lesson, on the welfare of the bright young people assembled before her. It was one of the pleasures of teaching. You could forget everything else.

★ ★ ★

What they knew so far was this: The gun was an AR-15. At eleven thirty, Nathan had entered the Millview Mall through the entrance by the food court, carrying a duffel bag holding two semiautomatic weapons and five spare magazines. He was a fifth-year senior, due to graduate in December, an Engineering major. (Maggie wondered about the reasons for the extra semester—failed classes, unfulfilled credits? Or something more fraught?) There was no word yet on why he'd done it. On the news, the same photo of him was shown repeatedly, over audio of the frantic 911 calls: *There's someone shooting! I think he just shot someone!* He'd killed at least three people and critically wounded another. The police had found him dead at the scene.

There were live aerial shots of the mall, of people who had been hiding in stores and in stockrooms now running into the parking lot where loved ones had gathered, clutching text messages confirming they were safe. In interviews, survivors were alternately shocked and weeping. They described the chaos, people huddling under tables in the food court or racing for the exits, the trampling of limbs. The sounds of screaming, then the tense, muffled quiet as they tried not to draw attention to themselves. There was the mother Maggie had seen on the Internet. She'd sat on the floor behind a jewelry kiosk, she said, breast-feeding her baby to keep her from making any sound; the baby now slept in her arms. Another woman had been in a Sears dressing room, and as she ran to the food court to find her son, she said, the security tag kept setting off alarms. The food court had been crowded, everyone said. The whole mall was crowded. Ninety degrees out. The mall was air-conditioned: It was someplace to be.

From Maggie's living room, fifteen minutes down the road, the helicopters over the mall were a faint but steady rattle. The kitchen phone rang frequently, the old rotary on the wall by the back door. Most of these calls were from Anna's classmates' mothers—not women Maggie was particularly close to, but they all checked in, a tribe of parents accounting for their children—while Anna hunkered down with her phone in the bay window, checking with friends to see if anyone knew anyone who had been there. It was not impossible, Maggie knew. Especially in the summer, Anna and her classmates were at the mall all the time. She found herself grateful, for once, that none of them rose before noon.

Before long, Anna had heard something: Kim's little brother's best friend, CJ. He'd been working at the Sbarro in the food court. Then, minutes later: a junior, someone named Laura, a friend of Janie's from the basketball team. They were both home now, Anna said, they were okay, but they had been there. Her voice was trembling, but Maggie nodded, kept nodding, trying to keep her as calm as possible. She could see how, for Anna, these personal connections were bringing the tragedy into ghastly focus, and was acutely aware of the anxieties that lay barely dormant inside her. In two days, Anna would be leaving, and Maggie was desperate to keep her from getting thrown off-course. Over the past year, she'd watched as her daughter pieced herself back together, as if seeing the path to college, she'd finally had the incentive to get better. She'd gotten off the Lexapro. She'd stopped starving herself, gained back some of the weight she'd lost. She had applied early to Bradford College in Boston and been accepted, the work ethic that had at times seemed obsessive, even symptomatic, paying off.

It was nearly three thirty when Maggie's cell phone finally buzzed once: *call me*, the screen said. Maggie glanced at her daughter, texting feverishly, then crept upstairs. "Hi," she said, and closed the bedroom door.

"Can you believe this goddamn thing?"

Maggie sank to the edge of the bed. It was still unmade from that morning, covers peeled back neatly at one corner, like a tabbed page of a book. "I know."

"Walked right into the mall and started shooting. Fucking Christ."

It was one of the things she appreciated about Robert: his directness, lack of filter. Tom was always so even-tempered that when finally he'd burst she was blindsided, but Robert's outrage relaxed her, most of the time.

"It's terrible," she said, her mind roaming for another word, a bigger word, one that would do the thing justice. "It's—unthinkable."

"You didn't have him, did you?"

In the open window, the curtains hung limp as tongues. The air didn't move. The house wasn't air-conditioned, so on rare days like this one, the heat collected like tide pools in the rooms upstairs.

"As a matter of fact," Maggie said, "I can't believe it, but I did." Then she laughed, though she wasn't sure why.

"Me too."

"Did you?" The sharpness of her relief took her by surprise. She sat up straighter. "And?"

"And nothing," Robert said. Maggie could picture how he looked, agitated, pushing one hand through his hair. "I checked my files. He was in my 101 four years ago and I don't remember a damn thing about him. A future killer sitting in my classroom and his name doesn't even ring a bell until I dredge up an old roster and see it sitting there." Robert was clearly bothered, but his lapse was justified. Introduction to American Government was enormous, a lecture course with a reputation for being one of the simplest routes to satisfying a Gen Ed. The class was so large and so popular that it was held in a small theater. There was no attendance policy. Exams were fact-based, objective, dots to darken and feed through a machine—it was nearly impossible to really get to know students in a class like this.

"It's different." She spread her free hand in her lap, bare and freckled, the nails rimmed with dirt. "A class like yours."

"Is it?"

"It's a lecture. It's so much more impersonal."

"What class did you have him in?"

"Comp, of course."

"Why of course?"

"Does this seem like a kid who was taking upper-level writing classes?"

"Why? Because he was a psychopath?"

"No," she said evenly. "Because he was an Engineering major. He wouldn't have taken any writing class but mine."

"You never know, though, do you?"

Maggie didn't reply; she was generalizing, yes, but she knew she wasn't wrong. She stared at the wall above her dresser, where the ceiling sloped steeply downward and the old flowered wallpaper was wrinkled and swollen, stained at the seams. Melted snow had crept through the roof last winter. Five, six feet of snow. Record-setting snow. Route 18 had been a tunnel of darkness, the ten-foot drifts on either side blocking the sun.

"So he was a freshman when you had him," Robert said.

The connection wavered, and Maggie angled slightly toward the window. The reception in here was notoriously shaky; Anna frequently complained that the bay window in the living room was the only reliable spot in the house. Before Robert, this hadn't affected her, as Maggie had never used a cell phone—she despised the cumbersome effort of texting, the electric warmth of metal against her cheek—but she didn't want to talk with him in front of Anna. "Right," she said. "A freshman."

"Was he a whack job?"

"I wouldn't call him that," she said, bristling at the term.

"What would you call him?"

Through the cast-iron grate in the floor, Maggie heard the low hum of the news, the sharp dip and rise of Anna's voice. "Well, I don't know," she said. "It was years ago, after all. Four years ago."

"Point taken," Robert said. Then, thankfully, moved on. Maggie liked this about him too: He never prodded beneath the surface of a thing, wondering what was simmering there unsaid. In part, this was just his personality—big and broad and external, not attuned to nuance—but it was also because their relationship was still relatively new. Because he didn't really know her. He wouldn't know, for example, that she never forgot a student.

"This is going to be hard on the school," he said then. "Enrollment will take a hit."

It was just the kind of thing Robert thought about and Maggie didn't. "But it didn't happen on campus," she said.

"Doesn't matter. He was a student. A current student. A killer in our midst, and nobody picked up on it."

Maggie gave a short laugh. "Sounds like an awful TV movie," she said.

"Bad for business is what it is," Robert replied, which struck her as crass, though he was probably right; after four semesters on campus, Robert had a keener grasp of university politics than she did after almost thirty years. For better or worse, Maggie had always stayed away from all that: She focused on the students, cared little about the rest.

Then he said, "I wish I could be with you right now."

It was disorienting on such a day, in such a moment, but Maggie felt a low flicker of desire. She closed her eyes and pictured Robert there beside her, his sure hands and strong shoulders. His thick hair, still brown but for two blasts of gray at the temples. Tom was a big man too, but lanky and unassuming. Robert was physical, vital, all volume and energy. He rode his bike to campus, swept her up in long kisses. He spoke what was on his mind.

"I want to see you," he said. "I want you, period."

She opened her eyes. "Well, you know," she replied. She let the words just hang there, bloated with implication—*well, you know, get a divorce. Well, you know, move out of your house.* Robert and his wife were separated but still living together—he occupying one part of the house and she another—though Maggie had played no part in their separation (by the time she met him, on a committee of all things, Robert had already been sleeping in his guest bed). He'd assured her repeatedly that the marriage was over, he just didn't feel he could leave yet. His wife was fragile, possibly depressed. He felt a responsibility to her; he was the reason they had moved to Stafford. Maggie felt uneasy about the arrangement, but understood it, even admired Robert for putting his wife's feelings first. She knew, though, that other people would make assumptions. It was why they never went out in public, why they met mostly in Robert's (larger, less conspicuous) office in Strathmere Hall. This summer, they had barely seen each other, with Anna home and neither of them teaching. A small town, a college campus: One never knew how things could be perceived.

Now he asked, "When does that daughter of yours leave?"

His tone was playful, but still, it bothered her. He knew she didn't like when he referred to Anna, not even lightly. "That's not what's keeping us from being together," she said.

"Oh, Maggie. A joke." He sighed. "I just wish I could see you, that's all."

"Well, I'm available," she said, but cringed at the neediness in her voice. Most of the time, being the one who was legitimately unattached was a safe berth, a role that reassured her. Other times, like now, it made her feel insecure, a high school girl waiting for an invitation to the prom.

"You know I hate this too," Robert said. "But I wish you'd let me in a little."

Outside, the maple stood red-tipped, motionless in the heat. Maggie didn't know how to reply. Tom had accused her of being closed off, but this was different. To put herself out there would be reckless, foolish. Until Robert left his wife, moved out of his house, there was no future here. Whatever he and Maggie were doing together remained within limits; sometimes their whole relationship felt scarcely real.

Then he said, "Okay then," with a suddenness that made clear Suzanne had just entered the room. "Thanks for calling," he added, and like that, he was gone. *Call Ended*, the screen confirmed. She felt stung, though she had no right. She'd told Robert she wasn't comfortable talking on the phone with his wife in earshot; even if they were separated, it seemed unnecessarily cruel. She placed the phone on one knee and fixed on the old oak dresser, the one that had been her parents' and listed to one side. She pictured Robert's house, a few blocks from the college, an elaborate Victorian she had several times driven by, not accidentally, on her way home from school. Pictured Suzanne appearing in his office doorway, sensing somehow he was on the phone. Maggie had seen her only once, at the university holiday party the previous winter, tall and pale, a native Southerner not cut out for the Maine cold. She'd spent all night by her husband's side. At the time, Maggie had known Robert only a little, but found him so dynamic that she'd been surprised to find he'd married someone so obviously uncomfortable at a party. Her shoulders were slightly stooped, as if curved permanently inward. *Fragile*, Robert had described her, and Maggie had thought, even in that glimpse, she saw what he meant.

Then again: There were two sides to any story. She'd heard this from Jim Whittier, the couples counselor in whose office she and Tom had spent seven excruciating hours. She preached it to her freshmen every semester, when teaching the significant personal experience essay— *everything is a matter of perspective*, she told them. *Every story of what happened is just a version of what happened. Memory is subjective. Fact and truth are two different things.*

Maggie closed her eyes. She was overwhelmed by the desire to lie down. Robert had stayed here at her house just once, early on. A Saturday in March, when Anna's weekend with Tom coincided with Suzanne's visit to her family in South Carolina. It had snowed, and they had stayed inside all weekend, in bed mostly, emerging to make coffee and feed the fire and retrieve the paper—ordinary things, but off-limits they had taken on the quality of a dream. Maggie had sworn, after Tom's affair, she would never be the other woman, and technically, she wasn't. Still, late Sunday morning, when Robert's car drove away, the sight of it had sent a storm of heat to her cheeks. How exposed they had been: Robert's brazen red Jeep rambling down her snowy driveway, flanked with winter maples, visible as a cardinal in a bare tree.

Over the course of the afternoon, the Nathan Dugan story grew more terrible and strange. An hour before the shooting, Nathan had posted a video on YouTube, describing his planned attack. The video was titled: *Greatness Comes to Those Who Wait.* The news had the sense not to show it—Maggie was especially thankful, with Anna watching—but reported that Nathan had been planning something bigger. In the food court, he'd fired thirty rounds and was headed toward the south end of the mall, with the Sears and the carousel, when the sirens outside grew audible and he turned the gun on himself.

The assault rifle, they reported, had been purchased at the Walmart adjacent to the mall on Route 18. Nathan had been employed there as a part-time stocker since March; he'd been fired the week before. According to the manager, he'd been making customers uneasy. On two occasions, he'd followed shoppers around the store. *Sort of like policing them*, the manager said, threading one hand through his hair. *I told him he couldn't act that way.* He explained that, when Nathan got defensive, he'd told him not to come back. *He was angry*, he said, stunned-looking. *But I had no idea he was this far gone.*

Inside Nathan's bedroom closet, police found fourteen firearms, several rounds of spare ammunition, and tactical gear including assault vests and silencers. He had been living with his mother, Marielle Dugan, in Reed, in the small, depressed neighborhood that sat behind the mall. The mother worked at the Big Lots in Millville. The parents had been divorced since Nathan was a child. He'd been raised by his mother, in New Hampshire; his father lived in Florida—this triggered a memory for Maggie. An essay Nathan had written for her class. About love for his father, maybe, a bonding trip they'd taken together. Hiking? Camping? Something. A former neighbor from New Hampshire reported that Nathan was often walking his dog, or with his mother. *You never saw him with kids his age.* This same neighbor recalled him patrolling the neighborhood with a BB gun, shooting mailboxes and trees.

The guns in Nathan's closet had all been purchased legally, over the past few years, some at the Walmart and others at a gun shop on Standish Road. Local news showed a picture of the gun shop: a red clapboard box, an American flag. There was a shot of Nathan's house too, small and square, painted an incongruously cheerful lemon yellow. A clip of Nathan's mother, standing on what appeared to be the front porch, looking shocked and small as she was bombarded with questions. *He's a good boy.* Another woman, no evident authority on anything, spat into a microphone, asserting she didn't believe any mother couldn't have known there was a serious problem. Easy to blame the mother, Maggie thought.

"Okay," Maggie said, turning the TV off. "Dinner."

Anna was still curled in the window, glued to her phone. "Really?" she said, glancing up. "That feels wrong."

"What does?"

"Acting like this is a normal day."

"Even on an abnormal day," Maggie said, "one must eat." She didn't feel like eating either, but hoped the routine—the food—would be good for Anna. She retreated to the kitchen and pulled the chicken off the stovetop, slid two potatoes from the oven, went to set the pans on the table. Then she thought better of it and filled two plates.

"I'm not very hungry," Anna said from the kitchen doorway. Her cheek was pink where she'd peeled it from the windowpane.

"You haven't eaten all day."

"I know. I've been too upset."

In the past, Maggie might have pressed the issue, but today she'd let it slide. In forty-eight hours, Anna would be starting a new life at college, and Maggie wanted to send her into it with as much confidence as she could.

"Well, you can keep me company, then," Maggie said, pulling back a chair.

Anna dropped into her seat at the kitchen table and set her phone beside her, briefly considering her food. Maggie studied her daughter's face surreptitiously, felt a pang of tenderness at the beads of sweat gathering in the tiny blond hairs above her lip. The kitchen was too warm. Thoughtless, to turn the oven on. Still, she began slicing into her chicken as Anna looked up, saying, "Did I tell you the latest about Laura Mack?"

In the absence of information about the victims, Laura's story was the main anecdote to have emerged from the afternoon; she'd overheard Anna rehashing it several times.

"You did." Maggie nodded. "Janie's friend."

"But did I tell you she heard the gunshots?"

"No," Maggie said, and paused, fork in midair. "No, I don't think so."

"She actually heard the shooting. And the people, you know, screaming. Dying, maybe." Her eyes welled with tears, a quick pool that surfaced then receded, and she shook her head hard. "I can't stop thinking about it."

This was not an idle comment; Maggie understood how her daughter's brain could get stuck on a thing, a needle skipping in a deep groove. "That must have been frightening," she said, carefully. "I'm just glad she's okay."

"I mean, she's alive," Anna said, pinching her bottom lip. "But she's not okay. She'll probably never be okay."

Her phone buzzed then, and Anna glanced down, picked it up.

"What time are you due at Kim's?" Maggie asked, forcing herself to take a bite.

"Soon." Anna looked up. "I need to shower, actually. I'm disgusting."

"Will you eat something later, at least?" Maggie asked—she couldn't help it.

"Don't worry," Anna said, scraping back her chair. Maggie traced the sound of her feet racing up the creaky staircase, the bedroom door shutting, mournful strains of that Adele song seeping through the floor. Then she set her fork down too. Briefly, she closed her eyes, felt the tension that had been collecting in her jaw all afternoon release in a slow ache. When she opened them, it was remarkably all still there—the high beamed ceilings, the soft pile of logs by the woodstove, the sun-bleached pillows piled in the window seat. It was on these days, the worst days, that Maggie was struck hardest by her affection for this old place. She was painfully aware that, in other rooms tonight, other houses, other mothers were not so lucky.

The ring of the phone startled her—probably another of Anna's friends' parents, she thought, even while she braced herself for the possibility of something worse—but as she picked up, she saw Tom's name on the machine. "Hi," she said, sliding the phone under her chin.

"Maggie?" He sounded panicked, breathless.

"Tom?" She moved the phone to her hand. "What is it?"

"You're home?"

"Well, yes—"

"And Anna's there?"

"She's right upstairs."

"She's okay?"

"Yes," she said. "Yes. She's here. She's fine."

Tom blew out a long breath. "I just heard," he said. "I was in a meeting all day. And no one called."

"Oh." Maggie paused. "I'm sorry. I assumed she had." She did feel sorry, and so refrained from pointing out the irony: Tom, a graphic designer, was forever glued to screens.

"I tried her phone five minutes ago—"

"She's here. She's in the shower. She's going out."

"Right." He expelled another breath. Maggie waited, letting him absorb the fact of Anna's safety, standing at the sink by the window. Just past seven, and the sun was already sinking behind the trees.

"Okay." When Tom spoke again, the panic seemed to have left him, in its place a tender matter-of-factness. "So, how is she?" he said.

Four years later, this was still the place Maggie and her ex-husband met and merged, the soft center of their bitterness: *How is she?* They both knew the potential it had to feed their daughter's anxieties, a thing like this. They had become wary, vigilant, after years of apparent ignorance. *None of those things struck you as unusual?* Jim Whittier had asked, in what would be their final session, and Maggie had felt a blast of fury—weren't therapists supposed to use language that was neutral, non-judgmental, non-blaming?—just before she began to cry.

Because the truth was, over the course of Anna's childhood, there *had* been things that marked her as extra-nervous, extra-sensitive. Little things. The way she'd sobbed over dead animals by the roadsides. The way she'd fretted about the fish in the fountain at the mall, afraid they might swallow the pennies and die. She'd always loved to read but couldn't bear books with sad endings, avoided small spaces and locked doors and darkness—but wasn't this true of many children? How was a parent to tell the difference between a phase and something more deepseated and real? By the time she was ten, Anna's fears had turned toward the hypothetical: fear of being homeless, being abandoned, kidnapped, abducted, shot. Sometimes she came into their room at night, frightened not by a nightmare but by a story of her own making, a fire she'd convinced herself was sidling through the walls or a robber she'd heard crawling across the roof. *It's all in your head*, Maggie would say, trying to erase her fears. Maggie's mode of response had always been firm and forward-looking, determinedly positive. For these hadn't seemed like problems, or symptoms. If anything, they seemed evidence of Anna's intellect and imagination. She was a straight-A student, a talented writer, a fast and dedicated swimmer. True, Maggie hadn't been inclined to poke too hard or look too closely—if Anna seemed fine, she was fine. It was impossible to imagine that she wasn't.

Later, Maggie would go picking through the rubble, turning moments over in her hands. The time she'd arrived to pick up Anna at Janie's house and watched from the car as she jumped rope, her movements light and buoyant, but on her face a driven sort of grimness. The time, after a swim practice, she'd discovered her counting tiles around the lip of the pool. But it was when Tom left that whatever trouble had long been brewing inside their daughter had hardened into fact: a rapid and distressing thinness. An obsession with swimming that was joyless and strange. A call from the coach when she collapsed one day after practice. *Panic disorder*, diagnosed Theresa Massey, the counselor at the high school whom Anna began seeing sophomore year. Tom, living in Portland by then, had proposed that Anna was acting out to give them a reason to be in contact, hoping their worry for her might bring them back together—*it's not uncommon*, he said, no doubt quoting the social worker girlfriend, in whom he'd evidently been confiding about their daughter. Maggie's daughter. *Fuck you*, she said. The outrage had nearly split her in two.

"She's spooked," Maggie said now, watching the sky. The sunset was incongruously, inappropriately beautiful, sweeping strokes of red and purple thickening into a band of deep gold. "Naturally. She's unnerved."

"Unnerved how?"

"I mean, unnerved in a normal way," Maggie clipped, but she couldn't blame him for asking. "She's okay, though," she said, adding, "They all are, from what I can tell."

"Thank God," he said. "I can't believe we're even having this conversation."

From upstairs, Maggie heard the shower shut off, a deep shudder in the pipes. The line went quiet, though she could hear Tom's breaths. Now that his panic had receded, the space between them felt once again vast, unswept and groundless. Maybe Anna hadn't been entirely wrong: Without their concern for her to unite her parents, a tide pulled back and left them stranded.

"Is she packed?" Tom asked.

"Getting there," Maggie said. From upstairs, she could hear the bumping of dresser drawers. "They're having a sleepover tonight," she offered.

"Oh?"

"The three of them. At Kim's."

"Well," he said. "That's probably a nice thing. Comforting, I mean."

"Right," Maggie said. She had felt the same way. It was endearing, the girls reverting to their adolescent rituals in the final few days before heading off to college. In junior high, sleepovers had been their Friday-night routine: renting movies from Reel Video, staying up all night whispering, eating pizza from Romeo's and slathering frosting on saltines. This was before boyfriends, before the divorce, before Anna would refuse to let pizza or frosting cross her lips. Even then, though, Kim and Janie had always stood by her, and Maggie was grateful for their loyalty. It was they who had sought out Maggie three years ago, showing up together at her office on campus, Kim wiping at her eyes while Janie did the talking, telling her they thought Anna might be *cutting*. (Maggie would never forget the pause she took before the meaning of the word sank in—foolishly, she'd first thought they meant skipping school.)

"Did you know him?" Tom was saying.

"Who?"

"This Dugan kid?"

Maggie detected a faint tapping sound. Naturally, Tom was at the computer. There was another sound too—the drone of a vacuum, or a hair dryer. She hated that she noticed, hated that she cared. She knew, of course, that Tom had had girlfriends (after the inevitable breakup with the social worker), but this new one, Felicia, seemed to have stuck. She was younger, and worked in marketing. Anna said they'd met online. Maggie didn't know much more than this, though evidently she would be meeting her on Sunday. She was coming to campus for drop-off, information Tom had relayed in an email titled *heads-up*.

Tom said, "Because I read that he went to the college—"

"Yes, I know he went to the college, Tom. He was my student."

"Oh," Tom said, and paused. "My God, Mag." Silence, this time a kind of awe, swelled on the line. The tapping ceased. Maggie closed her eyes. She could picture just how Tom looked when absorbing news that was sad or shocking: the moment's stillness, then the flexing of his hands, just slightly, as if making sure that, cast in the light of this newly altered world, everything still worked. "When?"

"Four years ago," she said. "The year you left," she added, then felt low. "Anna's freshman year of high school."

"Which class? Comp?"

"Comp, yes."

"Jesus," he said. "What was he like?"

Maggie stared at the darkening sky, strewn now with torn purple clouds. She knew she wouldn't be able to get away with the sort of non-answer she'd given Robert. Of all people, Tom knew how much she poured into her students. Of the many surreal aftershocks of divorce, this one had never stopped surprising her: Though her marriage had ended four years ago, and Tom now lived in Portland with another woman, it was he who really knew her—or knew her as much as any one person could really know another.

"Do you?" Tom was saying. "Remember him? Anything off about him?"

Off—this wasn't the right word either. It implied a student who was imbalanced, truly and unmistakably, and surely Nathan Dugan had not been that.

"Not really, no," she said. "Not exactly." She watched the night gathering outside the window. Soon it would be dark out, true dark. From the corner of her eye, she saw a shadowy movement in the garden. Quickly she crossed the kitchen and flung open the screen door, but by the time she stepped outside, the creature was running back to the woods.

Maggie had taught in a basement annex of the English building that semester: Room 14C. It was not a good room. Cold in winter, warm in summer. In the coldest months, the radiator had emitted ghostly clanks and bangs. The windows were narrow rectangles at the top of the wall, like holes in an aquarium lid, level with the brick footpath on the quad. Through them she could check the weather—the softly piling snow or pelting rain—and the rush of boots and sneakers, which would thicken and disperse between classes. From Room 14C, Maggie was aware of the world outside, though the world—save a thin band of light that fell on the footpath in the evenings—was, certainly, unaware of them.

She remembered that class, Nathan Dugan's. Even after twenty-eight years, each of Maggie's classes remained a distinct imprint in her mind: a sense, a shape. The configuration of chairs, the time of day, the size and appearance of the room. And the mood, which was about the distribution of boys and girls, shy students and talkers. Unlike Robert's lectures, a writing class was a delicate infrastructure; so much relied on the particular alchemy of the fifteen personalities in the group. From that class, Nathan's class, Maggie remembered Ashley Shay, a sturdy, red-cheeked girl from Washington County with a big laugh and an easy confidence— a girl who faintly glowed with self-esteem (which perhaps had been of particular note to Maggie then, as her own daughter's problems consumed her). Hannah Chaffee dressed like a hippie, in long skirts and braids, an eyebrow ring; she wrote a starkly moving essay about an abortion she'd had at sixteen (certain phrases still resurfaced sometimes for Maggie—*the gasp of the aspiration machine*). Katie Sutton had described the heartbreak of her parents selling her childhood home, a farmhouse— cedar logs, red door, lovely parents hauling wood and heating cocoa; it had been overly sentimental, and couldn't have been entirely truthful, but still Maggie had been charmed—jealous maybe—of the impossibly perfect light in which Katie still viewed her mom and dad.

They were that kind of class: sensitive and serious, a class of girls mostly, eager to share and listen, making it even more regrettable that Nathan was getting in the way. This, Maggie knew, was why she wasn't cut out for teaching high school, where more concern was directed toward the students who were disruptive—the sullen ones, the lazy ones, the ones who needed to be corrected and chased. In college, the students were responsible for themselves. Her job, as she saw it, was not to pay undue attention to the troublemakers but to minimize them, prevent them from ruining the experience for everybody else. Under the best of circumstances, it happened organically, for the other students were so invested in the class that the outlier was shamed into caring about it too.

With Nathan, it was different; his disruptiveness wasn't laziness or insolence, something he could be manipulated into changing. The very inattentiveness that made him uncomfortable to be around made him impervious to change. Maggie could only try to alleviate the uneasy feeling that was generated by his presence. More than Nathan himself, this was what she remembered: the feeling in the room. How, if he was absent, the atmosphere loosened. How, when he was there, it shifted and morphed to accommodate him, like a river around a rock. When she broke the class into small groups to trade papers, she took care to partner Nathan with students she felt might be less bothered by him. On the occasions he spoke in class, he'd usually start talking over someone, prompting Maggie to remind him to raise his hand, and the student to flash her a sympathetic look. From time to time, in classes with problematic students, Maggie would feel the others looking at her, trying to commiserate and empathize, to wince or roll their eyes; tempting as it was to indulge those moments of connection, they were nonetheless something she tried to avoid. With Nathan's classmates, though, Maggie sometimes let herself reciprocate—a tight smile, a quick nod, grateful, apologetic, an affirmation of how they were feeling, assurance that she felt that way too.

One such incident, that spring, was with Meredith Kenney. Meredith was the kind of student who was endlessly positive—praised every paper, agreed with every comment—because she either lacked a critical edge or was simply too nice to offend. Not surprisingly, her own writing tended to be safe, somewhat narrow, until, that April, her brother was killed in Afghanistan by a roadside bomb. Maggie had been notified by the dean of students, excusing Meredith's absences; when she returned to class, the death was on her face. But to Maggie's surprise, her first week back Meredith volunteered to read out loud about her brother—a flood of raw, shocked feeling—reducing her classmates to a stunned silence. It was Nathan who jumped in quickly, immediately pointing out the technical flaws in her description of the IED. The rest of the class turned, appalled, to Maggie. *That may be factually correct*, she said, cutting Nathan off midsentence. *But let's consider what's really important here.* She was filled with rage; it was almost freeing. Nathan didn't reply. So she let his ignorant comment land, like a foul smell in the corner, and pivoted away from it. Focused all her energies on Meredith, on her essay. On the other students, the better students, who now had their hands high, ready to commend Meredith for being so brave.

Maggie woke on the couch to the ringing of the phone. The windows were black; it looked late, felt late. She hurried to the kitchen and, upon seeing an unlisted number, felt the blast of worry she always did if the phone rang at night and Anna wasn't home.

"Maggie?" The voice was familiar but not immediately placeable.

"Yes?" She stood in the darkened kitchen, the phone in both hands. "Yes? Who's this?"

"It's Bill," he said. "Bill Wall. I apologize for calling at this hour."

"Oh—Bill."

"Did I wake you?"

"No, no," she said as her eyes moved to the clock—eleven thirty-nine. "It's fine. I was awake." She flipped the switch above the toaster and pulled the top of her bathrobe closed, squinting into the light of the hanging lamp.

"Not easy to sleep after a day like this," Bill said.

His voice sounded different, she thought, thinner than it did at school, though in fact she had never spoken to him on the phone.

"No," she said, "it isn't." She took a seat at the kitchen table, waited. Outside, the crickets chirped their sleepy, syrupy night song.

"I'm calling about one of your former students," Bill said, clearing his throat.

"Yes." Maggie paused, disoriented. "Nathan Dugan—"

"Well, no. A different student. A Luke Finch."

Luke Finch: Maggie stared at the nicked kitchen table as the memory gathered in her mind. Luke had been in that same comp class, Nathan's class. Thin-faced, narrow-shouldered. Huddled in his desk, chest pressed forward and knees locked. There was a melancholy about him, Maggie remembered, yet its source never made itself known. He spoke only if called on. He often doodled when Maggie was talking, though she understood this wasn't necessarily a mark of rudeness; for certain kids—shy ones, usually—it was a form of concentration, a distraction that actually helped them focus more.

"I remember Luke," she said.

"Same class as Dugan."

"Yes," she said. He was from Maine, she thought, north of Augusta. And then—maybe because today it seemed so indiscriminate, so plausible—she was seized with a quick fear that he was dead. "Is he all right, Bill? He wasn't—"

"No, no. He's fine." Bill cleared his throat again, as if gathering loose strands of thought. "He put something online," he said. "Something he wrote about that class."

Maggie leaned one hip against the counter. This was surprising. Like Luke himself, his essays tended to be quiet, unrevealing. "Okay," she said. "What is it?"

"A post on Facebook," Bill said. "You know, social media—"

"Yes, I'm aware of Facebook," she said, with a laugh. "I may be our resident Luddite, but not even I am that out of touch." Bill didn't laugh. Maggie was struck then by the peculiarity of the moment, these two parts of her life intersecting: her worn bathrobe, Bill Wall's voice on the telephone, the stick of butter softening on the table, bugs bumping gently against the screen. "What does it say?"

"He talks about Dugan," Bill said. "About that class, and things he observed about him. Some are relatively innocuous, but he also mentions some unusual behaviors. And he suggests Dugan wrote a paper that was potentially—well, incriminating."

Maggie tensed. "Incriminating?"

"That's the implication," Bill said.

"Is that the word he used?"

"Well, no, I don't think he—"

"I'd like to know his exact words. Please."

As she waited, Maggie could feel emotion welling inside her—heartbeat thumping, some unformed dread rising—and tried to remain empty, to stay on the surface. She reminded herself that, for Bill Wall, the word *incriminating* might apply quite broadly, especially tonight.

"Here it is," Bill said. "The Facebook post." Again, he paused, clearing his throat. "I won't read the whole thing. You won't have any trouble finding it. But he says here that Dugan wrote, and I'm quoting, 'a paper that was really weird. So today when I heard what he did there was a part of me that didn't feel surprised.'"

"'Really weird,'" Maggie repeated.

"Yes."

"Weird? Weird how?"

"That's what I was hoping you could tell me."

"I'm sorry, Bill, but I really don't remember," she said, and this was not untrue. What she remembered about Nathan Dugan was the quality of his presence. About his papers she remembered only the feeling of them, airless and dense. "He may have written something about his father," she said. "But I can't recall the details." She paused. "It's been years. Four years."

"Yes. Four," Bill said. Was he trying to imply that she'd been negligent? That she didn't pay attention to her students, didn't remember every single one of them? The irony—Maggie almost laughed out loud.

"It's a long time," she said. "Luke may not be remembering things entirely clearly."

"That may be," Bill allowed. "Nonetheless, his post is already generating a fair amount of attention. We should be prepared, just in case."

"Prepared?" A hum had started to gather in her ears. "Prepared for what?"

"It's not impossible it could lead to questions," Bill said. "About Nathan's performance in your class—his behavior, and what he wrote. Fortunately, these shouldn't be too difficult to answer. I assume you kept the required student writing samples."

"Well, yes," she said. In fact, she had a barn full of them—but there were hundreds. Thousands. Unlike most faculty, who accepted papers electronically, even required them, Maggie still insisted on hard copies: real, bound, to be read in their solid, substantive form. "I mean, I always do," she said. "I always have."

"Good," Bill said. His relief was palpable through the phone. "Let's meet tomorrow then, my office, and bring whatever you—"

This time, Maggie let out a short laugh. "Do you really think that's necessary? On a Saturday?"

Again, Bill paused, a silence that stretched so long Maggie wondered if he'd lost his train of thought. But when he spoke again, his tone was considered. "It will probably amount to nothing," he said. "But with something like this—you never can tell. It could get picked up by media outlets. It could blow up and go viral. You know how these things online can go."

In fact, Maggie didn't know. She had managed to keep her life largely and deliberately unburdened by technology. Eight basic cable channels, an answering machine, a flip phone her daughter decried as prehistoric. *Go viral*—the very phrase struck her as both menacing and silly.

"You know," she said, "lots of students write 'really weird' stuff, Bill."

"I'm sure that's true," Bill said. "But they don't kill innocent people."

Maggie said nothing. The hum was rising. "My apologies again for calling so late," Bill said, then confirmed the details for the next afternoon and wished her good night. For several minutes Maggie continued to sit there, receiver pressed to shoulder, then stood and hung up the phone. It was now almost midnight, but she was fully awake. Her heart was pounding, though she couldn't quite say why. In the window above the sink, she studied the reflection of the kitchen, moth-speckled, the lamp behind her like a bright moon. *Really weird.* That could mean anything. Not to mention these students were eighteen. Eighteen, and encouraged to write freely. It was frankly impossible that some of what they wrote wouldn't be really weird. And Luke Finch, with his shy bearing and benign doodles, might have had an especially low tolerance for weirdness. He might be overreacting to something he remembered, or merely thought that he did. *Memory is always subjective.*

Tomorrow, Maggie would ease her mind, confirm her instincts. For now, she peered into the darkness of the yard, but with the light on inside, she could see only her own reflection staring back.

Two

The party tonight was at Gavin's house, which was unfortunate but not surprising. For party purposes, Gavin's was ideal. It was isolated (even for Stafford), the last house on a dead-end road, where the noise wouldn't draw attention from the neighbors. Gavin lived with his dad, who traveled sometimes for work and had the added bonus of being largely oblivious, the kind of parent who wouldn't notice a new water ring on the coffee table or a bottle of watered-down rum in the liquor cabinet. Over the past two years, Anna and Gavin had been able to have sex in his basement without worrying that his dad would ever notice or care. It was a place she had thought she'd never see again; it felt strange, going back.

Kim and Janie had insisted it was fine, possibly obligatory, that Anna come to Gavin's party. It had been almost three months since graduation, when Anna had broken up with him on the football field. *It might be insulting if you don't go*, Janie had said, which made a kind of sense at the time.

Tonight, the prospect of going to a party of any kind felt wrong, even disrespectful, though Anna was grateful to have something to distract her racing mind. She'd spent all afternoon online. *Prayers for all the victims,* she'd seen repeatedly on Instagram, Facebook, Twitter. *So glad Laura is OK!!* Just before she'd left for Kim's, where the three of them were convening before the party, she'd gotten a voicemail from her dad—*call me back right away, Anna*—and been startled by the panic in his voice. When she returned the call, he answered, already choked up. Even his girlfriend had gotten on the line. *Are you doing okay, sweetie? We'll see you Sunday, okay?* Felicia was always overly affectionate with Anna (the opposite of her mother, who had never once called Anna sweetie), and while Anna often found her cloying, tonight she didn't mind.

Now, as they sat in Kim's room drinking orange juice and vodka, Janie read her text exchange with Laura. She'd been locked in the dressing room at the Gap. *Oh my God*, Kim said. *Poor Laura.* Anna didn't say anything. All afternoon she'd been thinking about what Laura must have gone through, how the gunshots must have sounded, like the hollow bangs she sometimes heard echo deep in the woods behind her house. How fearful she must have been knowing the shooter was still loose in the mall, that she might be his next target. Knowing that people were dying, that she was hearing the sounds of their lives ending—how Laura would carry around that memory, be traumatized by it, for the rest of her life. Now she imagined the Gap dressing room: Laura trapped inside, frightened face in the mirror, music playing, clothes heaped on the floor, the collision of the ordinary and the end of the world. Anna had always been afraid of things happening—stupid things, freak things, fears that in her rational mind she knew were (basically) unrealistic—but tonight, what she felt most of all was the not-impossibility of terrifying things.

She forced herself to focus on the rest of Kim and Janie's conversation—who else might be at this party and the implications of his/her presence—and then the three of them finished their drinks and approved one another's not-trying-too-hard outfits (jeans and T-shirts, minimal makeup) and drove to Gavin's house, arriving a strategic forty-five minutes late.

As Anna walked down Gavin's driveway, being there had an unexpectedly calming effect. His blue truck, his house where she'd spent so many nights in high school, the sounds of rowdy shouts and laughter rising into the night sky—the sameness reassured her. In the backyard, a comfortable cushion of about fifteen classmates was gathered loosely around a keg. As soon as she spotted Gavin, though, Anna felt guilty. She hadn't seen him since the breakup. It wasn't like she'd been deliberately hurtful—*I just think we're too different.* She hadn't meant to say it that way. She had assumed, abstractly, they would part ways before they left for college, but it had just come out, a blurt of feeling. She wished she'd done it differently. She noticed him notice her—he gave a short nod in her direction, she returned a quick smile—then, in a single motion, sweep his hair off his face with one hand and take a deep drink from his red cup.

"Ladies," said Brian Tucker, approaching them with three keg cups clasped in one thick-fingered hand. Tucker (they hadn't called him Brian since seventh grade) was a meathead who practically lived at the cheap gym on Standish Road. Right now, though, Anna was glad to see him. At some point, talk would turn to more serious things, but for the moment, the epitome of unserious: Brian Tucker. "About time you got here," he said. And then, to her surprise, he went up to each of them and hugged them. With uncharacteristic solemnity, he handed around the cups, saying, "Drink to your health, girls."

"What the hell is that?" Janie said skeptically, peering into her cup. It looked like windshield wiper fluid.

"Are you trying to get us drunk or something?" Kim added, trying to be flirty. She and Tucker had hooked up at the "morp"—the after-prom breakfast, which translated to pancakes served in the school cafeteria at two a.m. and took its name, ingeniously, from *prom* spelled backward—and though they'd had no contact since then, Janie and Anna had signed off on Kim hooking up with him again tonight if the opportunity arose.

"You guys are no fun," Tucker said, but conceded, "Tequila and Hawaiian Punch. But mostly tequila." He handed the last cup to Anna. "Hey, D-B. We weren't sure you'd come."

Anna tried her best to look unbothered. "Really? I was invited," she replied, even though it was Janie whom Gavin had texted about the party. But surely he'd known the invite would make its way to her.

"She's my date," Kim said.

"I thought I was your date," Tucker said, and Kim laughed wincingly hard. Anna took a swallow of the blue drink. It was too sweet, way too strong. She was suddenly regretting having come. *We weren't sure*, Tucker had said—did the *we* refer to Gavin? Had Gavin explicitly told Tucker he didn't want her there? Maybe Gavin hated her now; maybe everyone did. Anna's mind turned to the worst-case scenario, a technique she'd learned from her therapist, Theresa, to reassure herself she could survive any stressful situation. Tonight, in fact, the worst-case scenario was eminently survivable. The party was miserable, everybody despised her, and she left—left Gavin's, left Stafford. She was leaving anyway. She'd be gone, thank God, in two days.

Now Tucker and Kim were talking, angling toward each other pointedly. Janie, naturally, was recruited for a flip-cup game—her basketball skill translated to beer and quarters—but Anna declined. Janie raised an eyebrow—*you okay?*—and Anna nodded back, with more confidence than she was feeling. She watched Janie jog off toward the picnic table, where the players were gathering, then stole a look at Gavin, manning the keg. She reminded herself of Janie's assessment after the breakup—*he's fun but he was never on your level*, which had felt unkind but sort of true. Now, though, as if to spite her, Gavin was talking to Mindy Reddy. A *cotton candy*—this was the term Anna and her friends had coined for shallow, airy girls like her. *Candy*, for short. Mindy looked skinny, Anna thought, skinnier even than at graduation, and she dwelled briefly, anxiously, on the twelve pounds she herself had gained since May—then felt a blast of remorse for worrying about Gavin, or Mindy Reddy, or twelve pounds, on a day like this, a day when three people had died. Been *murdered*.

She forced herself to look away from Gavin and Mindy, take another swallow. The drink was revolting—it really was tequila, mostly—but the more she consumed, the less offensive it became. She glanced at the flip-cup game, where Janie was positioned between Claudia Jones and Tara Abram, both of them unmitigated *candies*, wearing those stupid shorts with words across the butts. Behind her, Gavin's iPod was blasting out the open window. A thin haze of gnats hovered above the scene. By next week, Anna reminded herself, this would all feel small, faraway. She imagined her future self, reflecting on nights like this with the same feeling she had reading her old journals: detached and forgiving, even a touch pitying. For in college, she knew, everything would change. She would have a smart, serious boyfriend with whom she had meaningful conversations. She would finally spend time on her own writing, get inspired. She would be a person who enjoyed parties, laughed easily. She would leave her old, panicky, calorie-counting self behind her. It was one of the promises of college: You could become someone else.

Kim appeared by her side, frowning. "What are you doing over here?"

"Nothing." Anna shook her head. "Getting drunk enough to deal."

"Got it," Kim said, and transferred the rest of her drink into Anna's cup. She'd come to check on Anna's drink but also, Anna knew, to check on Anna herself; Kim had many amazing qualities, but subtle she was not.

"Thanks," Anna said as Kim sank her head onto her shoulder. Sometimes her friends' continued vigilance made Anna feel pathetic, even a tiny bit resentful, but she understood: Being her friend had not always been easy. She'd made them worry. She suspected that, in some way, her constant state of crisis had actually made Kim and Janie closer with each other; she tried not to resent that either, just be grateful that they cared.

They stood quietly, watching the scene. "I think Tucker's into me," Kim said finally.

Anna smiled. "Of course Tucker's into you."

"Do you think it's a bad idea to hook up with him?"

"Didn't we decide this already?"

"I know, but it's not like we won't see each other—"

"There are like a million people on that campus," Anna told her, taking a swallow. "You can avoid him for four years if you need to. Go for it."

"Right," Kim said, then lifted her head and looked at Anna with eyes suddenly teary, smudging her eyeliner, which was applied in the usual quirky Kim way: little flourishes, like commas, at the outer edge of each eye. "This is going to be so weird."

"I know," Anna said, and it would be—she had not yet begun to wrap her mind around life without Kim and Janie—though for Kim, it was different. Anna was going to Boston. Janie would be in Maine, but at Bates, on a scholarship. Kim was stuck going to Central Maine State. Anna felt bad for her. Unlike Tucker, who was no doubt going because of his ridiculously low GPA, Kim ending up there was financial—her father had been laid off from the paper mill last winter, and the school was offering aid. It was ironic: The kids whose parents were Central Maine professors would basically never go there (to Anna's mom's credit, she had never even suggested it), while others' parents, like Kim's, didn't make enough money to send them anywhere else.

"How is it with Gavin?"

Anna shrugged. "It isn't."

"He keeps looking over here," Kim observed. "Maybe you should consider a nostalgia fuck."

"Um, no."

"Why not? You've already had sex with him, like, a hundred times, so once more doesn't really count."

"Thanks," Anna laughed, taking a sip, tucking her hair behind one ear. "In any case, I don't exactly see the opportunity presenting herself. He probably hates my guts."

"You never know," Kim said, glancing into her empty cup. "I need a refill. Be right back." She kissed Anna's cheek then made her way to the keg, where Tucker happened to be standing. Gavin was still there, wearing his bruised yellow-and-black Bruins cap, Mindy nestled in the crook of his arm. Anna took a prolonged drink of the blue stuff, trying not to care about all the calories she was consuming. Then Mindy abruptly detached herself from Gavin and ran over to throw herself at the person walking through the back door: Leo Blunt. Mindy gave him a long hug, and Leo patted her awkwardly on the shoulder. Leo was a nice guy, quieter than most of Gavin's friends, the starting pitcher on the baseball team—he also worked at the mall, Anna realized with a start. At the Verizon store. She felt a splash of nerves. She recalled seeing Leo there a few times this summer, his lanky pitcher's body awkward in khaki pants and a red collared shirt. The store bordered the food court. He might have been inside—waiting on a customer, bored—when the shots started firing. He might have tried to hide behind a display case, make himself as small as possible, believing those were the last moments of his life. He might have seen the whole thing.

Suddenly it registered that the entire party had gone quiet. The flip-cup game had paused. A hush had fallen over the group. Everybody was turned toward the patio, where Mindy had the floor. "It just doesn't feel real."

At first, nobody spoke. People held still, staring into the middle distance or wiping at their eyes. Anna located her friends. Kim was still standing next to Tucker, who had his arm around her. Janie was on a picnic bench, wedged between Claudia and Tara, her blue-jeaned knees pressed against their bare ones.

"I know," someone said. "I can't believe it."

"I was just there last night."

People nodded, commenting about when they'd last been at the mall, who they knew who had been there, or almost been there, that morning.

"Did anybody see the video?" Tucker said.

Anna shuddered. She'd heard about the video Nathan Dugan put on YouTube that morning but hadn't watched it. She couldn't imagine wanting to.

"It was down in, like, ten seconds," Gavin said. "But I read about it. The guy was seriously fucked up."

"I heard he took a mental leave of absence."

"My sister was in the same class as him," Tara said. "She's a senior."

"He was a loser," Tucker said heatedly. "End of story." He was rubbing Kim's shoulder, and Anna wondered if this was especially upsetting for the two of them, knowing they'd be at Central Maine next week. "He killed three people because he got fired. From fucking *Walmart*."

"It wasn't just because he was fired," Tara said quietly. "He'd obviously been planning it. It didn't come out of nowhere."

Meg Crowley spoke up. "My cousin works at the Walmart. She knew him. I mean, she didn't hang out with him, but she worked with him. She said he was unfriendly and whatever. But nobody knew he was this messed up."

Anna stared into the remaining inch of her drink. A dead bug was floating on top. This, she thought, was the most terrifying part: that Nathan Dugan had been plotting, roaming around the periphery of their lives—the mall, the campus—just waiting for the moment to explode, and nobody had seen it coming. That these killers walked the world, invisible and unstoppable, and your only hope was that you didn't cross their paths. Even her mother, so obsessed with her students, hadn't caught on to how disturbed he was. He could just as easily have snapped in her class—shot his classmates. Shot her. Anna shut her eyes, squeezing the image into black.

"Leo, man, were you there?"

Anna tried to refocus. Her pulse was skittering. All eyes were now on Leo, whose head was hanging, as if he couldn't bear to meet their eyes. "I usually open on Fridays," he said. His voice was faint, almost apologetic. "But I didn't today," he said. "Because of college. Yesterday was my last shift."

The group murmured in Leo's direction, and a few other girls ran over to hug him. Anna's heart beat just beneath her breastbone, light and quick, a trapped bird. She thought about what would happen if she spoke up about the connection to her mother, how the entire party would angle toward her—Anna didn't like drawing attention to herself but, perversely, when she got anxious, that sometimes made her want to do it. According to Theresa, it helped her feel a measure of control. She thought she understood, at least a little, those stand-up comedians who were really deeply unhappy or actors who were shy.

Then Leo continued, "I talked to this guy I work with." He looked pale. "The guy who picked up my shift. He said that one of the guards was hit. He was still alive when the police came."

It took a minute for Anna to process what he was saying. The victims' names hadn't been released yet, but the information was online everywhere: one person in critical condition, three dead.

"Which guard?" someone said.

"The nice one," Leo said. "Joe."

They all knew which one he meant; he had worked at the mall since Anna was little. Every December, he wore a string of colored lights around his neck, and he played Santa in the Christmas display. Once, when she and Gavin had been caught in the mall after closing—they'd been out on the fire escape behind the Foot Locker, where Gavin was working—he'd raised a conspiratorial finger to his lips and let them slip out an emergency exit without a word.

"Oh my God," someone said. Others started crying.

Anna looked at Gavin, but he wasn't looking at her.

"What a fucking asshole," Tucker said, with surprising vehemence. "I swear, if he wasn't dead already, I'd kill him myself."

Anna felt the air leaving her lungs. She glanced again at Gavin, but he had his arm around Mindy. Over by the picnic table, Janie was holding hands with Tara. Kim was rubbing Tucker's back. Then the music changed abruptly: a goofy dance song from back when they were in eighth grade. People looked around, laughed a little. The moment slowly loosened, the cool night air shot through with relief. Anna watched as the rest of the group decided it was permissible now to talk of other things. Kim leaned into Tucker, talking close to his ear—accelerated by talk of the tragedy, their hooking up tonight was all but inevitable. Gavin handed shots to Leo and Mindy, then the three of them raised their glasses and, with an air of ceremony, held them in the air. The flip-cup game gradually resumed, teams reassembling on either side of the picnic table. Anna wished that she were able to refocus, let herself be distracted. She tried draining her cup and, too late, remembered the bug.

When she set the cup down, trembling, she headed for the back door. She needed to be alone, to pull herself together. Inside, she paused in the sudden brightness of the kitchen; it was a kitchen she knew well. She steadied herself on the counter, blinking, as the room took solid shape around her: the empties piled in the sink, potato chip bag torn open on the kitchen table. It was the same table where, for two years, she had watched Gavin mindlessly, constantly, eat—midnight snacks, boy snacks, pizza bagels and Hot Pockets, Cool Ranch Doritos and Chips Ahoy. Things Anna never would have let herself consume in a million years. Maybe it was the absence of a mother (Gavin's mom had left his dad when he was little), but his was the most junk-food-filled kitchen Anna had ever seen. Anna would always claim she wasn't hungry, knowing Gavin wouldn't push it. He'd stuff his face, and she'd watch enviously, sipping her Diet Coke. "Coke tastes better," he said once, grabbing a can from the fridge, and she was so amazed by the simplicity of this decision—of choosing something just because it tasted better, for reasons of pure pleasure—she could have wept.

She was hungry right now, she realized. She was starving. She opened up the snack cabinet and scanned for something healthy, then impulsively grabbed six Double Stuf Oreos and ate them all without stopping to breathe. As the taste flooded her jaws, she felt better—steadier. But moments later, she was consumed with regret. Behind her, the door banged open, and Meg and Tara stumbled inside, giggling. Anna walked quickly in the other direction, down the stairs to the bathroom in the basement, not wanting to be seen. Past the old brown couch she and Gavin used to have sex on, the steamer trunk where he stashed his condoms. Mr. Newland's hunting trophies hung over the mantel. Deer heads, glass-eyed and frozen. At the wall, their necks stopped so cleanly, it was as if their bodies continued on the other side.

In the bathroom, Anna yanked the door closed hard and turned on the drowning hum of the fan. She washed her face and confronted her reflection: She looked huge. It was a thought she'd had, a mirror she'd confronted, countless times. It was the mirror she'd stared into after having sex with Gavin, irrationally worried the condom had broken and she might be pregnant or have caught a disease. The mirror where she'd turned sideways to study herself in profile, the fat on her stomach, her arms—hundreds, thousands of times. Now she gripped the sides of the sink and leaned in so close that the breath from her nose steamed the glass. She thought of Laura, staring at herself in the Gap dressing room, hearing the shots and the screaming and unable to get out. Of Joe the security guard, probably unconscious, hooked to machines. Her pulse was hammering. From the backyard, the drinking game erupted in a burst of cheering. She wished she could sneak out and leave. Wished she hadn't eaten those six Oreos. Wished she'd taken an Ativan before coming—Theresa had her take them only "as needed," but certainly a party at Gavin's on the night of a shooting qualified. She turned sideways and examined her profile and it confirmed what she knew: She had gained twelve pounds. She lifted the hem of her shirt and observed, horrified, the roll of skin that bulged over the side of her jeans. She calculated the width of her upper arm. She reminded herself that she was leaving. That if she wanted to, she could undo it. She could fix it. At college, no one would be watching her. She could exercise more, eat less: It was just discipline, just math.

Stop it, Anna—she squeezed her eyes shut, pressing her fingers against her lids until colors bloomed against the dark. She felt tears rise behind her fingertips. She reminded herself that twelve pounds didn't matter. That she didn't want to *be* a person for whom twelve pounds mattered— she wanted to free her brain to think about more important things.

She opened her eyes and stared into the mirror and spoke out loud. "Stop it, Anna," she said. "Stop." It was a strategy Theresa had given her for breaking the surface swirl of thought, and though it was kind of silly, it usually worked. "Stop it," she said again. The thoughts began receding. She took one more deep breath and smiled at her reflection— another mental trick that was embarrassing but effective—and when she turned and exited the bathroom, Gavin was standing not five feet from the door.

"Oh," he said. "Hey."

She laughed in surprise. "Hey." She was simultaneously relieved to not be alone anymore and worried he'd been listening.

"What's so funny?"

"Nothing."

"I didn't even know you were down here," Gavin said, which meant that he had. "I came for this," he added. He held up a bottle from his dad's liquor cabinet.

She laughed, but Gavin wasn't laughing. He looked upset, maybe even a little pissed off. Anna recalled his face, his look of surprise, and hurt, when she broke up with him three months ago, as they'd all milled around the football field in their caps and gowns. She'd surprised herself too; she hadn't planned on doing it. She'd hoped they might go hang out alone for a while after the ceremony, but then heard Gavin inviting people back to his house for an after-party. Anna didn't care about the after-party. Maybe it was the fervor of graduation, the talk of the future, but she'd felt a sudden clarity: not only that she wasn't meant to be with Gavin, but that she might find, at college, someone more like her.

"What are you doing down here?" Gavin said. He was pretty drunk, Anna saw, his cheeks red, his cap pulled low over his eyes, the brim landing at a sloppy, crooked angle.

"Nothing," she said. "Hiding."

"From?"

"I don't know, everyone?"

"How come?"

"I guess I'm not having a particularly good time." She raked her fingers through her hair. "No offense."

"None taken." Gavin held up the bottle by the neck. "Would this help?"

"What is it?"

"Wild Turkey."

"Yeah." She laughed again, pressing her hair behind both ears. She didn't like this feeling: sober enough to realize she was drunk, too drunk to do anything about it. Every move she made felt too obvious, too much. "I don't think so."

"What's the matter?" Gavin smiled a little this time. "Can't handle it?"

She'd always been susceptible to things like this—*I dare you*, someone would assert on the playground, at a sleepover, when she was a kid and afraid of literally everything. *Fine*, she'd reply. *I'll do it*. And she'd hate it, but she would. Dumb things. Prank-call the pizza place, walk up to a random boy in the mall, hold her breath underwater at Meer Cove.

"Fine," she said now, taking an emphatic step toward Gavin. She reached for the bottle and took a swig and instantly started coughing. "God, what *is* that?"

"I told you. Bourbon."

"*Bourbon?*" Her lungs blazed. "I didn't know Wild Turkey was bourbon," she said, and Gavin laughed, which she deserved. She pushed the bottle back toward him, swiping at the dribbles on her chin.

He stopped laughing, but a loose smile still hung on his face. "Hey," he said.

"Hey what?"

"I thought of you today."

"Oh, wow, I'm honored."

"I'm being serious. When I heard about the shooting."

She paused, confused—she thought maybe he was referring to her anxiety, realizing how shaken up she must have been, but Gavin had never been aware of her anxiety, not completely. He knew, of course, that she got nervous about certain things, quirky things—checking that the doors were locked or the hair straightener unplugged—and he'd known about the eating stuff (more or less), which hadn't seemed to faze him much (eating problems were so commonplace, so embarrassingly predictable—plus what guy didn't want a skinny girlfriend?). But the real, true depths of it were something different.

"You did?" she said.

"I wanted to know you were okay," he said, emphasizing each word as if he thought she might be too drunk to understand, and with a sickening feeling, it clicked.

"You mean you wanted to make sure I hadn't been *shot*?" Anna said. It came out so bluntly that it sounded like she was joking, but she was terrified.

"I didn't really think you were," he said. "But, yeah, it crossed my mind." He took his cap off and smashed it back on, then looked away. He seemed a little self-conscious. "I worried about it for a minute. I mean, isn't that a normal thing to worry about?"

It was, and that was the most upsetting part—the fact that, in Gavin's mind, her being shot in the mall this morning had actually been possible, that a world had briefly existed in which this had been a not-unrealistic thing to think.

"I guess you weren't worrying about me," Gavin said.

"No," she managed. "No, I was." She hadn't been, not specifically, but she included him in the general state of nerves she'd been swimming in all day. She reached for the ends of her hair, twisting a lock around her thumb. Her eyes skipped to the wall above him, the deer with their chins raised, antlers sprawled, gazes pointed somewhere over their heads. "Do you remember that time, with the security guard?" she asked him.

He frowned. "What time?"

"When he found us on the fire escape at the mall and—"

"Oh," he said, face clearing. "Right," he said. She watched as the memory returned. "He was a really good guy."

"Is," Anna corrected.

"Is. That's what I meant." Then he set the bottle down on the floor, and he looked at her more seriously, kind of tenderly. "Want to get out of here?" he said.

Anna hesitated. To get away from the party, away from her own restless, relentless head—this might be a good thing. She didn't want to be alone, didn't want to go back upstairs. She knew she wasn't going to hook up with Gavin, despite Kim's permission, but the prospect of being in his company, apart from all the others, was a comfort. With the exception of Kim and Janie, she was still more at ease with him than anyone there.

"Okay," she said. "Well, maybe." She paused. "What did you have in mind?"

"I don't know," he said. "We could take a drive."

"You think you can *drive*?"

"Fine." He shrugged. "Walk."

"Walk."

"Yeah. You know." He shuffled a few steps toward her. "One foot and then the other?"

"That's enlightening, thanks," she said. "But where—"

"Oh, who *cares*?" Gavin groaned, staggering backward in mock aggravation. He looked toward the stairs, as if he was considering abandoning the plan completely, then turned back to her and smiled and said, "I know. The Grange."

She let out a sharp laugh. "Are you serious?"

"Why not?"

"Um, it's a little extreme, don't you think?" She was trying to be coy, but only to disguise her nervousness. The Grange was an expanse of woods near the campus, dense and dark even by day. She couldn't imagine being there at night, and drunk.

Gavin placed both hands on her shoulders. "Come on, it'll be fun," he said, and looked at her closely, his expression soft and flushed and sweet, kind of needy. Gavin, she thought, had always made her feel pretty. If he'd noticed she had gained twelve pounds, he didn't care. "Please?"

Later, she would think that it was because she was drunk herself. Or because she was feeling grateful to Gavin for having been a basically nice boyfriend, or guilty about breaking up with him. Or maybe it was the nearness of college or her desire to get away from the party or the terrible strangeness of the day that had come before it, but she went.

The Grange sprawled from the edge of the campus to the Stafford town line. Occasionally, Anna heard stories about CMSU kids getting busted in there for partying, and there was a local legend about a Boy Scout who disappeared while camping. The forest spanned almost thirty acres. One edge bordered a cluster of student apartments; the other was two blocks from Gavin's house.

As they walked down the middle of the one-lane road, Anna inhaled deeply. The night air was cool, laced with woodsmoke, the sky filled with stars—instantly her head felt clear. This had been the right move, after all. The road was empty, and sleepy, and for a moment nothing else felt real—the party, the shooting, the fact that they were all leaving. Anna knew she didn't want to be with Gavin, didn't belong with Gavin, but for a split second she let the moment wrap itself around her, her sandals and his flip-flops slapping against the blacktop, the hum of the cicadas, Gavin's warm arm bumping hers.

"Did you not want me to come tonight?" she asked. They were walking by his neighbors' house, the old Abbotts, past the rotting wood-pile.

"No," Gavin said. "I did."

"Oh," she said. "Well, good. You realize that Mindy Reddy is an idiot, don't you?"

"Jealousy." Gavin nodded. "I approve."

"I'm not *jealous*," Anna said, checking him in the shoulder. "It's just that she's an airhead. I want to make sure you know who you're dealing with."

"Oh, I know who I'm dealing with," Gavin said, and checked her back.

But as they neared the woods, Anna's light mood began to dissipate. By day, there were signs posted about hunting regulations and hiking trails, but at night you couldn't see anything. The trees were a single mass, solid and black, blacker than the sky.

She stopped. "Are you sure this is a good idea?"

"Absolutely," Gavin replied, footsteps crunching evenly toward the trailhead.

Anna glanced over her shoulder. The lights of the party were no longer visible. She felt the telltale glimmer of nerves. It was a feeling she knew all too well, the way her hands began to tingle. She pictured running water. A spigot in her brain, trickle in her veins.

"Come on, wuss!" Gavin was calling from the mouth of the trail. Then she watched him step into the woods and disappear.

Anna looked around once more, hunting for any other light: the faraway stars, the smudge of moon, the dull squares of gold from the old Abbotts' windows. Rumor had it that, after their son killed himself, the Abbotts had disconnected their phone and TV; they almost never left the house.

"Gavin!" she shouted, and slowly picked her way toward the trees. She waited for her eyes to adjust, listened to the old rain dripping faintly from the branches. It was insanely dark. "Where are you?"

"Right here," he said, and his voice was just ahead, still close.

"Wait," Anna told him, stepping onto the path. "Wait for me."

Her strides were short and cautious. The ground sank a little beneath her sandals, still muddy from yesterday's rain. A branch snapped, making her jump. She tried to come up with the worst-case scenario, but it was terrifying: Worst-case scenario, a killer was hiding in the woods.

"Gavin," she said. "Let's go back."

"What's wrong?"

"This is dumb," she said. "These are woods where people hunt."

He laughed. "No one's hunting this time of night."

"But some people are crazy. Some people are completely crazy lunatics."

"I think you're a completely crazy lunatic," Gavin said.

She stumbled over a root. Ten steps in and she was completely blind. She was scared too, and starting to sweat in the cold, but to stop now wasn't an option because then she'd be alone. "Gavin," she said. "Gavin, I can't see anything."

"That's the point."

"No, I mean—*anything*." She reached both hands before her like a zombie, swiping at the air, and grabbed onto the back of his T-shirt.

He laughed again. "You're not wimping out, are you, Anna Daley-Briggs?"

She could hear, in his voice, the teasing curve of his smile. He wasn't being cruel; he didn't realize how seriously she wasn't kidding.

"Would it help if I sing?" he asked, then started belting in a loud, high-pitched voice. "'*Tonight, we are young*...'"

Anna's heart was pounding so hard she could feel her skin twitching. Gavin kept on singing and she wished that he would stop because if there was a murderer in the woods they wouldn't hear him coming. She willed herself to keep moving forward, the way she used to push herself when swimming: If she didn't go seventy-five more feet, something terrible would happen. *One more lap or.*

"Gavin," she said, but faintly. Her ears were ringing. Their footsteps, his voice, were growing distant. She hadn't had an attack in over a year, but there was no mistaking the sensation—the way she was simultaneously aware of what was happening to her, cataloging the symptoms—limbs losing feeling, sound dulling, senses leached away one by one—and unable to make them stop. She tried counting in her head but couldn't focus. She pictured the dead bug decomposing inside her, bits of antennae and wing. Soon, she knew, her senses would start failing. Already the deep black of the woods had faded to a sickly, feathery gray. Nathan Dugan's face swam up in her mind. His cap. His unsmiling eyes.

"Stop," she said, but Gavin kept going.

"Gavin!" she said. She was nearly screaming. She yanked at his shirt so hard that he pulled up short and she fell into his back.

"Jesus," he said, but she felt him turn to face her. "What?" She couldn't see him but she could smell the alcohol on his breath, which meant that he was close. He couldn't have been more than a few inches away.

"Gavin, we need to go back," she whispered. "I'm not kidding."

"Why?"

She heard a rustling in the leaves, an animal or a man's footstep, and dug her nails into his shoulders. "Gavin," she said. She was almost crying. "I'm serious." Her ears were ringing and she knew that if she didn't turn around now she would start hyperventilating. Desperate, she did the only thing she could think of to make him leave—she groped for his face and shoved her mouth against his. Instantly she felt the pressure of his tongue, and when within seconds he was under her shirt, fumbling at her bra, she said, "No—not here," and pushed him back toward the mouth of the trail. "Hurry," she said, holding his hand and trying to breathe normally, stepping on the backs of his flapping Tevas. When she spotted lights ahead—*thank God, thank God, thank God*—and they stepped into the street, she dropped Gavin's hand and bent forward and drew a few lungfuls of air, bracing her hands on her knees.

When she stood upright, Gavin was looking at her strangely. Anna wiped at her tears. She didn't say anything, and neither did he, except to ask: "Are you okay?" She nodded. Sensation was returning—her vision sharpening, the buzz subsiding in her ears. "You sure?" he said, and when she nodded again, they started slowly back toward the house. Gavin took her hand, not minding that it was limp and clammy, and after a minute started talking about his new roommate at UVM, who seemed like a pretty cool guy, a lacrosse player. Anna had never been so grateful for his solid boyness, his normalcy. As they passed the pile of damp firewood, he stopped and turned to her. "You still with me?" he asked, and then he kissed her, and she knew it was because he wanted to make sure she didn't get too sleepy or change her mind. But she wouldn't change her mind. Back in Gavin's basement, she would have sex with him just to prove she was okay—*a nostalgia fuck*, she would report to Kim and Janie later—then she would try to put this night, this whole day, behind her. In the morning, she would go home and she would finish packing for college, and when her mom asked about the sleepover at Kim's, she would say that it was fine, it was like old times.

Three

The old red barn looked romantic from a distance, but up close it was sagging, soft with neglect. The shingles were loose, the paint chipping. The roof was skimmed with moss and the gutters choked with damp leaves. Still, Saturday morning, standing at the kitchen window as the sky grew light, Maggie felt as if she were gazing at a postcard. That was just the sort of lazy cliché she instructed her students to avoid, but in this case, it was the truth.

It was just past dawn, a private hour. The sky was the color of wet lilac, the moon a pale wedge suspended just above the trees. Maggie had gone to bed well past midnight but slept fitfully, replaying her conversation with Bill Wall. Now she filled a thermos with coffee, ate a piece of dry toast standing at the kitchen counter. It would be hours yet before Anna made her way home. When she pushed open the back screen door, the air was light and cool, near weightless, an apology for its oppressiveness the day before. The morning sat thick and glittering, the only sounds the hum of unseen insects. As Maggie started across the wet grass, she saw that an animal had indeed torn into her garden overnight, dug its way under the wooden fence.

Immediately after last night's phone call, Maggie had gone on to her computer and managed to find—easily enough, to her surprise—the Facebook page of Luke Finch. Birthday: March 29. Hometown: Paxton, Maine. There were no pictures of her former student, at least none immediately visible. At the top of the page was a photo of two dogs, golden retrievers, and just below it, a post written ten hours before:

I had a class with this kid

Four years ago

Today he shot and killed three people

Then he killed himself

The bluntness was jarring at first, though within just a few lines, Maggie could tell that this was not the Facebook post Bill had described. It was not intended to grab attention, go viral. *I didn't really know him but I still remember him*, Luke wrote, and what followed was a litany of memories, an elegy of sorts.

I remember these big headphones he used to hang around his neck

The stress ball that he squeezed until his hand turned white

The way he sat with his two pointer fingers pressed together

Maggie had no memory of the stress ball (in fact, she found it hard to imagine), but she remembered the pointers. Indeed, he had sat like that.

He wore this big green coat all year, Luke continued, and here Maggie bristled—see? She'd known how distracting that coat had been.

The class I had with him was Freshman Comp with Daley

Her chest tightened at the sight of her name on the screen. That Luke referred to her by her last name only was vaguely disorienting; it had a jocular quality more appropriate to a football coach but here, she thought, might confer a hint of disrespect.

He always sat in the same seat in the front next to the window

Sometimes he brought his dog to class

He was always one of the first ones there

Was he? Maggie hadn't known this, but she wouldn't have. She always arrived a minute or two late, to let a class settle in.

He never talked to anybody and if he talked in class he kind of walked over people

At this, she felt an old sting of remorse—that it had been so obvious, that she hadn't better managed to control it.

He wrote this paper that was really weird

There: Maggie stared at the words, let herself absorb them. Read and reread them until they were drained of meaning. *Weird. Weird. Weird.*

So today when I heard what he did there was a part of me that didn't feel
    completely surprised
And I wonder what that means
If I knew deep down something was wrong with him
Maybe I should have been nicer to him
I didn't really talk to him but now I wonder if it could have helped him
If anybody else from that class is reading this please write back
#classmate #millviewmallshooting #nathandugan #freshmanyear

At twelve fifteen a.m., the post appeared to have been shared 1022 times.

Maggie had read it twice more, sitting under the faint buzz of the lamp over the kitchen table. Each time, she actually felt a notch more reassured. *Incriminating*—surely that had been too strong a word. Bill must have been feeling rattled, overly sensitive, his judgment colored by the late hour or the horrific afternoon. For it was clear that Luke was not trying to agitate or provoke. He was shocked and saddened, trying to process his feelings, connect with his old classmates. In fact, rereading what he'd written, alone in her quiet kitchen, Maggie felt unexpectedly moved.

As she neared the barn, the bottoms of her jeans were soaked and heavy. She stepped up to the wide, shallow puddle of mud by the door. When Tom lived there, the barn had been one of his ongoing projects— he'd planned to convert it to a writing studio for her one day—but in three years it had fallen into quick disrepair. Maggie hadn't been in here since May, and when she pulled on the rusty handle and stepped inside, she was assaulted by the smell—trapped heat, wood, mildew. Something vaguely animal. Dust idled in the shafts of light beaming through the high windows, alighting on the dead and broken things strewn on the mud-streaked floor: a rusty lawn mower, a three-legged table, a stack of old snow tires. Anna's bike leaned against the pile. As Maggie climbed the creaking ladder to the loft, the musty air rose with her. At the top, she surveyed the makeshift work space: a warped wooden chair, a desk made of a door propped on two old sawhorses, and the boxes. They covered nearly an entire wall.

According to the university handbook, all faculty were required to save samples of student writing: *to maintain, for purposes of assessment, an archive of student work.* It was one of many practices the previous dean had been lax about requiring, but under Bill's watch had been strictly reinforced. Assessment metrics had been created, syllabi bloated with policies that made the students glaze over on the very first day of class. Faculty grumbled these things, about Bill in general—his methods were tedious, vaguely litigious—and Maggie understood their fatigue; when she was in college, a syllabus had often been a single, motivating page. Still, she respected Bill, how seriously he took things. And secretly, the collecting of student work was something she enjoyed; it was something she'd been doing for years. She'd always liked leaving with a tangible souvenir at the end of the semester: a record of the hard work done, the progress made. A paper trail of students she'd grown to know and, yes, love. If she rarely looked at them, she still liked knowing that she had them. Now, though, as she faced the wall of boxes—pliant, slumped against one another like piles of sleepy children—she felt only trepidation. Instead of amassing accomplishments, suddenly it seemed she'd been mounting evidence.

This wasn't an entirely new feeling. Over nearly three decades, Maggie had naturally encountered her share of troubling student work. Depression, addiction, mental illness, profound grief—the significant personal experience essay, cornerstone of the Freshman Comp curriculum, invited this kind of thing. Maggie had learned, repeatedly, how much of teaching was more than just teaching: the sensitive topics that might quickly boil to the surface, the thicket of personal problems a teacher might find herself wading through, undefended and unprepared. Every year some of the younger, more inexperienced instructors would come to view their classes like sessions of group therapy, mention their students' problems at staff meetings with a flushed eagerness that looked more like excitement than concern. Maggie did not actively solicit such personal confessions, but her students offered them anyway. She was proud that they trusted her, proud to have fostered the type of class, year after year, that earned that kind of trust. For the freshmen, eighteen and homesick, she was the closest thing to a parent that they had. And usually, if she received a worrying paper, it was clear the student was telling her on purpose, asking for her help. Like Alison Bower, a bright, self-possessed young woman Maggie had watched unravel before her eyes— grades dropping, confidence disappearing, absences piling up. *I think the world would be a better place without me in it*, she'd written, setting in motion an urgent chain of events. *Have you thought about committing suicide?* Maggie had asked her—the recommended strategy, to her surprise, was to ask directly, but it worked. Then the teary confession, the phone call to the crisis line, the after-hours walk to the counseling center along icy footpaths, her hand bracing the girl's narrow back. She still had the card she'd received from Alison later, thanking Maggie for all she'd done for her, standing on the shelf above her desk.

This, Maggie thought, was why English teachers became the first line of questioning when tragedy struck on a college campus: They were the ones who read the students' papers, glimpsed their inner lives— the personal confessions, tendencies toward violence or self-loathing or despair. Why the entire Freshman Comp staff had once been required to sit through a meeting with the counseling center. *Concerning Student Papers*, it was called. In the meeting, the counselors had talked about identifying students in crisis, coached the writing teachers on what subtleties to look for: *expressions of extreme hopelessness, lack of empathy, suggestions of violence toward self or others.* This was shortly after the Virginia Tech shooting, Maggie remembered. Like everyone, she had followed the unfolding story in wordless horror. She'd watched one of the shooter's English professors interviewed on CNN, admiring her clarity and courage as she described the disturbing material she'd seen in his work. How she'd taken it upon herself to tutor him individually because his presence in the classroom was unnerving. How she'd alerted the school, and the police, who couldn't act unless the threats were more explicit—but of course they weren't explicit, Maggie had thought, indignant on the teacher's behalf. That was the problem; that was the point.

The memory of this now was unsettling, but in a small way, consoling—Nathan's work, while perhaps *really weird*, had been nothing like that. Still, as Maggie stood in the barn surveying the boxes, piled in a rough pyramid under the steeply slanting roof, nerves swept through her like a wave. She reached for the top of the pile, cursing herself for not dating the boxes, then grabbed a few and hoisted them onto the floor. Kneeling, she pulled the lid from the first box. On top sat a blue roll book with raised gold letters: TEACHER'S PLAN BOOK. It was the old-fashioned kind she'd always used, despite the pressure to migrate everything online. The names scribbled inside were too recent, but still Maggie browsed through the pile of revised, polished final essays underneath. She knew instantly they were a comp class—while students in her upper-level courses submitted formal, plain-faced final papers, the freshmen tended toward brightly colored folders, collages assembled from magazine pages. Some had price tags intentionally affixed, evidence of how much they cared. As Maggie picked through, proud, inspiring titles went flashing by. *One Writer's Journey. From Cowardice to Confidence.* A few handwritten notes fluttered loose from the pages. *Thank you for all your help! This was my favorite college class!!!*

These papers served to reassure her. This, she thought, was the teacher that she was. Her *best self*—for years, it had been part of her rationale to Tom for the long hours, the devotion to her students. She moved on to the next box, which was visibly older, cardboard furred at the corners. The papers inside were browning at the edges. Still, Maggie remembered every one. Sifting through the contents, she wondered what Anna would write about if given the assignment. *A significant personal experience.* There were so many difficult stories to choose from, so many unflattering lights—unshakable, naive, distracted—in which the mother character could be cast. Or perhaps Anna's most significant experiences were ones in which Maggie didn't even appear, feelings she'd never known her daughter felt. She recalled how, after Anna started seeing Theresa, she'd encouraged her to keep a journal, an idea Maggie liked; Anna had always loved to write. Maggie had allowed herself to peek inside the clothbound book only once—flipped through a few pages skimming lines about Gavin and Kim and Janie, convincing herself it wasn't an invasion of privacy if she wasn't actually pausing to read anything, until she alighted on *think Mom could have tried harder to make him happy*—then, startled, put it back.

Maggie paused now to swipe the back of her neck. The loft was suffocating; the windows didn't open, making the barn a greenhouse on a sunny day. When she and Tom had argued in here, it had been winter, and they both had been standing, boxers in a ring. She remembered the deep cold—the barn wasn't heated—and how they were screaming at each other, absurdly, dressed in their hats and coats. Even now, Tom's words echoed in the walls, pulsed like old injuries in bones. *Are you blind? Have you even noticed how miserable I am?* She remembered her shock at what he said, and at how he looked as he said it, pacing the old beams, face swollen in anger. It was a side of him she'd never seen before, never even known was there.

She twisted her hair off her neck, tying it up with a thick, slightly gummy brown rubber band, and lifted the lid from the next box on the pile. The pages inside were stiff, pinched with flaking metal paper clips. A small brown spider scurried down one side. As Maggie kept digging, one old essay after the next, her sense of fondness gradually began to morph into a kind of sadness—how aged it all seemed. All the old courage and optimism, the passionate opinions and personal stories— stories that at the time had felt so urgent and necessary, full of unleashed feeling—written by eighteen-year-olds who were now adults with children and spouses, relegated to these boxes, wilted and dank.

A headache was migrating across her scalp. Her knees ached. She picked the lid off the next box, velvety with dust, and when she opened up the roll book, her breath caught—*Dugan, Nathan. Spring 2012.* Carefully, she slid one finger along the row of boxes and check marks. B-, C+ on his major papers. Absent three times, never late.

For a minute, Maggie looked up and watched the dust drift in the sunshine. Of course he was there; she had known that he would be. The three absences surprised her—she would have guessed more, so palpable was the memory of her relief when Nathan wasn't there. She was afraid suddenly of what else she might have misremembered, what she might rediscover once she started looking. She was seized with the urge to abandon the mission entirely, close the box and return to the house— but no. She took a breath and resumed her task. And there they all were: that basement classroom, 14C. Hannah Chaffee's abortion. Meredith's lament for her brother. Luke Finch: a plain manila folder, an essay about his grandfather. *My grandpa was a kind man*: The plain language that on Facebook had felt appropriately spare, even respectful, in class—and perhaps especially that class, dominated by outspoken young women— might have been so understated it disappeared.

She returned Luke's folder, and already was nearing the bottom. She fantasized that by some twist of fate Nathan's work hadn't been saved with the rest of them—she could tell Bill that, unlikely as it sounded, it simply wasn't there—but just as she allowed herself a premature flicker of hope:

Nathan Dugan

Final Paper

May 3, 2012

Professor Daley

Freshman Composition Section 19

Maggie removed Nathan's paper and set it gently on her knees. Something about the actuality of it was startling: The same boy who would later walk into a mall with guns in a duffel bag, who would end his own life so gruesomely, had stuffed these very pages into his knapsack one morning before school. That same boy had sat in front of his computer and typed her name. He had been sitting in her classroom for an entire semester, within reach of her other students, of herself—it was not unrealistic to think something could have set him off. Maggie's reprimand after he criticized Meredith's essay? One of the quick looks she'd shared with the girls? She recalled the manager from the Walmart, saying he'd made people uneasy. Maggie had observed the same quality in Nathan but she had never confronted him, had avoided confronting him. If she had, might she have gotten to him in time? Steered him toward help? Or was it possible that, in this instance, her rare lapse in professionalism might actually have kept her students safe?

She stared at the title page, damp fingertips puckering the margins. Unlike the others, Nathan's paper had no cover, no clever title or colored binder. It had been typed on an old word processor, judging by the square font and green tint. A single staple was centered in the upper left-hand corner. Confusingly, when Maggie turned to the first page of his essay, she saw that this was the original draft, the version with her comments on it—Nathan had not bothered to revise it for the final. Not only that, he hadn't even made the superficial gesture of printing off a fresh copy. At the top, in a quick flourish, Maggie had scribbled: C+. The most neutral of grades, the most noncommittal. The look of the pages was much as she remembered—long unwieldy paragraphs, narrow margins—but when she turned back to the beginning—

The Hunting Trip

Maggie held very still. She stared at the sunlight that had crept over her knees.

On a Saturday morning in October my dad and me decided to go hunting. We left the house at 5:00 a.m. My dad was a corporal in the US Army. It was a ritual we had.

So Nathan had, in fact, written about his father. Maggie was comforted that—in this detail at least—her memory was correct.

My mother packed our lunches and said for us to be careful. My dad
said women always worry too much.

She flinched at the casual disparagement of women, then reminded herself this kind of gender bias was not terribly unusual. It was something she
encountered occasionally in her students—and challenged when she could,
encouraging these teenagers to think more deeply about their worlds—but
was a perspective difficult to isolate, it was so deeply ingrained.

My dad and me loaded the truck and drove to the woods off of Route
70 near the intersection of Route 70 and Route 18. We wore camo pants
and vests and face paint and carried daypacks which included: com-
pass, hunting knife, lighter, GPS, ammo, two rifles and a AR-15.

Maggie wiped her palms on her jeans. She reminded herself that these
were kids from the country, kids who grew up hunting—certainly this was
not the only hunting essay she'd received. Obviously hunting didn't make
you dangerous. Take the locals who converged on Dead River Market on
November mornings, filling their thermoses with coffee, dressed in neon
hats and jackets, guns stowed in truck beds. Take Dick Newland, some kind
of pharmaceutical rep who hunted on the weekends; Anna had once mentioned that Gavin's house was full of mounted heads.

But as she kept reading, there were other things, smaller things. Bits of
language—always, it was in the language. The clinical specificity of all the
ammunition Nathan had carried into the woods with his father (featureless,
except for his rank, and a brown Mazda B–Series truck). And the guns.

I have hunted with many different types of weapons including: pellet
guns and BB guns, bow and arrow, single shot 12 gauge shotguns,
22 gauge shotguns, 12 gauge auto, pump action shotguns, bolt
action rifles (sniper rifles), big game rifles, AR-10s and AR-15s. Some
people have no respect for using semiautos to hunt with or say it's
not PC but in the right hands they can be your best friend.

Her breaths were light and careful. For the next two pages, the paper continued in this vein: a glossary of different weapons, different uses and specifications. Guns for hunting, for combat, for sandstorms, survivalist scenarios—pointless tangents as far as the essay was concerned. The guns weren't on the page because they were relevant, or even because Nathan was trying to fill the required five pages, but because—Maggie sensed it in the quality of the sentences, the tunnel-like repetition, the tinge of relish—he simply liked thinking about them. He couldn't help but think about them, like the student with an eating disorder who lapses into lush digressions about food.

> If I had to choose one gun for home invasions I would go with a pump action shotgun because it can blast through anything so if I was positioned to annihilate invaders the penetration would give me the upper hand. If I had to choose one for hunting and SHTF though I would choose the AR-10 semiauto because it can disable a car engine and quickly neutralize multiple targets at close range.

And that was the end. There were no conclusions made, no insights drawn, not even a tidy, insincere final paragraph. The dad—along with the opening scene in the woods—had disappeared. The rest of the paper was single-minded, narrow in its focus, oblivious to its audience: thoughts dumped from head to page. This, though, Maggie reminded herself, was the quality of everything Nathan wrote; it was the quality of Nathan himself. Perhaps the military father was the detail she'd remembered because its presence at the time had reassured her, provided some context for Nathan's knowledge of weapons, cast him in a softer light. Proven that his oddly detached tone could apply to any subject, even a person he loved. Now, of course, in light of the past twenty-four hours, the lists of guns looked troubling, but back then they likely struck her as the work of a lonely kid who lacked imagination, who was prone to digressions, a kid whose writing—whose person—simply lacked awareness, lacked depth.

Maggie drew a breath. Then she returned to the beginning, reading again more slowly. This time, she paid attention to her own comments penned in the margins. Where usually she smothered students' papers with notes, these were sparse, only two or three per page; the weaker the essay, of course, the less there was to say. *Add paragraphs to help organize ideas. Avoid generalizations.* Most of her comments were broad, generic. She winced at the scribbled *vary word choice*, next to the word *annihilate*, used twice.

At the end of the paper, Maggie had scrawled: *Ultimately I'm not quite certain what this essay is saying about the title "hunting trip." What is its significance exactly? MD.* She regretted not writing something more—more thoughtful, more motivating—though presumably she'd realized by then that there was little point. That Nathan didn't take suggestions, that there were other more dedicated students she could be giving her time to, that his essay would come back exactly as it had been turned in.

"Mom?"

"Anna!" Maggie startled, palm pressed to her chest.

Her daughter paused halfway up the ladder. "Yikes."

"You scared me," Maggie said. "I didn't hear you." She wiped her runny nose with the back of one wrist, smelled the sour tang of her own skin. "I didn't realize you were even home."

"It's almost eleven," Anna said, clearly confused. "I was looking all over for you. What are you doing up here?" She stepped off the ladder, ducking under the gabled roof. "And why don't you open a window?"

"These windows don't open," Maggie said. "They've never opened."

"Well, that's helpful," Anna said. "It's like a sauna in here." She shoved her sleeves up to her elbows, slipped a purple elastic from her wrist. Briskly, she snapped her hair up in a quick, emphatic knot. "But seriously," she said, glancing around the room. "What is all this?"

Maggie took in the mess of loose papers and dusty boxes. "Nothing," she said, shaking her head. "I was just going through some old files."

"What's that?" Her gaze had stopped on Maggie's lap.

Maggie looked down at the pile of limp pages: the march of square green letters, the old staple bleeding rust into the corner.

"Oh my God," Anna said. "Is it by that guy? Nathan Dugan?" She looked at Maggie's face. "You kept it?"

"Well, yes," Maggie said. She gestured vaguely around the room. "Obviously, though, I keep papers from all my students—"

"What's it about?"

"Just—a day trip."

"What kind of a day trip?"

"Just a day he spent with his dad," Maggie said.

Anna pinched her lip. "Does he sound violent?"

"No." Maggie paused. "I wouldn't say that."

"Can I read it?"

For years, Anna had been curious about her students' essays—it fascinated her that they were allowed to write about such personal things for school—but Maggie had never let her read them. It would have been unfair to the students, and unhealthy for Anna. Now Maggie shook her head and said, "You know that wouldn't be right."

"But this is different."

"I still don't think it's a good idea," Maggie said, which was true. Until she'd discussed the paper with Bill, it was best to keep it to herself. Besides, she could tell by the look on Anna's face that the paper's very presence was upsetting her. "In any case," Maggie said, and forced a smile, a change of subject. "Tell me about you."

Anna paused with her lip. "What?"

"Your night. The sleepover. Was it fun?"

She looked over Maggie's head, seeming to consider the question. It was then that Maggie really registered how tired and tense her daughter looked—the black liner smudged beneath her eyes, the clothes she'd worn the night before. "Not really," she said. "We went to a party, actually. At Gavin's."

"Oh?" This was a surprise—not that Anna hadn't told her they were going, but that she was telling her now. It was also disappointing. Maggie felt saddened, disproportionately so, about the sleepover.

"But don't worry," Anna continued. "We're not back together. It was just a lame party that Kim and Janie seemed to think I should attend."

"I wasn't worried," Maggie said, though she had to admit, she was glad to hear it. Anna looked at the floor, the bright white squares of sunlight. Maggie waited a beat, and when no more information was forthcoming, tried "Was it hard to see him? Gavin? Was it—"

"It wasn't Gavin," Anna cut in, and when she looked up, Maggie saw there were tears standing brightly in her eyes. "It was just the whole thing. The whole night. Everybody was just—you know, freaked out."

She looked shaken, Maggie thought. She looked scared. She imagined the scene at the party, Anna's classmates speculating about the shooting, telling the kinds of stories that might have set her off. "Well," she said, careful. "That's only natural. That's understandable."

"I know that," Anna said miserably. She looked back down at the floor. It occurred to Maggie to wonder if anyone at the party had mentioned Luke's Facebook post—but if Anna didn't bring it up, she wouldn't either. Instead she ventured, "You didn't tell them he was my student, did you, Anna?"

Her head snapped up. "Why? Was I not supposed to?"

"No, no, I just wondered—"

"I mean, I told Janie and Kim."

"And that's fine," Maggie said. Her armpits were sweating, the backs of her knees. "But you know, about this paper, I think it's best if we not mention it to anyone else."

"Why not?"

"It's just—it's a sensitive situation," Maggie said. "Okay?"

"Fine." Anna shrugged. "I mean, what would I even say?" Then she was picking at her lip, and Maggie had to restrain herself from telling her to stop. From outside, she began to take in the distant sounds of late morning, the rumble of the tractor at the Lyonses' down the road and a truck rattling by on Route 18. It was their last morning together, the last day her only child would live at home with her. In twenty-four hours, she would be leaving for college. Maggie knew it was entirely likely Anna would never live here again. She felt a quick swell of—was it sadness? Fear? "You promise you'll be careful, Anna, won't you?"

A mistake—she knew this as soon as she saw the stricken look on Anna's face. "Oh my God. Like what? Like I'll try not to get shot?"

"No, no," Maggie said. "That isn't what I meant. I just want to know you'll take care of yourself. And you'll call me. If you need me."

Anna covered her face with both hands and inhaled through her fingers. "You're freaking me out," she said, then started for the ladder. "I need to pack."

"Okay," Maggie said. "I have to run over to school later, but I won't be long. I can help when I get back. And I was thinking, for dinner, takeout—"

"Kim and Janie are coming."

"That's fine. I assumed so. We could do Romeo's, for old times' sake."

"Right." Anna looked at her palms, squeezed them into fists. "I'm going down," she said. "It's too hot up here to breathe."

"Agreed," Maggie said, but her daughter had already begun to leave. She listened to her descend the creaky ladder, the gentle slam of the barn door, then the quiet. The essay in question still stared up from her knees—*quickly neutralize multiple targets at close range.* Maggie closed her eyes until they watered. Then she took a breath, folded the paper and stuffed it in her pocket, and made her way back outside.

From her front porch to the steps of Tilghman Hall, the road to campus was a virtually straight line. Maggie had always liked the simplicity of her commute: eleven miles linking work and home. She knew the road in all its variations, the way it transformed in different seasons—the edges softened by cattails and violets in early summer, the cocoons that grew on the trees each August like thick spools of yarn. In winter, the snow that mounted on the roadsides, the glimmers of black ice that once sent her car sliding and crashing, almost gently, into the Kirbys' wooden fence. She knew the exact point at which the old farmhouses yielded to the tackle shop, the dairy barn, the now-defunct general store, and the brief, garish stretch of commerce—KFC, Pep Boys, True Value, Taco Bell, the mall, the Walmart—before morphing into campus where, for six blocks, Route 18 was renamed University Row.

On a late Saturday afternoon in August, the sun was low and bright, the sky scudded with clouds. A few leaves were just turning—a flame of red, splash of gold. The car windows were down, the radio on. It was the first time Maggie had left the property since yesterday, and it felt disorienting to be outside. Here was the world, just as she'd left it. Her canvas boat bag sat on the passenger seat beside her, Nathan's paper zippered into the inside pocket. Since that morning, she'd run the lines through her head multiple times, and still felt that her reasoning was sound. She hoped Bill felt the same.

—victims in yesterday's fatal shooting in Reed, Maine.

Maggie made an involuntary sound, a small gasp, and reached to turn the volume up. As the trees swished by, under a beautiful summer sky, she listened as the county commissioner read the names of the dead. Betsy Crawley, from Reed, a mother of two small children. Frank Tremont, a high school math teacher in Essex County. Doreen Howard, from Millville, just nineteen. Joe Poole, mall security guard; he'd died that morning in the emergency room. Maggie didn't know any of them—though she would recognize the guard, surely—and felt a momentary sense of relief. Then the grief struck her, heavy as a stone. A mother of young children. A nineteen-year-old girl. An interview was now playing with the girl's fiancé. His voice was tearful and breaking. As she listened, Maggie could feel the weight of the tragedy subtly shifting: the shooting no longer a slow unknown unfolding before them but a terrible memory taking shape behind them, facts disclosed and assembled, hardening into the past.

As she rounded the bend in the road by Del's Dairy Barn, caught up in her thoughts, she abruptly hit the brake. A column of traffic stretched before her as far as she could see—eight or nine cars, at least—before twisting out of sight behind the trees. Maggie stopped hard behind a white pickup truck, Maine plates. She lowered the radio to a murmur. Usually this sort of backup signaled a slow driver or meander-ing tourist somewhere up ahead bogging down the lane, but these cars were stopped completely. Maybe there was tree work, an accident. She strained to see a flagger up ahead directing traffic, but there were no cars coming in the opposite direction either. She noticed the truck's engine was turned off—an ominous sign. Maggie turned hers off too. In the quiet, smaller sounds began surfacing. The chirp of crickets from the long grass by the roadside. Faintly, voices, a megaphone. She stepped out into the road, peering up ahead, and made out what looked like police cars, their sirens silently flashing, a scattering of traffic signs and orange cones.

The mall, she thought, and her first instinct was panic—was it hap-pening again? But of course the area around the mall would still be gridlocked. There would be media swarming the place; it had barely been twenty-four hours. Gawkers, maybe, or people leaving flowers and candles for the victims by the main entrance. She'd seen footage of the mounting pile on the news.

She returned to the car, angry at herself. She should have anticipated this and allowed extra time. She cast an eye around the front seat, as if a solution might appear before her. To her left, Del's was empty, a dirt parking lot with a scattering of wood-stump tables and chairs. A hand-lettered sign hung in the window: CLOSED. RIP. To her right, a plume of weeds, papery flutter of moths. Behind her, an SUV pulled up sharply, its silver nose filling up her rearview mirror. She checked her watch: three thirty-six. If she waited, inching her way past the mall toward cam-pus, she would be unforgivably late. She wished she'd thought to bring Bill's number; her flip phone wasn't connected to the Internet. Still, she dug it from her bag and tried dialing Holly, the admin, a number she had memorized, but on a Saturday there was no answer. She tossed the phone in the cup holder. Her best option now would be to thread her way through the back roads behind the shopping plaza and reconnect with Route 18. She turned the car on, and the radio bounced back to life, seeming louder than it had before. *It will take time for our community to heal from this senseless—* She turned it off and eased onto the shoulder, raising an apologetic palm to the other drivers as she bumped along in the lopsided trench, carpeted with gravel, until a quarter mile later the first cross street appeared: Parrish Road.

Maggie had passed this street countless times, but it was possible she'd never actually turned down it. It was in an unremarkable neighborhood of small, ranch-style houses made of clapboard and vinyl. A school bus sat parked in a driveway, a boat in another. The front yards were cluttered—lawn ornaments, toys, bikes, plastic pools, a salting of satellite dishes—as if compensating for the smallness of the houses by furnishing every inch of property they had. The house Maggie had grown up in, fifty miles west of here, had been small too, but unadorned. It sat on land, she thought; the land made the difference. A dog roamed a driveway, unchained, letting out a sharp bark as Maggie drove past. She flinched slightly as three teenage boys on bikes came careening down the street and whizzed by—stone-faced, stiff and upright, hands loose in laps.

At the next intersection, she made a left, then a right, attempting to stay parallel to the main road. Another long march of small, ranch-style houses, nearly identical, but set more widely, on just one side of the road. The other side was woods—mossy, untended, choked with blowdown. A beer can was tossed at the edge, a torn plastic bag. Up ahead, Maggie spied another roadblock, several cars and people, a small truck blocking the street, and again she felt a flare of panic—an accident? But no. These cars didn't seem damaged. The truck was maneuvering itself into a spot in front of the small house, lemon yellow—she froze.

On television, the house had looked bigger, but in fact the people gathered outside were congregated on a small patch of lawn. Maggie watched, unable to go forward, as some spoke into microphones; others stood with arms folded and stared at the house, as if challenging it to speak. She recalled seeing Nathan's mother on the news, but now there was no light or movement from inside the house, no evidence that anyone was there. Maggie felt a stab of sympathy, imagining this woman trapped in her own home. When a car drew up behind her, honking, Maggie saw the truck had pulled over, and that it wasn't a truck at all, but a news van. She drove past the house, keeping her eyes on the road.

By the time she reached the end of the block, she had lost her bearings. Ten minutes to four: At this rate, she would be half an hour late. Two turns later, she finally found a large intersection, Standish, which would connect eventually with Route 18. She leaned on the gas as she passed by a bleak stretch of storefronts: check cashing, gym, tanning salon. A small red building, a wooden sign shaped like a rifle—the gun shop. She startled as she recognized it, nestled inconspicuously next to a cheap motor lodge that advertised cable TV.

When she pulled into the parking lot beside the English building, it was nearly four thirty, but Bill's car was still there. She rushed inside. On a Saturday in August, the lobby was deserted but still had an anticipatory air—floors waxed and gleaming, bulletin boards neatened, sounds of grounds crews buzzing somewhere on the quad. Despite everything, the freshmen would arrive in four days.

"Bill," she said, arriving at his office door, slightly winded. "I apologize. The traffic by the mall—"

Bill was sitting at his desk, hands folded, staring absently at his computer screen. Maggie thought for a moment he was praying. The overhead light was off, the only light in the room coming from the desk lamp and the rim of sun around the window shade.

"Sorry," she said. "I'm interrupting."

He drew his glasses down to hang from the black cord around his neck. His eyes had a faraway look. "I was just reading the news. About the victims," he said. "The security guard, Poole. He was the uncle of one of our students."

"Oh," she breathed. "I hadn't heard. Who—"

"A sophomore. Samantha."

Maggie shook her head: not one of hers. "How awful," she said.

"And the girl, Doreen," he said. "Her fiancé is a senior. Arlen Mackey."

"Oh no," Maggie said. She recalled the sound of this boy, crying, on the news.

For another moment, Bill just stared at his computer. Even on a Saturday, he was wearing his customary tie and jacket, but up close Maggie could see how disheveled he was. The tie was slightly crooked, his beard in need of trimming, details unremarkable except for the fact that Bill was ordinarily so meticulous. She thought again about the thinness of his voice on the phone the night before, the lateness of his call.

He touched his tie then, the knot at his neck. "Please," he said. "Come in. And close the door, if you would."

Maggie couldn't imagine who in this vacant building might overhear them, but she pulled the door shut behind her.

"Tea?" He gestured to the low shelf by the window, where a hot plate sat among orderly rows of books, a framed picture of his three teenage children. Two boys and a girl, smiling broadly, arms slung around each other's necks like loose towels.

"I'm fine," Maggie said. "Thank you."

"My mother was a big believer in tea," he said. "The great curative."

Bill had a cup by his elbow, though it appeared untouched. Maggie took the chair across from his desk and placed her bag by her feet.

"Well," he said, then allowed himself a sigh. "I trust you found the Facebook post. At last count, it's been shared—" He pushed his glasses back on and returned to his computer, tapping the keyboard with one finger. "Two thousand one hundred and three times."

"Really?" Already the number was more than twice what it had been the night before—it felt large but abstract, oddly weightless. Maggie even laughed a little. "How are these hordes of people even finding it?"

"The mysteries of the Internet," Bill said. "Twitter, Snapchat, Instagram."

"You're speaking a different language," she reminded him.

"You have a daughter who's a teenager, don't you? High school?"

"College," she said. "She's about to leave for college. Tomorrow, actually."

"Well, I'm sure she could give you a social media tutorial before she leaves."

Maggie assumed that he was kidding, but Bill's expression had no humor in it. "Yes, well, I'm sure she could," she said. She might have added that she couldn't be less interested, but held her tongue. "In any case, I found it, yes. I read it."

"And did you agree?"

She hesitated. "Agree with what?"

"With how Dugan was depicted. How he was described."

"Oh—well. In part, I suppose." She had been working on laying out the fairest way, the best way, to describe him. "I remember him as quiet," she said. "Like Luke did."

Bill nodded, angling his chair toward the screen.

"He wasn't as engaged as his classmates," she continued, and when Bill reached for the keyboard, Maggie thought he was consulting Facebook again, but then he began typing. Taking notes.

She hesitated, and he looked up. "Don't mind me."

"Right," Maggie said, with a wry laugh, though she reminded herself that Bill, thorough as he was, probably took notes in every meeting.

"You were saying that Dugan was disengaged—"

"Yes." She paused, gathering her thoughts. "And well—that particular class, they were a close-knit group. A terrific group, in fact. But Nathan, he didn't seem as invested," she said, and as Bill resumed typing, she had a flash of the couples counseling sessions with Jim Whittier, the long stretches of quiet and one-sided conversations, the sense that every word was becoming a matter of permanent record. Maggie hadn't particularly liked Jim—was sure she'd sensed a subtle allegiance between the two men in the room—but she had to admit the sessions had been effective: They'd coaxed damning things to the surface, done what they were designed to do.

"The Facebook post," Bill said, looking up again. "It said he brought a dog with him to class."

"He did, sometimes."

"Why was that?"

"Do you mean—officially?"

"Was it an emotional support animal?"

"Oh, no, I doubt it. There was no official—paperwork, or anything," she said, fumbling. "I'm not really sure. And I'll admit, I don't think I ever asked. But the animal was well behaved, not disruptive. Sweet, even." She paused again. "I almost always get to know my students quite well, but Nathan, he was difficult to connect with."

Bill frowned. "He was isolated?"

"I don't know if I'd go that far," Maggie said. "But he kept to himself. He didn't participate too often. He wasn't responsive to feedback. In many ways, most ways really, he felt simply absent."

"Absent," he repeated, looking uncertain.

"He was there, of course," she said. "But uninvolved. Distracted. Clueless, maybe," she added, then regretted it. *Cluelessness* suggested a student who was sloppy, dreamy, lost-in-the-clouds, a student who with guidance could be brought around. "He lacked a certain sensitivity," she said. "The other students were actually quite nice with him, given the circumstances."

Bill was now studying the screen. "You said he was insensitive."

"Well, no—I said he lacked sensitivity."

He nodded toward his notes but, she noticed, didn't change them. "How so?"

Outside, the hedge trimmers were drawing close. "Well," she said. "Naturally, comp is a class where students write about personal subjects, and Nathan wasn't always so aware—so perceptive—about these things."

"Was he rude to the other students? Was he hostile?"

"No, not exactly," Maggie said. "He could be quite literal," she added, and by way of example, she recounted the way he'd reacted to Meredith's essay about her brother.

Bill raised his eyebrows. "He lacked empathy then."

"That's one interpretation, I suppose." *Isolated, hostile, lacking empathy—*

she had the feeling Bill was quoting key terms from a checklist. "I think I interpreted it as sort of disconnected," she said, then pressed her lips together. "Actually, I'm not sure that's the right word, disconnected—"

"And this didn't concern you at the time?"

She flinched at the note of judgment. *None of these things struck you as unusual?*

"If you're asking if I thought Nathan was dangerous, Bill, then no, I didn't, not then," she said firmly, but felt a quiver of self-doubt. She recalled the commiserating looks she'd received from the other students, the way the rest of the class had navigated around him, the deliberation with which she placed him in small groups. She hadn't thought him dangerous, but she couldn't say she hadn't been concerned. The concern, though, had been primarily for Nathan's classmates, for whom she had wanted to dilute his presence. In fact, to even imagine the scenario where her concern was expressed *to* Nathan, for Nathan, that simple pivot in perspective—to have taken him aside, seen him as the student in need of help—was nearly impossible to do, and this made her feel alarmed.

Bill had leaned back in his chair. The hedge trimmers were getting louder, making their way up and down the mulberry bushes flanking the building. He drew his glasses off, rubbing both eyes until the sound began to fade. His nose was creased with deep pink dents on both sides. "You know, Maggie," he said, "I consider you one of our most dedicated faculty."

"Thank you," she replied, feeling a fresh, floating worry.

"You've been teaching here for—what, twenty-five years?"

"Twenty-eight."

Bill nodded. He rested his fingertips along the edge of his desk. "So you know how things have changed. The mental health concerns on campus. The pressure to accommodate students. To protect them. It's the university of the twenty-first century," he said. It was a term Maggie disliked, but Bill spoke it neutrally enough that she couldn't tell whether he rejected or embraced it. More likely, neither: For Bill, policy was policy, fact fact. "Did you know, last year, one in every two of our students was medicated for anxiety?" he asked.

Maggie knew, of course, about anxiety in teenagers—far more than Bill could ever guess—but still, this statistic surprised her. "I didn't, actually," she said.

"We're in the midst of an anxiety epidemic. The students are anxious, parents are anxious. They send their kids to college and trust us to keep them safe." He smiled wanly. "Your daughter's headed to college. You must know what I mean."

"Well, yes," Maggie said, squeezing her elbows in her hands. "Obviously, though, it's not that simple. We can't guarantee the students' safety."

"Of course not. But we have a responsibility to try. And we need to do better. From where I'm sitting—frankly, you can't imagine the pressure. This tragedy didn't happen out of nowhere. Whatever measures we can take, whatever red flags we can be more vigilant about moving forward—this young man was on our campus not three months ago with what were obviously very severe problems. No doubt there were signs, and they were missed."

Panic was creeping inward. The clock on the chapel chimed five. On any other day, this was a sound Maggie loved—robust, collegial—but today it felt ominous.

"It's getting late," Bill said, sitting forward and pushing his glasses back on. "And I've steered us off-track." He tapped at the keyboard, sending a faint splash of light into the room. "Two thousand one hundred seventy-one."

The hedge clippers abruptly cut off, and in their absence, Maggie registered the sound of a light but steady rain.

"Let's get to the writing samples," Bill continued. "Nathan's writing samples. What did you find?"

As if from a distance, Maggie observed her hands, now curled in her lap like pale shells, the bluish glow of the computer screen. She felt the presence of Nathan's essay, leaning against her knee and waiting to be sprung. *Frankly, you can't imagine the pressure.* She was certain that, if she produced this paper, no matter what, Bill would deem it troubling, incriminating. That, in the face of his conviction, her rationale from this morning would sound woefully thin. And the prospect of the dean thinking Maggie—Maggie, a teacher whose dedication to, attention to, her students had come more easily than to her husband and her daughter—that he might think her negligent, even in some small way responsible for what had happened—it was impossible to bear. Too easily, she could picture the essay plucked from her hand, the dismay on Bill's face, and what she said was: "I didn't find anything, I'm afraid."

Bill's expression altered only slightly, a flinch in one eye. "You didn't find anything that concerned you."

"No," she said. "I meant I couldn't find anything at all."

"The required writing samples." He looked at her uncomprehendingly. "You didn't archive them?"

"I did," she said. "But unfortunately, I don't have them."

"I thought you said you kept them—"

"I do. I always do. But I store them out in my barn. And there was damage."

"Damage?"

"Rain," she said, the lie coming with unsettling ease. "It must have been those heavy storms, back in June. I didn't know it until this morning."

"And they weren't saved electronically."

"I'm afraid not, no," she said. "As I said, I'm not a technology person." This part, at least, was true.

Bill sat back in his chair and rubbed one palm back and forth across the top of his head. Maggie held still, trying to remain composed, and when Bill spoke again, his voice was thick with feeling. "I know people don't like the way I do things," he said. "All the policies, all the rules. But this is why they're important. Naturally, I'd like to believe there was nothing incriminating in that paper. I trust you would have caught it if there were. But now, without it, we can't know for sure. If more comes of this—" He nodded toward the computer. "We're in no position to respond. And say there *were* something, even something subtle, we could learn from it. We could know what to look for. Because if a red flag had emerged in one of Nathan Dugan's papers, had it been noticed, there's a chance a tragedy might have been avoided. It might have been caught."

Maggie cradled one hand inside the other. Tension was climbing up her spine. It was at that moment—she would remember it, later—that she thought about handing Bill the paper, correcting the lie she'd told, apologizing for her momentary lapse in judgment. Bill would understand; he was a decent man. But she couldn't bring herself to do it, imagining the fallout, the ensuing scrutiny—the essay, and her insufficient comments in the margins, picked over line by line. Quietly, she said, "You have to admit, Bill, this isn't something teachers are equipped for. We're not trained psychologists. We're hired to teach students how to write. It's not our job to know if they might be shooting people in a mall in four years."

Bill peered at her, in surprise, over his glasses. "There's no need to get defensive," he said. "We're all upset about what happened."

"I'm not defensive," Maggie returned. "I'm saying that often these aren't easy calls to make."

"But by your own admission, this student had some difficulties—"

"As do many students," she said. "As do most students."

"And now this Luke Finch remembers something being wrong."

At this, Maggie merely nodded. "I'm sorry," she said, "that I don't have Nathan's work to show you. I can tell you though, with absolute certainty, I never could have imagined he would do something like this."

"No," Bill said, and she was startled by the depth of sorrow on his face. "I can't imagine that you did."

Four

Suzanne had developed a theory, even before her own marriage started falling apart, that the people who put the most cheerful things on the Internet were the ones whose lives were the most unhappy. They were pretending otherwise (to the world, and maybe to themselves) by posting idyllic pictures of their husbands and children—date nights, summer vacations, first days of school. Suzanne understood this impulse, but also recognized that it was not without consequences. For sometimes, these same people would abruptly stop posting anything, and Suzanne would hear through her sisters or old friends that the husband was having an affair or the bank had foreclosed on their home or the youngest son had developed an addiction to Vicodin following surgery on his knee. Lately, this kind of thing seemed to be happening more and more. It was probably the age—fifty-three, a time in life when one's body began to falter, and the problems of one's children grew more dire, the problems in a marriage more intractable, and time seemed suddenly not so indefinite, as one began to weigh how happy one's life was against how much life was left.

Suzanne was careful to never put anything online that might misrepresent her life as happy, nor anything that might hint at all that was wrong.

To get too personal either way seemed in poor taste. She'd been raised by a mother who, above all else, valued privacy and propriety. (Her mother would have despised Facebook, Suzanne thought.) What Suzanne posted were nature photographs, mostly. She'd taken an eight-week course at the adult school back in Indiana, and for her birthday that year Robert had given her a digital camera. It was one of the few things Suzanne liked about living in Maine: There was so much to photograph there—the woods with their thin veil of new snow, a stubborn beach rose the color of a dog's tongue, a shaggy tree draped in fog standing by the side of the road. Sometimes, after an appointment at Central Maine Medicine, she would drive to Meer Cove and sit inside her car with the engine running, warm air blasting from the vents, and watch the sea smoke dance on the water, curling and twisting across the frozen surface like a ballet. It was exquisite, and impossible to capture with a camera—both the smoke and the way it echoed inside her, took the haze she felt trapped inside and lifted it off her like a coat, manipulating it into something beautiful and visible and filling her with a sweeping sadness that was, somehow, pleasurable too.

Her photos always received a polite flurry of responses (the beach rose had been particularly well liked), and in return she clicked dutifully through her sisters' children, old friends' and old neighbors' children, even when the preponderance of children made a darkness come nibbling at the edge. Mostly, though, the world online was purely an escape—a distraction. Except for those times when a real-world tragedy was so horrific that to post about anything else was heartless, or ignorant. She pitied her sister Julia, asking for beach-read recommendations on the same day as the bombing at the Boston Marathon.

The shooting at the Millview Mall hadn't generated the highest level of attention—four victims sadly no longer ranked that kind of coverage—but as Suzanne sat shakily in front of her laptop screen that Friday afternoon, it was enough to trigger a surge of messages from friends both actual and virtual who recognized the name of the small Maine town and wanted to make sure that she and Robert were okay. *Yes,* she typed back, *very close, just down the road. But we're fine. Yes, a student at the college, but R didn't know him*, she wrote, though this was not quite accurate. Robert had in fact taught this boy—Suzanne had recoiled when he told her—but said he didn't remember anything about him. She'd found this both amazing and unsurprising. Regardless, it wasn't something she wanted to admit to people; to say Robert didn't know him was true enough.

Now, Saturday morning, the house was quiet except for the sound of a somber newscaster on CNN. Robert had left the television on when he went running. Suzanne had thought he might skip his run this Saturday, out of deference to the tragedy, but no—to her husband, that would make no sense. *Would it change anything?* Suzanne returned to her laptop. She sifted through all the new messages, the relieved responses. So many, in fact, that she felt obliged to post a note of general thanks. *Dear Friends: Robert and I appreciate all of your concern. We are shaken, but we are fine, and we are grateful.*

As soon as the words were inscribed on-screen, she regretted them: *we are grateful.* It sounded so tidy, so made. This was why she was wary of putting anything on the Internet—it was so hard to get it right. She didn't want to risk sounding unaffected. Nor did she want to admit to the raw nerve the news had opened, or exploit their connections to the event. The fact that, yes, incredibly, Robert had taught this boy. Yes, it was a mall that Suzanne went to regularly, though not to shop (it was a depressing mall, and she'd never really shopped there) but to walk her laps when it rained. And, yes, it was the very town they lived in—though if she was being honest, except for a few kind nurses, she felt no deep connection to the place, to the entire state. She'd lived there just over two years and it had brought her nothing but heartbreak.

She left the computer for the kitchen, where she poured a glass of water, hands trembling, and removed her pill organizer from the sill. Before yesterday, the pain she'd felt had been mostly personal, but now it was spreading. Four people dead. She made her way through her morning dose. Vitamin D supplements. Tamoxifen, 20 mg. In late July, she'd had her final blast of chemicals. A clean scan. A quiet dinner celebration for two. Since then, she'd been following a strict regimen of hormone therapy. Vitamins, exercise. Laps around the neighborhood, the mall. Omega-3 fatty acids, 1000 mg, for inflammation, depression. Calcium and magnesium, 500 mg each, for bones. As she was swallowing the last pill, she heard, from the living room, the somber newscaster say *Doreen Howard*—she choked the pill back up, spat it into the sink and ran to the television. When she saw the girl's picture on the screen, she let out a cry, and sank to the couch.

It was early spring, the Empire Hair Emporium on Meer Creek Road. After more than a year in Stafford, Suzanne was still shopping for a passable hair salon, and though she'd gone to this one only once, she remembered the girl: Doreen. She was young—not much older than twenty-one, she'd thought then; in fact, she'd been only nineteen—and friendly, the kind of hairdresser who chatted the whole time she was cutting. This was something Suzanne usually found intrusive, and generally avoided by opening up a magazine, but that day, she hadn't wanted to be alone with her thoughts. She'd met with the surgical oncologist the day before, so it was nice to just sit and listen, bathed in mild chatter, away from the tests and doctors and the relentlessly falling snow.

Doreen, she could tell, was not chatting out of obligation. She was a friendly person, a cheerful person. She and her boyfriend had just gotten engaged. His name was Arlen—Suzanne noted the name because it wasn't one you heard. Doreen had paused to show Suzanne the ring: a chip of diamond whose smallness only made it more poignant. The wedding would wait a few years, Doreen explained, because they were saving money, but that was fine by her. *As long as I know I'll be his wife someday*, she said, in her voice a sincerity and fullness, and Suzanne had felt a quick affection for this girl, and also a tick of worry, thinking of marriage and all that came with it, things Doreen couldn't possibly yet know. The small disappointments, and big betrayals, and the surprises that befell you out of nowhere. The way you mourned the life you'd always imagined for yourself—the babies you wanted, closeness you always felt you deserved—and recalibrated your expectations: accepted that this was what it was, this was all it was, decided it was enough.

In the mirror, while Doreen was cutting, Suzanne studied her face: thick stripes of eyeliner, lavender lids, frosted lips. *Never leave the house without lipstick on*, Suzanne's mother had always told her, and in fact there was something about the lipstick her mother wore—a deep red knot against the gray haze—that seemed to gather her together, take the dull parts and give them definition. Beneath Doreen's makeup, her cheeks were a natural pink; she had a smile that suffused her entire face. She was so palpably happy—it was nice to be near such happiness. When she said, *I just feel lucky I get to spend the rest of my life with him*, Suzanne marveled at her certainty. Maybe Doreen knew more than Suzanne did about marriage, after all. Maybe she knew intuitively what she was doing, that she was choosing the right person, and her marriage would be the kind that lasted and lasted, devotion deepening with age. She seemed the kind of girl who would have babies easily—she was so young, for one thing. By the time Suzanne had started trying, she'd been thirty-eight.

Suzanne had closed her eyes for a long minute, and when she opened them Doreen, maybe catching this in the mirror, said: *I talk too much, don't I?* She smiled apologetically. *What about you?*

So while she had never made a habit of chatting with hairdressers, Suzanne found herself telling Doreen about her move to Maine. Two summers ago, she told her, from South Carolina—she skipped over the places she'd lived in between, college towns in Pennsylvania and Indiana so indistinct they'd barely left a mark. When Doreen asked what brought her to Maine, she guessed, *The college?* and Suzanne said yes, but quickly added, *for my husband, not for me*. Doreen nodded, as if in commiseration. Suzanne was tempted to tell her more. That she was deeply unhappy. That the biopsy had come back positive. That her husband, she was fairly sure, was having an affair.

The irony was, when Robert took the job in Maine, he'd been convinced Suzanne would be so happy there. A pretty little town, he proposed, only about an hour from the coast. *You love nature*, he said. He was referring, she supposed, to her photography, though Suzanne didn't take pictures of nature because it was beautiful; at least, not beautiful in the obvious ways. When they first arrived, he'd taken her on scenic walks and drives, to glassy lakes and rocky beaches, and she had to concede that compared with the other college towns, this one was picturesque. But it didn't change anything. Occasionally, she'd feel her dead mother knocking in her bones, the impulse to lie down in a darkened room—but this wasn't something Robert could understand. For him, sadness was a decision. When he came home from campus to find her in bed in the middle of the day, he looked at her with naked disappointment, but there was nothing she could do. It was all just so much effort—should it be so much effort? At this age? (Maybe that had been the pleasure of Doreen's company, the abstracted scrub of fingernails along her scalp, the chatter like warm milk—it was no effort, none at all.)

Over the next months, Robert stopped trying. No more hikes, no more breakfasts with his colleagues and their wives with whom he thought Suzanne might hit it off. He spent more time in his study, or on campus. He bought a mountain bike. He started working on a book about foreign policy, started taking running more seriously. He slept in the guest bedroom: two nights a week, then four, then all of them. Something had sidled into their house, into their marriage, and one day, Suzanne knew, it would burst open, but until then the best she could do was try not to provoke it. She lived in it and around it, spoke of it to no one. She was fifty-three: It was better than being alone.

It was January—start of the spring semester, though still the depths of winter—when she began to suspect Robert was having an affair. He was coming home late more frequently. Always with flimsy excuses, long meetings or needy students. A few times, when she walked into his study, he'd say hastily, "Right, thanks for calling," and hang up the phone. She didn't confront him. Though she was fairly certain he wouldn't lie about it—her husband could be direct to a fault—she couldn't bring herself to ask. Because if she did, she would know, which would mean she'd have to do something, and the prospect of actually getting a divorce was unthinkable—all the logistics, the pity, the shame.

Then came February. Still freezing. Still dead and dark out, still snowing, though they had more than done their time. She despised the cold, the way it seeped through the invisible cracks in the windows and made it impossible ever to get truly warm. For more than a year she'd been telling Robert they needed to install a woodstove, taping plastic over the big lovely windows and stuffing those awful padded snakes under the doors. In early March, on a whim, she booked a trip home to visit her sisters, hoping when she returned it would all have gone away: the snow melted, the cold lifted, her husband's affair purged from his system. But when she returned, the drifts were even more monstrous. They climbed, like ragged gargoyles, up the sides of the roads.

It was that week, her first week back, that the doctor found the lump. A routine exam, a doctor she'd seen recommended online. As she lay on the table waiting, dressed in a paper gown and staring at the popcorn ceiling, she experienced, ironically, a moment of pure but passing joy. Heat was streaming from the vents in the exam room. Extravagantly, luxuriously. She could have lain there all day. Then the doctor came in—a brief introduction, apologies for his cold fingers—and she saw his face go still. *Here's something*, he said, pausing. *Maybe I'm allergic to winter*, Suzanne replied. It wasn't like her to be flippant; she was embarrassed to have said it. Worse, the doctor humored her, smiling gently. *Let's take a look, just to be sure.* When the results came back, she was stunned. And scared. And also, in a very small, unspeakable way, relieved: because she knew now, given the man her husband was, any further speculation about their marriage, their future, would have to wait.

As expected, Robert shifted into action, contacting doctors and soliciting second opinions. There was no need; they all said the same thing. Lumpectomy and radiation. They compared Suzanne's tumor to various small unthreatening foods, a peanut and a pea. Suzanne told her sisters, who cried and panicked, then resolved not to tell anyone else. She insisted Robert do the same. He pressed the doctors to schedule surgery quickly. He surprised her with the woodstove. Soon she'd be filled with heat, more heat. The previous afternoon, at her appointment, she had gazed out the waiting room window: It was spring now, gutters dripping, but the old snow was still parked by the entrance in stubborn gray heaps. The woman beside her kept turning to smile, trying to strike up conversation. Suzanne wished that she would stop. Then the woman was telling her about a group she'd joined online. *It's private*, she said. *It's helped me. I'll invite you*, she added, as if it were a ticket to an exclusive party, and asked for her email address. Suzanne was taken aback but gave it to her, not wanting to be rude, wondering what it was about her that had telegraphed needing help so clearly. Later, when she climbed in bed with her laptop and found the invitation waiting in her inbox, she bristled but clicked ACCEPT—and to her surprise was flown directly to the page itself. She was amazed by what she found. Strangers, hundreds of them, confiding in each other about their cancers. Their side effects and treatments, help for getting through it, extremes of fear and resolve. Suzanne was stunned by their honesty. She kept on reading, worried she was invading their privacy but unable to stop. It was like stumbling upon a secret compartment of the Internet, a suite of hidden rooms. If she closed her eyes, she pictured a constellation of other houses, other rooftops, other lonely women staring at screens in the dark.

Now, not twenty-four hours later, as she watched Doreen's kind face in the mirror, still smiling, still ready to listen, it was all Suzanne could do not to open her mouth and vomit her own secrets all over the floor.

Instead, she confided in Doreen about the college—they had been talking, after all, about the college—and how she'd never really felt at ease among academics. She found them a little smug and self-involved, to be completely honest, Suzanne said with a laugh. Doreen nodded seriously, seemingly agreed. Then she told Suzanne that Arlen, her boyfriend—*fiancé*, she corrected herself—was actually a junior there, at Central Maine. He was majoring in business. He worked part-time at the Lowe's in Elkton. Doreen hadn't gone to college but read books on her own, she said, to expand her vocabulary. Suzanne had found this both touching and maddening, thinking of the chronic laziness among Robert's students (for some reason, it always seemed to bother her more than him).

At the end of the appointment, the haircut was all wrong (too puffy, too done-looking) and Suzanne was disappointed, because this meant she wouldn't be back. Nonetheless, she smiled and touched her hair and told Doreen it was just what she'd wanted. She felt a twinge of fear, imagining what her hair would look like later, after whatever treatments lay ahead. As she watched Doreen dust stray hairs from her shoulders, despair drenched her like a wave. She knew she would miss Doreen, already missed Doreen (which, even then, struck her as a strange thing to feel), and then found herself telling the girl that she was a photographer, an amateur, but still, if she and Arlen were ever interested, she would take their engagement photos at a discount—she wanted to say free, but feared it would sound like charity.

Now she wished she'd done it anyway. The television screen swam before her. In the photo of Doreen, she was standing on a beach. It was windy, and she was smiling, clutching her blowing hair back with one hand. Her smile was not just for the camera, Suzanne could tell, but for the person taking the picture. Then there he was—ARLEN MACKEY, said the caption along the bottom of the screen. Just a boy, Suzanne thought, not older than one of Robert's students. A square, earnest face. A cross around his neck, a gold chain. His fists pressed to his eyes. As Suzanne stared at him, she could not stop crying. The unfairness of it all—it leveled her. That some get to survive. That some don't.

By the time Robert walked in, she was curled on the floor—"Christ, what happened?" he said, rushing to her side. He thought she'd fainted, a side effect of the hormones. "It isn't that," she wept as he lifted her onto the couch. She told him about the victims—about the hairdresser, Doreen Howard—and as she was speaking, saw the quality of concern changing on his face. "You met her that once?" he said, gently, but that was entirely missing the point. Because, Suzanne admitted, her husband simply didn't understand her. Because it was possible, even after many years together, to know a person well but not at all. She tried to recall how she'd felt when she was younger—perhaps she'd assumed the knowing would come later; perhaps she hadn't realized it was missing. She could still summon the thrill (a luxurious gut roll that felt almost indecent) she'd felt the first time she brought Robert home to meet her mother and sisters and he'd asserted his intentions: complete his PhD, get a tenure-track position, marry her, have a family. He'd seen a point ahead and driven toward it. He'd split the cautious stillness of her childhood into a million little bits.

But to remember it now only filled her with grief. How young she had been, how trusting. How filled with hope.

Five

By the time Maggie returned to her car in the parking lot by the English building, the gray sky was purpling into evening. The rain was persisting. The landscapers were gone, the bushes trimmed and squared alongside Tilghman Hall. A few students—orientation leaders, athletes—moved across the quad in sandals and bright windbreakers, hoods drawn, unhurried despite the rain. Maggie sat behind the wheel, drops drumming on the roof, the canvas bag like an accomplice beside her on the seat.

It would be different, she reasoned, replaying the scene in Bill's office, if she felt the paper were unambiguously alarming.

If she truly believed it were a vital piece of missed information.

If Nathan Dugan were still at large, still living.

Or, regardless, if the information in the paper could change anything—for Nathan, or for his victims.

Maggie swallowed a wave of nausea. She fixed her eyes on a tall white spruce, glimpses of its pale trunk visible through the green. For a moment, she considered the unbearable possibility that she may in fact have overlooked something important, in Nathan's paper or his person. That her concerns had been focused in the wrong direction. She grabbed her phone from the cup holder and, before she could rethink it, called Robert's number. She'd texted him briefly that morning about the Facebook post, the pending meeting, and the prospect of talking to him now was reassuring. He would be practical, decisive. She would unload everything and ask his advice. If he instructed her to walk back inside Bill's office, come clean, she would do it. But the phone kept ringing. A Saturday, five thirty—he was probably at home with Suzanne. Still, Maggie stayed on the line, hoping he'd be so surprised to see her calling that he'd find a way to answer, when the front door of Tilghman opened and Bill stepped out into the rain.

Maggie kept the phone pressed to her ear, pretending to be talking, not wanting Bill to wonder why she was still sitting there. He walked quickly toward his car, shielding his head with a thin briefcase. It wasn't until he had climbed into the front seat and wiped the rain from the case that she saw him look up and see her there. She waved. A pause, a wave in return. Then he started his car and eased out of the lot, wipers flapping, down the hill to the main road.

Maggie hung up the phone and squeezed it in her lap. She registered the pressure in her chest and realized she wasn't breathing. With an exhale, she turned the key and switched her headlights on. She'd feel better once she was home, with the commotion of the girls upstairs. Kim and Janie were no doubt already there, helping pack the last of Anna's things. As she drove, the brake lights in front of her beamed a watery red. The blacktop shone. She proceeded slowly down University Row, under banners draped between wrought-iron lampposts—WELCOME NEW STUDENTS and HOME OF THE EAGLES!—the rain falling in sharp darts past the streetlamps' glow. Approaching the next intersection, she pictured just in time the scene outside the mall—the crowd of media and mourners, the road choked with police cars and flashing lights—and turned the wheel hard to the right, back the way she'd come: past the march of grim stores on Standish, their lit signs now flickering, and into the maze of humble back roads, cluttered yards and dripping gutters, until she saw, up ahead, the small lemon-yellow house.

The reporters had dispersed, the neighbors gone. There was surprisingly little evidence of the crowd that had so recently been there. As if on autopilot, Maggie eased the car onto the other side of the street, the wooded side, and turned the engine off. She clutched her hands in her lap. The yard was patchy, bald in places, in others overgrown with weeds. A Ford, hemmed with rust, was parked in the driveway. A single dim light shone behind the faded flowered curtains drawn across the living room window; one of the panes was broken. On the news, Nathan's home life had been described in dramatically gray tones—a working-class neighborhood on the fringes of a college town—and Maggie had thought it a lazy cliché but was struck now by how depressed this house felt. Whenever she imagined her students in their lives outside her classroom, it was always in campus spaces—the dining hall, the library and dorms—yet this, here, had been Nathan's other life. She pictured him climbing onto this broken porch, books dumped by the front door, TV on, big booted feet twitching on the carpet. From this angle, she could see that the yellow paint—so incongruously hopeful, bright against the stone-colored sky—stopped halfway down one side of the house; it was as if the job, a burst of optimism, had been abandoned halfway through.

Her phone buzzed. Robert: *Can't talk. S not good. Everything ok?*

Maggie returned the phone to the cup holder. If she told him where she was, he would surely tell her to drive away. She looked once more at the house, drizzle filming on the glass. Then the image came suddenly to life, the porch light snapping on as the front door opened and a shout sounded from the doorway: "I see you!"

Maggie stiffened. The words were muted by the window but impossible to mistake. A woman had stepped out onto the porch. Maggie fumbled to put the car in drive but as her hand closed around the keys, another shout came: "Hey!" She was waving one arm in a wide, slow arc. "I see you! Do you think I don't see you sitting there?"

The glass was fogging over with rain and breath. Maggie squeezed the wheel, staring straight ahead.

"This isn't some kind of tourist attraction!" the woman called out.

Maggie was tempted to just leave, but couldn't bring herself to do it. It would be cowardly, her second indefensible act of the day. Besides, she was the one who had chosen to drive there, sit there ogling this woman's house. A woman who, no matter the circumstances, had lost her son.

Maggie gazed ahead for another minute at the empty road—she would offer her sympathies briefly, she thought, then leave—and swung open the door. Gripping her bag, she stepped onto the woods' edge, soft with mud and pine. An empty plastic bottle, a shred of yellow caution tape. As she crossed the street, she kept her head down to avoid the woman's gaze, looking up only as she neared the porch. "Hello—"

"I'm done talking to reporters."

Maggie paused on the bottom stair. The woman was now back behind the door. It was open only about a foot, secured by a short metal chain. The thought crossed Maggie's mind—fleeting, oddly matter-of-fact—that she could be holding a gun.

"I'm not a reporter," she said. "I was Nathan's teacher. My name is Maggie Daley."

Marielle Dugan kept one hand on the door and one on the frame, the metal chain stretched taut between them. Through the narrow gap, Maggie could make out denim shorts, a white T-shirt, brown canvas sandals. The ribbon of face revealed bleached and cropped blond hair, a blurred line of blue eyeliner beneath each lid. She was tall, taller than she'd looked on the news—at least six feet, to Maggie's five-three.

"I apologize," Maggie said. "I didn't mean to—"

"What teacher?"

"English," Maggie said. "His freshman year."

"He never took English."

"He did," she said. "The freshmen. They all do."

"Well, he never mentioned you."

"Well," she said, and nodded. She wasn't surprised. "I remember him."

Marielle's face looked fleshy and slack, smooth except for the deep lines around her mouth and nose. In the flatness of her expression, Maggie was reminded of Nathan, though the specific features—a long face, wide eyes—bore little resemblance to her son.

"I didn't mean to bother you," Maggie repeated, fishing for the right words. "I just wanted to say I'm sorry."

Marielle Dugan said nothing, her expression unchanged. A soft brown basketball, like a piece of rotting fruit, sat on the porch by the door.

"I'm sorry for what you're going through," Maggie clarified. The woman continued looking at her, making Maggie uncomfortable. Still, she felt she needed to offer something else. "And," she fumbled, "I'm sorry if there's anything more I could have done for him." She turned to leave, as Marielle asked, "Like what?"

Maggie shifted on the stair, the old weak wood creaking beneath her feet. She was getting rained on but thought it better not to step onto the porch. Somewhere in the near distance, she heard the rev of an engine, a roar that abruptly surged then faded, melting into the damp air.

"Well," Maggie said. "I just meant—for Nathan. If I could have done something more to help him."

"How?" Marielle asked. Her eyes looked glazed, Maggie thought, a deep grief, or a medicated dullness. She considered the immense effort behind that bright-blue liner—the same spirit that had chosen the yellow paint, she was sure. Despite her unease, Maggie felt a stab of compassion for the woman standing before her. She thought of all the things she'd really like to know—*had you been worried about him? Had any idea he was capable of a thing like this? Do you think there was anything you might have done to stop it?* She imagined those were just the questions Marielle herself was asking, of herself and of the world.

"What I meant was," Maggie said, "looking back, I wonder if there were things about Nathan I might have paid more attention to. In my class." It was painful to admit this, but to her surprise, doing so filled her with a sense of rightness, of moral alignment. If there was anyone to whom she owed an apology, to whom she should take some responsibility, this was she.

Marielle Dugan, though, looked displeased. She moved one hand from the doorframe and settled it on her hip. "What things?"

Maggie searched her brain for something to offer here—simple, truthful, but not blaming. "I just meant—indications that he was troubled," she said.

But this was the wrong thing. Maggie sensed it even before she saw the hard look cross Marielle's face. She added, "That he might have needed—" as Marielle shut the door. Maggie thought she'd offended her but then the latch tumbled down and the door opened three feet. She could see Marielle more clearly: wide hips, belly round with middle age. The living room was dark behind her, except for the low light of a single lamp. On the mantel sat a gold-globed clock, a vase. Maggie was struck by the feeling of emptiness, the absence of any family or friends.

"What, did he disturb your class or something?" Marielle said. One arm was resting loosely across her waist.

"Well, no," Maggie said.

"Because he never got in any trouble in high school. Not on his own, anyway."

Over her shoulder, on the mantel, Maggie could faintly make out a framed picture of Nathan, looking younger and slightly thinner than he'd been that spring of 2012. Probably his senior portrait, Maggie thought: a tie, a buzz cut. The barest hint of a smile.

"No," she said. "He didn't cause trouble."

"Then what?"

"Well." Maggie hesitated. The rain was falling harder now, leaking from her hairline. There was no simple way to explain Nathan's presence in her classroom, not if his mother didn't understand that about him already. She tried to think of something fact-based, concrete. "I might have noticed his interest in hunting," she said.

"Hunting?" Marielle jerked her chin dismissively. "Everybody hunts."

"Yes, but—" She paused. "Given what happened."

Marielle gave her an uncomprehending look, and it occurred to

Maggie she might be in a state of denial, or shock, or some primal maternal protectiveness. She might be a gun enthusiast herself. Fourteen weapons had been stashed in a room just upstairs, not twenty feet from where they were standing. At this distance, it seemed impossible that this woman wouldn't have known, that she could have avoided knowing.

"It wasn't just hunting," Maggie said. "It was guns. How much he relished them." Then she amended, "How much he seemed to enjoy them, I mean."

Behind her, a car was approaching, seemed to be slowing, and then started honking, unleashing long, angry blasts of the horn. Maggie looked quickly over her shoulder. The car honked twice more but kept moving, tires hissing against the wet road. When she turned again, Marielle's eyes hadn't left her face. Over her shoulder, the living room looked darker than it had before. The picture of Nathan still hovered over his mother's shoulder, his expression more a smirk than a smile.

"You know," Maggie said, "I'd better be getting home—"

"Where do you live?"

"Right nearby," she said. "Just down the road."

"Reed?"

"Stafford."

"And you're a teacher."

"A professor, yes."

"You have kids?"

Maggie hesitated, but said, "I do. One."

"Boy?"

"A girl," she said. "A daughter."

"How old?"

"Eighteen," Maggie said, adding, "And she's leaving for college tomorrow, actually, so I really should be—"

"I guess you probably wouldn't like it if strangers came around asking questions about her," Marielle said.

"No." Maggie felt like she'd been slapped. "No, I guess I wouldn't."

"Acting like they knew her," Marielle said. Her eyes grew watery. She returned one hand to the doorframe, as if to bar Maggie from entering. "You don't know my son."

Maggie looked down at the soaked porch stairs. "I'm sorry to have bothered you," she said. "And very sorry for what you're going through." She gripped the bag against her shoulder, then turned and hurried across the lawn. Crossing the street, she felt eyes on her, and as she climbed into the car and drove away, back toward the familiar roads, she glanced once over her shoulder and saw Marielle's silhouette still watching from the door.

Six

Anna had resisted taking her Ativan that morning: a kind of mission statement. On that day of all days, she wanted to not need it anymore. Now, though, as she sat in the passenger seat, anxious to leave, her mind kept wandering to the bottle in the trunk, wrapped in a sweatshirt inside her old swim team duffel bag. It should have been a moment of pure antici-pation, but instead, she felt on edge.

It was six thirty in the morning—because it was a Sunday, her mother was insisting on getting an early start to beat the summer people—and she'd planned on sleeping most of the drive to Boston but felt painfully awake. She grabbed her phone, texting Kim and Janie. *Anybody up???* No response. The two of them weren't leaving until midweek. Anna clutched her phone in her lap and stared out the window at the front porch with its chipping wooden rockers, the big curtainless bay window, the house she'd lived in all her life. She thought of all the times she'd ridden up this driveway in Gavin's truck, a minute before midnight, mouth swollen from kissing, Gavin reek-ing of alcohol, lights blazing pointedly in that bay window as her mom waited up for her inside. She remembered standing on that porch, sobbing uncontrollably as her father drove away, her mother staring at her like she was an alien, beyond help.

She picked at her thumb. She needed to leave already—what could her mother possibly be doing? She looked at her phone again and tried to distract herself by roaming online, but everywhere felt fraught. The shooting was still the only thing anyone was posting about. Instagram photos of the pile of flowers outside the mall's main entrance. The candlelight vigil at Essex High, where Frank Tremont had taught. A Facebook post—it was written by another one of her mother's old students—that had popped up in her feed a hundred times. Janie and Kim had both read it—*Maggie has a cameo*, they reported—but Anna didn't want to, didn't want it gaining traction in her brain. Now, though, here it was again, taunting her. She knew that Theresa would encourage her to read it. To demystify it. *I dare you*—Anna clicked. Instantly she regretted it. The comments were intense and sprawling—she thumbed down, skimming past something about gun control, Nathan Dugan's YouTube video, the word *FREAK*.

Quickly, she blocked the post from her feed. Then she exited Facebook, exited the Internet. She retreated to her photo library, a reminder of the relatively calm existence she'd led in the months preceding Friday afternoon. There was a goofy video of Kim applying her eye makeup, selfies of the three of them on the rocks at Meer Cove. There was one of her and Janie at the mall, in the food court, laughing—Anna felt like throwing up. The picture had been taken just last Tuesday. They'd been shopping for new jeans for college. They'd stopped to split a smoothie. It was the last time Anna had been there, the last time she would ever be there. Because worst-case scenario, you go to the mall and someone starts shooting people. She was never going there again.

The front screen door banged shut. There, finally, was her mother, hurrying off the porch. She was gripping a thermos of coffee in one hand, her old scuffed boat bag in the other. She looked as tense as Anna felt. Anna knew her mother was concerned about her—yesterday, she'd basically said she didn't think Anna was capable of taking care of herself at college, which had both troubled and infuriated her—and last night, when she finally got home, she was so distracted she'd forgotten to get the pizza. *It's not like Maggie to pass up an opportunity to watch you eat,* Janie had observed, upstairs in Anna's room. The three of them had agreed that she must have been freaked out about the shooting, about her old student, and Kim had floated the theory that she was nervous about meeting Felicia (in all the strangeness of the past two days, Anna hadn't given this dreaded introduction the attention it deserved). Then they'd finished the last of Anna's packing and agreed upon Kim's Tucker-related strategy and shared a hug good-bye. *See you around campus, Maggie!* Kim had called as she was leaving, which made Anna feel inexplicably left out.

Her mother slid into the driver's seat. "Sorry," she said, shutting the door. She wedged her thermos in the cup holder and her bag on the seat between them. Then she turned to Anna, gripping the wheel in her small, freckled hands, and smiled a strained smile. "Feeling good?"

What could she say? Her insides were shaking. But she was leaving. She was finally going. It was easier to just say yes.

When they pulled onto campus four hours later, the quad was teeming with people. Most were dressed in identical blue T-shirts—WELCOME CREW—ready to greet the new students and help haul their stuff inside. Anna's RA, Isabel, was a junior, an Early Childhood Education major, and perfect-looking. "Welcome to your new home!" she sang, dropping them off at Anna's room. It was tiny, half the size of Anna's bedroom in Stafford. Naturally, she was the first one there. As she waited, alone with her mother, she suddenly realized how much she wished Felicia weren't coming, and hoped that her roommate (Alexis Riggio from Old Lyme, Connecticut) was next to arrive.

"Knock knock!"

It was Felicia, of course, ten minutes later, breezing through the door. "This is so exciting!" she said, wrapping Anna in a tight hug. Then she approached Anna's mother, smile bright and hand extended. "You must be Maggie. So nice to finally meet you. Felicia."

It seemed like not the right thing to say, though Anna wasn't quite sure why.

"Yes." Her mother looked surprised, and slightly amused. "You as well."

Their differences were immediate and striking. Felicia wore an ankle-length halter dress, a long silver necklace, and metallic sandals. Her arms were bare, her toenails painted a deep red. Anna's mom was wearing her standard jeans and a baggy sweater that hung from her small, hard shoulders like laundry pinched on a line. Then Anna noticed that she had in fact dressed up slightly: pale-pink lipstick, small silver ball earrings. The effort was probably on account of Felicia, yet her mother's accessories had such a small fraction of the effect, they only made the contrast between them more stark.

"Big day," Anna's dad said, kissing Anna's head. He was carrying a laundry basket with a giant bow on it.

"For you," Felicia said, beaming, and Anna thanked her. The basket was packed with food: bubble gum, kettle chips, microwave popcorn, M&M's, a truckload of Swedish fish—was this her unsubtle way of ensuring Anna keep eating? Anna glanced at her dad; he gave her an encouraging smile.

"So," Felicia said, still beaming. "Maggie. How was your drive? Any traffic?"

Her mother replied that the drive was fine, and Felicia nodded as if she'd said something interesting. "How long is that? Three hours? Four?"

Anna assumed that Felicia talking directly to her mother was deliberate, an attempt to defuse the awkwardness, but Anna wished she would stop. There was something sort of desperate about her cheerfulness, superficial and strenuous—it was just the sort of thing that would put her mother off.

"Three and a half, depending on traffic," her father answered, and Anna thought she detected a hint of irritation in his voice too.

Then there was a commotion in the hallway and Alexis Riggio burst through the door. The first thing Anna noticed was her size: a two, maybe even a zero, details that had not been so obvious when Face-Timing on her phone. She wore an enormous pair of sunglasses, PRADA marching along one arm in little white letters, a dozen purses dangling from her shoulder. "Roomie!" she squealed, throwing her arms around

Anna like they were old friends. Anna stiffened, wishing Kim or Janie were in the room to exchange a knowing look.

"Hi, folks," Alexis's father said, wheeling a huge red suitcase, luggage tags flapping from its handle. "Frank Riggio," he said. "My wife, Liz."

To Anna's surprise, Alexis's parents both hugged her. They were smiling. They appeared to still be happily married to each other. In fact, the entire family looked relaxed and tanned, as if they had just returned from a tropical vacation.

"Bunk bed preference?" Alexis asked.

Anna did have a preference—she was afraid that being close to the ceiling would feel like sleeping in a coffin—but thankfully, Alexis said she didn't like the bottom and hoisted her shoulderful of bags on top.

"I doubt there are enough drawers on this campus for all the clothes Allie brought," Mr. Riggio said. "Right, Al?" Alexis rolled her eyes, as if this affectionate teasing was so familiar it barely registered. She was already divvying up the dresser with the matter-of-fact familiarity of a kid who had gone to overnight camp. "Don't forget to make room for the Dustbuster," her father added, then addressed the room: "In a moment of delusion, we bought this kid a cleaning implement." Felicia and Anna's dad both laughed.

Anna's mother smiled. She didn't laugh. No doubt she was unimpressed by Alexis, who was unbuckling a suitcase filled with expensive-looking sweaters—she might be, at least slightly, a *candy*, Anna thought.

But Felicia chatted easily with the Riggios, the banter that had felt overeager fifteen minutes ago now seeming light and adept. She asked about their drive, recommended a few nearby restaurants, sushi and Vietnamese.

"Oh, you know the area?" Mrs. Riggio said. She fingered her necklace, made of thin gold links. "Didn't Allie say you lived in Maine?"

"We do," Felicia said. "In Portland. Tom and I. But I used to live in Boston."

Anna felt a prick of worry—had her mom even known that they were living together? Would she care?

"Well, Portland's not so far," Mrs. Riggio said. "You two can keep watch."

"Oh, we will," Felicia said, with a delighted laugh.

Anna looked quickly at her mother. Her expression hadn't changed but she looked more upright, shoulders back and chin raised. Standing beside the four other adults, Maggie was clearly the odd one out, and not just because she didn't have a partner. In Stafford, her plainness read as grounded and no-nonsense, but next to these two women, her short ponytail and limp sweater looked almost dowdy. Noticing again those tiny ball earrings, the pale effort of the lipstick, Anna felt a swell of pity roll through her.

As if reading her mind, Alexis's dad said, "So, Maggie, Allie tells us you're a professor?" Then he raised his eyebrows kindly, and Anna decided she would love Mr. Riggio forever.

"That's right," her mother said.

"Must be back-to-school season for you too, then."

"Almost," she said. "Classes start next week." Anna felt herself unknot a little, glad her mom was getting to showcase this part of herself. Mr. Riggio asked about her teaching, and Maggie sounded almost animated as she described her courses this semester at Central Maine State.

"Central Maine!" Mrs. Riggio interrupted. She turned to her husband, as if searching his face for confirmation. "Isn't that where that boy went? That shooter?" she said, and Anna's stomach turned.

"Which one?" He frowned.

"Just the other day. The one in the mall—"

"Yes," Anna's dad cut in. "He did."

"Oh," Mrs. Riggio exclaimed. She turned to Maggie, wide-eyed, fingers of one hand folding around her necklace. "Oh, Maggie, how terrible for you. How *unsettling*."

Anna felt a sharp dot of sweat under one arm. She wondered if her mother would tell the whole story—the truly unsettling version—but Maggie replied only, "Yes. It certainly is."

"He was still a student there, wasn't he?" Mrs. Riggio said, shaking her head in a kind of horrified wonder. "He was right under your nose. I guess you can feel lucky he didn't do anything at the school—although *lucky* is the wrong way to put it—but he could have. I mean, it was only a matter of time. A ticking bomb. It must be terrifying to even think about," she said, then paused, clearly wanting her to affirm just how terrifying this was.

Anna could see, in the tightness of her mother's jaw, that she sensed this woman's hunger for details and wanted to change the subject. Still, Anna wished she would relent a little, offer a notch more feeling. She'd learned this in high school: People love trouble—to be a part of it, gush over it, soft-voiced and wide-eyed—but give them just a glimpse and they'll be satisfied, move on.

"You didn't know him, did you?" Mrs. Riggio pressed.

To her dismay, Alexis was now paying close attention, clutching an armful of jeans.

"It's an enormous campus," her mother replied. "A state school." She had sidestepped the question, and Anna couldn't blame her—if Alexis's mother heard that the ticking bomb had been her student, she'd go nuts.

Then Felicia said, "Must be easy for problems to get lost in the shuffle in a school so big." Anna glanced at her—did she know about Maggie's connection to the shooter? Was she trying to make her feel better? Felicia gave her a knowing wink.

Anna's nerves were quickening. Her hands were tingling. Her dad was smiling at her sadly, and her mother's face was made of stone.

Mrs. Riggio was still talking. "Well, even so," she said. "There he was, for four years, just sitting in those classrooms. He was walking around the quad just like any normal person." She waved one hand, as if to take in the whole of campus, an agitated flutter. "He was probably living in the dorms. My God, I hate to even *think*—"

Anna blurted out, "This friend of mine, Laura, she was there." She felt everyone turn to look at her. She didn't meet her parents' eyes, unable to bear their stricken faces. Instead, her eyes flew to Felicia's. "At the mall. She was hiding in a dressing room," she said. "In the Gap. She heard everything. She was afraid for her life." Her voice was trembling.

"That must be scary, sweetie," Felicia said, and reached out to squeeze her arm.

"Poor thing," Mrs. Riggio said. "I honestly can't imagine what you all must be going through." Mortifyingly, Anna's eyes thickened with tears. "Aw, roomie," Alexis said, slinging an arm around her shoulders. Anna stared furiously at the floor. Her dad said, "We got very lucky." From outside, someone chirped into a bullhorn—"In fifteen minutes, all first-years on the quad!"—but inside the room it had gone hushed and still.

"That kid," Mr. Riggio said. "He's dead now, isn't he?"

Alexis's arm still hung around Anna's shoulders. The arm was cool, near weightless, but Anna's neck was sweating.

"He killed himself, right?" Alexis's dad was still addressing Anna's mom, apparently seeing her as the authority on the subject. "Suicide?"

"He did, yes," she said.

Felicia added, "They usually do."

"What was his deal?" Mr. Riggio said angrily. "Was he mentally disturbed or just one of those kids who's pissed off at the world—"

"Dad," Alexis interrupted. "I know this was a terrible thing. And I feel sorry for these people. But it's our first day of college. Can we please talk about something a little less morbid?"

Mr. Riggio chuckled. "That's our girl," he said. "Poster child for sensitivity." But Anna was grateful. She smiled at Alexis, who rolled her eyes as she unlatched her arm from Anna's neck. Below their open window, engines started revving. An eager tumble of voices rose from the quad. Inside, the parents' conversation turned briefly to lighter topics, but Anna just wanted them all to leave. Her dad said, "Remember, we're just a phone call away." Felicia hugged her extra-hard. Her mom stood waiting by the window, gripping her sweatered elbows in her hands.

"Bye, Mom," Anna said, when everyone else had headed downstairs.

Her mother's eyes roamed once more, quickly, around the room. Then she said, "I guess it's that time," and gave a little laugh. "Okay." She kissed Anna's cheek. "Don't forget to call me," she said. Then she started down the hallway, her old canvas bag hitched to one shoulder. As Anna watched her go, she was seized with a surprising feeling of sadness, and worry, picturing her mother driving back to that empty house, down those long quiet roads, nothing to occupy her but her endless spin of thoughts.

Seven

L uke knew the feeling of not being noticed: It was how he moved through the world. As a kid he'd been so quiet people tended not to register his presence, sitting in the corner of the living room, or in the back of his dad's truck, to the point where sometimes—*Luke, honey, you're staring*, his mom would say, and he'd snap out of it, embarrassed.

What he remembered most about his English class freshman year was Meredith Kenney. She was the kind of student Luke could never hope to be. The kind who always raised her hand in class and seemed to genuinely care, and somehow made this seem admirable instead of annoying. Her eyes were different shades of green on different days, like sea glass. Once, that semester, she'd read an essay Luke had written about a family trip to Deer Isle when he was little, and left comments in the margins in her neat, round handwriting. *Great job, Luke. Your relationship with your mom is so sweet. ☺ Can't wait to read what you write next!*

That Meredith took his dumb papers seriously embarrassed him, but that she took her own so seriously impressed him. Toward the end of the semester she'd written an essay about her brother, who had been killed somewhere in the Middle East, and read it to the entire class out loud. The room had been silent except for the sound of her voice, which shook and faltered, sometimes dropping to a whisper. At one point the overhead lights, on motion sensors, snapped off, and a few people twitched their feet and hands to bring them back. Luke knew the abruptness of losing a person without warning—how they were there, then suddenly just gone—but he couldn't bring himself to write about it, much less read about it out loud. As he listened, his admiration for Meredith Kenney translated into personal shame. It was this alone that made him try harder on his next paper: an essay about his grandfather, who had died of a heart attack three years earlier. After he read it to the class, he looked up to find Meredith smiling at him sadly. *I'm sorry, Luke.*

They had never had another class together, and in a school so big he rarely saw her. Junior year, he heard she'd transferred to a college in Massachusetts to be closer to her family; remembering her brother's death, Luke thought this made sense. Since then, he had Googled her occasionally but hadn't found her. Facebook turned up dozens of Meredith Kenneys, but as far as he could tell they were all somebody else.

When Luke heard the news about Nathan Dugan, it felt like a punch to the throat. It was a Friday in August, still and sweltering, the kind of heat they rarely got in northern Maine. He'd worked the five a.m. shift at Dunkin' Donuts and was sitting in his room, too hot to do anything but poke around on his computer, when things started appearing on Facebook and Twitter, links to headlines like SHOOTING AT ME MALL and SUSPECTED GUNMAN STUDENT AT CENTRAL MAINE.

Luke clicked one of the links and when he saw the picture, he froze.

That morning, Nathan had walked into the Millview Mall with a duffel bag packed with guns and ammunition and started shooting. The mall was right near campus—Luke had been to it once, spring of senior year, when April Peale dragged him along with her to go shopping for a dress for graduation. Nathan had killed at least three people there, then shot himself. No one knew why. As Luke roamed online, alone in his silent house—his father was at the auto body and his brother still in bed at nearly one thirty—he pored over descriptions of what happened, of a YouTube video Nathan had posted that morning, and grew nauseated. His mouth filled with spit, and he kept swallowing it down. His stomach hurt the way it used to when he was little, pain growing bigger and darker, like ink in water, until it was so intense he had to run to the bathroom and throw up. Then he brushed his teeth and splashed his face, and when he returned to his desk it was almost unthinkingly that he began to type.

He wasn't too active on social media, though he constantly checked his accounts. Now and then, he would post one of his drawings on Facebook or Instagram and tag it *#nature* or *#art* or *#justscrewingaround* and it would get four or five comments and likes. Aunt Millie, his mother's only sister, who liked everything. Matt, his best friend from growing up, who now had an apartment with his college roommates down in Portland: *nice dude*. Occasionally, Luke heard from one of his fellow ES majors. But he never got more than a few responses, and that was fine. He didn't expect anything more. That, he thought, was the Internet in general: a lonely landscape, a largely barren place but with these rare bursts of not-loneliness, these moments of connection that made it worthwhile sometimes.

That afternoon he started writing, not really thinking, just wanting to connect to anyone else who had known Nathan and might understand how he felt. As he typed, random memories kept popping into his head. The boxy headphones Nathan used to leave hanging around his neck. The way he sat, index fingers pressed together on his desk. The dog he sometimes brought to class. That creepy paper, that big green coat. The stress ball he would squeeze until his knuckles went white. He tagged it *#nathandugan* and *#millviewmallshooting* and *#freshmanyear* and wrote: *If anybody else from class is reading this please write back.*

After he posted it, he sat in silence. He was vibrating. He almost never talked about personal things online, or in general—April used to urge him to talk about his feelings, something he didn't miss about her—

and his first instinct was to just delete it. What if someone was offended he was posting about Nathan, or thought he was remembering him wrong? But it wasn't like anyone would really read it. Maybe, with luck, he'd reach a few old classmates. He realized he was hoping mostly to hear from Meredith Kenney, hoping his post would find its way to her through the online alumni chain. (*Aw*, he imagined, that sympathetic smile.) He changed his privacy settings to "public," just in case.

Instead of Meredith, though, within minutes, other comments began appearing. Matt, and Aunt Millie, but random people too. Marissa Calabasas from high school, who now lived in Boston: *OMG! Must be so upsetting it's someone you actually knew Luke!* Someone named Liz, a friend of Marissa's: *Sounds like he was a budding psychopath even then*...Heather Doyle, who he'd worked with at Dunkin' Donuts that morning: 😨

Within fifteen minutes, his post had 17 likes, 8 comments, and 6 shares. For a while he just sat there, hitting refresh every few minutes and watching the numbers tick upward. 25 likes, 13 comments, 12 shares. 52, 28, 25. The attention was nerve-racking, but kind of exhilarating. Around five thirty, he left his room, retrieved the dogs from the back-yard, and topped off their water bowls. Then he made himself a ham sandwich, ate half and gave the dogs the rest, and returned to his desk. 98 shares. 111. 131. 153.

At six thirty, when his father's truck came rumbling down the driveway, Luke went downstairs. His brother, Brent, was there too, kind of hovering near the couch. When their dad walked in, he dumped his stuff on the kitchen counter and came into the living room and looked surprised to see them both standing there. For a long minute he looked at them, and Luke just watched him, wondering what he'd say about the shooting. He remembered the way he'd gazed up at his father the day of his mother's accident, and over and over in the weeks and months after, just waiting for him to say something that would help. He felt that way now, like he was ten again, waiting, but what his father said was: "You two are on your own for dinner." Then he walked out to the porch and Luke heard the wheezy couch springs as his father sat down, the twin thumps of his work boots hitting the floor.

Luke looked at his brother, and for a minute their eyes locked. His brother already had his car keys in his fist. He was probably going to meet up with his dumb friends, Mike and Layton, and though usually Luke hoped they hung out somewhere else, tonight he wished for a minute that Brent would stay. Then his brother breathed, "Have fun," and headed for the door and was gone. Luke listened as his father turned on the TV, the muffled sound of the news through the living room wall. His brother's truck went tearing down the driveway, timing belt squealing. A woman was saying: *All of a sudden I heard this sound like balloons popping—* Luke went back to his room and closed his door and sifted through the new comments.

Hang in there Luke <3

You're expressing EXACTLY how I feel about people like this—how do you know when to do something? Who's dangerous and who isn't? How can you know for sure??

Just glad your safe!!!

As the night grew darker, the comments appeared more quickly, and more of them were from strangers. Luke pictured people in rooms all over the state reading what he'd written on their computers and their phones. It was kind of thrilling, to be this point of connection, but sometimes unsettling. *Stop giving this fucking loser the fame he was looking for! Someone should have paid attention to him sooner!* A few people had posted links to Nathan's YouTube video, which gave Luke a twang of panic—but to his relief, when he clicked, it was gone. *This video has been removed.* Soon, he reminded himself, the numbers would stop climbing, the focus shift to something else. But for now they just kept growing. 212 shares. 259. 326. It felt like one of those elementary school science experiments, the crystals that form overnight in jelly jars, a living thing.

By midnight, his post had been shared 1000 times. Luke stared at the number, overwhelmed. When it ticked to 1001, he stood up and walked downstairs. His brother wasn't home yet. His father had turned on an old movie, a western. Luke held the back door so it didn't slam, and as he stepped outside, the temperature dropped at least ten degrees. He paced the perimeter of the yard, taking in the familiar night sounds: the hoot of an owl, the river lapping through the trees. He thought about the people who must know by now their family members were among the victims, had gone to the mall that morning and happened to be standing in the wrong place. He remembered, the day of his mother's accident, the oddness of seeing the police climbing his porch steps—their saddened faces, hats in hands—and how, as they began speaking, he'd closed his eyes and tried to force time backward, rewind to that morning, himself in bed and his mother calling from down the hall. She was going grocery shopping, she said, and did he want to come? No, he didn't. He was sleepy. *It's after ten, lazybones*, she said. She had paused in his bedroom doorway, wearing her blue button-down, sleeves rolled to her elbows. She'd smiled tiredly. She'd said, *Okay, honey*. It had all just happened; she had just been there. Luke would have given anything to get a do-over, to alter the space-time continuum. But he couldn't, of course. His mother, the drive home from Hannaford, the drunk driver in the oncoming lane at eleven fifteen in the morning—it wouldn't be undone.

He stopped walking and stood still, listening to the sound of his own breathing. He stared at the stars until they dissolved. When he went back inside, the house was silent. The dogs were in their spot by the stove, the day's dishes still piled in the sink. As Luke climbed the stairs and returned to his computer, he wondered if it had all vanished in his absence, but there it was—1128. 1175. 1201.

There was another reason, one he didn't admit on Facebook, why four years later Nathan Dugan was so stuck in Luke's brain. It was a thing that happened in English class that year, just after spring break. He remembered the timing of it because he'd been unhappy to be back at school again—he didn't much like his roommate, a hockey player, and hadn't made any real friends yet—and it had been nice (or if not nice, at least relatively easy) to spend the last two weeks back home. By senior year, he would have found his niche—a major in Environmental Studies, a brief, not-too-serious relationship with April, who subsequently and kindly broke up with him because she was going home to New Jersey, but not before he spent senior week basically living in her apartment and feeling okay, even almost confident, about his standing in the world—but on that day in late March, as he gathered his stuff at the end of class, he'd felt his usual unease. The sensation was a contradiction: the feeling that he was both completely invisible and acutely, terribly seen. He grew overly conscious of the space his body occupied, of how his face looked and what his arms were doing, how he stuffed one hand in his pocket in a way that was meant to look casual but felt obvious and strange. The pocket too small, or his hand too big. As he walked toward the door, backpack on shoulder and hand in pocket, Nathan Dugan had been standing there, his dog beside him, a friendly Lab with one chewed-up ear that Luke often had the urge to pet but never did. "Hey," Nathan said, too loudly, as Luke approached.

Luke realized that Nathan had been waiting for him. He glanced around, uncomfortably aware of the other kids leaving the room. He drew his hand out of his pocket. "Hey," he replied.

Nathan was wearing his winter coat, even though the weather was springlike. His headphones were dangling around his neck, arms stiff at his sides. He was a pretty unusual kid, although Luke didn't mind him as much as his classmates, who exchanged loaded looks anytime he spoke. He had a habit of interrupting people, what Luke's mother might have called *unable to read the room*. When Luke was little, babbling to her about his ant farm or his bike tricks while she was trying to pay bills or make dinner, she had said this about him sometimes too.

Now, though, Nathan was focused on him, and in his abrupt way he said, "We should hunt sometime."

Luke saw a few other kids look over, and hoped they hadn't heard him. He had no clue why Nathan would single him out for this dubious honor. Because he wrote that essay that mentioned trout fishing with his grandfather? Because he and Nathan both lived in Maine (but lots of kids did)? Maybe it was just that Luke seemed like someone who wouldn't say no. In fact, Luke did consider it for a second—he didn't have many friends, and though he didn't want to be friends with Nathan, he felt kind of bad for him. He missed his own dogs and wouldn't have minded hanging out with this one. But as Luke stood there, his sympathy quickly soured. The expression on Nathan's face, it bugged him. The way he was just looking at him, silently, waiting for an answer. His skin looked kind of sticky. Kind of desperate. Loneliness rose off him like bad breath. Luke had the feeling that if he said yes, he might never shake him, and he didn't want to be associated with him. Didn't want to catch it. And suddenly, there was Meredith Kenney, smiling at Luke as she squeezed out the door behind Nathan's back. Luke returned the smile, and she widened her eyes and grimaced: *Yikes,* she meant.

"Yeah, I don't think so," Luke said.

It came out meaner than he'd intended, dismissive. Luke watched as Meredith was swallowed up by the crowd in the hallway, and when he looked back at Nathan, his face had closed over—not even angry, or hurt. Just gone. Nathan put his headphones on and shuffled his big hood up and walked away without another word. Luke stood there for a minute, pretending to fish for something in his pockets, to put a little distance between them. He felt mostly relieved, but also guilty. He hadn't meant to be a jerk to Nathan. He understood it had been a big deal for him to ask.

A few weeks later, when he'd been stuck in a group with Nathan and read his creepy essay about hunting with his father, Luke's relief came back. He let himself off the hook for being rude, even complimented himself on his instincts. He was glad he hadn't been alone in the woods with this guy. Now, though, hearing about the shooting, it was the feeling of guilt that returned. He kept thinking about Nathan's expression in class that day—it was needy, insecure. It wasn't the face of a killer. Somehow, though, four years later, he was so angry or lonely or just messed up that he was bragging about shooting people on YouTube, that getting fired from his stupid part-time job had pushed him over the edge. Luke couldn't shake the feeling that it didn't have to happen. Not that he really thought he could have changed anything. He knew that. But he wondered if in some small way his rejection had affected Nathan, made something tighten at his core. One more tiny moment, added to an accumulation of tiny moments. Like the volcano he'd made in seventh-grade science, how each ounce of vinegar you dripped through the hole in the top brought the whole thing a notch closer to blowing up.

It had been too much to hope that Meredith Kenney would appear among the responses, and she didn't. But the numbers were going through the roof. By Sunday morning, there were almost 300 comments, and the post had been shared more than 4000 times. The numbers freaked him out a little, but it was too late now to take it back. To Luke, the Internet had always felt like a relatively safe place: real but not real, like a padded room. Now, in random moments, sitting in front of his computer, eating a microwave pizza or picking at his chin, he felt suddenly exposed, convinced he could be seen through the screen.

Still, for the next week, if he wasn't at Dunkin' Donuts, Luke was parked in front of the computer, refreshing the page and watching the comments snake and sprawl. He read every one. At this point, most of them were people he didn't know. Some were reacting to his original post but others were just sounding off in all directions, the page a dumping ground of angry opinions—about the GOP, NRA, Walmart. *What do we expect in a country where buying a machine gun is easier than buying a pack of cigarettes???* There were countless theories about Nathan and what was wrong with him. It turned out he'd been posting on crazy gun websites, pretending to be in the military or something. *Losers like him will do anything to feel powerful because they've been ignored all their lives.* There was a flood of outrage about all the guns in Nathan's bedroom, about the stupidity of Nathan's mother. Sympathy for the victims, for their families. Sad-face emojis. A few times, somebody legitimately connected to one of the victims appeared, and it was startling, like bumping into a famous person. A student of the math teacher, the fiancé of the teenage girl. Arlen Mackey. He was a student at Central Maine too, a senior, although he sounded much older, posting: *Thank you all for the prayers and support.*

Then there were the sick conspiracy theorists who thought the shooting hadn't happened and was part of a government hoax perpetrated by anti-gun groups. And there were what Luke's mother would have called Jesus freaks, quoting the Bible and inspirational sayings like *God has a plan* and *it may not be clear now but everything happens for a reason* (Luke had heard that one when his mom died; he hated it then and hated it now).

But the ones that made Luke really uneasy were the people who felt sorry for him.

You're a nice person Luke Finch! Don't feel guilty!

People are just wired that way.

Lots of people knew him not just you . . .

Do NOT beat yourself up about this my friend! <3 <3 <3

This worried him most: that people would think he'd written the post because he was just fishing for consolation, or praise. That some inaccurate, alternative version of him, someone he couldn't control, was coming to life on the screen. So when among all the strangers and the wackos, his old classmates appeared, Luke was relieved to see them there. Kevin McAllister. Katie Sutton. Hannah Chaffee. Ashley Shay. Surprisingly, Luke remembered every single one of them, and in most cases pretty personal details about them, things he must have learned in that Freshman Comp class. That Kevin had had some kind of heart problem as a little kid and wasn't allowed to run in gym. That Hannah had had an abortion in high school that her parents didn't know about (and yet Luke did—it occurred to him how odd this was). The *significant personal experience essay*—this was pretty much all he remembered ever writing in that class, and some kids had really put themselves out there (in hindsight, they'd probably all gotten better grades than Luke did; his most significant personal experience he'd kept to himself).

Now here was Hannah Chaffee, four years later. As a freshman, she'd had long dark hair that always smelled like burnt coffee. In her profile picture, her hair was white-blond, chopped at the ears.

Hannah Chaffee: *omg I've been thinking about that class a lot luke . . .*

so disturbing

Kevin McA: *dude was a FREAK*

Luke smiled. It was nice, to hear their voices. To not be alone with it. Although he hadn't replied to any of the other 312 comments (to do so hadn't even occurred to him), to his classmates he typed back.

Luke Finch: *I guess so yeah*

Luke Finch: *good to see you guys*

Hannah Chaffee: *you too!*

Then Katie (now Kaitlyn) Sutton chimed in: *hi luke (and everyone)!*

Luke didn't remember anything Katie had written about as a freshman (though he'd heard later, through April, that she had an Adderall addiction senior year). He remembered her as kind of annoying, a kiss-ass to the teacher. It was possible she hadn't spoken to Luke once that entire semester, but now she wrote: *Don't feel bad about not talking to him Luke. Everyone was afraid of him. You weren't the only one.*

Luke Finch: *hi katie, thanks yeah*

Kaitlyn Sutton: *I remember that crazy coat—good memory*

Kaitlyn Sutton: *and the dog . . .*

Ashley Shay: *omg so weird*

Hannah Chaffee: *awww I thought the dog was cute!*

Kaitlyn Sutton: *you're right about that paper too! it was insane!*

Hannah Chaffee: *which paper??*

Kaitlyn Sutton: *not 100% sure what it was about but think it was really gory . . .*

Kaitlyn Sutton: *right luke???*

Luke Finch: *yeah maybe*

Kevin McA: *wasn't it about a zombie apocalypse or something?*

Hannah Chaffee: *I don't think I read it . . . ?*

Kevin McA: *ZOMBIES ATTACK*

Ashley Shay: *lololol*

Kaitlyn Sutton: *all I know is it freaked me out!!*

★ ★ ★

"Would you mind telling me what's going on?" his father said. It was Saturday, late morning, and the three of them were in the kitchen. His father was standing by the sink, draining a third cup of coffee before he left for work. Brent was slumped at the table, playing Fruit Ninja on his phone. Luke sat across from him, the dogs flopped by his feet. "Ray told me his kids read some thing you put on Facebook," his father said. "About that shooting."

Luke reached for a day-old doughnut from the box in the middle of the table. "Probably," he said, pulling it in half.

His father stared at him over the rim of his coffee cup. "What did you do that for?"

"I don't know." He shrugged. "I didn't think anyone would really read it."

"Then why'd you write it?"

"I don't know," he repeated. He fed a few bites of doughnut to the dogs. His father had some older-generation idea that whatever happened on a computer behind a closed door was something unsavory or worse.

"Well, Ray told me all about it, and then other people at work said they knew about it too. Customers," he added, pointedly.

"You're famous," Brent said, smiling into his phone.

It was a joke, or an insult masquerading as a joke, but Luke wanted to fire back that he was a little bit famous, in a way. That his Facebook post had been shared more than ten thousand times since last Friday. If you Googled *Nathan Dugan*, it was the eleventh hit.

"Just stay out of it," his father said to Luke.

"I'm not doing anything. People are just finding it. What am I supposed to do?"

"Take it down, dumb-ass," his brother said.

But he didn't want to take it down, although once or twice he almost had. Occasionally there was a comment that sounded so enraged, and so enraged at Luke specifically—*Why are you sympathizing with this monster, you fucking moron? You're part of the problem!!*—that the force of the emotion jolted him through the screen. His stomach started hurting, and

he'd have to lean over his knees and close his eyes and focus on something immediate and real: the texture of the scratchy carpet between his
toes, the whistle of a cardinal in the trees. In those moments he'd think
about just deleting the post, and it was tempting—that return to silence,
to being no one. But he didn't. For one thing, it would look conspicuous, like he couldn't handle the attention. For another, after all this, he
couldn't resist letting it stay up long enough to find its way to Meredith.

"People are just reading it," Luke said. "I can't help it."

"Well, you shouldn't have written it in the first place," his father said.
He set his cup down and wiped his mouth with the back of his hand. He
looked angry; a single wrinkle, like a backslash, had appeared between
his eyes. Luke wanted to tell him he should consider being happy: His
antisocial son—*a loner*, as he'd once memorably called him—was finally
getting some attention from the world. But he said nothing, scraping his
chair back and heading to the door, the dogs on his heels.

"What time do you go in?" his father asked him.

"Noon," Luke said, then let the screen door shut with a bang. He
knew his father was well aware of his schedule. It was like he didn't
trust Luke would show up at fucking Dunkin' Donuts unless he asked
him, when it was Brent who was the actual slacker, getting stoned in his
room, working a few nights a week at the pizza place—not that it mattered. Luke didn't care. Soon enough, he'd be out of there.

He decided to walk the dogs the long way, across the road and down
the path that wound around the river. His dad would have left by the
time he got home. When he crossed the street, the dogs ran ahead,
scrambling down the bank and nosing around in the rocks. As Luke hit
the path, he inhaled and began running. The air was crisp and clean and
smelled like just-turned leaves. There was a hint of sadness in it too—
the end of August. He swore he could name the month of the year, almost the exact week, by the feeling in the air. That morning, the air
reminded him of the start of fall semester, the season he'd grown accustomed to heading back to school. Next week, the new semester would
start without him. He'd never have predicted he would miss it but now

the thought of those six-hour labs, the permanent red dents around his eyes from the goggles, awoke an ache inside him. It was lonely, being home. Worse, it was embarrassing. Some people from high school had been around over the summer but now most of them had gone, and the few still left were working dumb jobs like his. Once he had enough money saved, he'd buy a used truck and head down to Portland. Maybe crash at the apartment Matt had gotten with his USM friends. He ran hard, harder. His breath scraped his throat. The tops of the oaks were bright red and yellow against the hard blue sky. He ran as far as the bridge, sucking air, breathing in the sweetness of the river water. It was like the air was crying, he thought—a weird thought.

When the phone call came, almost a week later, it took Luke by surprise. It was early on a Thursday morning, and life was back to something like normal. The Facebook post had quieted down, as he'd known it would eventually; strangers still left comments, but they were more sporadic, and often from the same few people. It was kind of disappointing to see it end, but mostly it was a relief.

That morning, Luke had the eight a.m. shift at Dunkin', and his father was leaving for the auto body, and they were both kind of silently maneuvering around the kitchen the way they did on Thursdays, coffee brewing and spoons tapping cereal bowls. His dad was just bagging up his lunch when the phone rang.

"Who?" He listened for a minute, then handed the phone to Luke. "For you," he said. "A newspaper." He raised his eyebrows, as if Luke had rigged the call himself.

"Hello?"

"Luke Finch?" It was a girl on the line, sounding chipper for not even eight in the morning.

"Yeah?"

"My name is Julie Brody," she said. "I'm calling from the *Maine State Sentinel.*"

Oh: a newspaper, but not a real one. The *Sentinel* was the student paper back at school. Luke had never really read it but remembered piles of it appearing every other week in the student union. Occasionally he'd thumbed through a copy in April's room.

"Is now a good time?" Julie said.

"For what?" Luke glanced at his dad, standing in the middle of the room, halfway between phone and door. He usually gave Luke a ride to work on Thursdays.

"I was hoping I could ask you a few questions for an article I'm writing about the aftermath of the shooting at the Millview Mall," she said. "I promise it won't take more than a few minutes of your time."

His father tapped an imaginary watch with his index finger. Luke checked the square white numbers on the oven: 7:43.

"I apologize for calling so early," Julie was saying, "but I tried this number several times in the past week and there was no answer. I just have a few questions about your Facebook post."

Luke pictured Julie Brody: an upperclassman, judging from her tone, which was clipped and confident, almost like she was acting the part of a reporter. At this hour, she must be calling from her dorm room, probably having set her alarm. No one woke up this early back at school.

"I saw it online," she continued. "A few days after the shooting. And I have to tell you, I found it very moving. What you wrote, it really made me think. And then the response you got—it occurred to me this would make a fascinating article. There are so many compelling angles here."

"Angles?"

His father frowned, as if the word had confirmed his deepest suspicions.

"Like what?" Luke said, shifting slightly toward the wall.

"I mean, there are so many," she said. "Your memories of Nathan Dugan, of course. And what it's like to be sitting in class with a person like this, and then all the attention online—the reaction was kind of tremendous, don't you think?"

It was a quarter to eight. His father was never late. Luke waved at his dad to go without him—he could ride his bike, like he did most days anyway—and his dad gave him a look, a long hard eyeful, then picked up his lunch from the counter and started slowly toward the door.

"Luke?" Julie was saying. "Are you there?"

"Yeah," he said as the door slammed on his father's back. "Sorry. I'm here."

"I was just saying, the online response was pretty remarkable," she said. "Why do you think people responded so deeply to what you wrote?"

Luke listened until he heard the crunch of his father's boot soles on the driveway, the point where the gravel met the grass. "I don't know," he said as the truck door cringed open. "People just want to know what he was like, I guess."

"Your post was shared over ten thousand times, right?"

"Yeah," Luke said. When he heard the engine start, something relaxed in his chest. "Something like that, anyway." Though in the past twenty-four hours there had been almost no new activity, the overall totals were still out of control. Now that it was over, sometimes Luke found himself just combing through all of it, reading here and there, almost nostalgically.

"It was closer to twelve thousand, actually, I think," he said. Then, worried it might sound like he was bragging, he added, "It's been pretty crazy."

"It's not crazy in the least," Julie Brody said. "It goes to show how much what you wrote affected people."

Luke let out a small, awkward-sounding laugh. "I don't know about that."

"Well, I do," she said. "You were honest about your feelings, and people respond to honesty. What I want to know is, what first compelled you to sit down and write it?"

Then she fell silent, and Luke felt her waiting, wanting him to say something good. "I don't know," he said, adding, "It was just one of those things." Still Julie said nothing, because clearly this was a terrible answer but he didn't know what else to say. He couldn't admit his real reasons for writing it—that he felt guilty for once being a jerk to Nathan Dugan, that he was hoping to connect with a girl he'd had a crush on freshman year. He thought back to that afternoon, the crippling pain in his stomach, and tried to offer something better. "It was just upsetting to hear," he said. "Somebody you knew."

"Well, of course," Julie said. He could feel her nodding through the line. "Your original post was written the same day as the shooting, wasn't it? You must have written it basically just as soon as you heard—"

"Pretty much, yeah."

"So the news hit you really hard."

"Sure." Luke laughed again, then wished that he hadn't. He hoped it didn't sound callous, but the question was just dumb. "I mean, it was pretty horrible—"

"Oh, of course it was. But I meant the identity of the shooter, specifically. When you heard it was your old classmate, Nathan Dugan," she said, quoting, "'I didn't really know him but I still remember him,'" and something about the way she delivered this line—with a tragic sort of emphasis, like his Facebook post was a piece of literature or something—made him queasy. "What do you think it was about Nathan that made such a lasting impression on you?" Julie said, and Luke felt a sliver of worry: Did it seem abnormal, how well he remembered Nathan? Did it imply that he'd been watching him in class or obsessed with him or something? *Luke, honey, you're staring.*

"I mean, he was pretty hard to miss," Luke said.

"Still," Julie pressed. "You paint such a vivid picture. Four years later, he really stayed with you—"

"Well, yeah," he interrupted. "But it wasn't just me who noticed him, though."

"What do you mean?"

Stayed with you—this bugged him too.

"I mean, there were a lot of us who felt that way."

"What way?"

"Just, that, you know, he was kind of disturbing."

"By *us*, you mean other students—"

"Yeah," Luke said. "Kids in the class."

Julie paused. "You're saying you talked about him at the time? About how disturbing he was? With your classmates?"

"I don't know if we talked about it. You could tell, though."

"How could you tell?"

"You know—people whispering, making faces, that kind of thing." He pictured Meredith, cringing as she squeezed behind Nathan and out the classroom door. Then he looked at the clock: 7:54. "Look, I'm going to be late for work—"

"Oh, no! Just ten more seconds!" Julie said. "You mentioned this paper. In your post, you mentioned a paper that Nathan wrote—can you tell me what it was about?"

She fell silent again, waiting, but this time Luke didn't rush to answer. Her thirstiness was putting him on edge. It wasn't like he was some official authority on Nathan Dugan—in truth, he barely remembered Nathan Dugan, and what he thought he remembered he was now starting to second-guess. Was it true that Nathan had worn that big coat year-round? That he'd sat with his fingers pointed—*gunlike*, one of the comments had described it—or had Luke's brain just conjured that up because it seemed right?

He looked at the kitchen wallpaper, a pattern of different fruits in vertical stripes. "I think it was about hunting," he said. "The paper. But honestly, I'm not sure."

"Hunting?" Julie repeated, and Luke detected a new note of eagerness in her voice. "Really? That's a pretty frightening coincidence, isn't it?"

"Yeah, but like I said, I'm not positive. You should look at the comments. A couple other kids mentioned it. They remember it too. Some of them said they thought it was about guns, or war, or one guy thought it was about zombies. Kevin McAllister. He might remember more than I do."

"Well," Julie said. "No matter what, it sounds like lots of students were aware there was a problem."

"Yeah." Luke nodded into the phone. "Right. It definitely wasn't just me."

"Doesn't that make it even more mystifying that other people missed it?"

"What do you mean?"

"The professor, for instance," Julie said. "This was Maggie Daley, right?"

That was what they'd called her, Luke thought. Maggie. He had forgotten her first name. He hadn't been one of her favorites, like Katie Sutton, but he'd liked her well enough. She seemed to get that he was shy; she left him basically alone. The thought of her now was kind of comforting, like being alone in a room with troublemakers and suddenly having an adult open the door.

"Did she ever address Nathan's behavior?" Julie asked him.

"Address his behavior?" Luke said. "Like how?"

"Anything, really—did she mention it in class?"

"No," he said. "Not that I remember."

"What about this weird paper?"

"I don't think so—"

"Did she talk to *him* about it?"

"I don't know," he said, and paused. "I mean, how would I know that?"

"Well, do you think she *should* have?"

"Maybe," he said. "Yeah, probably."

"If he was writing about guns, after all."

"Well, yeah," Luke said, his eyes on the clock as it slid to 8:01.

Eight

In the days following the shooting, Maggie checked the Internet multiple times a day. She had never been bothered before by her slow connection; if anything, her technological inefficiency was a point of certain pride. But those endless minutes, waiting for the screen to load, felt torturous, as she worried what she might find. She tried to distract herself with thoughts of the upcoming semester, the new students whose names and majors she'd received by email—one of them had already contacted her, wanting to get a jump on buying books—then, suddenly, the little wheel stopped spinning, the screen was awash with words, and she scrolled into the depths.

It was her first exposure to a Facebook post, and she was amazed by how it unfurled and expanded, shoots from a vine. Sunday night, when she got home from Boston, there were over 350 comments. By Monday morning, nearly 100 more. Luke's reflections had sprouted conversations, and those conversations sprouted conversations, tangents and sidebars, unruly and unstructured, one long thought unraveling in many directions—*threads*, the surprisingly perfect term. Many of these remarks were insensitive, if not outright ignorant, confirming one of Maggie's objections to the Internet: Anyone could publish anything here. Nonetheless, she would follow a thread as it gained momentum, attracting other voices, an irate and righteous chorus, like a rock hurtling down a hill.

Over the weekend, new information had emerged about Nathan's online presence. A search of the laptop from his bedroom turned up frequent visits to websites dedicated to guns and weaponry and other high-profile shootings, where he'd posted hundreds of long critical rants under an alias—a *handle*—traced back to his email address. Maggie shuddered, remembering Nathan's critique of Meredith's essay: Had that been the seedling of this impulse, now full-blown? His alias was SergeantX. *Did he think he was some kind of military supervillain?* the commenters weighed in, denouncing him as *fake, a wannabe, delusional.* Maggie's mind turned to the paper still smoldering in the pocket of her bag—if Nathan's essay had felt ambiguous, his online writings sounded like a clear barometer of his instability. On the Internet, though, she supposed such things could simply go unnoticed, or be mistaken for any other furious screed. Anybody was reading them, yet nobody was.

About Marielle Dugan, new details had also surfaced. Not only had she been living with her son, renting a house near the college; she had sold her house in New Hampshire to move there with him before his freshman year. She maintained that she'd had no idea what her son was planning, that he was capable of such violence, sparking another avalanche of blame. Obviously, people wrote, she knew something was wrong with him. Why else would she have moved with him? She must have known that he was dangerous. That he needed to be helped, to be watched. *If the mother had any doubts about his mental health she had a responsibility to get help for him. Either she's an enabler or she's a moron. Or both!!!*

Maggie read these comments with a quick heart. She too felt guilty about Nathan, about what she might have done differently, what warning signs might have escaped her notice. And she was just the teacher, a college professor. For a mother to not recognize something was so deeply wrong with her child—it was a sickening thought. Maggie had known that guilt herself, though on a far lesser scale. Yet she struggled to square her instinct for empathy toward this mother with her memory of speaking to Marielle Dugan the day after the shooting. The entire encounter—the sagging porch, the half-painted house, the blast of bitterness as Maggie left—were details so surreal they felt like something she had dreamed. She hadn't told anyone she'd gone there, not even Robert. Very early Sunday morning, he'd texted her, asking about the call she'd made the night before, but Anna was waiting in the driveway—there wasn't time to explain. She managed to type a short but painstaking text back, telling him she'd fill him in when she returned. But the next day, when finally they managed a proper conversation, the urgency of her call outside Tilghman had faded; she was wrung out from dropping Anna off at school. When Robert asked about her meeting, she didn't mention Nathan's essay; if she hadn't told Bill, she decided, she needn't tell anyone. And Robert didn't have the time anyway. Suzanne, he said, had been taking the news of the victims badly. But the new semester was starting next week; they would be seeing much more of each other soon.

For now, Maggie remained alone at her computer, wading through the stew of threads and headlines and, occasionally, bumping into herself: *What I still don't get is why that idiot Professor Daley didn't do anything.* It was a shock each time: to see her name invoked by strangers, floating on the waves of the Internet, visible to billions and available to be wielded in whatever way they wished. *Obviously it's the fault of the killer but anybody who knew he was dangerous is partially responsible too imho.* The comments shook her in their ire, their casual certainty. What unnerved her even more, though, were the ones that began appearing from her former students, all members of that same comp class. Katie Sutton, Kevin McAllister, Ashley Shay. They were the same students whose sweet, vulnerable essays now sat in her barn, growing soft with mildew. To read their comments felt like eavesdropping on a party, hearing what the students really thought and how they spoke.

Hannah Chaffee: *omg I've been thinking about that class a lot luke . . . so disturbing*

Kaitlyn Sutton: *you're right about that paper too! it was insane!*

Hannah Chaffee, who had written so movingly about her abortion. Katie, who had always taken notes so diligently, calling *thank you!* to Maggie as she left the room. Maggie remembered Katie as mature, almost peerlike, but maybe she'd misread her; most of her comments felt tossed off and shallow. And then there was this: *Don't feel bad about not talking to him Luke. Everyone was afraid of him. You weren't the only one.*

Maggie stared at that line. *Afraid.* Had Katie chosen such a strong word unthinkingly, under the influence of the shooting, typing quickly into her phone? Or had Maggie's students really felt this way? It alarmed her, the possibility that they had been so unnerved by Nathan's presence, that her efforts to defuse it had failed so completely. Perhaps she just hadn't been fully present that semester. Too worried about her daughter, too distracted by her own coming-apart life. Perhaps, that difficult spring, her class had served as a reprieve for her, a needed affirmation, making her all the more inclined to pretend Nathan Dugan wasn't there. Or perhaps she simply hadn't wanted to deal with him, wanted to be finished with him and to focus on the other students—the more rewarding, more appropriate students. Deliver Nathan his C+ and return him to the world.

Sunday evening, the night before the first day of classes, Maggie received an email called *request from student.* She expected to find one of the names from her list. But the student was a senior, Juliet Brody. She was an English major, though she'd never taken one of Maggie's classes. *I am writing a story about your former student Nathan Dugan for our first issue of the Sentinel and would like to speak with you about his performance in your class. Please call me at this number.* On first read, Maggie found the email jarring—not the fact of the article, which wasn't so surprising, but the tone of it, which was inappropriate, presumptuous. *Sent from my iPhone.* Maggie thought it best to ignore. She knew this student, Juliet Brody, would ask what she remembered about Nathan, and she didn't want to lie again.

Part Two

Nine

Anna's first essay assignment was to choose a twentieth-century poet and closely analyze the way(s) a recurrent theme or symbol manifests in his/her work. It was for her first-year seminar, The Preoccupations of Poets. First-year seminars were small, cleverly titled, and taught mostly by grad students; hers, Siena, was working on her PhD in Comp Lit. Siena was kind of heavy, but pretty—Anna was impressed by the way she seemed to own her size, wearing fitted dresses with tall boots and bright tights and scarves. In class, she'd shared a few of her own poems, which she'd had published in online journals. In high school, Anna had hated speaking in class, but Siena's seminar felt different, less like a class than a conversation. She could imagine Siena becoming a kind of mentor figure for her as time went on.

For her essay, Anna decided to write about the preoccupation with solitude and otherness in Elizabeth Bishop. She devoted way too many hours to it, but it was her first college paper—and an English paper, for Siena—so she was determined to do well. When, at the end of the next class, Siena slid their essays facedown across the table, Anna flipped to the last page and was stunned: B-. The margins were filled with blue-penned notes, underlines and arrows that quickly swam off into the margins. "Until next time, guys," Siena was saying as Anna stuffed the paper in her backpack. To her horror, she felt tears gathering behind her face. She bit the inside of her cheek and hurried outside and onto the quad, where she found an empty bench and bent over her knees, opening the paper again and madly skimming, twisting her bottom lip. *Lovely writing but I wish the feeling came through more. Push this idea further? Potentially interesting, but not clear.*

When some guy sat down beside her, she swiped at her eyes, startled—couldn't this person see she was in the middle of a meltdown? In her peripheral vision, she saw a blue-jeaned leg, scuffed black boot, paperback book splayed upside-down on his knee. "What'd you get?"

Later that day, recounting this meeting for Alexis, the arc of the story would take on a high gloss—how, before Anna realized she liked James, she thought James was the most arrogant person she'd ever met. In reality, Anna's first impression of James was how skinny he was (sadly, even with guys, it was the first thing she saw). "Excuse me?" she said.

"On the paper." His face was hidden behind his sunglasses, which were mirrored and disconcerting.

"What paper?"

He pointed his chin toward her lap. "That one right there."

She pinched her nails into her palms. "Are you asking me what I got on my paper?"

"So you didn't get an A."

He was a collection of affectations, Anna told herself: the wrinkled short-sleeved button-down, the glasses, the phone weighing down his shirt pocket, even the book, which was the sort of paperback you might find in a used bookstore, swollen, pages yellowing.

"How do you know?"

"Because if you got an A, you'd just say you got an A," he said. "Don't get me wrong. I'm not suggesting I think grades have any real significance. But you obviously do, so you must have done badly—or, not actually badly, but badly for you, because you probably got straight A's in high school." He pushed his sunglasses on top of his head. His eyes were sort of smiling, but she couldn't tell if he was kidding. They were light brown, the color of balsa wood. "B minus, right?"

Anna didn't reply right away—*I didn't want to give him the satisfaction*, she would report later to Alexis, but in fact she was too caught off-guard to speak. When she did, she tried her best to sound airy and unfazed. "You guessed it. Congratulations."

"And?"

"And what?"

"And who gives a shit about a B minus?"

"I do."

"How come?"

"Oh, I don't know, because I want to do well? Because I care about this class? Because I worked hard on the paper and have never gotten less than an A in English in my entire life?"

"Ah." He nodded. "I knew it. You're an overachiever."

"What's wrong with being an overachiever?"

"Nothing," he said. "If that's what you're into."

"Why wouldn't overachieving be what I'm into?"

"Apparently, it would."

"Great. Thanks for clearing that up." She spoke briskly, but there was a new feeling, a low thrumming, in her gut.

"What's the class?" he asked.

Her eyes dropped to her lap—*phrasing is awkward*. "Poetry. My first-year seminar."

"If it makes you feel better, nobody gets an A on their first paper for first-year seminar. To motivate you to do better and all that bullshit."

"I find that hard to believe."

"Suit yourself." He shrugged. "Perfectionism is kind of your thing, right?"

"I don't have a thing. What's *your* thing? Quick, unfounded generalizations?"

"Truth-telling. Challenging the status quo. Exposing the hypocrisy that plagues modern society." He smiled. "Although according to the

official rhetoric of this institution, I'm majoring in Film and Poli Sci."
He pulled the phone from his pocket, holding it level with his chin.
"What about you?"

"What about me?"

"What's your major?"

She paused. "What are you doing? Are you filming me?"

"For posterity," he said. "An archive of our first meeting."

"Well, that's normal," she quipped, but felt suddenly self-conscious,
aware of her face. "To answer your question, I don't have a major. I'm
a first-year. Like I said when you apparently weren't paying attention."
The camera was making her anxious. She looked at it directly and stuck
her tongue out, and he laughed, which pleased her. Talking to him felt
something like a competition, like she was skating on the surface of herself and trying to keep up. "But eventually, English and Psychology."

"Why English and Psychology?"

"Well, my mother's an English professor, so that's probably some sort
of Pavlovian thing—"

"And Psychology because you have a fucked-up family?"

"Potentially," she said, a ripple of adrenaline in her veins.

"So," he said. "Let me guess. You want to be a shrink."

She laughed. "Um, wrong."

"You have something against shrinks? I've been shrinked."

"Sure. Me too." It wasn't something she wanted him—or anyone—
to know about her, but it felt like they were locked in a game of one-
upmanship, playing honesty with a stranger and seeing how far they'd
go. "That doesn't mean I want to be one."

"So an academic," he said. "A prof. Like Mom."

"No," Anna said. "God, no."

He raised his eyebrows. "Why's that?"

Anna rifled through the reasons—the fact that she'd watched her
mother's teaching gradually consume her, that her mother had always
been halfheartedly "working on a book" but as far as Anna knew had
never written a word—but said only "I have a complicated relationship

to higher education." And: "Actually, I want to be a writer." Then held her breath. This wasn't something she'd admitted to many people either, but he nodded seriously.

"I can see that," he said. "And in case you were worried, grades on papers in bullshit first-year seminars are not a predictor of future writing success. You can fail all your English classes and still go on to have an outstanding career. In fact, some failure might be healthy for a perfectionist like yourself."

"Noted," she breezed. "Thanks for the tip."

He slipped his phone back in his shirt pocket. Then he looked at her closely, kind of wonderingly, and later, Anna would think that what first attracted him to her was her seeming bite and boldness, the willingness to go toe-to-toe with him, though in reality, this crisp, cavalier exterior was just the flip side of her nerves.

He stuck out a hand. "James. Intrusive asshole who interrogates women who clearly want to be left alone."

"Anna," she replied. "Perfectionist who has a breakdown if she gets less than a B plus."

He let go of her hand but still sat there, studying her, as if deciding something, while Anna struggled to maintain a look of cool indifference, hoping he'd walk away before she cracked and her true self spilled out. Finally he fished the phone back out of his pocket and said: "May I have your number, Anna, please?"

James Baird-English, Alexis reported. *Junior, Film/Poli Sci double major, freakishly smart, kind of political, no known addictions and/or baggage, went out with a grad student.*

"Wait," Anna said. "Grad student?"

"So?" Alexis shrugged. "That's a plus." They were splitting a pizza and sitting on the floor of their dorm room in Hightower, on the shaggy multicolored rug Alexis had ordered online. It was just how Anna had imagined college would be: the rug, the pizza, even the way they were sitting, cross-legged, bare knees touching. Except that, on the inside, the pizza was making Anna's heart race. She was distracted by Alexis's knee, which was half the size of hers. It turned out Alexis was actually one of those people that celebrities claimed to be, the kind who was naturally tiny, could eat anything she wanted and not gain weight. Anna tried to accept Alexis's carelessly shared snacks and not let on if they were making her feel panicked. For as much as she'd already confided in her new roommate, Anna had told her nothing about her struggles in high school and had no plans to. Her intermittent inner freak-outs about all the junk food she was consuming, the high-calorie beer she was drinking, the occasional bursts of lingering online activity about the shooting—these were all part of the life she'd left so deliberately behind.

"That means he's experienced," Alexis was saying, reaching for another slice. "That's a good thing. Plus, smart. And smart people are better at sex."

"Oh?" Anna laughed, forcing a bite. "Is that scientifically proven or something?"

"Haven't you ever heard that? It's a definite thing." Alexis often offered up lines like this, pronouncements on the way life was, but she had the goods to back it up: eight years of camp, five sexual partners (her term), various international travels (she'd spent half the summer with a single aunt in Italy), and casual encounters with drugs at her elite private school, which she referred to with eye rolls, as if they were childish fads she'd outgrown. Alexis herself was off the market (which of course only made guys more interested) and had a boyfriend named Willem (Willem!) who went to Vanderbilt; they sexted regularly, something Anna hadn't known people actually did.

"Anyway," she continued. "The girlfriend was unstable. The grad student. That's what Breck said." Between Alexis's school and camp, she was well connected on campus; after hearing about Anna's conversation with James that afternoon, she'd tapped her upper-class sources like a private eye. "She transferred after the breakup, apparently."

"Really?" Anna said. This information was weirdly exciting. "Unstable how?"

"Breck didn't say."

"Didn't or wouldn't?"

"Both," Alexis said. "But never fear, roomie. We have our ways." She dropped her half-eaten slice back in the box and blotted her fingers on the rug (Anna had been appalled at first by Alexis's personal habits but had since chalked them up to her growing up with maids) and grabbed her laptop. "Let's look him up."

This was one of Alexis's strengths: She always had an answer, always had a plan. She never seemed less than confident about anything. At parties, she steered Anna around warm sticky basements, homing in on guys to introduce her to. Alexis herself didn't do anything too recap-worthy, and any minor exploits she owned so thoroughly that they never felt juicy. But she was a reliable source of gossip about the other girls in their hall: like Violet Sharma, who had had sex with both Mike Hack and his roommate at the same party. Hilary Macintosh, whose nose had started bleeding (study drugs, Alexis surmised) in the middle of Intro-duction to Eastern Thought. Violet's roommate, Carly Smith, was so unsocial as to be fascinating in her own right: She went to bed at nine thirty, Violet reported, even on the weekends (a supposed inner-ear problem), had never had sex, never drank.

"Bueno," Alexis announced. "It's public."

Anna edged closer. Alexis was scrolling down James's Facebook page. His profile picture looked like some kind of psychedelic solar system. Under Lives In, he'd written: *State of Perpetual Disillusionment*. Under Studied: *Whenever the Eff I Felt Like It at Collwood HS*. Anna found this clever, but Alexis zipped by it in search of more pertinent information. There wasn't much to be had. Links to articles and petitions, mostly. *Un-masking the Media* and *Stop Corporate Greed NOW*. Alexis flipped through James's photo albums, most of them pictures he'd been tagged in by other people, and Anna watched years of his life go whipping by: James at graduation, arms looped over two girls' shoulders; James leaning out a car window pointing to a sign that said ENDLESS MTNS NEXT 6 EXITS; James sitting by a campfire, giving a blurred finger to the camera; James, looking younger, raising an OCCUPY sign in a crowd in New York City; James taking a picture of the person taking the picture.

"He doesn't post much about himself," Alexis summarized. "But there are no lingering pictures of him and the girlfriend. So that's good."

She flicked through his mobile uploads: a ticket stub for a film festival, a bumper sticker that said DON'T JUST SIT THERE MAKE SOMETHING HAPPEN, a pair of mud-crusted boots sitting in a field. And there was his profile picture again—not a planet, Anna realized, but an eyeball. His eyeball. The nice brown color that had been fixed on her earlier was threaded with thin red and blue veins that made the eye look vaguely electrocuted, like a fortune-teller's ball.

"He's definitely eccentric," Alexis pronounced, then returned to her slice. "But no serious red flags, roomie. And Breck said he was cool."

Anna was left staring at the photo of James caught on the screen, one that had probably been taken in middle school: acne-ridden, glasses-wearing, sitting on a bald brown couch with two other acne-ridden glasses-wearing teenage boys. Subtract the glasses, cut the hair, and erase the acne, and there was James: another, perhaps truer version of James. On his face was a twist of a smile, a trace of insecurity. Looking at it, Anna felt guilty, as if she were peeking at a painful past James would surely not want seen. Her mother was always denouncing technology, and Anna was always defending it, but then there was this: The most awkward phase of your life still available, visible, with a few clicks.

"Don't worry," Alexis said without missing a beat. "That was taken a long time ago."

Since arriving at college, Anna had had little contact with her mother. With her father, even Felicia, she texted now and then. But Maggie had an ancient flip phone on which texting was basically impossible, and didn't like email, so their only real option was talking on the phone. The times her mother called, Anna had been studying, or hungover. After three messages, she'd stopped leaving them, the red missed calls piling up in a silent reprimand. Anna had listened only to the first one. *Anna, how are you doing?* An ordinary question, but coming from her mother, it was soaked in concern. It was enough to make Anna feel defensive and put off calling. That Tuesday, though, the day after she met James, her happiness was making her feel magnanimous. Her mother answered on the second ring: "You're alive."

Anna was lying in bed, toes hooked in the coils on the underside of Alexis's mattress frame. "That's a little extreme, isn't it?"

"Did you get my messages?"

"I got them," she admitted. "I've just been really busy."

"You need to call me, Anna," her mother said, and though this irritated her a little, she said, "I know. Sorry."

"I was getting worried."

"I said I was sorry," she added, but then felt guilty, hearing the fretfulness in her mother's voice. She pictured her alone in that quiet kitchen, sink ledge lined with ragged balls of steel wool, a pile of bruised oranges in the cracked blue bowl on the table. Then the reception grew fuzzy, and she felt another pang of annoyance: That entire house was a technological black hole.

"So," her mother asked. "How are you doing?"

"Good," Anna quipped. "Great, actually." She provided a quick inventory of her classes: Intro to Psychology, Nineteenth-Century American Novelists, World History, Preoccupations of Poets. "My first-year seminar," she explained.

"Ah."

"It's taught by a grad student."

"Is it?"

"That's how it is here," Anna hastened to add. She'd heard her mother criticize some of the younger teachers in her department for being too casual with students, too friendlike, and even though she still smarted a little, thinking of Siena and her paper, she didn't want Maggie to get the wrong idea. "She's really smart," she said.

"I'm sure she is," her mother replied. "And the workload? It's manageable?"

"Totally," she said, digging a finger into the mattress frame. She wasn't going to mention the B-. She considered mentioning James—her mother, she thought, would probably appreciate his intellect. She'd always thought Gavin cared too little about the world, but James was Gavin's opposite: He seemed to care almost too much.

Then her mother asked, "How's that roommate?"

That roommate: So she hadn't liked Alexis. Anna wasn't surprised. "She's great, actually," Anna told her. "You kind of have to get to know her." As if on cue, the door opened and Alexis walked in, tossing her backpack on the floor and saying, "Can we go to lunch, please? I'm starving."

Anna pointed at the phone.

"And it's going well?" her mother asked. "Living with someone?"

"It's bueno," Anna replied. Her mother paused at this, but Alexis smiled. "She's the perfect roommate," she added, prompting Alexis to arch one brow. Anna mouthed, *My mom.*

"Well," her mother said, then lapsed into quiet. Anna heard a crackle of static on the line. "It sounds like you're really settling in there," she said, and despite the poor reception, Anna thought she sounded a little forlorn, compelling her to ask: "So what's going on at home?"

Immediately, she regretted it. As soon as her mother started talking, Anna's patience began to ebb away. It was always this way. Whatever sympathy she felt for her mother in the abstract, or sitting in Theresa's office, tended to erode in the wake of actual life—the hours she spent marking papers, or the way she clutched the steering wheel when driving, or her habit of editing her sentences while she spoke.

"Some of them are promising," her mother was saying. "They have promise. So they'll come around. They always do."

She was talking about her classes, of course. About her students.

"It's still early. Not even October—"

Alexis was rolling her wrist in impatient circles—*hurry, hurry, hurry.* Anna winced, holding up one finger. Then the phone quivered, a text message incoming. Anna held the screen away from her face and registered the 607 area code—*Can't stop thinking about you*, it said.

She bolted upright, banging her head on Alexis's mattress frame. "Um, crazy person?" Alexis laughed, and Anna extended the phone, widening her eyes. Alexis peered at the screen, then let out a scream and clapped a hand over her mouth. It buzzed twice more.

Hope that doesn't freak you out

This is James btw

Anna's mother's voice was still leaking from the phone. "Oh my God, hang up," Alexis whispered. "Hang up, hang up, hang up." Anna pressed the phone to her pulsing ear. Her mother was saying, "So it seems to have died down but—"

"Mom," she interrupted, "I'm sorry, but I kind of have to go."

Her mother paused, but when she spoke again, she sounded wounded. "Go?"

"It's just that I have class—"

"But I just asked you a question, Anna," her mother said.

"What was it?"

"Weren't you listening?"

"I was, but I didn't hear it," she said. "It must be the reception."

"I asked if you ever saw this Facebook post," her mother said.

"Facebook post?" Anna asked, rolling her eyes at Alexis, who was looking at her, incredulous.

"A post on Facebook, Anna," her mother said. "Did you not hear what I just said?"

"Sorry, I just didn't hear the last part—"

"I left you a message about it," she said. "Days ago."

"I must have just forgot."

Her mother paused, then spoke evenly. "This post," she said, "was written by one of my former students. On the day of the shooting," she said, and Anna felt a spike of alarm. Alexis was still staring at her, but Anna looked away. "His name is Luke Finch. He was in my class. Nathan Dugan's class. He wrote about him—Nathan—and what he wrote was viral, evidently—" But Anna could feel herself tuning out, in self-defense. She kept her eyes on the floor, the carpet with its pattern of brightly colored squares, avoiding her roommate's eyes. Alexis had been part of that terrible conversation, their first day on campus, but the shooting hadn't come up since then, and Anna preferred to keep it that way. Conveniently, Alexis didn't appear too interested in knowing. She didn't seem anywhere near as affected by these sorts of things as Anna was—Alexis paid attention in the moment but then had the ability to get beyond it, to let troubling things flow past her and move on.

"It's subsided now, it seems. I just wondered if you'd seen it. I take it that you didn't," her mother was saying, just as the phone buzzed again—*What are you doing in 15?*

Alexis grabbed the phone, read it, then thrust it back toward Anna's ear. "Seriously," she hissed. "Hang up now."

"Mom, listen," Anna said. "I really have to go."

Her mother fell silent again. The phone burned against Anna's cheek. The reception was still crackling, like a small fire hidden somewhere along the invisible tunnel that connected school and home. She closed her eyes, blocking out Alexis's frantic gestures. She felt sorry for her mother, attempting to navigate that intense Facebook post on the slow computer in her study, but she couldn't afford to keep worrying about it, not when she was getting overwhelmed herself. "I'll call you later," Anna told her. "But I wouldn't worry about it. That kind of thing is popular for twelve hours and disappears. It sounds like it already has."

James proposed they meet at a coffee shop six blocks from campus. It had brick walls and exposed copper pipes and faded furniture with embroidered pillows, some with little sayings sewn on them: HOME IS WHERE THE HEART IS and IGNORANCE IS BLISS. People were lounging on chairs and couches, tapping on their laptops; most looked like they'd been living there for days. James was waiting by the counter, wearing another in his collection of wrinkled button-downs. His appearance seemed deliberately haphazard; or maybe it was the lack of deliberation that was deliberate.

Anna ordered a nonfat latte, James a rooibos tea.

"Really?" she laughed, but he looked serious.

"What?" he said.

"I don't know. I guess I assumed you were more of a black coffee guy."

He wagged a finger at her. "Shallow generalization of the brooding artist. Tsk, Anna. Tsk." Then he picked up his mug, a stainless-steel one he'd brought with him, and headed for an empty couch. She followed, worried she'd offended him—she blamed Stafford. She blamed Gavin. She blamed Gavin and his incessant, generic Coke-drinking.

As they sat, James leaned toward her, whispering, "You know I was kidding."

"Oh," she said. "Honestly, I wasn't sure."

"It takes way more than that to offend me," James said. Then he leaned back on the couch, crossing his legs at the knee. "Okay," he said. "Pick a topic."

"A topic?"

"A good one."

"Um. Okay." She skimmed through her mental inventory about James, wanting to avoid anything that might betray the depths of her online research. Finally she said, "Where are you from?" realizing even as she asked the question how uninteresting it was.

But James smacked a palm on his knee. "Right. Yes. Let's get the basics out of the way so we can talk about the real stuff," he said. "I'm from New York, but not New York City. Lest you assume I'm a black-coffee-drinking Williamsburg hipster. I grew up three hours from Manhattan in a rich, culturally bankrupt suburb filled with people who prefer to ignore how fucked-up the world is in favor of watching the *Real Housewives* and *Fox News*." He smiled. "Now you."

"Me." She was trying to orient herself, to fall into his rhythm, volley back.

"You're from Maine," he said.

"Yes." She was flattered that he knew this. "From a town called Stafford. It's pretty small. And pretty rural."

"How small and how rural?"

"I'm not sure, population-wise—"

"Livestock?"

"No livestock," she said. "We have a barn, though. It's red. And more or less dilapidated."

"Nice," he said approvingly. "Actual rustic, not that fake countrified bullshit. Number of minutes to the nearest Starbucks?"

"Probably fifteen," she said, and winced. "But that's because we're also right next to a college town—"

"Oh, right, right. Because your mom's a professor." He tapped his temple. "See? I pay attention." He pried the top off his mug and removed the dripping tea bag, one of those fancy silken ones with leaves inside, and laid it on a napkin, which it devoured in a quick red stain. "Is she any good?"

"Is who?" Anna said.

"Your mother."

"What, as a professor?"

"Sure." He shrugged, stirring a finger in his tea. "Is she challenging? Liberal? Open-minded?"

"How would I know?" Anna said, but of course she did. She had observed her mother's classes, times when she was off from school and spent the day with her on campus. She was always surprised by how animated her mother would become in front of students, gesturing emphatically and pacing around the room. In such moments, Anna found it hard to imagine her back home marking papers, tucked into the rocking chair, head bowed, scribbling comments so ardently her whole arm shook. "I mean, her students seem to like her," Anna said. "I hope they do. They're, like, her whole life."

James smiled. "Jealous?"

"Yeah," Anna said sarcastically, though she sometimes was.

"She teaches literature, right?"

"Composition, mostly. It's a requirement. All students have to take it."

"Oh," he said with a knowing nod. "You mean Personal Tragedy 101."

Anna laughed. Growing up, she and Kim and Janie had frequently sneaked looks at her mother's students' papers, piled on the coffee table or the kitchen counter, covered in her tiny handwriting. Her mother hadn't known, and wouldn't have liked it if she had, but it was impossible to resist. Reading those papers was like peeking inside someone's diary. There were your standard-issue personal experiences, grandparents' deaths and parents' divorces and eating disorders. Then there was the boy who burned his arms with matches, the girl who had been raped by her babysitter, another girl so anorexic she'd grown fur. That students would divulge such personal things to a teacher, to her mother, Anna had found incredible, though also kind of painful—that these students, kids not so much older than she was, confided in her mother so much more openly than she did. (The fact that the anorexia essay was where she'd gotten some of her own ideas was something she'd never admitted to anyone, not even Janie and Kim.)

"My brother had a class like that," James was saying. "At his community college. It was a joke. I mean, it's a tragedy contest, right?"

Anna shook her head. "I know."

"You just exploit the shitty stuff that's happened to you, because how can you write about your lifesaving stay in rehab and get less than a B plus?" As Anna wondered if he was still referring to his brother, James continued, "Your mom must read some crazy shit."

"Honestly," Anna said, lowering her voice conspiratorially, "you wouldn't believe some of the things they write."

"Try me." James sat forward, rubbing his palms together in anticipation. "Tell me about the worst offender."

"Alison Bower," Anna said—she didn't have to think. But in the next moment, a memory returned: her mother in the barn, the morning after the shooting, Nathan Dugan's paper curled on her knees.

James said, "Motherfucking Alison Bower," and slammed a fist on the table in mock outrage. Anna forced a laugh. "What was her problem? Misbegotten Tinder hookup? Parents didn't love her enough?"

"Actually, she was suicidal," Anna said. James paused; his face seemed caught between expressions. Anna straightened the smile off her face. "I'm sorry," she said. "I take it back. It isn't funny. It's just that my mom got kind of obsessed with her." Another image came rushing back, this one honed through repeated analysis in Theresa's office: the November night her mother had come home late from taking Alison Bower to some kind of campus crisis center. She'd curled on the end of the couch, visibly shaken, while Anna had felt annoyed, invisible, hungry; she hadn't eaten for two days.

"How did she deal with it?" James asked.

"She didn't—I mean, she's fine. She's alive."

"No, I meant your mom."

"My mom?" Anna paused. "I mean, she got her help. And I guess, saved her life, basically." She didn't admit to all the rest: how Anna had come to resent Alison Bower, and also envy Alison Bower. How, over the years, she'd loomed as this enigmatic and (according to Theresa) symbolic figure: the troubled, talented teenager her mother had rushed to save. It occurred to Anna that Alison Bower—that all her mothers' students, years of them, stacks and stacks of them—had been, always, the same age she was right now.

"She got lucky then," James said. "Most of the time, the people who really need help can't get it. It all depends who you are." He seemed about to say more, but instead shook his head hard, as if clearing water from his ears. "Too dark for a first date, right?"

"Not at all," she said quickly.

"You should know I have a tendency to take things way too seriously."

"So do I," Anna said, and James paused to smile at her, linger on her. She smiled back, savoring his use of the word *date*.

"Okay," he said finally, picking up his mug again. "So your mom is a willing receptacle for eighteen-year-olds' personal tragedies. What about your dad?"

They talked for the next two hours. Anna told James that her dad was a graphic designer living in Portland and had a newish girlfriend who was the exact opposite of her mom. She learned that James's parents were both remarried (divorced when he was six) and that he had one brother (older, recovering addict, college dropout, currently living with his mother), plus three half-siblings, his father's kids from marriage number two. They touched briefly on their past relationships (Anna calling Gavin *kind of mainstream,* James describing his ex as *chronically victimized,* which Anna absorbed with a concerned nod, not letting on that she'd searched for her picture online), then alighted on politics (Anna vaguely identifying herself as liberal, and James speaking passionately about democratic socialism, which she made a mental note to Google later on), and they compared their hyphenated last names. James's mother's last name was the one after the hyphen, which was less common—she used to be a feminist, he said, a freethinker, before she moved to the suburbs with his soul-sucking corporate dad. Anna told him how, in Stafford, her last name was such a novelty that her classmates had nicknamed her D-B.

"Sounds pretty fucking insular," he said.

"Oh my God," she breathed. "It was."

Then James leaned forward, pressing one finger to her knee. "Can I ask you something?"

"Yes."

"This is a very important thing I've been thinking about."

Anna nodded, aware of the pressure of his fingertip, the size of a dime.

"What do you think will happen when all the kids with the hyphenated names start reproducing? What will their last names be?"

She smiled a little. "This is a very important thing you've been thinking about?"

"Why not? I mean, just say, for the sake of example, we get married."

Anna's heart dove in her chest, but she stayed composed. "You and me," she said.

"You and me. What would our strategy be? Combine all four?"

"No way," she said. "Too cruel. Think about how hard it would be to monogram towels."

"Oh, right." He nodded. "I hadn't fully considered the towel angle."

"Maybe we'd have to choose our two favorites."

"Or fuse all four into one giant portmanteau."

Portmanteau—it was one of her favorite words.

"And here's another thing," he said, cupping her knee. His thumbnail was inked with blue. "What do you make of the ratio of kids with hyphenated names to kids with divorced parents? Because it seems to me, in my carefully conducted anecdotal research, more kids with hyphens have parents who are divorced. Do you agree?"

"I guess I've never really thought about it."

"So, say I'm right." He smiled. "Then the question becomes, are the parents who go with the hyphen less mainstream to begin with, so they're more willing to break up if the marriage goes off the rails, or did they hyphenate because they sensed at the beginning they wouldn't stay together? So both spouses were preemptively staking their claim?"

Anna shook her head. "No way."

"Why?"

"That's too depressing."

"The whole fucking world is depressing. The question is, is it true?"

"It can't be true," she said. "I mean, if it is, it's seriously subconscious. It would be too sad if people got married sensing they wouldn't stay together."

"I bet it happens way more often than you think."

"Maybe so," she allowed. She looked into her mug, a simmer of caffeine in her veins. "Actually," she said, "when I was little, I used to have this anxiety dream—a sort of premonition, as it turns out—that my dad was going to leave." As soon as she said it, she wished she hadn't. Just offering up the word *anxiety* made her feel vulnerable, as if James could now peek into corners she didn't want seen.

But James replied by giving her knee a light squeeze. "So it was your dad who wanted out," he said—which is how Anna found herself opening up to him about her parents' divorce. About how, in hindsight, they had never really seemed to love each other. How her mom was preoccupied with school, and her dad was having an affair. How it was February, freshman year, sitting in the front seat of his truck, snow dusting the windshield, that he'd told her he was leaving, and she'd felt a crack run down the center of her life: There was life before this moment, there was life after. As she spoke, James was listening so intently not a muscle was moving in his face. She was amazed that talking to him could feel so easy (though she of course edited some parts out: how the night in the truck had been Valentine's Day, and like an idiot she'd thought her dad might be giving her a present; how the night he left she cried so hard she had to breathe into a bag; how there followed years of related anxiety attacks and food issues and a failed attempt at cutting; how hurt she'd been that her father had moved three hours away from her, and how she felt this obligation to protect her mother, and yet, illogically and immaturely, didn't blame her dad for leaving so much as she blamed her mom for making him so unhappy that he left).

"Sorry," she said. "That was a lot to unload on you—" But James reached out and took her hand.

"I like you, Anna," he said. Then he kissed her, right there on the couch. An hour later, when he walked her home, still holding her hand in his, the long light on the quad dusky and golden, leaves quietly turning, Anna felt so full, so replete with happiness that she was buzzing—like anxiety, if anxiety could feel good.

Ten

After twenty-eight years, Maggie knew precisely where a class should be at every point in the academic season. Week Four: when the flush and novelty of the new semester wears off. The workload is more intense, the routines more familiar. The students' initial wariness turns toward cautious interest and the latent talent begins to surface, the guardedness to fall away.

But this semester, something wasn't right. Maggie's freshmen were not there; they were far from there. Their first set of essays had been lacking in the expected ways—vague, generic—and that was fine, even useful. Correctable. Later, they would see how far they'd grown. But the next batch was even weaker—hasty and halfhearted, margins gaping and type size ballooning—tricks so obvious she couldn't help but take them personally. She'd sat through countless staff meetings listening to colleagues complain about the epidemic laziness among their students— their eroding writing skills, the gadget-obsessiveness, the growing sense of entitlement—and had felt defensive on their behalf. When Marta Crane complained that her students no longer seemed motivated, Maggie felt a quiet sense of superiority: *That's on you.* If the students don't care, the teacher hasn't inspired them. She rejected the notion that this generation was somehow fundamentally different from those that came before it. Eighteen was eighteen.

But now Adam Gillis occupied a corner of her classroom with knees sprawled, Red Sox cap shadowing half his face. Popular and good-looking, but a dedicated slacker—an unfortunate combination, for it gave his shallow presence weight. Kara DiCiccio had boasted about her first essay, *I wrote it in literally ten minutes.* Maggie knew that such disclaimers came from insecurity, but still, it was audacious, and lazy. Jess and Nicole, the roommates, were forever whispering and peering at their phones. If Maggie tried breaking the class into small groups, they dissolved into socializing. Twice already she'd had to tell students: *I have eyes, therefore I see you texting*—a line that in the past might have elicited an apologetic cringe, but with this group it was as if the reprimand had been issued through an intercom. The offending phone would slide into a pocket until, minutes later, it crept back out.

Some kids are just bad apples, Robert would say with a shrug when Maggie sat in his office after class prattling on about her students. She always needed time to review a class, transition gradually from that world back to this one. When she and Robert first started spending time together, she'd liked the prospect of being with a fellow academic, someone who could appreciate those instincts, but Robert saw teaching differently than she did. He found Maggie's obsessiveness endearing, mildly amusing. For him, good teaching was about delivering an impressive lecture. Of his own students, he rarely said a word.

Maggie acknowledged that, this semester, she might be distracted. Shaken by the shooting, by missing Anna, by her fraught wanderings on Luke Finch's Facebook page. She still checked it sometimes—on the computer in her office at school, where the connection was reliably quick—though she found nothing new, or noteworthy. When after repeated attempts she finally got in touch with Anna, she mentioned the post, and Anna seemed not even to have heard of it. In the semester's first faculty meeting, Bill had addressed the shooting, their shared connection to Nathan Dugan. He'd spoken to the police, he told them, and relayed any information he had. He reminded them to read their students' work carefully—Maggie was certain he glanced in her direction—to report any concerning subjects, concerning behaviors. Some younger faculty nodded solemnly. *But what's the point of reporting it?* Marta Crane complained. *Nobody does anything unless there are actual threats made.* For once, Maggie agreed with her. Through the frustration, though, she allowed herself a moment of relief—Nathan's essay, however strange, hadn't threatened anyone.

Today, Maggie resolved, she would turn her class around. It was not too late. It was not even October. She would focus on the students who showed glimmers of early promise, like Andrea Gardner, whose essay about her high school boyfriend was clichéd but earnest. Or Pete Brown, whose work was rushed and sloppy but had a voice. *You can't change them*, Robert told her, but Maggie knew this wasn't true. She'd had her share of challenging students and had always gotten through to them. Or, almost always.

"Good afternoon!" Maggie announced as she entered the room. A quick scan revealed two absences, neither one critical. Andrea was fanning herself with one lacquered hand. Nicole and Jess were whispering, heads bent over a laptop screen. Adam slouched, sleepy-eyed, in the corner. Maggie faced the board and wrote in tall, deliberate letters: ANGER, HUNGER, NOSTALGIA, then faced the group as chatter began dying down.

"Today, we turn our minds to places," she told them. "Places that carry some sort of personal importance for you. Places that are specific and memorable and emotionally resonant." She pointed at the board. "Take five minutes, right now, and describe a significant place you associate with each of those three words."

"You mean write it down?" This was Kara. Phone on desk, whine in voice.

"Yes. This is, in fact, a writing class," Maggie said, but smiled. "And lose the phone, please."

Slowly, they stowed away their electronics and unearthed old-fashioned pens and notebooks—a medley of tearing loose-leaf and unzipping backpacks, a few lost souls asking to borrow missing items from their neighbors. Maggie paced the aisles, trying to inject some energy into the room. "First! A place that you associate with anger. And remember," she said, "write without censoring yourself. Without crossing out. Whatever comes to mind."

It took a few minutes, but hands began moving, heads lowering over pages. In the age of laptops, Maggie still insisted on pen and paper; she believed in the pressure of hand to page, in escaping the diabolical barrier of screens.

"Next," she said. "Hunger. Summon your hunger-inducing place in all the detail you can muster. Don't overthink it. The first place that comes into your head."

"Now I want Taco Bell," someone muttered—Pete. Goofy, but harmless. Maggie smiled again. In her cache of exercises, this one was as reliable as any: She could recite both parts, hers and theirs.

"And lastly," she said, a few minutes later. "A place that evokes nostalgia."

Andrea raised her hand. "What if we can't remember it exactly?" She was wearing a baseball cap and CMSU sweatshirt, but her face was made up as if for a party, eyelashes carefully curled.

"Then just write what feels true," Maggie told her. "Remember, fact and truth can be two different things."

She observed, with satisfaction and a measure of affection, the hands scribbling, breaths deepening. Even Adam seemed reasonably engaged, fist wrapped around one of those fat plastic pens the local bank gave away free. Then Maggie noticed Jess and Nicole hunched over something on Nicole's lap—a phone, undoubtedly.

"Jess," she snapped. "Nicole."

They looked up, sheepish. "Sorry," Jess said as a few students lifted their heads.

Maggie stopped in front of the girls' desks, on which she saw they'd each written exactly nothing: two open notebooks, both blank. "Tell us about one of your significant places," Maggie said.

The two traded a cringing look. *I can see the expressions on your faces*, Maggie almost said, but stopped herself before she lost them completely.

"Um," Jess said. "What was the question again?"

"A place," Maggie said, still patiently. "Evoked by one of the three words on the board."

"So like a place that makes you hungry," Andrea offered.

Pete said, "Like the fine dining hall cuisine."

"Ew." Nicole wrinkled her nose. "That place is vile."

"Excellent. Evoke it for us in all its vile detail, Nicole," Maggie said, drawing a few knowing chuckles. She was happy to meet them on their level, if it meant she could carry them somewhere else.

"Okay," Nicole said. "Well, the frozen yogurt tastes like plastic."

"There is literally nothing normal there. The cereal is covered in actual dust."

"The tacos are dogshit in a shell."

"No way," Adam said, speaking voluntarily for the first time all semester. "Those tacos are fucking tasty." The students looked at Maggie, wondering if she would react to the swearing, but she said, lightly, "He wakes," earning a small laugh herself. "Okay," she said as she returned to the front of the room. "Let's hear from someone else. Nostalgia."

The room went quiet. Maggie was undeterred. She had learned, through trial and error, to let a silence happen; her class would get uncomfortable before she did.

It was Andrea, again, who dutifully raised her hand. "I wrote about this beach on Cape Cod my family used to go to when I was little," she said. "Should I just read it?"

"Please," Maggie said.

"It's really rough," she warned, but plunged gamely ahead. She wasn't wrong—the place Andrea was describing might have been any beach town anywhere—but it was heartfelt and, Maggie was secretly grateful, not good enough to deter anyone else.

"Thank you, Andrea," Maggie said, nodding. "Another. How about anger?" To her surprise, Kara DiCiccio raised her hand. "Yes? Kara?"

"Mine's about the Millview Mall," she said. "Where that shooting happened."

Maggie paused, taking her in: Kara's chin was raised, defensive, her color high. She was a commuter, Maggie recalled. It would have been her nearest mall growing up.

"Of course," Maggie said, trying not to sound thrown. She had no desire to open up the subject of the shooting but she did want to encourage Kara, who had never raised her hand before, who until now had shown only the barest interest in the class. Obviously, this mattered to her. "Would you like to read?"

Kara took a breath and blew it out, then picked up her notebook with two hands. "A place that makes me angry is the mall where some sick asshole started shooting people." As she read, Kara's eyes never left the page. Her delivery was rushed, barely concealing the tremor in her voice. "The mall was a place I went my whole life. Now it's the place where four innocent people lost their lives. I don't count the shooter because his life wasn't worth living. I knew one of the victims. It was my algebra teacher from high school." She stopped then, glancing up, and Maggie nodded: sympathy, encouragement. Kara shakily recounted memories of Mr. Tremont, her disbelief when she heard his name on the news. "This monster stole his life from him and from all of them," she said, and then looked up again at Maggie, tears in her eyes.

"Thank you," Maggie said, and she meant it. She surveyed her students, lapsed into a respectful silence, waiting for their professor to speak. For once, she had the entire room's attention, but she was struggling to find the words, to even form coherent thoughts. "To be robbed of something that you loved——" There was a break in her voice. Oddly, the parallel that came to mind was that of Anna and her swimming: how much joy it had given her, before it turned on her. Then Jess, of all people, raised her hand, and Maggie nodded, relieved. "Jess, you wanted to read?"

"Oh——" Jess said. "No. This is kind of off-topic, actually." She looked around the room, and the room looked back, and Maggie steeled herself for what she suddenly knew was coming. "Wasn't that guy—the shooter—wasn't he in your class?"

Maggie's first thought, however shaken she felt, was that it was important to appear composed. She had invited the topic and, not surprisingly, this was the result. At the faculty meeting, Bill had encouraged them to facilitate conversation in their classrooms, make students aware of the counseling services on campus. Be vigilant, be available and open. If Maggie's class had heard somehow that Nathan had been *her* student, had taken this same class just four years ago, naturally they'd have questions. Maybe they'd read the post on Facebook. Maybe they just hadn't felt comfortable bringing it up with her until now.

Maggie leaned on the desk, where she could see all thirteen faces. "He was," she said. "It was an excellent group, actually. A dedicated and hardworking class." She couldn't help herself—to dip into the pool of past students and assert how different they could be.

"What was he like?" Jess asked.

Maggie considered the question, the audience. "Quiet," she decided. A neutral word: not provocative, not untrue. "He wasn't as engaged as his classmates."

"What did he write about?"

"Well," she said. "I can't go into detail about other students' work—just as I wouldn't talk to anyone outside this class about your work," she added, but if her hope was to convey how much she respected them, how seriously she regarded the integrity of their work in the class, they appeared unmoved.

"The article said he was deeply troubled," Jess offered, and it was then that Maggie understood: the article. Of course. That email. Juliet someone. After writing to Maggie, she'd left the same message, word for word, on her office phone; Maggie hadn't returned her call.

"I see," she said. "Well, I haven't read it yet—"

"It came out this afternoon."

"Yes. Of course. I knew about it, but I haven't seen it, so I don't know exactly what was written," she said, a bit more briskly than she'd intended.

The students glanced at each other, then back at Jess, their unofficial spokesperson. "Well, there's this other kid," Jess said. "He was in the class too. And he put this thing on Facebook—"

"You mean Luke," Maggie said. "Luke Finch."

"You remember him?"

"Of course. I remember all my students. And I read his Facebook post."

"Okay, yeah. Well." Jess hesitated then, and winced slightly, and it was this that made Maggie go preemptively numb. "In the article he said this guy Nathan wrote this paper for your class that was pretty disturbing. It was haunting. It basically said that he was messed up, and the other students all knew it—"

Maggie completed the sentence: *but you didn't*. She tried to keep her expression neutral, to remain in character, not betray her alarm. Not let on that the very essay was sitting right there, still burning a hole in her canvas bag. *Haunting*—no doubt Jess had lifted this word from the article directly. Before she could respond, Maggie needed to see it, to read it. She considered asking if anyone had a copy—it may well have been what the girls had been huddled over earlier—but that wouldn't be appropriate. She didn't want them watching her react. Which was precisely what they were doing now, a room full of eighteen-year-olds regarding her closely, a bit anxiously, even Adam Gillis, and she remembered then how young they were.

"This was a terrible thing," Maggie said. She looked deliberately at Kara, whose eyes had returned to her desk. "Naturally, there are strong feelings about it—deservedly so. I haven't read the article yet, so I can't speak to what's in it, but I think it's safe to say I don't remember Nathan quite the way Luke does." Her head felt light, but she pressed on. "That's human nature, though, isn't it? Right? I was Nathan's teacher and Luke was Nathan's classmate. Our perspectives on him were quite different. It stands to reason that we'd remember him differently four years later. It's inevitable, really."

It was a weak attempt to shift the conversation, turn it into a so-called teachable moment, and the students saw right through it. When Adam dislodged his phone from his pocket, Maggie didn't care, the distraction so banal that she was grateful.

She dismissed class fifteen minutes early and when she stopped by her office, an email from Bill Wall was waiting on the screen. *Please contact me at your earliest convenience.* For the moment, she ignored it; she had to. She couldn't talk to Bill until she knew exactly what the article said. She hurried to the student union, where at least a hundred newspapers sat in slippery piles by the main entrance. CLASSMATE REMEMBERS KILLER. The headline was a bright red. Below it floated a pair of photos: Nathan Dugan, Luke Finch. Both of them looked like high school portraits, probably retrieved from their freshman year viewbooks. At the sight of Luke's photo, Maggie's old student came back to her more clearly. The hunched shoulders, shy sweater. Nathan's photo was familiar too, though it took a minute to remember where she'd seen it: on the mantel in Marielle Dugan's living room.

Maggie was tempted to just stand there and tear through the article—tempted, for a moment, to take the entire pile—but was conscious of the students grazing in the vicinity, glancing now and then in her direction. She grabbed a single copy, shoved it in her bag, and walked back out the door.

Her breaths were shallow as she made her way toward Strathmere Hall. At five thirty, the quad was already beginning to darken, the clock on the chapel glowing like an eye. Just one week ago, it had been light out at this hour, but now the shadows were bowing across the footpaths. It was the time of day Maggie always thought the campus looked most poignant, the very essence of college—a world-within-a-world—but tonight it felt like a rebuke. "Evening, Maggie," she heard, and looked up, startled—Marta Crane. Was she looking at her with suspicion? Disdain? Marta was just the type to have read the article and formed a quick opinion on it. By the end of the first faculty meeting, she'd requested an office on the second floor to minimize the chance of being shot at her desk. Maggie could only imagine how she might have handled actually *teaching* someone like Nathan. "Have a good night," Maggie said, and kept moving, trying to ignore the growing seed of panic in her chest.

She pulled open the glass door to Strathmere, thin as a window but surprisingly heavy, then rushed up the stairs, down the glass-walled corridor to the faculty offices on the second floor. "Hi," she said, shutting his door.

Robert was standing in front of his desk, sleeves pushed to his elbows. At the sight of him, she felt briefly comforted, then registered the grim expression on his face. "Have you read it yet?"

There was a copy of the *Sentinel* in his hand. Maggie unshouldered her bag and set it on a chair. "I just got out of class," she told him. "I haven't had the—" but before she could reach for her own copy, he'd handed her his.

CLASSMATE REMEMBERS KILLER

By Juliet R. Brody

Have you ever wondered about that person sitting next to you in English class? That quiet kid you never really got to know? For Luke Finch, the answer to this question was a devastating shock when he heard that a Central Maine State student, Nathan Dugan, was the killer in the August 21 shooting in the Millview Mall.

Nathan Dugan was a senior majoring in Engineering who was planning to graduate this December. Luke Finch only had one class with him: Freshman Composition, taught by Professor Maggie Daley. Though the class was four long years ago, Luke's memories of it were so vivid and so disturbing that he felt compelled to post them on Facebook the day the shooting happened. "It was upsetting," Luke said, recalling that fateful day. "Somebody you knew."

Maggie read on, with a sinking heart, as the article overpraised Luke's *incredible sensitivity,* his *astonishingly vivid* cache of memories—*from the stress ball Nathan regularly squeezed to the fact that he rarely spoke, the recollections of Luke Finch clearly point towards a deeply troubled person who was lurking underneath.*

As of press time, the Facebook post has been shared a remarkable ten thousand times. Luke said, humbly, "It has been pretty crazy."

But perhaps it's not crazy in the slightest. Because Nathan Dugan was clearly an unforgettable presence. Said Luke, "The guy was pretty hard to miss."

Therefore, it's no surprise that other classmates have been coming out of the woodwork to contribute their equally worrisome memories of Nathan too. The most haunting was a paper of a personal nature written by the future killer for Professor Daley's class. Asked what the paper was about, Luke cannot claim with certainty but ominously hypothesized, "I think it might have been about hunting." Other classmates confirmed that they remember the paper was violent. Speculations about the subject include zombies and war.

One thing is definitely certain, however; they all agree that Nathan Dugan was a person with a disturbing inner life. In fact, Luke claims they were all worried about him at the time. "A lot of us felt that way," he insisted. "I wasn't the only one."

Professor James Rush in the Engineering Department also taught Nathan, although he doesn't remember his violent tendencies. He points out that his students don't write essays of a personal nature, however. "It's a different sort of course," Professor Rush emphasized.

Despite several attempts at contact, Professor Daley, the Freshman Composition instructor, declined to be interviewed for this article.

"Jesus Christ," Maggie breathed.

When asked if his writing professor ever addressed Nathan Dugan's alarming tendencies in class, Luke said he had no memory of this happening. Asked if he thought his professor had been negligent, Luke admitted, "Probably, yes."

Clearly, in hindsight, that intervention was necessary—not only that, it might have prevented a tragedy.

Maggie stared at the page until the words bled together, too shocked to speak. She looked, incredulous, at Robert, leaning against his desk. "How did this happen?"

He shook his head. "Beats me."

"I don't even know what this is—it's exploitative. Manipulative."

"Agreed."

"It's defamation of character," she said. "Not to mention, an objectively awful piece of writing."

At this, he chuckled. "It's the student newspaper, Maggie."

"And?"

"And they might not have your journalistic standards."

"Well, then, they shouldn't take on a subject as important as this," Maggie snapped. Robert, she thought, always expected too little of the students. *Not only that, it might have prevented a tragedy*—it was like a line lifted from a television show. "This is totally irresponsible."

"It's bad," Robert said. "Okay. But is it true?"

"Is what true?" She looked at him, looking at her. "Which fucking part?"

"Was he as messed up as they say he was?"

"I don't know," she said. "This was four years ago, remember?"

"Well, did she really contact you? The reporter?"

"She's a student, not a reporter—"

"You know what I mean. Did she?"

"She left one message," Maggie said, an edge in her voice. "And emailed me once. From her phone."

"And you declined to comment?"

"I didn't decline. I just didn't respond."

"And is there a difference?"

"Of course there's a difference. There's an enormous difference. Decline makes it sound like I refused, or resisted—"

"Okay, then, why didn't you respond?"

Maggie could feel her tension mounting but fought to stay on top of it. She pinched the skin on the back of her hand. "She left a cell phone, Robert," she said. "Her personal cell phone number."

"And?"

"And it didn't seem professional. Or appropriate, even, calling a student to discuss another student, especially in a situation like—I have no idea what Jim Rush was thinking. Not to mention, this was four years ago. Who knows if any of us remembers him accurately? Do I want to go on record saying something that may or may not be true and have it show up in print? Especially in the hands of this—what's her name again?"

"Julie Brody."

"Juliet."

"She goes by Julie," he said. "I had her."

"You had her? She's an English major."

"Well, then, she's an English major who's politically engaged. She's actually not a bad kid. She's just—passionate about things."

Maggie stared. "You're defending her?"

"All I'm saying," Robert said, "is maybe you should have just explained why you didn't want to be interviewed. You could have nipped this thing in the bud. Because the fact that you just ignored her comes off sounding a little weird."

"Weird." Her eyeballs felt hot. "Weird? What does that mean?"

"Weird means weird. Strange. You know what it means."

"No." She let out a short laugh. "I truly don't."

Robert gave her a measured look. To the extent they'd ever argued—they weren't arguments so much as debates—Maggie was the one who remained even-keeled while Robert grew heated, but now the dynamic had shifted: As her temperature rose, he became practical and grounded. "Maggie," he said. "I think you're missing the point."

She stared at the page. *Despite several attempts at contact, Professor Daley, the Freshman Composition instructor, declined to be interviewed.* What Robert didn't know was that in avoiding the interview Maggie *had* been trying to stay honest, but that didn't matter. He was right. It did sound weird, and surely Bill Wall would think so too.

Quietly, she said, "You know the sort of teacher I am, Robert."

He cracked a small smile. "Obsessed to a fault?"

"I'm being serious," she said. "You know how committed I am to my students. How much I care about them." Her voice caught, and Robert stepped toward her, wrapping her in his arms.

"It's going to be fine."

"You just said yourself—"

"It's not that bad," he said, with such conviction that she almost believed him. He drew her in close, tucked her hair behind her ear. "You just need to get ahead of it," he said. "Get in touch with Bill."

"He already emailed—"

"Okay, then. Call him back and tell him what you told me. A student contacted you and it didn't seem appropriate. Bill is all about appropriateness." He paused, lips grazing her hairline. "He'll see this article for what it is—immature, written by a twenty-year-old kid—and nobody who knows anything will take it seriously and soon it will be forgotten."

He leaned down and kissed her, and for a moment, Maggie gave herself over—to the warmth of him, the weight of his hand on her hair, the pump of his heart, steady and certain beneath the panicked gallop of her own. Then she pulled away.

"Robert," she said. "I need to tell you something."

He moved to kiss her neck. "I'm listening."

"I'm serious," she said. "It's about that essay. Nathan Dugan's essay. I might have made a serious mistake."

He pulled back a little, looking at her. "Okay," he said, and waited.

"The essay that the students remember," she said. "I have it. I found it."

He paused. "What do you mean you found it?"

"The morning after the shooting. Out in my barn."

Robert studied her, gaze shifting from side to side. "And that's the reason you didn't want to talk for the article?"

"Yes," she said, but she couldn't look him in the eye.

"How bad is it?"

"Honestly—I don't even know anymore."

"What do you mean, don't know?"

"I mean, it's not that clear-cut. It's certainly less clear-cut than—" She gestured toward the paper on the chair. "At first I thought the essay was just kind of—obsessive. Like he was. But now—I don't know. It's so colored by what happened, by the shooting, it's hard to be objective—"

"It can't be that hard," Robert said, cutting her off. "Does the guy sound violent? Does he say he wants to kill people? Threaten to shoot up a public place? What?"

"No, no—" She took a breath. "It's nothing that explicit. It's not explicitly threatening. But it does—it involves guns," she said, and Robert let out a moan, dragging one palm down his face. "It involves hunting," she amended. "It's about hunting. With his father. But the thing is, Robert, remember, a kid from rural Maine going hunting, that's not unusual. That's not uncommon. It's not like that's out of the realm of—"

"What did Bill say?"

"I didn't show Bill," she admitted, filling with shame. "I fully intended to, but I just, in the moment—I didn't. I couldn't. Because I thought it might look bad," she said. "Might make me look bad." When she glanced at Robert again, his face was rigid with worry; it looked almost like anger. "You think I might have missed something," she said, in a whisper. "What if I did? Am I—what, Robert? What? Could I have *prevented* this?"

"Hold on," Robert said, raising one hand. "Don't get ahead of yourself." He pushed the hand through his hair, exhaling, but spoke sensibly, firmly. "Big picture," he said. "There were lots of people who interacted with him. You weren't the only teacher he had. This paper wasn't the only thing he wrote. What about all that stuff online?"

"That's different," she said. "That's on the Internet. It's out in outer space. This was an actual paper turned in for an actual class, to an actual authority figure—"

"Okay. Okay." He still sounded calm, but a seam of worry had appeared across his brow. "Can you show it to me? I need to read it." He looked at her, and when she didn't reply right away, he said decisively, "I need to read it, Maggie, or I don't know what the hell I'm talking about." And she knew that it was true. That surely, when she told him, she had known that he would ask to see it—had even, on some level, wanted him to. Though a part of her was terrified, another part was desperate for a second opinion, for the relief of unloading that weight from her bag, handing the paper to someone else.

She walked to the chair, unzipped the inside pocket of her bag, and returned with the thick paper square. "Here," she said, placing it in his palm.

Robert chuckled. "Well," he said. "That was easy. What, were you afraid to let it out of your sight or something?" As he unfolded the wad of pages, he added, "Feels like you're passing me a note in algebra class," and Maggie felt fleetingly reassured. But as Robert registered the title, his face went still. "Christ," he said.

"Just remember," Maggie said, but weakly, "you have to pretend you have no context. Pretend you're reading this four years ago—" though within seconds she could see there was no point. She watched Robert scanning the pages, mouth tightening at the corners. Maybe this had been a mistake. Robert was so matter-of-fact, and had no real experience with personal essays—not only that, he was moving through it quickly, too quickly, pupils darting back and forth.

"Are you really reading it?" she asked him.

"I'm skimming it. I just want to get a sense of it."

"But you won't understand the ambiguities—"

"Ambiguities?" He looked up sharply. "Maggie. I'm looking at an encyclopedia of firearms here."

She was stunned into quiet. Just then the office phone began to ring. Robert glanced at the number and reached for it. "Hi," he said. "Yeah. I'm just finishing up."

Maggie averted her gaze, as if to give them privacy, but there was no place to safely rest her eyes: the bike propped against the wall, the phone in Robert's hand, the paper in the other. He sat on the edge of the desk, angled slightly away from her. "Everything's fine," he said, voice softening as it did sometimes when talking to Suzanne. "How did it go today?" he asked her, and suddenly Maggie needed to get away. One more second in that office and she would scream, or sob. She stood, looking at Robert, who looked back at her, eyebrows raised. She considered grabbing the essay from his hands, showing it to him again some other time—but no. She had asked for his opinion, and she wanted it. She deserved it. She trusted him. And if she snatched it back while he was on the phone with his wife, it might come across as petty, or jealous. Instead she grabbed a block of Post-its, tore one off and scrawled *call me*, the pen's tip biting through the paper, and pressed it to the page in his hand. Then she ripped off another, scrawled *sorry*, and stuck it on top of the first. Robert held up one finger—*wait*, he mouthed—but she grabbed her bag and left the office and hurried down the hall. It was fully dark out now, and her reflection in the glass was disorienting, as if there were another woman moving in tandem beside her, a more frayed and vulnerable version of her, walking side by side.

Eleven

To Kim and Janie, James Baird-English could best be described as the diametrical opposite of Gavin Newland in every way. He was obviously smarter. He didn't follow sports and didn't watch television (and not just because he didn't have one: The decision had a faintly moral tinge). If Gavin was mainstream, James wasn't afraid to go against the grain; he embraced it. He was passionate and principled and unafraid to speak up about things. Objectively, James was maybe less attractive—Gavin was cute in a universal, backward-baseball-cap-wearing sort of way—but James's looks were less generic. *An acquired taste*, Alexis described him, a phrase that Anna repeated to Kim and Janie, adding, *and he looks nothing like those old Facebook pix*—knowing that they could, and surely had, scrolled through his photos, including that painful series on the brown couch.

It had been ten days since they'd met, and they'd seen each other seven times. This consisted largely of hanging out at James's place, a real apartment five blocks from school: There was a landlord, a neighbor who was a single mother, a mailbox bearing his name on a curling piece of Scotch tape. James didn't go to campus parties (he considered the fraternity system primitive and patriarchal), and as with most of his stances, Anna thought she agreed; at least, she didn't disagree. James more or less avoided campus except for classes, and even those he seemed to attend on a need-only basis (*I'm a paying customer, right?*), so they defaulted to hanging out at the coffee shop, or at his apartment, eating dinner (some version of pasta) and having long in-depth conversations and almost having sex. The apartment itself was objectively depressing—a narrow bed with an itchy mustard-yellow blanket, a tiny kitchen with one working burner—though Anna found herself charmed, and somehow calmed, by the fact that James owned things like a colander and a vacuum, that he'd stocked his cabinets with eight kinds of tea. Still, when she returned to Hightower—to Alexis and their dorm room and the cozy checkered rug—it felt, at least a little, like she'd been holding her breath.

Alexis registered her complaints with this new arrangement: *You never hang out here, roomie!* Anna apologized—she truly did miss Alexis—but she didn't mind the fact that James wasn't frequenting their room. She knew he'd find their life in Hightower immature and silly (the thought of him being there when Alexis announced news of some fresh gossip made her cringe). With Alexis, she could allow herself to be glib, or lazy, but James was so intense that Anna always felt an obligation to rise to his level. To stay quick, stay interesting, take everything as seriously as he did. It was just easier, to be with him alone.

In the off-hours Anna did find herself at home, she and Alexis spent most of their time discussing James: most pressingly, when to have sex with him. Date number eight, Alexis proposed. It was a Wednesday night, so they'd probably be drinking but not drunk, and Anna had been seeing him for over a week, even though it felt much longer. But the hesitation Anna was feeling wasn't about the timing. She knew that sex with James would trigger an entire catalog of new worries—pregnancy, STDs, HIV—but didn't want to admit this to Alexis. *If it was in any way slutty, I'd tell you*, her roommate assured her, adding that Violet Sharma had so far had sex with five guys in the month of September. In college, Alexis reminded her, to have sex with a person you legitimately knew and liked was actually somewhat rare.

That night, the Wednesday, James made spaghetti carbonara and they drank a bottle of cheap red wine. The wine made Anna's nose sting, like swimming underwater. The pasta she hardly tasted, distracted by the visible sheen of grease.

When they were finished (she'd drunk half the wine, managed to empty half her plate), James took her hand and led her to the bed, then perched on the edge beside her. "I want to show you something," he said.

"Okay."

"This," he said, reaching into his shirt pocket, "is the raw footage for my first film." He handed her his phone. On it were dozens of videos, all of them basically identical: the same guy, dark-haired and overweight, sitting on a plastic lawn chair, a tweed couch.

"That's my big brother," James said as Anna studied him. It was disconcerting: He was James, but an older, thicker version. "My film is going to tell his story," he explained, as Anna thumbed slowly down the screen. There were easily over a hundred videos. In many of them, the brother was wearing the same red hooded sweatshirt. His facial hair differed slightly, from beard to goatee. "It's going to take his life story and use it to expose the massive failures of our system," James told her. "A real human story. Just truth. No bullshit."

"That's really moving," Anna said, and it was, in a way—if not James's brother, then how much James obviously cared about him.

"I wanted you to know about it," James said. "Because it's important to me. And you're important to me."

Anna felt a little leap in her chest. "You too."

He took the phone from her hand. "Good," he said, and kissed her. "Don't move." Then he stood up and began making minor adjustments, lowering the shades and lighting the white pillar candle on the bedside table. It was equal parts nerve-racking and sweet. Anna climbed under the covers, caught in that disorienting moment between knowing you're about to have sex and actually doing it, her skin cold, her body still her own. When James crawled into bed beside her, he kissed her collarbone, her shoulders. He peeled off her jeans and kissed the insides of her knees. He looked at her seriously, eye whites glowing in the darkness. "Tell me what you like," he said, and Anna felt too awkward to respond even if she'd had any idea what to say. She and Gavin had never talked during sex, had barely even looked at each other, but James was so attentive it was stressful. "That feels good," she managed, and he whispered, "Try to relax," so she closed her eyes and tried, and it felt nice, basically nice, but then she found herself worrying that he could feel the fat on her stomach, and sucking in slightly, then alighting on Alexis's theory about sex and smart people—briefly missing Alexis, imagining how she'd tell her all about this the next morning—and thinking how abnormal it was to be missing her roommate at a time like this.

Thankfully, James produced a condom without her asking. When he was finished, he collapsed, groaning, then sagged on top of her for what felt like minutes. Anna worried he might be leaking inside her. She was uncomfortably aware of how their bodies matched up next to each other: hip-to-hip, chest-to-chest. She had easily twenty pounds on him. She could count his ribs when he breathed.

Finally he rolled off her, tossed the condom on the floor, and propped himself on one elbow, studying her. "Hi," he said. "I'm James."

She laughed a little. "Anna."

"Can I ask you something, Anna?"

"Sure."

"Have you ever had an orgasm?"

"Excuse me?" she said, startled. "Of course. I mean—I think so."

"You would know for sure," he said.

"Oh," she said, suddenly defensive. "Well, okay then."

"Don't worry. Lots of women don't have them until their twenties."

"I wasn't worried," she said, though inevitably she would be now.

She pulled the blanket to her chin. The wool was making her itch. James reached for the glass of water on the bedside table, next to the fat candle whose flame was flickering madly, wax rolling down the sides. "Are you on the pill?" he asked, taking an audible swallow.

"Why? Is that a requirement for having sex with you or something?"

"Of course not," he said, holding out the glass. "Sip?" She could see, even in the half dark, the dust on the rim.

"I'm good," she said. "And, no, I'm not. On the pill." She didn't add that this wasn't because she was unafraid of getting pregnant (she was terrified) but just that she was more afraid of getting fat.

"What about STDs?" he said, and she felt a kick of nerves.

"What about them?"

"Do you have any?"

"Um, no," she said, with a strained laugh. "Do you?"

"None that I know of. But I haven't been tested in a little while." He balanced the glass on his rib cage. "When's the last time you were tested?"

"Never," she said tightly. "Untested. Probably riddled with diseases. Sorry to disappoint you." She'd thought about going, of course, but the prospect of the needle, the excruciating two-week wait for results—she didn't think she could survive it.

"You're not disappointing me," James replied seriously, kissing her on the cheek. He took another swallow of the dust-water, then reached across her, returning it to the nightstand. "You should go, though. I'll go with you. We're going to be doing a lot more of this, right?" he said, and settled an arm around her shoulders.

The bedside clock glowed one fourteen. She wanted suddenly to leave. She surveyed the floor and began mentally gathering her things—jeans, bra, backpack, Alexis's shirt. She could make up an excuse—she didn't feel well (not a lie), had an early class tomorrow. That part was easy. The harder part was getting home. She weighed the desire to be back in the dorm with Alexis against the risk of walking alone in the city this time of night, but at this point she didn't care; the desire outweighed the fear.

"Walk-in hours at the health center are on Friday mornings," James was saying. "We could go this week."

"I'm really not good with needles," she managed.

"Oh, come on, Anna."

"No, really—"

"It's just a little pinch," he said, then clipped at her waist with two fingers—a roll of fat. As he leaned in to kiss her again, she sat up on her elbows and said, "Actually, I think I might just go home."

Anna felt him go still behind her. "What's going on?" To her surprise, his tone was flat, clearly annoyed.

"Nothing."

"Then why are you leaving?"

"I don't feel very well."

"Since when?"

"And I have a test tomorrow."

"Anna," he sighed. "Come on." Abruptly, he pushed himself out of bed and pulled on his boxers. She watched, paralyzed, as he disappeared into the bathroom: pale spill of light, splash in the bowl. But instead of getting back in bed, he sat on the very edge of it, not touching her. She was alarmed by the absence of his attention, the void it created, the sudden, desperate feeling it woke inside her. She had ruined this, she thought. It was ending. It was over that fast.

"Sorry," she said. "Forget I said it. I'll stay."

James was studying his hands, clenched in his lap. "Look. I like you, Anna. I think I've made that pretty clear," he said. "But if there's something on your mind, you have to tell me. If I'm going to be with someone, it has to be honest."

She nodded quickly. "I know."

"I realize I can get intense about things. But if something's not worth getting intense over, I don't see the point."

"I get it," she said. "I feel the same way."

He looked at her, then reached out and touched her chin. "I'll go with you," he said. "Friday. We'll go together."

Anna could only nod again, feeling cornered, unable to admit to him how much this scared her, how having him go with her would actually make it worse. He blew out the candle and crawled back under the cover, folding his pillow in half and stuffing it beneath his neck. He faced her, one arm flung across her ribs, one leg resting on her leg. "I'm glad you're here," he whispered. He was asleep minutes later. Anna lay there, immobile, his breath warm against her face. She watched the candle smoke twine silently toward the ceiling, hoping the hot wax didn't drip onto the bed and start a fire. Pictured the oily, uneaten pasta still sitting on the table. She closed her eyes and tried to be normal, rational. She reminded herself that this was what she'd wanted: a relationship that was meaningful and real. This was what she had been hoping for. As she listened to his breaths deepen, she crunched her stomach ever so slightly in and out, in and out, hoping the movement didn't disturb the sheet.

The next day, all day, Anna's thoughts were circling. *Everyone freaks out unnecessarily about getting tested,* Alexis said. Logically, Anna knew she had no reason to be worried—she and Gavin had always used condoms, pausing to fumble in the steamer trunk—but she also knew it didn't matter. That there were always exceptions. Freak things.

That night, she told James she had too much studying to come over. She skipped dinner and went to the library, the fourth floor, where people went to do real work. It was actually quiet there, the only sounds the skitter of laptop keys, the occasional cough or creaky chair. No one talked on phones, or to each other. Anna opened her assignment for Intro to Psychology and her eyes glazed over the same paragraph three times. She twisted a strand of hair around her thumb. Crunched her stomach in and out, in and out. She needed to get some food. She hadn't eaten since lunch, and that had consisted only of frozen yogurt and Special K. Her stomach felt hollow, but the ache was reassuring, familiar. She promised herself she'd go get a snack when she finished this chapter. *In Piaget's preoperational stage, the child struggles with logical thinking*—the line dissolved like sugar into tea.

Over the edge of her laptop, she saw her antisocial hallmate, Carly Smith, sitting in a nearby carrel, face half hidden by the divider. She appeared to be typing, shoulders back and chin down. One eye was visible, peering through her owly glasses. Beneath the desk, Anna saw that she was wearing furry purple slippers, but her ankles were crossed as primly as a queen's. The image was so absurd that for a moment Anna was distracted—she made a mental note to describe this to Alexis later—but then her phone began to buzz, inching across the surface of her desk. She clamped a hand on it. *Missed Call Mom.* She didn't leave a message, naturally. Anna set the phone back down and resumed her reading—*in Piaget's preoperational stage*—tightening the hair around her thumb and trying not to think about tomorrow, but five minutes later the phone was writhing again. Carly Smith's half face peered up at her. She snatched the phone, then saw that it was Kim.

The sight of her old friend's name made her suddenly, deeply lonely. She wanted to talk to her but couldn't answer, not in the quiet zone. And maybe this was a good thing. Because if she did, Kim would know something was wrong, and Anna didn't want to have to explain. Even though Alexis had endorsed the joint trip to the health center as *weirdly romantic*, Anna was certain Kim would find the whole thing just weird. Probably find James weird. Already Anna had been getting this impression from group texts with Kim and Janie, and had started omitting key details accordingly, like his habit of scribbling notes on his forearms to avoid wasting paper, or sometimes, in the coffee shop, taking videos of strangers, or once announcing *I choose to be poor* (in the moment, Anna had nodded appreciatively, swept along in the tide of his conviction, but later realized this was something only an actually rich person could ever say).

To Anna and Alexis, James's candor was mostly appealing—*tell me what you like* was already their new in-house catchphrase—but Janie had laughed at the line, confused. *Ooookay*, she said. *Way to put it out there, dude.* To be fair, Anna had felt a similar bewilderment when Kim talked about Brian Tucker, with whom she was now, incomprehensibly, officially going out. Earlier that week, she'd told Anna that he was actually much smarter and more sensitive than they'd given him credit for. *And it's just nice to be with somebody from home*, she'd said, a sentiment Anna couldn't begin to share. Anna tried to picture James meeting Tucker, meeting Gavin, but it was unfathomable, the merging of two different species; the disconnect amused her. What worried her was the prospect of Alexis one day meeting Janie and Kim; she wasn't at all sure they would get along. What did it say about her, Anna, that it was so hard to imagine her three closest friends being friends with each other?

Her phone buzzed. *Voicemail Kim.*

Disappointingly, the message was only nine seconds long. Anna pressed the phone to her ear. *Hey, I know you're busy having sex with your new boyfriend but call me when you can, okay?* She smiled. It was probably an update on Tucker's newfound depth of character. Anna would call her back tomorrow, when the appointment was over. But she listened to the message twice more, just to hear her voice.

The plan had been to meet on a bench outside the health center after their appointments, but by the time Anna stepped out the sliding doors and into the sunlight, she felt dizzy and raw. Historically, Anna's worries about a thing always outweighed the thing itself, but in this case the appointment had been far worse. It was more than just the needle. There was the quiz about her sexual history, the lecture about safe sex practices and the sheaf of fear-inducing brochures. By the time she'd had blood drawn—rubber tubing wrapped around her arm, nurse tapping bluntly for a vein—her hands were water. The needle went in, and the syringe filled slowly. *I think I need to lie down*, she said, and then everything was blurring around the edges and she knew that she was fainting but couldn't stop.

She woke lying down on the table with feet propped on her backpack. Her forehead was wet and warm. The nurse, now slightly more kindly, asked what Anna had eaten that morning (apple) and went to get her juice and saltines. Alone, she sat up. A damp wad of paper towel dropped to the floor. She stared at the posters on the wall before her, a black-and-white photo of a girl's pained face. DEPRESSION HURTS. Next to it, two pairs of bare feet, one polished and one hairy, poking out beneath a blanket. PULLING AN ALL-NIGHTER? GET TESTED! She remembered the time, junior year, her period was late and she lived for five days in a state of abject fear—convinced her nausea was morning sickness, the occasional flutter in her belly a medically impossible kick. When finally she got up the nerve to take an EPT test, she and Kim and Janie had crammed into the bathroom, holding hands and watching the stick turn—a minus sign. They had celebrated with wine coolers, joked about narrowly averting the spawn of Gavin Newland. Thank God. Thank *God*! Later, Anna had read online:

Menstruation doesn't occur sometimes when the body has too little fat to carry a child. It's the body's way of protecting itself.

She bent forward and pressed her head between her knees. The smell of her jeans was faintly cottony, and it reminded her of home—the slow clouds of steam that blew past her bedroom window when the dryer rumbled in the mudroom—and tears pooled in her eyes: that this was her life now, sitting in a clinic getting blood drawn to check for potentially fatal diseases, a poster of a sad-faced teenager hanging on the wall. She wished she'd never let James put her up to this. Wished she'd taken an Ativan that morning. Wished she were back in Stafford, in her old bedroom, or Gavin's basement, easy undemanding Gavin, watching *Anchorman* for the hundredth time and nursing a Diet Coke.

When finally she left the building, squinting into the sudden brightness, the sight of James on the bench sent a blast of resentment through her: the booted foot, the sunglasses. Even the exposed gauze taped to the crook of his elbow seemed designed to provoke.

"What took so long?" he said, walking toward her. "Are you crying?" Then he stopped. "Jesus, you're not—"

"No," she said. "Of course not. And anyway, you don't find out for two weeks." The crook of her arm still pulsed faintly. "I fainted. I told you I'm not good with needles. I got dizzy and the nurse gave me juice and was really worried about me. She wouldn't let me leave."

"Oh." Then, "Come here," he said, and stepped toward her, reaching for her hand. She hated this. Hated him, suddenly. She walked away, arms tucked across her chest. "Anna, come on. Where are you going?"

"Class," she managed, though poetry didn't start for another hour. She continued past the dining hall, the student union. James followed. She was tempted to keep lapping the quad just to see at what point he would give up, but her anger slowly ebbed, and after a few minutes, she began feeling silly. When he reached for her again, she stopped. "Come on," he said. "Can we talk?"

She followed him to a bench near the library, under a sprawling maple. The tree had leaves the size of hands. They sat close but not touching, facing the quad, which was red and golden, splashed with sunlight. It looked like the stage of a play. He said, "What's going on?"

It was a cool afternoon, but Anna's face was burning. *If I'm going to be with someone, it has to be honest,* James had said. She watched the students strolling along the brick paths, sunlight filtering through the branches, and knew she had to tell him. Worst-case scenario: He took it badly; he broke up with her on the spot. If so, she knew Alexis would gladly meet her back in the room to explain why she was better off without him. She wouldn't have to worry anymore about STDs, or this pressure she felt to impress him all the time, to never just relax and be herself. The worst-case scenario was survivable—in some ways, it might be a relief.

"Well, so"—she was trying to keep her tone light, despite the flush prickling her neck—"I was thinking about what you said, the other night, about being honest, and in the interest of full disclosure I should probably tell you that, back in high school, I struggled with some things."

She fixed her eyes on a long crack winding along the bricks, but sensed his nod. "Okay," he said.

"I mean, it was nothing cataclysmic," she said. "It was eating stuff, mostly. An eating disorder, officially." She glanced over at him, palms pressed between her thighs. "Please don't freak out."

"I'm not freaking out," James replied. In fact, his face, beneath the sunglasses, looked unbothered, possibly even unsurprised.

"It's a cliché, I know. It's embarrassing."

"How bad was it?"

She shrugged, tears rising sharply. "Bad, I guess."

"How much did you weigh?"

At this, she couldn't help but laugh. It was a question, the question, nobody ever asked. "One eighteen," she said. "And now I'm like one fifty. So, there you go. I'm not starving myself anymore. I'm over it. Obviously."

"How did you get over it?"

"I had, you know, a therapist," she said. "A nutritionist. But mostly, I just realized I was thinking about it too much. It was taking up too much space in my brain." This was partly true. It was also an answer she thought James might appreciate. In James's brain, there probably wasn't an iota of wasted space.

But James was slowly shaking his head. "It's such bullshit," he said. "Another false narrative perpetuated by the media. Selling a celebrity culture that warps people into thinking they have to attain these unrealistic standards of perfection."

Anna made a small, halfhearted non-sound. She knew James was being supportive, but the fact that he saw her as vulnerable to these *standards of perfection* made her feel gullible. And that he obviously saw her as falling short of them made her feel, absurdly, hurt.

"Anyway," she said. "I just thought that I should let you know."

"I'm glad." He smiled, giving her knee a squeeze, and as much as she'd dreaded telling him, his reaction left her feeling empty. Maybe, in the hierarchy of the world's problems, things worthy of solicitude, eating disorders ranked among more shallow and unserious.

Anna stared out at the quad. "And, well," she said. "Since I'm confessing past afflictions, in the interest of full disclosure I guess I should probably mention I had some issues with anxiety too."

James chuckled. "Who doesn't? If you're a rational, thinking member of this country you'd better be feeling a little fucking anxious."

"Yeah," she said. "But this was more than that. It was real. It was scary. Like panic attacks."

James looked at her, pushed his sunglasses on top of his head. "Really? What were your triggers?"

"Um, everything?" Her laugh was a catch in her throat. "Robbers. Fires. Highly improbable abduction scenarios."

"B minuses," he said, and she smiled, grateful for the joke.

"And needles," she added. "And sexually transmitted diseases."

"Anna. Jesus. You have to *tell* me these things. If you don't, how am I supposed to—"

"I know," she said. "That's why I'm telling you now. And I mean—it's not like I can't handle it. I handled it, didn't I?" She felt light, shaky with emotion. James picked up her hand and put it in his lap, rubbing his thumb along the inside of her wrist. He was looking at her closely now, expression folded into concern. Clearly, anxiety was a more respectable problem, darker and messier, more intellectual somehow.

"Are you medicated?" he asked.

She shook her head. "Not anymore. I was."

"Klonopin? Ativan? Zoloft? Lexapro?"

"Lexapro," she said. "And Ativan."

"My brother was on that."

"Oh," she said. "Right." She paused. "Well, now I take it only for real emergencies."

"How frequent are real emergencies?"

"I mean, never, basically. I haven't had one in almost a year," she said, but then remembered that night in the Grange. It had been only August, not even a month ago, but already felt surreal, a distant memory of a different person. It was almost not worth mentioning, but she had decided to be honest, and she had come this far. "Actually," she admitted, "if we're being totally thorough, there was a minor incident that happened this summer. Not a full-blown panic attack. Just—a little thing."

"A little thing," James replied. He squeezed her fingers once more, then let go, propped a boot on the opposite knee. "Let's hear," he said.

"Do you remember that ex-boyfriend I told you about? Gavin?"

"Mister Mainstream."

"Right," she said, with a jolt of remorse. "Well, there was this party at his house, right before I left to come here. A going-to-college, good-riddance-to-high-school kind of thing, and we decided to go for a walk. Just the two of us." She stole a look at him, hoping for a trace of envy, but he was looking down, peeling the gauze from the inside of his arm. "So we took this walk," she went on. "In the woods near his house. And it was just incredibly—spooky. It was eerie. It was pitch black. It's hard to explain, but you literally couldn't see your hand in front of your face." James said nothing, and she felt a stab of regret—for telling such a stupid story, chipping away at her credibility. "I realize it sounds completely childish," she said, and

James didn't contradict her. He looked distracted, even bored. The gauze pad, white but for a single dot of blood, perched on his knee. "But also," she said, "it had been a really stressful day. Because of this shooting."

James turned to her and frowned. "What shooting?"

It alarmed her, to have said it, but James was now listening carefully. "It was a few weeks ago," she explained. "In the mall, in my hometown. This guy just walked in and started—"

"Hold on," James said. "Nathan Dugan?"

For some reason, this made her laugh. "You know about it?"

"Of course. It was national news."

"Oh," she said sheepishly. "Right."

James angled toward her, sliding one knee up onto the bench. "That was in your hometown?"

"Well, not technically the same town. But only a few miles from my house. I go to that mall all the time."

"Anna." James stared at her for a full minute. "Holy fucking shit."

"I know." She knew that it was wrong: using the shooting to deflect attention from her stupid panic attack in the woods that night, to explain it, justify it—but it was true. And also, it was working. She could see the boredom disappearing, the interest deepening on his face.

"Did you know any of the victims?"

"No," she said. "No, thank God. But a good friend of mine, Laura, she was there." No matter that the extent of her friendship with Laura Mack was drinking with her at the basketball team parties she occasionally tagged along to with Janie. Whenever Anna let her guard down and thought about the shooting, even for a second, it was that dressing room her mind rushed into: the mirror, the screams, and then the frightening silence, the sense of the walls closing in.

"There, where?" James asked. "Right at the scene?"

"No, not exactly." For some reason, she stopped short of mentioning the Gap. "She was in the mall, though. She wasn't far. She heard it all."

"Jesus Christ."

"I know," she said. "I hate even thinking about it, actually—"

"That's how these guys operate, though," James cut in. "Crowded public places, random victims. Maximum anxiety. So nowhere feels safe."

"Yeah," Anna said. She hadn't thought of it in quite those terms, but this explanation made a terrifying kind of sense. For that was the fear, the core of it: that these things could happen anywhere, to anyone. No warning. You could even know the person and still not see it coming.

"Well, anyway," she said. "That's why I was freaking out that night, at the party. I mean—we all were. It was the same day as the shooting. Everyone was really shaken up."

"Yeah," James said. "Of course."

He was looking at her closely now, almost admiringly, as if her proximity to this event cast her in a new and more interesting light. Much as Anna didn't want to keep talking about it, the promise of James's reaction was too much to resist. "And actually, the most disturbing part—this is truly crazy—he was my mom's student."

"He?" James paused. "He, who?"

"The, you know, shooter."

James raised his eyebrows and held them there. "Dugan."

"Yeah."

"Nathan Dugan was your mother's student."

"Right."

"Anna," he said. "Holy shit."

"I know." She felt a rush of something uncomfortably like pride. "What did I tell you? So—"

"Wait, hold on. When did she teach him?"

"I mean, he was a fifth-year senior. So, four years ago, I guess. But she definitely remembered him." She drew a breath. "Anyway, you can understand why I was so freaked out—"

"And what did she say?"

"She said he was, you know. Different."

"Obviously," James said. "What else?"

Anna racked her brain for the few words her mother had parsed out in the kitchen that afternoon. "She said he was kind of tightly wound,

I think. He didn't have friends. But she didn't say a whole lot. She was annoyingly evasive about it, actually."

"Why would she be evasive?"

"Well, no, not evasive, I just mean—she didn't say much. That's how she is." She paused. "But he definitely sounded strange."

James looked disappointed there wasn't more to report, and Anna felt annoyed retroactively that her mother hadn't been more forthcoming. She knew she shouldn't keep talking, her mother had actually asked her not to, but she blurted, "The next day, though, I found her looking through some old stuff in our barn and she had dug up this old paper that I'm pretty sure was his."

It worked: James shifted back toward her, the energy returning to his face. "Paper?" he said. "What kind of paper?"

"You know, for Freshman Comp—"

"One of those personal tragedies?"

She let out a mild laugh. "Yeah, probably."

"Probably?" he said. "Did you read it?"

"Well, I wanted to. Obviously. She wouldn't let me."

"Wouldn't *let* you?"

"I mean, there are issues around it. Ethical issues. She doesn't let people read her students' stuff."

James frowned. "You told me you read tons of those papers."

"Yeah, when she wasn't looking. She would never have let me if she'd known—"

"Did you ask?"

"Of course I asked. But my mom follows the rules. That's just how she is."

At this, James scoffed lightly, then sat back on the bench, surveying the quad. Anna's palms were damp, and she pressed them to her thighs. "Wait," James said, turning back to her abruptly. "Maybe it was the paper that guy wrote about online. On Facebook."

Anna felt a surge of panic but managed to shake her head. "I highly doubt it."

"But you saw that post, right?"

"I don't know," she stalled, remembering the scary spill of comments she'd glimpsed once and hidden from sight. "I don't think so."

"Yes, you did. You must have. The guy talked about this class he had, a writing class. And Dugan wrote some paper—fuck. It probably was." He stared at her. "How could you not read it?"

"I'm not a big Facebook person," she lied.

"I mean the paper, Anna. That paper might be really important. It might shed light on this guy's motives or his mental state—"

"It doesn't exactly matter now," she snapped. "He's dead. He killed himself. You know that too, right?"

This didn't warrant a response; clearly, James did. "Things turn up after the fact," he told her. "That's how these things go. These guys leave a paper trail because they know it'll get found eventually and they'll be famous. I mean, you read about the crazy shit he put online, right?"

"Honestly," she said, "I haven't been following it too closely."

"How is that possible? It was your mom's student. Your own town. You want to be a *writer*, for God's sake."

"I know," she said, stung. "I just—it's the anxiety. Like I was telling you. Sometimes knowing makes it worse." Her pulse was tripping in her veins. "Plus," she added, "my mother actually asked me not to tell people about it. I probably shouldn't have even told you."

"Why would she ask you not to tell people about it?"

"It's just, you know," she said. "It's a sensitive subject."

James gripped the back of his neck, then sat forward, elbows on his knees. He studied the ground as if considering a chessboard. "Maybe there was something in it she didn't want you to see."

"What do you mean?"

"Maybe it was some kind of a manifesto."

"It wasn't a manifesto."

"How do you know? You didn't read it. She wouldn't let you."

"I know because I know," Anna said. Sweat was blooming under her arms. "Because I'm telling you, my mother is just like that. She's a private person. An ethical person. And I know because there's no way one of her students wrote a—a manifesto—and she didn't do anything about it. Like I told you, she's obsessed. And when I asked her she *said* it wasn't about anything. She said it was about hanging out with his dad or something—"

"His dad?" James pounced. "His dad wasn't around. He lived with his mother. Which is why she got ripped apart online. When you know there were plenty of other people who were fully aware this guy needed help. Because that's how the system works. It protects some people and ignores others—"

"Why do you know so much about this?"

"Because it's a national crisis!" James practically shouted. "Because it's important. Because I read. Because it interests me."

"What does? Shootings?"

"No, Anna. Not *shootings*. Just—the world. What's actually happening in the world. Which most people choose to ignore." He spread both hands in an exasperated flourish. "Life. Real life."

"Why are you getting angry at me?"

"I'm not *angry* at you." He pulled at the skin beneath his eyes, then dropped his hands to his lap. "I'm just saying. This shit is a big deal and you're acting like it isn't."

"That's not true," Anna said. She fought the urge to pick her lip to shreds. "Did I not start this whole thing by telling you it was serious? That's the whole reason I was so freaked out, the night of Gavin's party."

"Well, you're right to freak out. Everybody *should* be freaking out. Most people just choose to look away and ignore things until something happens and they're forced to confront it. In fact, you should freak out more."

Across campus, the bell on the chapel was gonging. Her heart was pounding. Students exited the buildings, backpacks slung on shoulders and phones pressed to ears, heading to lunch or confirming plans for later. A weekend, a Friday. Anna felt as if she were looking at them from a vast distance. A girl walked by in sweatshirt and sunglasses, speaking into her cell phone: *I just wanted to hear your voice.*

"I feel kind of sick," Anna said. Her voice sounded unsteady, even to her.

"Sick as in you don't want to talk about this?"

"No," she said. "Sick as in sick. I fainted at the health center, remember? And my arm," she said. "It still hurts." She located the throbbing in her elbow, distant but still there. "I'm going to go back to the dorm."

"I'll come with you."

"Actually, I just want to be alone."

She stood up, hoisting her backpack to her shoulder, and James looked up at her face. "Anna, if you're upset, you can tell me."

But Anna was finished telling James things. Since meeting him, it felt like all she'd done was tell him things. "I'm not upset."

He studied her for another minute. "Okay," he said. "Well, call me later."

"I will," she said, and as she walked away, wished she could unsay it.

The dorm room was empty. Alexis wasn't home yet from Art History. That meant she'd gone to lunch after, which meant she wouldn't be back for at least another half hour. More, if she lingered in the dining hall with her friends from class. Anna felt shaky: nerves, or hunger. Hunger, more likely. She'd eaten nothing all day except the apple and four health center saltines. She assessed Alexis's junk food stash and what remained of Felicia's gift basket but the thought of actually eating repulsed her so she chugged a bottle of water and stuffed her mouth with gum.

She wished Alexis were there, and she didn't. Because she needed her to analyze what had just happened but it would be hard to fully explain without getting into things she didn't want to talk about, i.e., the anxiety/eating/shooting—they had melded in her mind as one panicky, pulsing thing: all the subjects she'd planned on keeping to herself and that, once spoken, had predictably blown up in her face.

Her phone started buzzing inside her backpack. Anna couldn't handle talking to James. But when she dug out the phone, she saw that it was Kim again.

Text Message Kim: *Hey girl*

Text Message Kim: *Tried calling*

Text Message Kim: *Did u see this?*

Anna watched the little dots that meant more was coming. Then a series of three quick photos appeared. Together, they made up a newspaper page.

Text Message Kim: *Your poor mom!!*

Anna stopped chewing, the hinge on her jaw suddenly freezing. She reached into her mouth and removed the wad of gum and dropped it in the trash. Then she clicked on the first photo: It was the front page of the *Sentinel*, the student paper at Central Maine. CLASSMATE REMEMBERS KILLER. A light snow of panic flurried in her brain. She absorbed the article in fragments, like flashes of an X-ray machine.

Professor Maggie Daley

so vivid and so disturbing

ten thousand times

most haunting was a paper of a personal nature written by the future killer

Another buzz.

Text Message Kim: *Did she say anything to you???*

. . .

. . .

. . .

Anna's heart was an ocean in her ears. Her mind flew back to that morning after Gavin's party, how she'd roamed the house and couldn't find her mother anywhere. How, when finally she tried the barn, she'd discovered her kneeling on the floor, looking upset, a paper on her knees. *I think it's best if we not mention this to anyone.* At the time, it hadn't struck Anna as strange. That was her mother: private person, taker of precautions and abider by rules. She wanted to write back and tell Kim about it, but now she felt afraid. She'd told James and already she regretted it. She could just imagine Kim telling Tucker, and Tucker telling his new Central Maine friends. She crunched her stomach in and out as she watched the little dots that signaled Kim was typing, and braced herself for whatever was coming, but when the words blinked to the surface, her eyes filled.

Text Message Kim: *How's your man?*

Text Message Kim: *Miss u friend* ☺

Twelve

The affair continued: Suzanne was sure of it. Robert seemed distracted, even more so than before. For a while, that summer, during treatments, she had thought it might be over. He was around the house more, and attentive, accepting. Gone was the need to apologize for disappearing to her room, gone the sense that she was always disappointing him. Their relationship was sexless, but private and tender, absent of expectations. In a strange way, Suzanne felt happier than she'd been in a long time.

Since the start of the new semester, though, Robert was back to staying late on campus. A few times, she'd seen him glance at his ringing phone, then shove it back in his pocket with an inattention that was conspicuous. At home with her, he often seemed annoyed. He thought her reaction to Doreen Howard was unhealthy—*extreme*. Suzanne frequently reminded herself of the response she'd received from the online support group when, finally, she'd dared post something. *You are stronger than you think.*

Robert's schedule was predictable, almost to the minute. Every Saturday at eleven he went for a run. He returned an hour later, fingers pressed to his wrist, Saturday *Times* clamped under his arm. While he was gone, Suzanne conducted a thorough search of his things. It was a habit she'd taken up a month ago, the weekend after the shooting, and already it had grown more efficient and refined. She began in the bedroom—Robert's bedroom, the guest room—and, starting with his wallet, inspected everything that had exited or entered the house with him in the previous week.

It was a mostly pointless exercise, but it helped to feel she wasn't doing nothing, and because her husband was not a detail person (was not, in truth, cut out for having an affair), bits of evidence surfaced here and there. A blue wool thread. A strand of medium-brown hair (long—it pained her). A receipt for food on a Thursday night, enough for two. Suzanne had deduced that must be when they saw each other, during Robert's supposed office hours—he had never held evening office hours before—and though anytime she called, he answered, there was something guarded in his voice. M—that was the letter she'd twice spied come up on Robert's cell phone before he pretended not to see it. She assumed M must be someone at the college. A few times, when he was in the shower, she'd attempted to read his text messages but didn't know his password and had no good reason to ask; she'd guessed a few combinations, all wrong, then gave up.

Suzanne had told no one about her suspicions—she would have told the online group but it didn't feel right, when people were dealing with matters of life and death—though as she searched, she often found herself talking to her dead mother in her head. Not about her marriage, but about her childhood. About the careful way their house had felt after Suzanne's father left. Above all, her mother hated being made a fool of, hated being embarrassed. Lately, Suzanne had come to see the quiet vigilance of those years as a kind of sadness, and her mother, plagued by headaches, as clinically depressed. She was amazed at the effort it must have taken to keep up appearances, to keep things looking right.

The house was so quiet it seemed to hum with it. Suzanne performed a quick search of Robert's wallet—loose bills, lunch receipts—then turned to the week's worth of clothes piled on the cedar chest. She turned out pant pockets, inspecting their contents with the detached precision with which she did a load of wash. In the corduroys Robert had worn on Tuesday, she found a Sudafed tablet (he had complained of allergies) and a plastic coffee stirrer, like a tiny sword. A receipt (smoothie, energy bar) from the student union was stuffed in the pocket of his jeans. As she turned toward the door, she caught a glimpse of her reflection in the vanity mirror—for a moment, she didn't recognize herself. Her hair was short now, and striking. When it started growing in, she'd dyed it dark brown. Her mother had always said that, with her height, she could have been a model if only she'd had more confidence. Staring at her reflection, Suzanne felt a quick gathering of tears. She wanted nothing more than to crawl into the bed and draw the shades. But she glanced at the bedside clock—it was nearly eleven thirty. Robert would be back before she knew it. She drew a steadying breath, and continued downstairs.

The study was an addition built off the living room and appended to the rest of the house by a short, enclosed bridge. When they bought the house, this feature had struck Suzanne as charming, like something out of a fairy tale, but she had grown to hate it. The bridge only emphasized their separateness. The study was hexagonal, large windows on five sides: Depending on the weather, it was the warmest or coldest room in the house. This morning, it was cool and foggy and it reminded her of home, though the South Carolina fog was thicker. Maine fog, she knew, could burn or blow off at any time.

She sat down at her husband's long, L-shaped desk. To the west, the study overlooked the backyard, the stone patio, and the grove of winter firs; to the east, it faced the wide, leafy street. Suzanne would have positioned the desk to face the peaceful span of yard, but Robert had done the reverse. His email had been left open, as usual. She skimmed the inbox but found nothing. Even Robert was not that careless. On the desktop, she noted three empty mugs, a stack of exams for 101. Peeking from the bottom of the pile, she saw the school newspaper, the word KILLER in garish red letters. Suzanne stopped and slid the paper out. CLASSMATE REMEMBERS KILLER. Below the headline sat photos of two boys. One she recognized as Nathan Dugan, though it wasn't the picture she'd seen endlessly on the news. He was younger here; he was even faintly smiling. In the more recent pictures, he looked bigger, and his skin had worsened. The other boy, the classmate, appeared entirely different. Studious and shy, nestled in a heavy sweater. He looked like he was cold. *Have you ever wondered about that kid sitting next to you in English class?* Suzanne unfolded the paper and dropped her eyes beneath the fold. Apparently, in a class the boys had had together, Nathan had written a paper that was *violent* and *haunting*. It had worried the other students, but the teacher hadn't done anything about it. She'd even refused to be interviewed for the article. *Asked if he thought his professor had been negligent, Luke admitted, "Probably, yes."*

As she read the last line, Suzanne felt a lash of anger—at this teacher, who should have known better, at the world of academia, which seemed to attract smart but self-involved people like these. She was enraged, but there wasn't time to stop and indulge the feeling. She hadn't yet touched Robert's briefcase, and it was ten of twelve, according to the clock on the computer. She refolded the paper, arranging it exactly as she'd found it, tucked under the stack of exams with the word KILLER just visible underneath.

The briefcase sat on the floor beside the filing cabinet. Suzanne had chosen it herself, a gift when he got his first job teaching; the leather was hard and shiny then, but now it was fashionably worn. Its unbuckled pockets flapped like tongues. She reached into one of the soft side pockets and rifled through it: more exams. In another, a spare pair of reading glasses, a napkin, a fistful of pens. The zippered pocket in the center contained only a single paper, seamed with squares, as if it had been folded and reopened. Two Post-it notes were stuck to the front.

sorry

call me

Suzanne placed the paper in her lap. For a minute, she just stared. The handwriting was small, cramped cursive, feminine-looking. A quick flush crawled over her skin. The top of the *c* was torn where the pen had ripped through the page—in haste, or anger? The heat crept under her hair. For a moment, she allowed herself to believe there might be an innocent explanation, but the truth settled in her bones, sickeningly clear. To find these notes was to stumble upon a primary source: not just proof of the affair, but of the emotional life that went with it, the fact that her husband, whom she saw every day strapping on his briefcase and biking to campus, was in another relationship so legitimate that he apologized and was apologized to—it left her feeling freshly betrayed. Though she'd suspected all along, to know for sure was a different thing entirely; she realized how much she had been clinging to that sliver of doubt.

She stared helplessly at the Post-its, heart pounding. Her arms felt weak. Her eye fell on a sentence crawling out from beneath one of the yellow squares—*ammo, two rifles and a AR-15*. Suzanne paused, then suddenly picked up the paper, flipping to the title page. When she read the name on the front, she gasped.

Her first instinct was to avert her eyes, as one would from a bloody animal on the side of the road, but she forced herself to look. At the date: *May 3, 2012*. The course: *Freshman Composition*. The teacher: *Professor Daley*—she recognized this name. It was the teacher from the article, the one who had ignored the essay. She paged quickly through the entire thing, feeling nauseated—*no respect for using semiautos to hunt with or say it's not PC but in the right hands*— At the end, she threw the pages on the desk, hands trembling. Why did Robert have this? What was wrong with him? Why would he have brought this into their home?

Because, she thought furiously, this was what Robert did. Let ugliness into their marriage, just invited it right inside, like flinging rats on the living room rug.

Dizzily, her eyes drifted through the comments in the margins—the handwriting was small, cramped—and her breath stilled.

The final detail shuddered into place: M.

For a moment, she stayed sitting there, in the thump and sweat of her discovery, staring out the window at the quiet street: the red blaze of the oak tree, pale slab of autumn sunlight breaking through the fog. She wished she could freeze time, go back and pretend she didn't know, but she turned to the computer. Eleven fifty-seven. She pulled up the school website, typed in *Daley*, and waited for the photo to appear on-screen. Her first thought, uncharitably, was that Maggie Daley wasn't pretty. She was plain. Thin lips, hair pulled back in a simple ponytail. Long, yes, and medium brown. She was wearing what looked like a flannel shirt, unprofessional, the sort of thing one threw on to do yard work. *Mousy*, Suzanne's mother would have called her, in so doing removing the sting of envy, but as Suzanne skimmed her faculty bio—degrees and publications, an award for teaching—her very plainness felt threatening. She was the opposite of Suzanne, and the fact that this was the woman Robert was drawn to, this was what he was looking for, left her feeling bereft all over again. Maggie Daley may not be pretty, but she was smart and she was accomplished. And selfish, Suzanne reminded herself, insecurity hardening into indignation. The woman was selfish, and she was negligent. Not only was she carrying on an affair with a married man—a married man whose wife had cancer, she thought, in a rare blast of self-pity—she'd ignored a student who was clearly violent, and who later went on to murder four people, including sweet Doreen Howard at the beginning of her long, happy life.

A check of the clock: eleven fifty-eight. Suzanne stood up and walked to the copier by the window—rage made her actions precise, purposeful, not a wasted motion—and pressed the paper beneath the lid. She watched as the pages baked in the machine, peeling off one by one onto the tray, then refolded and returned the paper to Robert's briefcase, gently pressing the Post-its back on top. Next she made a copy of the newspaper article, taking one of Robert's highlighters to the last few sentences and smothering them in wet gold. *Clearly, in hindsight, that intervention was necessary— not only that, it might have prevented a tragedy.* She considered including a note—*I felt you deserved to see this*—but trusted she didn't need to. She wrote only, *With deepest sympathy,* then retrieved a manila envelope from Robert's filing cabinet and slid the pages inside, still warm. She addressed the envelope to Arlen Mackey, c/o Lowe's Hardware Store, Elkton. Then she pasted on five stamps, more than it would need, and left the house in the opposite direction from where Robert would be coming. The morning was a little chilly, but today the chill felt motivating, as she walked the eight blocks to the post office and dropped the envelope in the mailbox with no return address.

Thirteen

Anna had read the article in the student newspaper and immediately called her mother, who assured her there was nothing to worry about. *Exaggerated*, she said. *And poorly written*. Once Anna had calmed down a little, she could see that this was true. She reminded herself that Nathan Dugan and his essay being creepy wasn't so surprising. She'd read enough of her mother's papers to know they were often personal—jarringly so. The more upsetting part was the implication that her mother could have done something to prevent what happened later. This, Anna knew, was impossible: that a student had written something that would have required Maggie's attention and she'd missed it.

Kim admitted that the article had caused a minor stir on the Central Maine State campus, but also acknowledged it was only the student paper; no one cared all that much. Tucker, she said, hadn't even read it. (*Wait*, Janie joked. *Tucker reads?*)

Anna had no intention of telling James about the article, not after yesterday's conversation. She didn't want to encourage his interest—it seemed to border on excitement—but when she heard a knock at the door Saturday morning, not yet ten o'clock, Anna knew that it was him.

"Go away," Alexis groaned.

Anna's first thought, foolishly, was that James had discovered she'd gone out the night before. When she'd texted him, around seven thirty, she'd said she felt too sick to do anything, but then Alexis had dragged her out to a party anyway. A fraternity party, the kind of party James hated. *Perfect*, Alexis said. *You don't have to worry about him showing up.*

Now, from the top bunk, Alexis raised her voice to a sleepy shout. "This better be necessary!" she said, and James opened the door.

"Oh," he said. He was dressed in jeans and a black T-shirt, ragged at the hem. Anna noted several blue-penned scribbles on his arms. "I didn't think it was that early," he said, but paused on the threshold for only an instant before walking to Anna's bed. When he bent to kiss her, she wondered if he could taste stale beer on her breath. "Did you get my texts?" he said.

Since their conversation the day before, James had sent several messages, most of them links to stories about the shooting he'd found online. Anna hadn't read them. "I think so," she said.

"You think so?"

"I got some of them. But maybe not all of them."

From the top bunk, Alexis offered, "You were sick. You were probably asleep."

James ignored this, kneeling on the floor beside Anna's pillow. "Have you seen this yet?" he said, and held out his phone. Anna propped herself up on her elbows and looked at the screen. CLASSMATE REMEMBERS KILLER. She didn't know what was worse: that the article was now online and James had found it, or that Alexis was there listening.

"Yeah," she said quickly. "I saw."

"It's about your mom, right?" he said, adding, "Maggie Daley." It bothered her, to hear him say her mother's name. "It's about that Facebook post. I told you."

From above, the bedsprings squeaked as Alexis jumped to the floor. She was wearing rumpled boxers and a white tank top that was basically transparent, though neither she nor James seemed to care. "What's going on?"

"It's an article," James said. "About the shooting."

"What shooting?"

James looked at Anna, incredulous. "You didn't tell her either?" He stood and faced Alexis, as if too amped to stay on the ground. "There was a shooting, in August, in Anna's hometown—"

"Oh, right, right," she said. "I forgot."

"You *forgot?*" James exclaimed, and fake-shot a gun at his own head. "Jesus. We're not talking about reality TV here. This actually happened," he said, then rattled off the pertinent data. "Mall food court. Four victims. Shooter was a Central Maine State student. And Anna's mom was his teacher."

"Really?" Alexis said, raising her eyebrows, as Anna's heart sank. "She didn't mention that. That's crazy."

"When was this?" James frowned.

"The day we moved in," Alexis said, with a glance at Anna. "But maybe it was just too upsetting for her."

"Yeah," Anna said quickly. "She doesn't like making a big deal out of personal stuff like that."

"Well, too late," James quipped. "Because now these other students from her class are saying he was clearly fucked up and she ignored him."

Anna shook her head. "That isn't what they said."

James read aloud from his phone. "'When asked if his writing professor ever addressed Nathan Dugan's alarming tendencies in class—'"

"Yeah, I know," she said, clambering out of bed. She felt at a disadvantage, being the only one not standing. "I read it."

"And?"

"And that's one person's memory. One person's opinion."

"Anna," he said, putting an arm around her shoulder. "They remember that he wrote a fucked-up paper. It's obviously the one she found."

Alexis turned back to her. "What is he talking about?"

"Nothing."

"Not nothing," James said. "There was a paper this guy wrote—"

"Years ago," Anna said.

"Years ago. That's the point. He was a freshman. And after he goes on a shooting rampage, she finds this paper and won't let Anna see it. And now these kids from that class are saying he wrote a paper that was violent. Remember? On Facebook. It was everywhere," he said, a trace of victory in his voice.

"Let me see," Alexis said, grabbing for his phone. Anna despaired as she watched the article change hands: the contents of her life at home pouring from one person into the next.

"Look." Anna was trying to project confidence, but her voice was shaking. "I talked to my mother yesterday. She said this whole thing is totally exaggerated."

"What else did she say?" James was looking at her intently.

"That's basically it." She shrugged, felt James's arm move, a warm weight across the back of her neck. "The article is over the top. It was written by a student. It's not, like, real journalism. And I mean, so he was weird. So what? That doesn't mean she could have done anything—"

"Why not?" James cut in. "She helped all those other students. The suicidal girl. Alison."

It startled her, the casual mention of Alison Bower. Anna had forgotten she'd even told him about her.

"Who?" Alexis asked, but Anna said, "That was different."

"Why was it different? Because she was a nice straight-A student and this guy was the freak in the back of the class?"

Anna's mouth had gone dry. Alexis looked at her, looked at James. "There's always a freak in the back of the class," she concluded, then handed James his phone. "We were actually just on our way to brunch."

James dropped the phone back in his pocket, where it glowed through his shirt. "Right," he said. Then he looked around the room, as if noticing for the first time where he was standing—the walls above Alexis's desk shellacked with postcards from Italy and photos of her prep school friends—and finally circled back to Anna. "Sorry," he said, and pressed his lips to her temple, speaking into her hair. "I was just fired up. I'll see you later?"

Inside her head, Anna was shouting that she didn't want to see him later. Didn't want to go to his depressing apartment. Didn't want to eat whatever greasy carbs he cooked. Didn't want to have sex with him, which, having happened once, naturally would be expected again. The line rose to the surface of her brain—*I think we're just too different*—but she couldn't bring herself to speak.

"Call me," James said, and Anna nodded, and he kissed her again and left.

When the door shut, Alexis turned to her, eyebrows arched again. "Well, that was bizarre," she said, and Anna was unsure whether she was talking about the article or James.

"I know," she said, pausing. "Please don't mention this to anyone. The stuff about my mom, I mean. I shouldn't have even told him."

"Clearly." Alexis studied her for another moment, but whatever she was thinking she kept to herself. "Come on," she said. "Let's eat."

Anna claimed she wasn't hungry, citing her lingering hangover, and picked at a bowl of dry Special K. They'd been joined in the dining hall by Violet Sharma, which ordinarily Anna would have found a nuisance—Violet had a talent for hijacking the conversation—but felt, this morning, like a reprieve. As Anna nursed her cereal, Violet bitched about Carly, who was now leaving little territorial Post-it notes on things: her granola bars, her gum. *Did you ask to take these?* Anna nodded absently at her stories, sipping at a glass of Diet Coke. "Yesterday I found one on a box of Kleenex," Violet continued, and Anna felt a quick stab of resentment, of envy, for worries as meaningless as these.

As they were leaving the dining hall, the three of them parted ways, Alexis and Violet heading back to the dorm and Anna to the library. She was going to work on her next essay for poetry. *In a five-page paper, analyze three distinct examples of the poet's preoccupation with the natural world.* But she couldn't concentrate.

Text Message James: *Just looking at this kid's FB post*

Text Message James: *Jesus there are 500+ comments here*

At library, Anna tapped back. *Essay due Mon.* She tried to focus on the blur of notes on her laptop screen.

Text Message James: *Your moms students are on here too you know*

Text Message James: *Lots of them*

Text Message James: *Def remember him as unstable*

Text Message James: *When are you coming over??*

Anna sent back noncommittal answers. *Still at library. Still feel kind of sick FYI.*

Outside, the sky over the quad was darkening. It was seven o'clock, and the library was virtually empty. Anna pinched her lip, staring out the window. At one point, the lights on the quad all snapped on at once.

Text Message James: *Jesus people are ignorant*

Text Message James: *They blame dugan's mother just because she's an easy target*

Text Message James: *When plenty of people didn't do shit*

Text Message Alexis: *Where r u roomie? Not still at library? Come home PRONTO!*

At seven thirty, Anna made herself leave. She dropped her phone in the bottom of her backpack and zipped it shut and for a moment, as she stepped out of the library, the cool night air made her eyes fill. It was so still, and so quiet; in the brief window between people eating dinner and going out, the quad was basically empty, and the absence of everything felt like a gift. The sky was purple, softly foggy. It was a Saturday and you could sense it: the way, before parties, the atmosphere feels simultaneously sleepy and alert. But as Anna walked toward the dorm, a long unlit stretch, her pleasure in the emptiness veered toward nervousness. Call boxes stood along the brick paths, glowing in the darkness, square black poles topped with blue lights, the white word EMERGENCY running down each side. The shadows of the trees yawned across the grass. Anna recalled the tips she'd long ago memorized for women walking alone at night: *Tie long hair back so attackers can't grab it. Walk with a sense of purpose. If you're alone in an elevator with a stranger look him in the eye so he'll think twice about attacking, knowing you could identify him in a lineup* (though that one had always struck her as flawed: What if, because you looked him in the eye, he decided to kill you instead?). She tried to walk with purpose but was worried about the clop of her boots against the brick, alerting strangers to her presence—like that one, there, sitting alone on a bench. She paused. What was he doing, just sitting there? Was he hunched over suspiciously? Was he hiding something? Watching her approach? Theresa had told her she had a vivid imagination, an instinct for observing details and spinning narratives, that it was part of what made her anxieties so acute. *You definitely have the makings of a writer*, she'd said. Then the guy stood up abruptly, reaching inside his jacket, and Anna's lungs burst through her chest—a gun. But no: a phone. Of course a phone. Always a phone. The guy wandered off. Anna resumed walking. Her boot heels were deafening. She imagined someone following noiselessly behind her. Imagined James, in his apartment, waiting for her call. The prospect of going over there, or of telling him she wasn't—both options filled her with dread. She gave her lip a vicious twist and glanced over her shoulder at the empty path behind her. *Stop it, Anna. Stop.*

By the time she reached Hightower, she just wanted to climb into bed and stay there but the dorm was buzzing. Music blaring, hair dryers droning. Girls wandering to and from the bathrooms, getting ready to go out. In her room, Anna found Alexis drinking a Corona and flat-ironing her hair. This was one of Alexis's most enviable talents: Her thick hair, once pressed through the straightener, came out shiny and flat as fresh tinfoil.

"Finally," she said, setting down the iron. "Where have you been?"

Anna let her backpack slide off her shoulder. "Library."

"I thought James had kidnapped you or something."

"Ha ha," she said. "I was working on my essay."

"On a Saturday night? You giant dork." She reached behind her to open up the mini-fridge, handing Anna a bottle, then pointed to the open Chinese food cartons inside. "Eat," she instructed. "And get changed. And get drinking. There's a party at Breck's house and you're three beers behind."

Anna paused, staring at the fridge. She was starving; she hadn't eaten since brunch that morning. Alexis picked up her straightener and clamped a hank of hair and the iron began hissing, unleashing a plume of steam.

"James wants me to come over," Anna told her, just as the phone started vibrating inside her pack. Reluctantly, she dug it out: *Where art thou???*

Alexis set down her iron again. "Is that him?" she said, and stood up, removing the phone from Anna's hand. She frowned, swiping quickly through his recent messages. Anna didn't try to stop her. Finally she looked up, saying, "You're not going over there, correct?"

"I don't know," Anna admitted.

"Anna," Alexis said. "Do you really want to be with this guy?"

"I don't know," she said again. Then: "No."

"You don't owe him anything. It's been what, like, a week?"

"Twelve days."

"Well, anything less than two weeks, you're allowed to break up by text." She considered the screen, then typed quickly, and held it up for approval: *I am sorry to put this in writing but I know it would be difficult to say. I have given this a lot of thought and while I like you I do not feel comfortable moving fwd right now.* "Yes?"

"Wait, no—" Anna said. "Let me see."

She clutched the phone in both hands. She felt anxious, of course. And guilty. And torn. For though it had been only twelve days, it felt longer, and to send a text this important seemed unkind. At the same time, she could feel already the relief of having sent it; she knew how hard it would be to say out loud. She reread the message, tinkered with it. Changed *fwd* to *forward*. Inserted a *truly* before the *sorry*, a *really* before the *like*. Then she handed it back to Alexis, who nodded. "Bueno," she said, and tapped SEND.

Anna's chest tightened like a rope yanked hard. By the time Alexis had handed her the phone, it was already ringing. "Oh God," Anna said, and Alexis reminded her, "You don't have to answer," but she took a breath and picked up. "Hi."

"Is this a joke?"

She had been braced for James to be angry; instead, he sounded hurt. Anna looked down at an orange square of carpet. Just hearing James's voice brought him into sudden focus, out of the realm of the abstract and into the real: James, who just three days ago she had wanted to have sex with. James, who had cooked her dinners. James, whom she had let herself confide in, really open up to. The truth was, he knew far more about her than Alexis did. She remembered that first afternoon in the coffee shop, the way her heart leapt as they talked, the warm pressure of his hand on her knee.

"I know," she said. "I'm sorry."

"You don't feel comfortable moving forward? Since when?"

"I don't know." She looked at Alexis, who was standing there listening. "I guess today."

"Was this your roommate's idea?"

"No." Her eyes dropped back to the floor. "I just—I think we're just really different."

He let out a wry laugh. "You're kidding, right?"

"I'm just not as passionate as you are. I'm not as opinionated about things—"

"Oh no. Of course, it's my fault," he said. "That's perfect. I should have known."

"That's not what I meant. If anything, it's mine. I *should* care more about—"

Alexis made a throat-cutting gesture.

"Look," James said. "Anna. I get that you're easily freaked out. You're an overachieving type-A who grew up in a small town with an over-protective family, which is why you're unable to deal with fucking reality," he said—it was startling in its briskness, and mean, like a sharpened stick. "But I don't know what you think you're accomplishing here. You think if you break up with me, all the upsetting things in the world will just disappear?"

Anna paused in the silence. She looked at Alexis, who gave her a firm nod. "I just don't feel comfortable," she repeated.

"Well," James said. "God forbid you feel uncomfortable. We wouldn't want that."

When she hung up, she cried. But not for the obvious reasons. Not because she felt sad about losing James, or regretted breaking up with James, but because she'd told him things about herself she had planned to tell nobody, and now he had them. He owned them. To be yourself around someone was a trap, she thought. A trick.

Alexis rubbed her back in circles as they chugged the rest of the Corona, ate the Chinese food. They consulted on Anna's outfit, and she alerted Kim and Janie. "Don't worry, roomie," Alexis promised as they left for the party. "We'll find you a nice, normal boy."

Text Message Kim: *If it helps I always thought he sounded too intense* ☺

Text Message Janie: *Good riddance!*

Text Message Janie: *(too soon?)*

★ ★ ★

For the next five days, it was as if James had disappeared. He didn't text her, didn't call her. Anna drowned herself in homework, partied with Alexis. Crunched her stomach in/out, in/out. Thursday, when his text appeared, her stomach leapt—*Text Message James*. For a moment Anna almost missed him. But it was a link to another article, a worse article, and two words: *READ THIS*.

Fourteen

Maggie was sitting in her office with Andrea Gardner—that childhood beach essay was, against the odds, turning into something interesting—when the phones began to ring. First her office phone, then her cell phone. "Go ahead and answer," Andrea said kindly, but Maggie brushed the calls away. She smiled at Andrea and posed the usual questions about her essay: "Why is this piece worth writing? What is it really trying to say?" Andrea nodded, diligently taking notes. The minute she left, Maggie shut the door and listened. With each message, her alarm rose another degree. The first had been left the day before, a reporter from the *Reed County Intelligencer*, asking to speak with her about a paper written by her former student. Then, fifteen minutes ago, Bill Wall telling her to contact him. Five minutes later, Anna saying, *Call me back as soon as you get this*, a thread of panic in her voice.

Maggie Googled *maggie daley nathan dugan*—noting the very improbability of their names together in the search bar, and the resulting spill of results. The most recent had been posted two hours earlier. It was from the local paper, the *Intelligencer*, the headline KILLER'S HOMEWORK RAISES RED FLAGS.

Just one month ago, 21-year-old Arlen Mackey, a senior at Central Maine

State University, was engaged to marry his childhood sweetheart, Doreen Howard, a 19-year-old hairstylist from Reed. The article went on to describe how someone—*an anonymous sender*—had mailed a package to this boy, Arlen, the fiancé of the shooting victim, earlier that week. The package contained an essay written by Nathan Dugan for a college composition class—*Professor Maggie Daley, the instructor, could not be reached for comment*—along with the article from last week's *Sentinel* and a brief sympathy note. The implication was clear: This was the essay from Luke Finch's viral Facebook post. *Mackey went on to speculate that one of his classmates might have sent the essay, perhaps Luke Finch himself.*

For Arlen Mackey, the outing of this four-year-old essay is proof that Nathan Dugan's violent tendencies had deep roots. "It shows the way his mind worked," Mackey continued. "It shows he was already planning. He was thinking about this even back then."

Patricia Brooks, a psychologist who studies the pathology of shooters, says it's not unusual for an inclination toward violence to emerge in written form. "There are almost always signs, if people are looking closely," Brooks says. "Sometimes they are quite obvious. Writing that glorifies violence is certainly one place they can emerge."

Read the full text of Nathan Dugan's essay below.

Maggie felt a tunnel of adrenaline engulf her, legs to scalp. Her eyes jumped to the bottom of the article and there it was: "The Hunting Trip." Not just the text but an actual scan of the physical paper, folds and all, that she had handed Robert a few days before. There was the drive to the woods, the litany of guns. Her handwritten comments in the margins, the noncommittal C+. She stared, disbelieving, at the screen. How had this copy ended up in this boy's hands? It couldn't have been Robert. After last week's argument in his office, they'd both been carefully apologetic. When they spoke on the phone, a day later, Robert said he'd reread it, and that although in his opinion the paper seemed *unhinged*—his word—his advice was to do nothing. Practically speaking, there was no point. She had planned to retrieve the paper when they met tonight after class. Had he inadvertently left it sitting somewhere in public? In that coffee shop he liked? Maggie tried his cell phone. Voicemail. Tried his office. She heard laughter in the hallway and was reminded of the pending appointments with her students, then dashed off an email canceling the rest of her office hours, and class later that afternoon, and was just trying Robert's phones again when there was a quick rap at the door. She held still, fearing the dean, but heard: "Maggie. It's me."

When he stepped inside, Robert looked ashen, slightly winded. His shirt collar was dark with sweat. He shut the door, tossed his briefcase on the floor, and dropped to a chair, the one usually reserved for students. "It was Suzanne," he said, then added, "My wife," in case there was any doubt.

Maggie held herself in place. Despite her panic, she remained acutely aware of the world outside: the students in the hallway, the Thursday taking place on the other side of her door. "You showed her," she said, managing to speak calmly.

"No." He shook his head. "No, of course not."

"How did this happen then?"

"She found it," he said. "In my briefcase. And made a copy—that's why I didn't know. Obviously I would have told you."

"But why—"

"When she saw it, she pieced it together. About us." He grimaced. "Apparently she'd had her suspicions for months."

"But—" Maggie's thoughts were careening in all directions. "You're separated. Living together but separated." She looked at him. "That's what you said."

"In my head, we were, I guess," he admitted. "More than in hers."

Maggie's first response was fury, but mostly at herself. *Living together but separated.* These words, like so many, were permeable, fickle, open to interpretation, able to be bought. And here she was thinking Robert had been doing the right and responsible thing, being sensitive to his wife's feelings. She had believed his story; she had wanted to believe it.

Yet on some level, hadn't she known? Maggie recalled sitting in his office just last week, the tender sound of Robert's voice on the phone. She had either been naive about the reality of the situation, or chosen to ignore it, which was almost surely worse.

"She just told me this morning," Robert said. Slumped in the chair, eyes on the floor, he reminded her of an irresponsible student. "She found the paper and when she saw that it was his, and saw your name, she somehow put two and two together—remember I told you she was having a hard time? After the victims? The girl, the hairdresser—she knew her. That's why she mailed it to her boyfriend."

He rested his elbows on his knees, and Maggie stared at his scalp, the rim of sweat around his hairline. "Fiancé, you mean."

"Right."

"Arlen Mackey," she added. "He's a student here, you know. A business major. A senior." She knew it didn't really matter, but for some reason it felt important that he have the details right.

Robert looked up at her. "I don't know what to say. I'm sorry. She just did this because she wanted to punish me."

"Please." Maggie let out a short laugh. "She wanted to punish *me*."

Robert dropped his hands, let them hang between his knees. He seemed to have lost some of his physical clarity, features gone blurry, indistinct. "Have you talked to anyone yet?" he asked.

"Like who?"

"Bill? The newspaper? In the article, it said they tried to reach you."

"They did but—"

"You ignored it again."

"No," she said tightly. "I didn't ignore it again. I didn't get the message. Not until just now. Today. I guess it doesn't occur to them, if you don't call right back, you didn't get it. That not everyone is attached to a phone twenty-four hours a day. That you should wait until you actually speak to someone before you assume they have nothing to say."

Robert gave her a deliberate look, but said nothing.

"Where is it?" she asked him.

"Where's what?"

"The paper. The original. You said she made a copy—"

"It's right here," he said, gesturing to his briefcase.

"I want it back," she said.

Maggie felt her jaw clenching as Robert reached for the briefcase, unzipped the pocket, and handed her the essay. It was still unfolded, one corner bent, crumpled slightly—she felt a spasm of protectiveness as she pressed it flat.

She opened her desk drawer and slid the essay inside, just as the office phone began to ring. She looked at the extension. Bill again. Last week, after the article in the *Sentinel*, Bill had been mostly sympathetic—he'd acknowledged that the story had gone too far—but he hadn't been pleased to learn that Maggie had ignored Julie Brody's attempts at contact. *Please pay attention to the students,* he'd said. She could hardly bear to face him now.

"That's Bill," she said, but made no move to answer. Robert didn't seem to expect her to. She shut the desk drawer, and they sat in silence until the ringing stopped. Then Robert said, "He'll want to know how it got out."

The apprehension on his face was undisguised, brow creased with worry, for it was easy enough to imagine where that conversation could lead. "I already told him I didn't have it," Maggie said. "I told him it was lost. Damaged, in a storm." A ridiculous story—she felt ashamed to recall it. "So to admit to him now—"

Robert nodded, as if confirming her assumptions. "It wouldn't be good," he said, and rubbed at a spot between his eyes. "Look," he said. "It could have been another student who still had a copy. Maybe it was this other kid, the Facebook kid. Or maybe it was in Dugan's house. Maybe it was the mother—"

"No one would believe it was the mother."

"Well," Robert said. "Regardless." He sat up straighter, and she could sense his energy returning. He swept one hand through his hair. "It's not your job to know. As far as you're concerned, your student wrote a paper four years ago. Maybe you should have acted on it, maybe not. That's a moot point. But to tell Bill you found it, and lied about it—don't jeopardize everything over this."

It was the word *lied* that jarred Maggie the most, although there was no denying it was the correct one. That was what she had done, what she would do again. For the alternative was impossible to imagine, the permanent damage to her reputation. She hated that she'd done it, but couldn't undo it: another lie, or the same lie, growing deeper and wider, like the rings of a tree.

From the hallway, there was a burst of noise—class being dismissed on a Thursday; for some, the unofficial weekend beginning—and seconds later, a knock at the door. Robert's eyes locked on hers, but she knew it wasn't Bill. The knock was too hesitant. A student, she thought, one who'd been in class and didn't know that office hours had been canceled. Without discussion, they both stayed quiet, listening to the choreography of sneakers shuffling, pack unzipping. A paper appeared like a receipt slid beneath the door. Maggie bent to retrieve it. "The Importance of a Ballfield" by Adam R. Gillis. A title page, even a middle initial. The fact that this neatly typed, correctly formatted paper was from Adam, of all people, made her feel like breaking into tears.

The sneakers retreated, melting into the commotion on the other side of the door. But when Maggie looked to Robert, his attention had gone elsewhere. "There's something else I haven't told you," he said. "About Suzanne."

It alarmed Maggie, how quietly he spoke. She braced herself, tried to detach herself from the moment, but was helplessly rooted in her own skin. "Okay," she said.

"It's the reason she's been kind of irrational lately," Robert said, then ran one hand roughly down his face. "She's been sick."

"Sick," Maggie repeated. "You mean the depression," she said, understanding as she said it that it must be something more.

"She's fine," Robert said, the way one preempts news of a car accident. "But she had cancer. Breast cancer."

"Breast cancer." A low sound, a buzzing, climbed into her ears. "When?"

"She's going to be fine," he said again. "It's in remission."

"When was she diagnosed?"

"The drugs, though. She hasn't been herself. She's been very emotional. Her attachment to this girl, for example—"

"Robert," Maggie interrupted. "When?"

He forced himself to look at her. His eyes were a sharp blue, the lashes stuck together in wet points. "March," he said.

"March." She stared. "So she had cancer when we—"

"She asked me not to tell anyone."

"Well, wasn't that noble of you," Maggie snapped. Her anger felt swift and sure, oddly light. She didn't bother pointing out the flaws with this code: that he was upholding his ethics, keeping his promise to his sick wife, even to the woman he was cheating on her with. "You should have told me," she said. "Then at least I could have known what I was doing. I could have made a decision—"

"She asked me not to tell anyone. I promised her I wouldn't tell anyone. She didn't want people knowing."

"And who would I have told? I didn't exist."

"Maggie," he said, and shook his head. "That isn't true."

"Now I'm not only a woman who was involved with a married man, I'm a woman who was involved with a married man whose wife has cancer," she said. Her voice shook with anger. "You turned me into something worse than I am."

Robert rested his head in both hands. He looked genuinely remorseful—whether because he'd stayed with his wife or cheated on her, Maggie couldn't say. "What I told you about our marriage," Robert said hoarsely. "All our problems, it was true. They were all true. But this is why I never felt that I could leave her," he said, and for a moment Maggie thought this had all been preamble to his telling her that now that his wife was cured, he was free. But what he said was "I just wanted you to know this wasn't like her," and there it was: the irrevocable shift.

Robert was pivoting toward his wife, protecting her, defending her. It was over between them, Maggie thought. Of course it would be.

On a Thursday evening, Tilghman Hall was nearly empty. Walking the corridors, Maggie glimpsed classrooms in endearing disarray, desks pushed in random configurations, whiteboards covered in scribbles, trash cans piled high with empty coffee cups and plastic water bottles. The air smelled of sweat and berry lip gloss. When she entered the administrative annex, everyone had left for the day except Holly. Maggie walked past her desk, gesturing toward Bill's office. Holly was scrolling through Facebook. "He knows you're coming," she said.

Bill was standing by the window. His chin was down, glasses hanging from the chain around his neck. She heard a tinny clinking sound, like a quickly dripping faucet, and realized he was making a cup of tea. "Please," he said. "Come in."

Maggie sat in the same chair she had last occupied six weeks ago. On that day, Bill had been shocked and disoriented, uncharacteristically unkempt. Now, as he returned to his desk and settled his cup on a coaster, his bearing was proper, sober, straight.

"When we talked before," he began, "you said you'd looked for Nathan Dugan's writing but couldn't find it."

The lack of preamble caught Maggie by surprise. "I did," she said. "I mean—yes, well, not that I couldn't find it. That I no longer had it."

"But obviously someone had a copy," he said.

"Yes." She shook her head, trying to suppress the rising tide of guilt. "I can't imagine who," she said. "I wish I could."

Bill was frowning. "And why was it sent to this young man? Arlen Mackey? He's a student here, you know," he added, as if this made it all the more incomprehensible.

"I know," Maggie said. "It's awful." An insufficient word—it was more than awful. This boy's life had collapsed at his feet.

"I find this greatly concerning," Bill said.

"It is," Maggie replied. "He's so young—"

"I meant the essay. Dugan's essay. It's very disturbing."

She had anticipated Bill's concern, but not this level of candor, of sureness. "I suppose it is," she said. "It is now, certainly—"

"I fail to see how, at *any* point, this essay wouldn't have raised alarm," Bill interrupted. "A student wrote about weapons, Maggie, in elaborate detail, and you ignored it."

"Well, no," she said. "I didn't ignore it. I guess, at the time, I just didn't find it that—disturbing."

"Well, then, that concerns me greatly too," Bill said.

Maggie was trying to regain her equilibrium. On the quad outside, students passed by, laughing, on their way to dinner. She was overcome with emotion—tenderness and terror—feelings so acute they left her paralyzed. "I understand it looks bad," she managed. "But please know I take this very seriously. I can assure you, contrary to what you're probably thinking, I'm actually quite good at recognizing students who need help."

Bill seemed not to have heard her. He was studying his tea. "We'll be instituting a set of new policies," he said.

Maggie blinked at him. "Policies?"

"From now on," he said, "if a student writes about any inflammatory subject, faculty must report it."

"Inflammatory subject," she repeated. "Such as?"

"Any material that alludes, directly or indirectly, to feelings of sadness, anxiety, anger, violence, hopelessness—"

"But that's every student, Bill. Every paper."

"That's the policy," Bill said.

Maggie's mind swam with half-formed objections. Such a policy would be imprecise, reductive, impossible to put into practice—and if a paper didn't check at least one of those boxes, could it possibly be worth writing?

"I am deeply sorry," she told him. "If I underreacted. With Nathan. Certainly any paper that mentions guns, or implies any sort of violent behavior—I'll be much more aware. But I don't see how we can possibly—if students know we're reporting every paper that hints at any kind of trouble, anything painful or personal, they'll stop opening up, stop caring—and I wouldn't blame them. That's not a classroom that's safe, Bill. It's sterilized. I can't teach that way."

But Bill appeared unmoved. He said only "We can't take any chances." Then he examined his hands, palms down on the desk. "I've always respected your dedication to your teaching, Maggie," he said, and she felt a peremptory dread. "But I think you might consider taking some time."

Maggie looked up, stunned. "What do you mean?"

"An administrative leave of absence," Bill said. "I won't require that you take one, but I'm urging you to consider it seriously. I've always liked you, Maggie, but we all need to get out from under this. For the school, and the students. And for you." Perhaps registering her shock, he added, "It wouldn't be permanent. But I believe it's the right thing to do." He paused. "Give it some thought," he said.

Maggie didn't need to give it some thought: The proposal was out of the question. To leave midsemester, even voluntarily, would be an indictment, an admission of something. Lack of fitness, lack of judgment. An embarrassment in front of her colleagues, her students—how could Bill possibly think it would be better for her to abandon them halfway through the term? There was no way she'd agree to it, but the very fact that Bill considered it a reasonable course of action left her shaken. As she exited the building, Maggie was reduced to a handful of objectives: get across campus and into her car without falling apart.

In the parking lot, she placed her bag on the seat and fumbled the key into the ignition. As she followed the eleven-mile road home—the stretch of campus, the mall, the road narrowing with trees—it all looked familiar and foreign at the same time. *Destabilized*: This was the word Theresa Massey had used to describe Anna when she first met her, and it seemed the right word now, the world having lost some essential reliability, its balance tipped, foundation gone. Even if Maggie had made an error in judgment—at this point, she was willing to admit this was true—a leave of absence was the sort of punishment leveled at a teacher who was untrustworthy, a liability—a Hank Dow, she thought. Some years ago, Hank had taken a leave after a student accused him of sexual harassment. He hadn't come back; it was not the sort of thing from which a reputation recovered. Unthinkable, that Bill would put her in such company. Maggie had devoted her life to her teaching, to her students, often at the expense of other things—it needed to have been worth it. It was incomprehensible that she would be accused of not doing enough.

The car jounced hard over the potholes, but she was too distracted to avoid them. She wished she could talk to Robert but of course she couldn't—not ever, but especially not now. She pictured him at home with his wife, who would be eyeing his phone. His wife from whom he was not separated, from whom he never had been, who had been sick while— A truck approached, flashing its headlights. Maggie hadn't dimmed her high beams. The truck passed with a hard shudder. The car swayed slightly, and she gripped the wheel. When she reached her mailbox, she didn't bother stopping but drove straight up the long rutted driveway. It was fully dark now, the trees soaked into the sky. Inside, the first thing she did was check the machine: a message from Anna, left hours earlier. Maggie had already tried her twice.

She considered food but couldn't imagine eating. Instead, she locked the doors, something she never felt the need to do, and retreated to the old computer upstairs. She watched as the screen woke, excruciatingly slowly. Wished she'd taken Anna's advice and gotten something faster, or upgraded her Wi-Fi—to be behind the times, she understood now, was to be punished. She bit her nails and watched and waited as the Internet connected, the little wheel spinning. She would read the article again, try to see what Bill was seeing, prepare to defend herself if needed. She watched as the article loaded one line at a time, like an unfolding paper doll. *Just one month ago, 21-year-old Arlen Mackey—* The screen froze. Then the page wobbled as the article was peppered with links to other things: the story in the *Sentinel,* an interview with Arlen Mackey, the headline TRIGGER WARNINGS: ANATOMY OF A TEENAGE SHOOTER.

Maggie's cursor hovered above the link. Unsteadily, she clicked, and watched the page start filling. *In some teenage males, the line between unusual behavior and potentially violent behavior can be murky, but there are often signs.* She waited as the screen froze, unfroze again. The little wheel was like a blueprint of her brain, a pirouette of her nerves. *Many times these young men have mental health disorders, such as chronic depression, which can cause them to isolate themselves.* Maggie raked swiftly through her memory, rifling through hundreds of students. Any number of them had seemed isolated, for any number of reasons—sadness, shyness, emptiness. Luke Finch, for that matter, had seemed isolated too. And yet. *These teens may also exhibit aggressive and antisocial behaviors, such as inappropriate outbursts or angry rants online.* She remembered the way Nathan had talked over his classmates, the way he'd reacted to Meredith Kenney. *In some cases these isolated individuals find a sense of belonging in online communities devoted to the glorification of high-profile shootings. This identification with antiheroes can stem from feelings of inadequacy or rejection and lead them to emulate these figures to gain attention and respect.* Her mind raced. She thought again about the swagger in Nathan's paper, about her mild, insufficient notes in the margins. About her attempts to minimize him, make the other students comfortable around him—could she have contributed to his feeling left out, depressed, unseen, the very feelings that eventually drove him to such a desperate act? Could she have fed his rage, his desire to leave a mark? *These shootings, however, are not impulsive. They are planned, months or sometimes years in advance. Almost always, intentionally or unintentionally, information is leaked.* Her eyes burned with tears. Was it actually possible that the essay Nathan submitted for her class had been a part of his long-term planning, his compendium of research, just waiting for a moment to light the match? That the particular strangeness that was Nathan Dugan had, in fact, been a laundry list of distinct red flags? *You're not the only one who knew him,* Robert had once assured her, but maybe the truth was that she was the one who'd gotten the most telling glimpse, been shown the window no one else had seen, and not only had she not helped the situation, she had inflamed it.

When her phone rang, she jumped at it. "Anna?"

"Mom?" she said. "You've seen this, right?"

Anna's voice sounded small. "I have," Maggie told her, swallowing her tears.

"You're not the one who sent it, are you?"

"No. No, of course not."

"Then who did?"

Maggie blinked at the screen. She didn't want to lie to Anna, but saw no other choice. "I'm not quite sure."

To her surprise, Anna replied, "But it was the one you found that day, right? In the barn?"

Maggie's mind traveled back to that shocked morning, the day after the shooting—the barn filled with dusty boxes and reams of papers, the stifling heat—then the memory realigned, expanded and reassembled itself: Anna had been there.

"Yes," she admitted. "Yes, it was."

"You said it was about his father," Anna said. "But you said it was about a day trip. You didn't say it was all about guns."

Maggie didn't recall saying any of this, but trusted that Anna would remember. Surely her own instinct then, as always, had been to downplay the situation, redirect the conversation. "I'm sure I just didn't want you worrying," Maggie said.

Anna made a scornful sound, but she stayed on the phone. "Then how did it get out?" she said. "Did someone come in our barn? Did someone steal it?"

"I doubt that." Maggie forced a light laugh. "There's probably no use speculating. It could be anything."

"Maybe it was one of your students," Anna pressed. "Maybe it was that guy on Facebook—"

"We may never know," Maggie said. "Try not to worry," she repeated, needing to stanch this train of thought. For there was a shake in

Anna's voice—it was slight, but there—and Maggie blurted, "Are you eating?"

"Mom," Anna said. "Oh my God."

Helplessly, Maggie closed her eyes.

"I'm eating, yes, I'm eating. Constantly, in fact." Anna paused. "Alexis just came in. I better go. I'll talk to you later."

"Tomorrow," Maggie said quickly. "Call me tomorrow." A click, and she was gone. Maggie returned the phone to the cradle. She pressed her wrists to her temples, pictured her daughter in her dorm room four hours away. Reminded herself that it was understandable, tonight, that Anna might sound rattled—how could she not? Still, she would call Tom, ask him to go check on her. Drive down to Boston and take her to lunch. It would be good for him to see Anna, good for her to be seen. A comfort, right now, to hear Tom's voice. But it was getting late—she would call him in the morning. Maggie faced the jumble of words crowding the screen. The original article was now cluttered with videos, ads, and sidebars, a newly trending headline, the link pulsing like a live wire: HOW CAN YOU HELP YOUR TROUBLED TEEN?

Fifteen

A week ago, when the *Sentinel* came out, Luke had read the article once, then immediately tried to erase it from his mind. But certain details still clung to him like burrs. Certain words. *Humbly. Incredible sensitivity.* He hated his high school picture, that stupid sweater, side by side with Nathan's picture. He felt guilty about his teacher. In the article, Julie Brody had made it seem like Luke thought Maggie had been irresponsible. *Asked if he thought his professor had been negligent, Luke admitted, "Probably, yes"*—had she even asked him this? If she had, Luke didn't remember it, but he knew he never would have answered so confidently. Never would have said *Probably, yes*. Never would have used the word *yes*, period. Yet somehow, at the end of the article, that line came out sounding like the entire point.

He tried to undo it, to make amends, returning to Facebook and posting a new status update. *The reason I wrote about Nathan Dugan in the first place is because one time he asked me to hang out with him and I said no and I felt bad about it.*

He couldn't bring himself to admit the rest—that if only he'd been nicer, Nathan might not have felt so desperate and lonely and the people he killed might still be alive.

Still, when the new post appeared on-screen, he waited for some kind of swift karmic reprimand, but this one generated only a few responses, smiley faces and likes. *Good that you didn't hang out with someone like that,* wrote Aunt Millie, and Katie Sutton chimed in: *CLEARLY you did the right thing!*

The messages from the reporter arrived three days later, and Luke was too freaked out to reply. It didn't matter. Four days after that, when the article appeared—a different newspaper, a real newspaper—there he was. Someone had mailed Nathan's essay, the original copy, to Arlen Mackey. *Mackey went on to speculate that one of his classmates might have sent the essay, perhaps Luke Finch himself.* Luke stared at the line, stunned. Would people actually think he'd done this? Kept Nathan's paper all these years? He considered contacting the reporter and asking him to print a follow-up, to clarify that Luke hadn't sent it, had nothing to do with it—but that, he had learned, could backfire too. You could say one thing, mean one thing, and they could make it sound like something completely different.

With the release of Nathan's essay, Luke's original Facebook post saw a renewed surge of activity.

You were right about that guy's paper!

"really weird"—an understatement...

job well done ☺ ☺ ☺

The praise felt upsetting, unearned. Luke wanted to correct them but was now afraid to write anything. He'd already tried explaining himself and gotten only a dribble of comments; it was like everything was backward, everyone reacting to the wrong things.

He received an email from one of his old ES professors. From April Peale, who was now working for some online entertainment magazine in New York. *Hey there,* she said. *I hear you're an Internet celebrity now?!*

Even his dad had heard about it. "Looks like you were onto something with that teacher," he said—ironically, for this, his father seemed to respect him. His father had always had a clear sense of yes and no, right and wrong, weird and not weird. It seemed that Luke had fallen, for once, on the right side of things.

When a friend request popped up from a Meredith Johnson, he almost ignored it until he glanced at the message: *Hi Luke! Remember me?*

It took him a minute. Johnson—that was why she'd been so hard to find.

Hey Meredith! he wrote back. The sight of her new last name was disappointing, but he was still happy to have found her. *Of course!*

When he asked how she was, Meredith told him that the wedding had been last summer, in her hometown near Boston, right after graduation. She worked as an assistant in a doctor's office. Her husband, Jason, was a structural engineer. Then she asked what Luke had been up to and he couldn't bring himself to admit the most basic facts about himself: that he'd been living at home, working at Dunkin' Donuts. Instead he wrote, *Moving to Portland soon.* She replied, *Cool! Glad to hear you're doing so well!*, and just like that, it was over. Luke reread the exchange twice, but its power ebbed each time, the magic of her name on his screen fading away.

The next morning, when Luke woke up, his stomach was hurting. He texted Heather from Dunkin' and asked her to cover his shift. *No prob— feel better!!* He heard his dad leave for work, then spent the day in his room. He returned to the Facebook post, wading through new comments about Nathan's paper. The guns were the main thing people were reacting to and, given what had happened, Luke supposed that made sense. The surprising thing was, the paper itself wasn't actually as bad as he'd remembered. It was about hunting, but that didn't mean anything. Luke hunted. So did his dad, his brother. So did basically everyone he knew. To him, the paper's peculiarity was more about the way that it was written. Reading it was sort of like watching a game of Grand Theft Auto, violent and impersonal at the same time. He recognized this feeling, or something like it—mindless, noisy, numbing—from spending hours online in his room.

Now, though, these people were saying Nathan was a robot, a sociopath—this upset Luke more than he understood. When the dogs scratched at his door, he took them outside, but instead of going on a proper walk, he just let them roam around the yard. His stomach was pulsing. Overhead, the sky looked like a thick gray pancake with a single stripe of watery blue at the horizon. As if the clouds were a skin that could be peeled back to expose a whole different sky. As he stood there, Luke was seized with the knowledge that he needed to get out—out of the house, out of Paxton—then he rounded up the dogs and went back inside. "What are you doing home?" his brother muttered. Luke didn't answer. Back to his room, back on the computer. He leaned forward, cushioning his stomach with his knees. Did a quick search of Craigslist, cheap trucks/cars within fifty miles. A page of ads appeared: the same truck over and over, a rusty Ford Bronco or Dodge Ram parked on a melting patch of snow. Then he returned again to Instagram, Snapchat, Facebook. There was Meredith Kenney, at happy hour with her co-workers. Five smiling faces pressed together. A photo of the margaritas, the heaping pile of nachos. *Grateful for good friends!* After hoping so much to connect with her, he wished he'd never found her. Her office, her husband, her cheesy sayings. She wasn't how he'd remembered her. It was just as possible he'd been wrong about Nathan. *There are almost always signs, if people are looking closely*, the psychologist in the article had said—the line haunted him. People, in this case, being him.

Over the next few days, Luke went into work but his stomach hurt so much he clocked out early and biked home. He roamed the Facebook post, not because he wanted to, but because he had nowhere else to go.

Kaitlyn Sutton: *once I read the paper it totally came back to me*

Hannah Chaffee: *it feels so angry . . .*

Kevin McAllister: *I still say there were zombies involved*

Kaitlyn Sutton: *it's scarier than zombies imo!!!*

Luke let the comments wash over him without responding.

Meredith Johnson: *to be honest guys I don't even remember it*

Kaitlyn Sutton: *prob b/c you weren't in his group??*

Hannah Chaffee: *or because you were grieving sweetie*

Hannah Chaffee: *it was right after your brother . . .*

Meredith Johnson: *thats true*

Kaitlyn Sutton: *omg mer do you remember when you read this incredibly moving thing in class and he was so amazingly rude to you??*

Meredith Johnson: *was he? no!!*

Kevin McAllister: *jesus that's RIGHT*

Hannah Chaffee: *oh I remember that too . . .*

Luke remembered Meredith reading, and it being moving. But the rest of it, the part about Nathan, he had barely retained. Meredith had been in shock—what was his excuse? How had he become the person whose memories had triggered this entire conversation? It was clear he shouldn't be trusted. There might be something wrong with his brain.

Kaitlyn Sutton: *I remember even maggie was pissed off at him*

Hannah Chaffee: *I felt bad for her honestly*

Meredith Johnson: *me too!*

Hannah Chaffee: *he created such negative energy*

Kaitlyn Sutton: *but don't you think that's why she should have seen how messed up he was???*

Mindy Reddy: *fyi I went to high school with her daughter anna and she was pretty messed up too!*

Luke stiffened, staring at the screen.

Kaitlyn Sutton: *really? messed up how?*

Mindy Reddy: *eating disorder*

Mindy Reddy: *pretty serious I think*

Kaitlyn Sutton: *yikes*

Mindy Reddy: *yeah it was really sad to watch*

Kaitlyn Sutton: *def sad*

Meredith Johnson: *now I feel bad for the daughter* ☹ ☹ ☹

Luke's stomach was an alert dot of pain. His first thought was: This was his fault. He had done this. Here were the facts, incredible but true: He had written a stupid post on Facebook and his professor had been trashed because of it, and now it was spreading to her daughter while Luke hid like a coward, doubled over in his room. He hadn't even realized Professor Daley was a mother. And her daughter—she didn't deserve this. It wasn't fair, wasn't right. And he was to blame. With one numb click, he deleted the thread. Blinked at the screen. He clicked again and deleted the entire post—1044 comments, gone. It was freeing, but not enough. He typed *anna daley* into the Facebook search bar and swept through the results but couldn't find her. There were plenty of Anna Daleys, but none who was the right age and hometown. There was an Anna Daley-Briggs, though. She was from Stafford, the town right next to campus. Before he could talk himself out of it, Luke opened the message box and stared at the cursor, palms damp, wondering if he had the courage to write what he needed to say.

Sixteen

Worst-case scenario: Student writes troubling essay, teacher misses it, student later kills four people.

On a Saturday morning in October my dad and me decided to go hunting. As soon as Anna started reading, she didn't want to keep going but couldn't stop. She sat on the edge of her bed, twisting her lip, hunched over her phone. She pictured Nathan Dugan typing at a desk next to a closet full of guns. Pictured Laura Mack in the Gap dressing room, face in mirror, sounds of gunshots, unable to breathe.

When Alexis came home, she slung her backpack on the floor and announced: "Lunch! Don't tell me you're not hungry, roomie." Then she looked at her another beat, and Anna worried she had seen the article, heard about it, could read it across her face. Alexis frowned. "And stop doing that thing with your lip," she said.

Worst-case scenario: Student writes troubling essay, teacher misses it, student later kills four people, troubling essay is sent to local paper which reprints essay in full.

—

Text Message James: *So? Did you read???*

In the dining hall Anna ate an apple and drank a Diet Coke and didn't mention the article to Alexis. Because if she knew, they couldn't not talk about it, and she didn't want to talk about it. Didn't want Alexis spreading the gossip to her hallmates who might start whispering about her mother or looking at her strangely. Anna needed to keep the two things separate: school life, real life. Let the two intersect, and no good could come of it.

Text Message James: *The paper is pretty incriminating*

Text Message James: *Now we know why she didn't want you seeing it*

Anna waited to call her mother until Alexis was in the shower. "Don't worry about any of this," her mother said, hilariously.

Text Message James: *Did you talk to her? What did she say??*

Anna didn't respond. She knew it would only encourage him. Then Alexis burst in, swathed in a giant towel, two beers in each hand. Not low-calorie, but who cared. Anna chugged three. She hadn't eaten since lunch. She was buzzed before they left the room. She was wearing her favorite of Alexis's shirts, purple satin with spaghetti straps. As they were walking across the quad, bare-armed, goose-pimpled, elbows linked, her phone rang. Alexis glanced at the screen. "Seriously," she said. "Is that James again? He's starting to freak me out."

The next day Anna sat through poetry, half paying attention, then spent the rest of the afternoon in the library, on the quiet floor, buried in her homework and hiding from her phone. It was only once she left that she checked the screen: sixteen new text messages, splash of light in the dusk.

–

Text Message James: *So I guess you're just not responding?*

Text Message James: *You can't just keep pretending unpleasant things don't exist anna*

Text Message James: *You have to admit this paper is fucked up*

Text Message James: *It proves this guy was unstable and your mother knew it*

When Anna stepped into her room, Alexis took one look at her and said: "Oh God. What now?" Anna opened her mouth but was stopped by the expression on her roommate's face: eyebrows arched, stiff and wary. Anna knew this face. It was expecting her to be in crisis, braced for it, and weary of it. Alexis crossed the room, removed the phone from Anna's hand, and studied it for less than a minute. "You're blocking him," she said.

For the rest of the night, Anna didn't hear from him. Like magic. He was gone. She and Alexis split a pizza and Violet brought over rum-and-Cokes and by the time they got to the campuswide, Anna was wasted enough to hook up with a guy called Smitty who stuck his tongue down her throat. Alexis chuckled at the story before they went to bed, munching on a Pop-Tart, but mused: "Be careful." Her voice floated from the bunk above. "You don't want to seem like a slut."

The next morning, Anna woke early, with a roaming sense of panic. It took a moment for it to sharpen into focus: the essay, her mother. James. She checked her phone but the only new text message was from her dad. *Hey, how about we do lunch soon?* Anna stared at the bottom of Alexis's mattress, moving slightly as she breathed. She felt bloated, disgusting. Her head was a brick. Her face was huge. She cast her eyes around the room—the empty bottles and cans, the pizza box—then got up and dug her bathing suit from the dresser and slipped out of the room. Outside, she followed the path through the woods from the quad to the fitness center. The morning was cloudy. Her steps were almost silent, the ground padded with pine needles and purple leaves. The center was deserted at that hour, especially on a weekend. The locker room empty, the air thick with the sharp smell of sweat and chlorine. She inhaled deeply, and her heart clutched, flooded with the memory of swimming—to disappear underwater and forget yourself, trace the black lines on the pool floor until your eyes hurt. She took off her sweats and stepped on the scale in just her bathing suit. It was the kind they had at doctor's offices, with the little sliding weights on top. The scale stood next to a long mirror, a thin mirror (smart, Anna thought, for a locker room full of girls). She nudged the weights until they were lined up evenly. Her weight: 152. Her image in the mirror: repulsive. Even in a thin mirror, especially in a thin mirror. The soft slope of her lower back, bulge under her arm, rim of fat wherever the elastic of her suit hit skin—she'd had no idea it had gotten this bad. She'd been trying so hard to be normal, be happy. *Happiness is fattening*: It was another of Alexis's truisms, cast off airily as ash from a cigarette as she ironed her hair or stuffed food in her mouth—which she could afford to do, because even happy and in love Alexis would never gain a pound.

Her head was bleating in her ears. *Stop it, Anna. Stop.* She closed her eyes then opened them and attempted to smile at herself, but it made the flesh bunch up around her cheeks. Which made sense—the drinking, the pizza, the pasta. Of course she was fat. Since coming to college, people wouldn't stop making her fucking eat.

Seventeen

If anyone had asked, she would have told them there was no hunting trip. There was no father. The paper was a made-up story. That was the truth.

No one did, even after all the questions they *did* ask her. The reporters, the police, the people gathered outside her house. That first afternoon, when she got home, the street was filled with them. She'd been at work when the news broke—a shooting at the Millview Mall. One of the other cashiers saw it on her phone. Then the police appeared, looking for her; they'd been to her house, and a neighbor had told them where she worked. When they said Nathan's name—*we believe that he*—she felt a thick, sickening dread. Silently, she rode with them in the police car. They tried talking to her but she couldn't hear them. Couldn't speak. She identified the body—a photo of his arm, an old scar. *Do you want to go back home?* they asked. *Or somewhere else?* Where else would she go? They took her back to her car in the Big Lots parking lot. *Don't leave town*, they said. Twenty minutes later, when she pulled into her driveway, she kept her head down, moved as quickly as she could through the crowd of reporters and up to the porch. *Did you know that he was violent? Why do you think he did it?* She didn't have an answer. She turned to the microphones, finally, said something—

she couldn't remember what. Inside the house, the police were turning everything inside out, but the disruption was almost a relief. It kept the strangers from coming right up to her door.

Ping: an email alert. For the past two months, the sound had gone off on her computer in the sewing room each time her son's name appeared online. She'd get an email letting her know what was said about him and where. He must have set it up that awful morning, before he left the house. Marielle had wondered, again and again, why he'd done that. She believed, she needed to, that her son was trying to look out for her, make sure she wasn't in the dark. Those first foggy days and hours, it was all headlines about what he'd done to those people. To himself. A video he'd put online. Interviews with his boss from the Walmart, the people from the mall. An interview with herself, standing on her own front porch. *He's a good boy*, was what she'd said.

Was he at home when you left for work this morning?

There were two cops in her house, and two FBI, from a special task force in Boston. All men, of course.

Yes, he was home, she told them. The words felt mealy in her mouth. That morning, she'd left for work, ten thirty, like every Friday. She'd seen the stripe of light beneath his door.

What was his demeanor? How was he acting?

No different. Nothing out of the ordinary. The night before, he'd seemed actually kind of happy, more talkative than usual, but she didn't mention this.

Did he say anything to you before you left?

She wished she could tell them different. But the truth was that he hadn't. She'd tapped on his bedroom door, told him she was leaving. "Okay," he mumbled from inside. She never even saw his face. She couldn't tell them how much this hurt, later, that knowing what he was about to do, knowing he was leaving her, after twenty-two years together, he hadn't said something more.

★ ★ ★

They searched his room, the entire house. Evidence, they called it. A crime scene. They marked yellow tape around her porch. She stood in the living room as his things were walked out. His computer, his phone, the guns.

Were you aware that he was in possession of the firearms, Mrs. Dugan?

She had known he had a few, but not nearly so many. When she told them no, they gave each other a look they thought she couldn't see.

Did you know he was fired from his job last week?

Yes, she knew. She wasn't that clueless. He'd come home early that night, and angry, saying he was being unfairly blamed. *He said it wasn't his fault*, she told them. *He was in trouble for something he didn't do.*

There were things they didn't take: his old skateboard. His fish tank with its dirty filter. In his top drawer, an index card with a single sentence on it. She'd seen it there once, doing laundry, and been surprised, pleased, that her son, who had struggled, still believed that things would get better. *Greatness comes to those who wait.*

Did Nathan have any contact with his father?

At that one she almost had to laugh. *And good luck finding him*, she said. But they did, right away. Ping: There he was. He lived in Florida. He had a girlfriend; the girlfriend had a little son. Marielle wondered if the boy was his. He said he hadn't been in touch with Nathan in twenty years, and instead of making him sound like a deadbeat, the news made him sound like a hero. How she longed to set the record straight.

Ping. You'd think she would get numb to it, but each time felt like when you bang your funny bone. Ping. It went off faintly, from the sewing room, like he was in there playing video games. For every article, there were opinions from strangers. Everybody had their theory about him. That he hated girls because he never had a girlfriend, hated authority figures because his dad had left him, idolized the military because his dad was in the army before he was born. That he was trying to impress his father, resented his mother, had spent his life being ignored. But Marielle hadn't ignored him. She had devoted her life to him, moved to be with him, but for this, too, people seemed to think she was a horrible mother. That she was enabling him, or in denial. There was that interview with that old neighbor of theirs from New Hampshire, the one who used to complain about Nathan's dog barking too early, too late; she'd always had it out for them. Marielle remembered when they put Sergeant to sleep last spring. It was Nathan who sat stroking his head, asking how they did it, what they were giving him and how it worked. A drug to stop the heart: The body just shuts down.

There were things she couldn't say: that this was a boy whose father had just up and left. A father who said he wasn't cut out to have a family, that she was too smothering. Ever since then, it had been just the two of them, her and her boy. She used to bring men around sometimes, but saw how attached he would get, how crushed when they stopped coming. The last one had actually said Nathan was part of the reason— *there's something wrong with that kid*. She'd burned with rage. Maybe that was because he hadn't had an easy life. Maybe it was because of men like him. So she stopped seeing anybody, decided she could play both parts.

That first night, a rock came through her window. The crash woke her and then there were a few slow minutes, like clawing her way up out of dark water, almost peaceful, before it all came back.

There were other things: that one boy, the one with the birthmark, he hung out with freshman year of high school. They mostly played video games and BB guns, marching around the neighborhood. They went out hunting sometimes, with the other boy's father. Once Nathan had come home excited, blood on his cheeks. He didn't wash it for two days. Soon after, this boy stopped coming over. Marielle never knew why—

when she saw his mother at the supermarket, she could have stabbed her with her eyes.

That Saturday morning, the police were back on her porch. They asked about the broken glass but didn't seem to truly care. Then they showed her the video: Nathan sitting in front of the computer in his bedroom, in front of the blue curtains she had made when he was little. He was holding a gun. It had been posted online at ten fifteen yesterday morning.

Ten fifteen—it might have been the very second she was knocking on his door.

She'd taken one of her pills that morning—they made her numb, tired—but still, as she watched, a pain began to grow.

Nathan was explaining what he was about to do: the layout of the mall, the timing. The exits, random targets. The people who didn't respect him. After a while, she stopped hearing it.

Greatness comes to those who wait.

The video had been taken off the Internet, the police said, because leaving it there was like publicizing it, making them famous. *And that's what they want.*

They—she understood, through the shock and the pain, she had no right to him anymore. He was no longer hers. He belonged to the world.

How did this kind of anger find its way into her son?

How could it get that bad, if he started out good?

If he'd always been loved?

She had nowhere to turn, no one to ask.

Ping. She'd thought, at first, he'd set it up to protect her, help her, but now it was starting to feel like a torment. Lately it was all about this article in the college newspaper, this boy from his English class. The boy had thought Nathan was strange—disturbing. All the kids did. But Marielle had always known kids like these. When Nathan was nine and ten, she'd sit on the bench at the park and watch the boys skateboarding—how maybe at first they'd talk to him, then start giving each other looks, and Marielle would stare at them, hoping for once he'd be folded into the group instead of shut out. She could remember it still: the sharpness of hope. The hate she felt when they walked away. Sometimes they shoved him, whispering and laughing, making sure the other kids didn't play with him either. Junior high, he came home with his eye bruised—*nothing*, he said, and slapped her hand away. The kids from this English class were more of the same. They'd ignored him, and so had the teacher. She was the same one who had showed up at the house that day. A professor, she'd said. She lived in one of the nice houses up the road. Marielle didn't remember all of it, but she remembered this. She'd said that Nathan had problems, that she should have done something for him, and this article said the same. Marielle had known that she was only apologizing to make herself feel better. No wonder Nathan had hated college so much, being around people like that.

Why did you decide to relocate with him when he went away to college?

Was this so hard to understand? She wanted to be near him. He was all she had.

She heard twice from her sister down in Exeter, once from one of the other cashiers, but that was it. Her boss called and said her working there was making customers upset. She didn't have a funeral for him. She was afraid no one would come to it, or only reporters would, or protesters. She couldn't bury him because they didn't want him polluting the cemetery. His ashes were on her mantel, in her mother's vase.

There had been times, lately, when she felt like she didn't know him. Since starting college, he'd changed. He'd stopped smiling. He had bad acne; she got him medicine, but he said he didn't want it. Once it scarred, he seemed to like how it looked. He started squeezing those stress balls with the smiley faces—he'd order them from Amazon by the box. Sometimes they'd burst and the beads would dribble into the floorboards, like the BB pellets she used to find back in New Hampshire, in the grass, the cracks in the wood. He was constantly on the computer. Sometimes she tried to get him to come take a walk like they used to, but it was like he didn't even hear her, like something had swallowed him up. His grades were dropping. She tried to talk to him about it once but he got angry at her. He'd always been skinny, but all of a sudden got heavier. Whenever he asked for money, she gave him what she could, but finally told him he needed to get a job. He was angry about that too. He started at the Walmart. He started talking about enlisting. Last year he failed some classes and was put on academic probation; she'd already paid for the extra semester. She saw him sitting at his computer once, smile on his face and mouth half open, as if he was deep in conversation, and wondered who he was talking to.

When the police told her about the victims—their names and faces—it was a hammer to her heart.

That her boy could have hurt these people. Killed these people. If she took a step toward it, it disappeared.

The body just shuts down.

Ping. Ping. Ping. Ping. She would have liked to turn it off but couldn't. It would have felt like she was rejecting him, giving up on him. But she only checked now on days when it went off like crazy, like today. KILLER'S HOMEWORK RAISES RED FLAGS. This one was about a homework assignment, a paper he wrote for an English class. When she saw the type, square and green, she recognized his old computer. The same one he'd used in high school, the one she used now. A few years ago she'd helped him buy a new one, a good one, the one the police took. *On a Saturday morning in October my dad and me—*

★ ★ ★

What she couldn't say was that she hadn't lost just this boy, she'd lost all the other boys he'd been. The boy who had always loved dogs; she guessed they were easier than people. The one who chose his own dog from the pound because of that one ragged ear, who named him Sergeant to make him tougher. The one who loved to play checkers. Who used to go on walks with her after dinner, scraping long sticks behind him on the street. But no one wanted to hear about those other boys; this last boy had erased them so thoroughly it was like they'd never existed. She was angry at him for taking them away. For making it so she couldn't grieve for him. She wasn't allowed to, not when he had taken other people's children. A mother who lost her child—it was the very worst thing. You had to be a member of an exclusive club, for the world to have no sympathy for you at all.

The paper was written for that class. For that English teacher. *My dad was a corporal in the US Army. It was a ritual we had. My mother packed our lunches and said for us to be careful. My dad said women always worry too much.* As she read it, she felt furious. She felt slighted, left out. But what bothered her most was that he'd idolized his father, pretended they were close to each other, put him front and center. That this was what the world would read and think was true.

A few reporters showed up again. She closed her curtains, floated in the shadows. She was running low on pills but was too ashamed to go refill them, so she'd started cutting them in half to make them last. Time passed. She remembered a time the power went out, a lightning storm, and he'd held Sergeant's head in his lap until it was over. The pinging, she heard it constantly now, in her head, or from behind the closed door. She closed her eyes and drifted in and out of sleep and imagined he was in there, her younger sweeter boy, the one she knew.

★ ★ ★

When she woke one day in the darkness of the living room, there was a car pulling up outside. She heard the bang of a door and sat up straight. Peeling back the curtain, she squinted out the broken pane. The car was sitting at the end of her driveway, someone walking across her lawn. She was ready to ignore them, shout out if she had to. But as her eyes focused, her heart seized—it was a boy. A young boy, skinny, hands in pockets. As he climbed up the stairs, he disappeared from view, and the house shook a little as he stepped onto the porch and knocked on the door. She opened it only partway, left the chain on. But the boy was smiling. When he started talking, she heard only part of what he said. *How have you been doing, Mrs. Dugan?* And: *I'm really sorry about what's been happening.* And: *I want to hear about Nathan.* This boy was looking at her with no anger, she thought, no blame. Just sweetness. A good boy.

Part Three

Eighteen

It was Maggie's class who showed her the video. Later, this would strike her as appropriate—even somehow poignant—that her last act as a teacher at Central Maine State should be in her classroom, surrounded by students, watching her fate play out.

But in the moment, when she arrived in the room and found them all gathered around a single laptop, her first instinct was a gratified rush—look at the shared camaraderie, the class finally getting on track. Then she registered the uncertain looks on their faces. She recognized the woman on the screen.

Marielle Dugan was sitting in what Maggie knew to be her living room. Behind her stood the mantel with the framed picture, the gold vase. Her face was bare, lined deeply. Faded blond hair, now dark at the roots. There was still a vagueness in her eyes, but her brows were arched.

So what did you think of that paper? the reporter asked. A male voice, offscreen.

Marielle shook her head slowly. *What did I think?* She paused, moving her jaw, as if summoning the words. *He made the whole thing up. He never went out with him. He hasn't seen his father in twenty years.* A small note of triumph in her voice. *You can check. That's a fact*, she said. *And they act like I'm the one who's a bad parent. They think something's funny about me moving here. But I just wanted to be close to him. I loved my son.* Her face sagged then, as if pried abruptly open. A moment passed.

The reporter asked: *And what's your impression of his teacher? Professor Daley?*

Marielle touched a shaky pinkie finger to the corner of each eye. *The teacher? She showed up here too.*

Did she.

Another nod, more vigorous. *She came here telling me she was sorry for messing up with Nathan. She said she could have done something for him. She could have saved him—she has a kid too, she said.*

The reporter paused. *Did it surprise you, that another mother wouldn't see how important it was to help Nathan? A teenager who clearly needed her help?*

Then Marielle's eyes grew watery, and she touched her chin with trembling fingers. *I told you this wasn't all my fault.*

In her classroom, listening with her students, Maggie stopped absorbing the words Marielle was saying. She registered only the tones: indignant, proud, pained. Vaguely, she heard, "Maggie, are you okay?" It was Kara, looking at her with concern. The entire class was turned toward her, but this time she couldn't attempt to conceal her despair. She thanked them, for some reason, then she let them go.

Shooter's Mother Speaks Out. This was the title of the video that had appeared on YouTube. At home, Maggie watched and rewatched it until the shock dulled and the panic set in and it struck her fully, stark as a précis: what she had done, and how foolish it had been. She didn't reply to the text from Robert, the call from Bill; since their conversation the week before, she had more or less avoided him. Now she knew she had to face him, but first she needed to evaluate the interview on her own. She parsed it line by line. The screen froze, unfroze. *She came here telling me she was sorry for messing up with him*—surely this was not what Maggie had said. She'd walked onto Marielle Dugan's porch to express her condolences. Maybe, in her numb state, Marielle had misunderstood her. Maybe she was twisting her words deliberately—she herself had been scrutinized and criticized, perhaps unfairly. Or maybe Maggie's own judgment was so compromised that she couldn't see it clearly. She had been wrong already, in ways she never could have imagined. Maybe this wasn't what she had said, but was in fact what she had meant.

What troubled her more, though, was Marielle's assertion that Nathan's essay had been a fabrication. *He never hunted with his father.* It was spoken with such matter-of-factness that Maggie felt certain she was telling the truth. And in fact, it was not uncommon for students to embellish their personal experiences, but Nathan was so literal that the possibility had never occurred to her. Now, though, she wondered what might have been lurking beneath those particular fictions, that display of bravado in the woods—being abandoned by his father, feeling powerless, ignored, forgotten. She'd always prided herself on her ability to read between the lines. A good teacher: She had poured herself into it, believed it completely. But maybe she'd never been that good. *Obviously this teacher knew there was a problem and did nothing*, said the comments that swarmed the screen. *She should be fired, end of story. She's a liability.* Maggie didn't resist them, accepted them as truth. For if she'd misread Nathan's paper, surely there had been other papers—seemingly autobiographical ones that had been invented, true ones hinting at trouble she had misread, overlooked. *Did it surprise you, that another mother wouldn't see how important it was to help Nathan? A teenager who clearly needed her help?* Yet that same ignorance had translated to her life with her family. Her troubled daughter, her unhappy husband—what else had she missed?

On Friday, she got in her car, drove to campus, and walked to Tilghman. She passed by a few colleagues and was certain she saw judgment on their faces but tried to maintain a neutral smile, let the rightness of her decision tide her along. She needed to leave with her dignity intact. She concentrated on putting one foot in front of the other, following the path of dusty tiles as she made her way to the administrative annex, past Bill's assistant and toward his open office.

"With a student," Holly told her, and Maggie stopped outside his door. "I'll wait."

From inside, Maggie heard fragments of Bill's conversation. London, Dublin, Oxford. She recognized the voice of the student: Lisa Grenier. She'd been in Maggie's comp class two years earlier. Maggie loved her. Not a polished writer, but a serious worker. The first in her family to go to college, she'd approached the class with the urgency of someone who took nothing for granted. "Maggie!" she said when she emerged.

Despite everything, Maggie smiled. "Lisa. How are you?"

"Just talking about studying abroad." She pointed to Bill. "He thinks England or Ireland. For literature. I'm a little nervous but I think I want to do it."

"You're the perfect candidate," Maggie told her, and she was. "Let me know where you end up going," she said, and Lisa promised that she would. As she walked off, enormous backpack hitched to shoulders, Bill nodded toward his office and Maggie followed him inside and shut the door.

"I'm sorry I haven't returned your calls," she said, still standing. "But I've been thinking that you were right. That I should take time off."

Bill looked surprised for only an instant before relief crossed his face: that he wouldn't have to raise the subject again, wouldn't have to press for it. "Please," he said, and gestured to a chair.

Maggie sat, and instead of making his way around his desk, Bill pulled up a chair beside her. He crossed one leg over the other, studying his knees. "I'm assuming," he said, "that means you indeed paid a visit to Mrs. Dugan."

"I did," Maggie said. She was determined to remain calm, despite the quiver in her voice. "It wasn't something I planned on doing. It was an impulse. I passed by her house accidentally, but, yes—I did." She paused. "It was poor judgment."

"It doesn't seem like you," Bill allowed.

"It wasn't," she said. "It was right after our meeting, so I had a lot on my mind—I suppose I felt somewhat responsible."

Bill didn't try to persuade her differently. "You've been teaching a long time" was what he said. Then he sighed, threading his hands on his knee. He went on to explain the terms for the rest of the semester: an administrative leave with pay. He would take care of identifying a replacement, contacting human resources, and notifying her students. Maggie floated toward the ceiling, absorbed every other word.

When Bill was finished, she said, "I want to apologize if this has reflected poorly on the department."

He gave a sober nod, as if accepting condolences. "Well, I regret that it's had such repercussions for you too. Not just here. But personally," he said, and she imagined him reading the ugly comments about her online. Then he asked, "How's your daughter?"

She blinked. "My daughter?"

"Didn't you tell me she was heading to college? A freshman?"

"She was," Maggie said. "She's enjoying it." At least that's what she could tell. After that shaky phone call, Anna had been sounding better, and Tom had gone to check on her. "I'm just hoping none of this is affecting her too much."

Bill nodded. "Maybe it's good that she's away." There was a longer silence, but Maggie felt no call to fill it. Bill was looking at his lap, fingers of one hand clasped in the fingers of the other. He cleared his throat. "My son Ethan," he said. "He didn't have an easy time in high school. He struggled with depression. But he's at school now. A sophomore. At Colby. He's doing much better."

It was the only personal detail Bill Wall had ever shared. "That's good to hear," Maggie said, and they lapsed into quiet. No longer dean and professor, but two natural introverts, worried parents. The worry never ceased, Maggie thought, from the moment they were born. It just deepened, changed shape.

Inside her office, Maggie sagged briefly against the wall, holding her hands against her eyes. She drew a deep breath and scanned the room. There was surprisingly little she felt the need to take. A few books, mugs, a folder of research. She removed Nathan's essay from her desk drawer and pressed it deep inside her bag. Then she scooped up her thank-you cards, Alison Bower and the rest, and dropped them in the trash.

She sat down in front of her computer. Bill had said he'd notify the students, but Maggie needed to email them herself. *I write with some unexpected news.* She typed fast, hands trembling. She added that she regretted not telling them in person. She was genuinely sorry to be leaving them. She was proud of what they'd accomplished in just a few short weeks. *I will miss this class.*

Nineteen

I

Over the past two weeks, Anna had established a few simple rules for herself. Drink eight glasses of water each day. Take the stairs instead of the elevator whenever possible. Eat small portions. It was all about moderation. Exercise more, eat less: just math.

She had read once, in a magazine in the doctor's office (ironically, a nutritionist), that the formula for dieting was to have your daily caloric intake equal your current weight, times ten. 1520 calories: This seemed reasonable, not-obsessive and not-extreme.

At six thirty every morning, she went swimming. At that hour it was just her and Ralph, the guy who swiped IDs. Alone in the pool, Anna could swim without stopping. She focused only on the surface of herself: head turning, mouth opening, side of palm grazing ear, breath going in/out.

She hadn't heard from James, not since blocking him. If there was a knock on her door, she worried it might be him, wanting to talk to her, but it was only Hilary needing to borrow batteries or Violet wanting to steal food and complain about Carly, who had taken to sleeping with a white noise machine next to her bed. *She's so depressing*, Violet said.

Alcohol was a problem: so many empty calories. Yet to forgo all alcohol was out of the question, of course. She invested in cheap vodka, 40 calories per serving. Cut out beer, for the most part.

Cut bread. Cut pasta. Cut snacks in general, especially when drunk.

The snacking part was tricky, with Alexis around, but not impossible. Anna told her she was just trying to be healthier—*so I can fit into your clothes!*

Claudia Jones tagged you in a post on Facebook. It was Claudia from high school, posting a link to that article, the essay. She'd even been thoughtless enough to include a comment: *Is this your mother Anna Daley-Briggs???* Anna untagged herself immediately, heart thudding against her ribs.

She walked to the Save-A-Lot and returned with five bags of three things: Diet Coke, rice cakes, sugar-free gum.

She walked to Liquor Land, where she bought a backup bottle of vodka with Brian Tucker's brown-haired older sister's old Maine state ID.

Links to the article appeared a few more times. *Thinking of u, Anna!* And: *your mama???* She squashed them as soon as they appeared, like stomping ants.

Worst-case scenario: Student writes troubling essay, teacher misses it, student later kills four people, troubling essay is sent to local paper that reprints essay in full and random people won't stop posting it online.

Anna decided to get off Facebook completely. Turn off all notifications. Tunnel vision: She would wipe it from her mind.

—

In the fitness center, early morning, she swam until her lungs ached. At the end of week one, she returned to the locker room and shed all excess—peeled off suit, emptied bladder, scrubbed self dry—and stepped onto the scale.

151. Just one pound, but she felt lighter already.

II

Her routine, after swimming, was to consume one cup of dry cereal (120 calories) and three cups of black coffee (0). She crunched her stomach in/out beneath the table. At that hour in the dining hall, she was virtually alone.

There was a clarity, a sense of accomplishment, that came on the other side of hunger. She felt competent and productive. Near buoyant. *If that's what you're into*, James had said—why yes, she was.

An A - on her poetic-obsession-with-nature essay. *Great improvement!*

Results from the health center: STD-free!

She stopped eating after three o'clock because, really, there was no reason to. If she could make it from dinner to the end of the day without food, she could make it from midafternoon.

When she called home, Anna tried to ask her mother how she was, but Maggie immediately changed the subject. *How are you doing?* The meaningful emphasis was enough to make her scream.

Text Message Dad: *Still on for lunch this Sat right?*

Before parties with Alexis, Anna pre-drank four vodka-and-Diet-Cokes, then arrived sufficiently drunk to hold one beer and nurse it for the rest of the night.

At the fitness center, she kept her eyes open, staring at the ribbony black line on the pool floor. Twenty-three laps, twenty-four. She added one more lap each day, letting the line guide her back and forth.

Saturday morning, she swam twenty-five laps and ate 120 calories and weighed 149 pounds. Her dad arrived just before noon. He was alone. He said Felicia wasn't feeling well. He said hello to Alexis, who was headed to a study session. Met her RA, Isabel, who called Anna a beautiful person inside and out (what was that supposed to mean?). Then they went, the two of them, to a pub he'd found on Yelp. As she scanned the menu, Anna picked her lip—there was literally nothing healthy here—then stopped when she saw the worry cross his face. So she recalibrated, refocused, told him how much she was liking college so far, about Alexis and her poetry seminar, and watched the worry soften into relief. *She seemed a little distracted at first*, he'd later tell her mother. *But happy. She looked healthy.* Guiltily, Anna knew that anytime she was just a little thinner, a little more toned, her dad would misread it as her looking good. She ordered fries and a chicken sandwich, to seal the deal (she would let herself eat it, she thought, most of it, then not eat again until tomorrow morning), but had only forced her way through six bites when her father said: *So I guess you've heard what's been going on with Mom.* Her throat began to close. *That article*, he said. As always, his timing was impeccable. Maybe, for him, the food was a comforting distraction; for her, it was like being ambushed twice. *I know it's probably unsettling*, he said, and she realized this was the reason that he'd come, the reason Felicia hadn't. She made the mistake of looking down at her plate: repulsive. Fries glistening in the sunlight beaming through the window, chicken wan and fleshy. Like all food, look too closely and it breaks down into its component parts: slime and veins. *It'll blow over*, her dad was saying. *I don't want you to let it slow you down.* She pictured the food in her stomach, revolving in slow circles, like one of those metal spits in gas stations. The thought of it, the actuality of it, was revolting, almost incomprehensible: that the same chicken, those same fries that had just been sitting on the plate were now inside her. She could practically feel her face blowing up. *It won't,* she said.

III

It was easy enough to turn 1500 calories/day into 1200, and 1200 into 1000.

There were only 60 calories in an orange, 40 in a cup of sugar-free Jell-O. Zero in black coffee. Celery (almost negligible) was tolerable if dunked in dressing (fat-free).

She crunched her stomach in/out whenever it wouldn't be noticed: lying in bed, sitting in class, walking across the quad.

Twenty-eight laps, twenty-nine. In the water her body felt weightless, secondary. Her legs were thin pale blades.

Dad had a nice visit, her mother reported. *He said you're doing really well.*

If she noticed Alexis looking at her oddly, she might realize she was twisting her lip, or pinching the caterpillar of fat on her knee, or chewing a bite of her rice cake fifty times. One night she came home from the library to find a little vial of berry lip balm on her pillow, like a mint in a hotel.

Still no James sightings. She was surprised, but maybe it wasn't so surprising. He didn't go to parties, attended class only selectively. Still, if she let herself wonder too long, her mind ran wild. Maybe he'd dropped out. Maybe he was gone. Maybe dead.

—

Maybe, she thought, James was hiding out in his apartment, maybe planning his own shooting—was that the reason he was so interested in them? Knew so much about them?

Stop it, Anna. Stop.

She was becoming acutely aware of mirrors again: the thin one at the fitness center, fat warped one in the girls' bathroom. The world was made of mirrors, if you were looking. Freezers in the Save-A-Lot, car windshields, the glimmering surface of the pool.

At night, in bed, the tally: laps (thirty-two), apple (calories: 100), frozen yogurt (calories: 100), Rice Krispies (120, no milk).

She remembered something Theresa once said about addiction: Learn it once, and it's like riding a bike, it all comes right back.

IV

This thing with your mom, Janie texted. *It's getting kind of crazy no???*

Evidently Nathan Dugan's mother had come out with this unbelievable claim that her mother, Anna's mother, had shown up at her house. That she'd come there the day after the shooting, apologizing for not helping him. An interview with her was on YouTube. *It made me sad to watch it,* Kim said. Anna didn't/wouldn't/couldn't afford to watch.

She called home right away. *I can't believe that woman would make this whole thing up like that.*

Well. Her mother paused. There was a touch of something in her voice, an unsteadiness. *She didn't make up all of it. But I didn't apologize for—that isn't what I said. What I meant.*

—

Worst-case scenario: Student writes troubling essay, teacher misses it, student later kills four people, troubling essay is sent to local paper that reprints essay in full and random people won't stop posting it online, then student's mother does YouTube interview that makes teacher look even worse.

Anna tried to focus on her classes. On eating, and not eating. She didn't talk about the video/shooter/shooter's mother, not with anyone. She avoided all social media. Still there was the sense of a thing, like a fly buzzing, always, just outside the frame.

At least it was easier to hide her eating/not eating from Alexis, who was pledging now officially. Last week, she'd come back to the room clutching a symbolic beer bottle, having been conferred the status of a future sorority member. *Congratulations*, Anna said, with what she hoped was a trace of sarcasm. Alexis smiled at her, sort of sadly, it seemed.

She decided to subtract one food item each day. Ketchup: unnecessary. Juice: borderline decadent. Sugar in coffee: replaceable with Splenda, potentially cancer-causing but calorie-free.

Her calmest moments were buried underwater: echo of breath in her head, chop/glide of limbs, pressure of fingertips meeting the slick tiled edge. She stared at the black line at the bottom until her eyes burned.

146 pounds: At this rate, she could drop twenty by Christmas break.

Her mother called as she was walking home from Liquor Land, plastic bags tugging at her wrists. *I wanted to let you know I won't be teaching for the rest of the semester*, and Anna stopped in the middle of the street. *You were fired?*

No, her mother said. *It was my decision. I'm telling you because I don't want you to hear about it—*

Should I come home?

Of course not, her mother said curtly. *Why would you do that?*

Anna called Kim, called Janie. No answer. She drank a vodka-and-Diet-Coke, drank two more, and stared at the carpet, at the pattern of shaggy colored squares. She looked for some logic in the arrangement of orange/red/blue/green/yellow but there was none there.

When Alexis came in, Anna was penciling on eyeliner. *Oh,* she said, and winced. *The party is for pledges only. I thought you knew.* Anna didn't know. Had she known, she would not have consumed three anticipatory 40-calorie vodka-and-Diet-Cokes. *Sorry,* Alexis said. She was looking at her apologetically. She was wearing the purple satin shirt. Anna capped the pencil and told her she'd been thinking about staying in anyway; she actually wasn't feeling good.

After Alexis left, she was angry. 120 wasted calories—she was furious at herself. And hungry. She was painfully aware of Alexis's junk food drawer: Smartfood, Pop-Tarts, seemingly thousands of Swedish fish.

She plugged her mouth with gum, pushed in more when the flavor started dying. Her jaw clicked like a metronome.

In/out. In/out. She did crunches on the checkerboard rug. She kept her head entirely inside a yellow square, feet entirely inside a red.

Text Message Janie: *Did you guys see what Mindy put on Facebook?*

Anna felt a fresh bolt of alarm—what now? She was still off Facebook but couldn't resist checking. When she opened it, what she found was a photo album: fifty-four pictures from the party at Gavin's back in August. Anna had no memory of Mindy taking pictures at that party. Then again, somebody was always taking pictures. There were Gavin and Mindy, sipping from the same red keg cup. Janie posing with the flip-cup girls. There was Kim, leaning into Tucker's arm. And there was Anna, standing on the porch, alone. For a minute she didn't even recognize herself. Her mouth was half open, eyes squinty, face enormous. Why the fuck would Mindy post this? Because she looked fat and sad and drunk and clearly Mindy wanted to embarrass her. She messaged Mindy before she could rethink it: *could you remove this ridiculously bad pic of me immediately? THX.* She felt heady, vibrant, defiant with anger. She untagged herself, vanishing the photo, and found herself staring at the YouTube link that had surfaced like a stubborn weed. *Shooter's Mother Speaks Out.* From the hallway, she heard shrieks of laughter. Her face pounded with blood. She clicked the image, enlarging it, and found herself staring at a still shot of Nathan Dugan's mother, sitting on a couch. Her face looked soft and stunned. It had been viewed 438,000 times. Anna stared at her, kept staring, like holding a foot in a pot of scalding water. *I dare you,* she thought, then clicked. *What did I think?* Mrs. Dugan said. The sound quality was airy, filmed on a phone. *He made the whole thing up.* A voice off-camera asked a question, and Anna nudged the volume higher. *They act like I'm the one who's a bad parent. I loved my son.* The offscreen voice said: *And what's your impression of his teacher? Professor Daley?* Anna froze. The line sailed through her body like the aftershock of a plucked hair, a prodded nerve. She rewound, relistened. *And what's your impression of his teacher? Professor Daley?* There was no question it was James. Panic scissored up and down her spine. *The teacher? She showed up here too,* she said, and Anna felt her fear rising, her own inexorable internal tide.

V

Worst-case scenario: Student writes troubling essay, teacher misses it, student later kills four people, etc. etc. etc., student's mother does YouTube interview with ex-boyfriend of teacher's daughter who just wanted to stay as far away as fucking possible from any of this.

—

This time, she texted *CALL ASAP* and Kim and Janie got back to her in minutes. They both sounded drunk; it was after eleven thirty. *I can't believe he did this to you!*—Kim. *What a smug asshole*—Janie. But there was something else in both their voices, an incredulity that wasn't about James but about Anna: that she could have been with someone like this.

When she called James, she tried to keep it together but she was dissolving. *How could you do that?* she said, and started to cry. James answered surely, almost serenely, as if he had been waiting for this conversation. *I had a responsibility, Anna*, he told her. *I did what needed to be done. People can't just treat people that way*, he said, and Anna had no idea if he was talking about her mother or herself or both.

When she called home the next morning, she tried to tell her mother what she knew about the video, to say she was sorry, but the words lodged in her throat. Instead, her mother casually mentioned she'd canceled the Internet. *I guess I'm becoming even more of a hermit without you here.*

In an essay of five pages, put forth an original thesis that describes the changing role of the self in contemporary poetry. Support your thesis with examples from our texts. (And have fun!)

The checkerboard rug: It bugged her. To call it a checkerboard was actually not accurate because there was no pattern to it.

She could make it from the bed to the dresser by stepping inside six squares, dresser to the door in three. She stepped only in the yellow squares—or, no, never the yellow. Only the red, only the green.

Alexis no longer talked about them rooming together sophomore year. No longer called her *roomie*, as though to disavow the relationship in advance. She was busy with pledging, though forbidden to speak about it.

She came home at two in the morning with Magic Marker on her face, dirt under her nails, and cleaned up silently, patiently, with an almost sanctimonious air—and she looked at *Anna* with pity? Like *she* was the one with the problem?

When Isabel saw Anna in the hallway, she commented that she'd been looking down lately. And that she'd heard Alexis was pledging. *If you're lonely, you know my door is always open!*

At parties, with random girls from her dorm, she sized up other girls' bodies: that one's toned arm, this one's sticklike thigh.

She considered the Ativan in her sock drawer but didn't want to lose her edge.

Text Message Kim: *Come back and visit this weekend! Gavin's coming. Re-union!*

Text Message Janie: *If I didn't have practice I would so be there . . .*

Their texts made her lonely, made her furious. She couldn't bring herself to reply. She was irrationally jealous of Janie's new friends from basketball. Of Tucker, of all people, whom they now apparently called Brian. *We miss you*, Kim said, *we* being she and Tucker/Brian. That weekend Kim sent a picture: her and Tucker and Gavin, Kim in the middle. They were standing in the middle of a road, pine trees thick on both sides. The Grange. Anna knew the exact spot, where the woods backed into freshman dorms. She could smell the air inside the picture. She could feel it on her arms. Tucker and Gavin were holding beers, arms around Kim, who was holding up two fingers in a peace sign. Kim was wearing too much makeup. Gavin had slightly longer hair. They were all flushed and drunk and smiling, the flash of the camera a spasm of silver against the dark.

VI

At 500 calories/day, Anna could still function admirably, though by nighttime it was getting hard to concentrate. Her head hurt. Her legs, from all the swimming.

One more lap or you'll fail your psych exam. One more lap or the building will catch fire.

She was satisfied if she lost a pound, despairing if she didn't. 139. 138. 138. 138. She slid the little weight beneath her finger, trying to line it up perfectly. Sometimes this took five, ten, fifteen minutes.

Text Message Janie: *Where are u??*

The rug was making her crazy. The squares, she had them memorized. One red square, one yellow. *Step on a crack and break your mother's back!*

You're looking good, Ralph said one morning, and she was elated all day.

On the phone with her mother, Anna made herself sound upbeat, sound happy. *Things are really good! Just busy!* If she put her mind to it, she could be convincing. If her mother knew what was going on she would come and drag her home.

Maybe you should talk to someone, Alexis said, once. It was night, and they were both in bed, Alexis speaking into the dark. *About your eating thing.* Anna didn't move. She pretended she was asleep but stayed awake for hours, staring at the bottom of the mattress, in/out.

Text Message Kim: *Call me back please . . .*

It was possible, if she paid attention, to just fit her foot inside each square. She stepped deliberately, carefully, avoiding letting heel/toe go over the edge.

She snapped at Ralph for taking forever with the fucking ID machine, which was malfunctioning, although obviously he knew just who she was.

When she came in one night, Alexis was sitting on the top bunk with fellow pledge Esme. They were eating Chinese food. (Esme was stick-thin too; everyone was.) They went abruptly quiet when Anna entered. Clearly they'd been talking about her. Anna was tempted to climb in the bunk below them, but she couldn't bear to cross the fucking rug. She went outside, lapped the quad twenty times. When she came back they were, of course, gone.

Siena asked her to stay after class one day. *Nothing bad!* she said, a little too gaily. When everyone else left, she told Anna she was concerned. There was worry, real worry, on her face, and Anna fought the sudden urge to break down and cry—for putting her favorite teacher in this position. For being this student. Siena was saying she was a great student, a great writer, but lately she seemed quiet, distracted. Thinner, too—later that was all she'd heard.

Sometimes in bed, she had to pee but it was too daunting, the journey from bed to door.

She chewed so much gum her jaw ached.

She felt her hipbones—knobs.

She hit 135 and felt glorious even though she understood this weight loss was all really about fear and control and blah blah blah.

Message from Janie: *Anna this is really getting old*

Step inside a white square, and something horrible might happen/will happen/might happen. To her father, to her mother. Her mother might die, or Kim, or Janie. Or Alexis. She didn't mean these things, but they stole into her mind and played on repeat, like bad songs.

Message from Kim: *Helllllllooooo?*

Was she swimming or was she drowning? They felt like the same thing. She was a lead weight. She was a stone. She was water, inside and out.

VII

The main thing she'd learned in therapy was that everything was really something else. Her worry about the locks on the door or the burners on the stove wasn't actually about the locks or about the burners: It was fear. The anorexia wasn't about food: It was control. The first time Theresa explained it, Anna had pictured those pans in darkrooms, the photo submerged in liquid, image emerging. *Subtext*, her mother might say, but it was more than that. The underlayer. The other, truer thing beneath.

Anna dreaded swimming. Instead of keeping her outside her head, it only sucked her in deeper. She had started going to the pool at all hours. She wished she could stop going, but she had to go, couldn't not go, even though she hated the repetition, the smell, the black lines, the near-inability to climb out.

She was so hungry that her throat hurt. She pictured her throat screaming for food and this made her feel pleased for a moment before she remembered that herself and her throat were the same thing.

If We Had Known

Text Message Kim: *I'm really starting to get worried*

The rug was unbearable. She rolled it up and shoved it under the bed.

Text Message Dad: *Happy Halloween!*

Anna had forgotten about Halloween, hated Halloween: an excuse to scare people/dress like sluts.

As she was leaving the fitness center, she heard: *Hey.* She stopped. Forty-eight laps and her legs were gone. *Over here.* It was James. He was walking by, walking toward her. He looked remarkably unchanged. Jeans, boots, sunglasses. *What are you doing here?* Anna said, dropping her hand. She'd been picking at her lip. Her first thought: Had he seen her picking? Second: Was he going to the fitness center? He never went to the fitness center. If James started coming to the fitness center it would throw off her entire routine. Third: Was he spying on her? He was looking at her sadly. *Oh, Anna*, he said.

When she returned to the room, the rug was back. She stood on the very edge. She had rivers in her veins. Outside, kids were heading to the dining hall. Anna clenched her stomach in/out, in/out. She was starving. Literally empty. What she wouldn't give for a slice of the cold pizza Alexis had left in their mini-fridge. Just one. She would savor it, revel in it, make it last an hour. *Don't you dare.*

She closed her eyes, wishing it were later. Wishing there were an off/on switch in her stomach/brain. She missed Kim and Janie. Missed Alexis. Missed home, though it no longer felt safe—she couldn't even feel homesick anymore. She thought about calling Kim or Janie, but it was dinnertime, and a Saturday. They were probably furious with her anyway. Probably eating/drinking with Brian Tucker/the basketball team. The night gaped before her, a cave in the woods. There was a party at Alexis's sorority later, for Halloween. Anna dreaded parties: rooms of arms and legs. But that morning Alexis had asked if she was going, and when she said yes, answered, *Cool. See you there.* Anna was happy that she'd asked. She'd sounded sincere. And though the prospect of the party was overwhelming, the thought of staying in the room alone was worse: the rug, the pizza. She didn't think she could survive it.

At seven, she poured herself a Diet-Coke-and-vodka. An hour later, she'd had four. She changed into jeans and a strapless black shirt and penciled on eyeliner whiskers, then stepped inside four red squares and left the dorm. As soon as she hit the air, her head began spinning. It was cool, too cool for strapless, and a little early, only eight thirty, but Alexis, she knew, would already be there. The night smelled sad but also crisp and slightly smoky. Dry leaves crumbled beneath her feet. She was a full block away from the sorority house when she felt the thump of music from the basement. Her lungs shivered. When the house came into view, lights blazed in every window, but as she walked inside, there was hardly anyone there. She was too early. She scanned the room and spotted Alexis, playing beer pong with Esme. They were dressed as matching Starbucks baristas. When Anna started toward her, Alexis looked up and turned to Esme and said distinctly: *She came.* Anna paused midway across the room. Somebody knocked into her elbow, said sorry. When Alexis met her eyes, she looked guilty, and Anna spun around and headed for the door. Vaguely: *Anna, where are you going?* But she didn't stop, and Alexis didn't chase her. She walked home, sky blurring into the trees. Past the fitness center, the English building, the pair of benches: the one where she'd met James, the one where she'd spilled her guts to James four weeks/four hundred years ago. When she arrived at the dorm, it felt deserted. The silence pressed into the stairwell, the entire building, the half-empty bulletin boards and harsh strips of dry fluorescent light, every pore of campus between the throbbing sorority house and the lip of the rug where she now stood as if toeing the edge of a diving board.

She just wanted this night to be over: fall asleep and wake up, reset, start again. She made it to the dresser (three squares, blue), where she stood with both feet inside a square and dug the orange bottle from her drawer. She poured out three. No, five. Her hands trembled. Not the whole bottle, not even close, but enough to knock her out until morning. She made it to the door (four squares, yellow) and down the empty hallway to the bathroom (twelve steps, black and white tile, black tiles only, step out and your roommate might die, will die, maybe you want her to die—*stop it, Anna, stop*). She faced the mirror, pulse hammering. Only at nine thirty on a Saturday night would she ever find this bathroom empty. The sink ledge was crowded with tampon wrappers, shampoo bottles, beer cans. The air felt prickly and damp. She splashed her face, scrubbed off the whiskers. Then she stared at the mirror and forced a smile but it looked so sad and fake and small and fat that it made her feel like bursting into tears. The smile collapsed. She turned and lifted her shirt to examine her profile just as she heard the shuffle of footsteps and someone opened the door.

Carly Smith, of course: the only girl who would possibly be here at this hour on a Saturday. "Hey," Anna said, letting her shirt drop. If Carly had caught her examining her fat, she didn't show it. She was wearing sweats, those ridiculous purple slippers. "I didn't think anyone else was here," Anna said. The pills were sticking to the inside of her fist.

"You thought wrong," Carly replied. The sarcasm surprised her. Carly's slippers sloughed against the tile. She carried a plastic shower caddy, a shower cap, toothbrush in a plastic holder, and something about all of this struck Anna as so prim as to be almost brave.

"What did you do tonight?"

"You're looking at it."

"Yeah." Her head bobbed. "Me too." She thought Carly might be pleased to hear this, feel a spark of kinship, but she barely looked at her.

"I seriously doubt that. You reek of alcohol."

"Well, yeah. That's because I went to a party—"

"Exactly."

"I know. I was there for literally ten seconds but I left," Anna said, as Carly unscrewed a thing of moisturizer. A blue tub, the kind her mother used. "It wasn't a good scene." Again, nothing. Carly stuck her fingers in the tub and the smell made Anna's eyes water. Anna had always felt bad for Carly but now she longed for Carly—to be friends with Carly, confide in Carly, maybe have her life. "And also, there are some crazy things going on at home." Carly didn't look at her and Anna snapped, "Do you just not like me or something?"

"I don't know you well enough to not like you," Carly said. Her cheeks were two white moons. "But I do know you're just talking to me because you're drunk and there's nobody else around."

"Like who? Alexis? I never hang out with Alexis anymore. I barely even see Alexis."

She snorted. "There's a real loss."

"You've never even talked to her."

"I don't want to talk to her. How about she talk to me?" She washed and dried her face. "They talk about you, you know," Carly said.

"No, they don't," Anna said. But of course they did. Quieter, she asked, "What do they say?"

"You should probably ask her yourself," Carly said. Then she walked into a stall and left Anna standing there. Her eyes stung. Screw her, then. Carly was a nerd, and not even a nice nerd. One of those nerds with an arrogant streak—the worst kind.

Anna unclenched her fist, where the pills had stuck to her palm and stained her skin blue. She grabbed a bottle of warm beer, swallowed all five, and licked her palm. On her way out she grabbed the moisturizer— *I dare you.* It was done.

Back in her room, Anna walked to the dresser (three squares, green), stashed the tub in her sock drawer, then made it to the bed (two squares, red). She turned out the light. She swam in the darkness, waiting for the pills to tug her under. She pictured a long mirror, an endless march of faces. Kim and Janie and Alexis. And Carly. Laura Mack, in that dressing room, terrified, committing herself to memory. Alison Bower—hers was a face Anna had never actually seen. What she pictured instead was her mother, the night she came home from taking Alison to the crisis center and curled up on the other end of the couch. She looked pale, and shaken, as if she'd just had blood drawn. *There was a close call tonight,* she said.

Twenty

Maggie's life had been emptied from the inside: no Anna, no
Robert, no students. Even the strangers on the Internet were
gone. Once on leave, her first act had been to call the cable company and
have them disconnect the Internet. Disconnect the cable TV, while they
were at it. Technology: monstrous as she'd always known that it was.

Those first few days, her house felt unfamiliar, like a town after a hurri-
cane, quietly wrecked. She called only Anna, wanting to tell her before
she heard about it elsewhere, fearing that in this surreal new world in
which the details of Maggie's life were available for public consumption
Anna might read the news online. To her surprise, her daughter's response was: *Should I come home?* Maggie felt a sharp sadness—that Anna
might think she needed to care for her mother—and though a part of
her leapt at the proposal, she replied, in a tone that was shorter than she
intended: *Of course not. Why would you do that?*

It was disorienting at first, not having access to the Internet. Funny,
since this had never mattered to her before. Now, though, she was aware
of what might be out there that she was missing, the way you might

wonder what was being whispered about you across a crowded room. Monday morning, she knew word of her leave would be circulating the department, but if the news landed she barely felt it, the plop of a rock in a faraway stream. As the day wore on, her thoughts receded. Late afternoon, she received a text from Robert—*this is not legally enforceable*—but didn't bother to explain. That this wasn't about rules, what they could and couldn't do. She simply wrote back, *my decision*, and left it there.

Mostly, though, the isolation felt like a reprieve. There was a certain bliss attached to being cut off from the world, to simply not knowing. She could no longer pore over the news, no longer wade through the opinions of strangers. No longer watch the video of Marielle Dugan, though in the past week she'd watched it so many times she had it memorized. Maggie's only regular contact was with Anna. Since Maggie had been home, they'd spoken nearly every day. She supposed her daughter felt sorry for her, worried for her, though she never said so directly. Sometimes Maggie detected something in her tone that felt a little forced, a little fervent— although Tom had reported, after their lunch, that she seemed good. A little stressed maybe, but good, basically good. She looked healthy. Her RA seemed competent. *And she ate?* Maggie asked. *She ate*, he said.

Beyond that, she deliberately limited her contact with the outside world. If she had to run an errand, she went early, when she'd be less likely to run into anyone. Time spent outdoors was restricted to the property around her house. In the morning, she worked in her garden. In the afternoon, she walked the driveway to retrieve the mail. If the phone rang, which was infrequent, the machine answered, messages slipping into its depths.

For Maggie, though, to be alone in her house was not to feel lonely. Even during her divorce, especially then, the house had been a comfort, a constant. She knew the place as intimately as another person: the damp blisters of paint on the bathroom walls, the tricky faucet on the old clawfoot tub, the labored breaths of the hulking radiators as they tried to start on cold nights, huffing and finally catching like a struck match.

When, late one afternoon, she heard a car approaching, she hurried onto the porch. Then stood there, arms folded, watching as the red Jeep pulled to a stop. "Does your wife know you're here?" she asked.

Robert seemed about to walk up onto the porch, but reconsidered and stayed where he was, hands in pockets, at the bottom of the stairs. He wore a tie and jacket; he must have come from campus. Maggie didn't invite him in. She didn't want the memory of him being there.

"I just wanted to see how you're doing," he said.

"I'm fine."

"I text you, and you don't respond."

"That doesn't mean I'm not fine," she said. He frowned, as if trying to evaluate the truth in this. Maggie pushed a quick hand through her hair. "So, am I a laughingstock?"

His face softened. "Don't worry about that."

"Ah," she said, with a quick laugh. "So I am."

"Nothing serious," he said. "Nothing to lose sleep over." But even Robert couldn't make this sound convincing. She could have pressed the point but decided she didn't want to know.

"How's Suzanne?" she asked, then clarified, "Her health, I mean."

Robert looked abashed, but said, "Better." He squinted at the sky. "She wants to move back home—or at least, in that direction. It's been sixteen years. So I'm going on the market," he said, then looked back at her. "She hates the cold."

Maggie did not betray the sadness she was feeling. That he was staying with his wife, that he was leaving—wasn't this an old story? She was a fool for ever believing it might end differently.

"She's had a hard time, being here," he said.

"Well, that seems like the right thing to do, then," Maggie said. She gestured toward the house. "I better get back."

Robert gave her a melting look. "You can call me, you know," he said. "I worry about you," he told her, and seemed about to step forward, maybe to hug her, but she thanked him for coming and turned to the door. Back inside, she listened, heart pounding, to his car driving away.

★ ★ ★

Day by day, in her empty house, the absence Maggie felt most keenly was her students. Convinced as she'd been about the rightness of leaving, she had underestimated just how much she would miss having them in her life. Tuesday and Thursday, she imagined the freshmen gathering for class, considered where they would be at that juncture in the semester. Working on their next set of essays. Extra-tired, extra-caffeinated, preparing for the midterm grind. For twenty-eight years, Maggie's life had been so shaped by the rhythms of the school year that without it, the days collapsed around her. This was not the short-term rigor of a sabbatical, nor the pleasant, temporary bagginess of summer. She had stepped out of life's current, while that old life continued without her, eleven miles down the road.

She tried to stay occupied. She made a to-do list of things around the house that needed freshening and fixing. The loose shingles on the barn. The cracks wrinkling the paint on her bedroom ceiling. She noticed the curling wallpaper in the kitchen, the shadowy water spots in the hall, things Anna had regularly pointed out but that Maggie, blinded by affection for the house, had quite literally never seen. The list was endless, but as the first week bled into the next, she had trouble doing anything; her initial motivation dissipated into aimlessness, vague fretfulness. *At loose ends*—suddenly clichés she'd always disdained made sense, were in fact the ideal expressions of how she felt. Time moved with the quality of simultaneous quickness and slowness she associated with being a new mother, the individual hours stretching on forever while days disappeared whole. Even the house itself, old reliable sanctuary, no longer felt like a comfort. She was newly aware of noises, small sounds that in her solitude grew distorted—the trickle of water in the pipes like a light rain, the rattle of the boiler a knock at the door. She wished for a television sometimes, if only for the blanketing distraction. In the evenings, she listened for creatures in the garden, and often threw open the back door, squinting into the dark. She never saw anything, but back inside she swore she heard them, tunneling beneath the fence.

At night, she dreamed of trains. She was traveling alone, by a window, but when she turned to look at her reflection, her face was blank. She dreamed of teaching. Of standing in front of the classroom, but the wrong classroom, filled with students she didn't know. When she woke, heart racing, it was impossible to get back to sleep. She stared at the ceiling and remembered Anna's childhood nightmares, the way she'd rush into their room having scared herself with a story of her own invention. *It's just in your head*, Maggie used to tell her, and she saw now how unhelpful this had been, for the problem was exactly this.

One early Sunday, Maggie dreamed the dream of the classroom and woke in a sweat. The bedside clock read just past five. It was still dark, and silent, the silence loud with many things. The thick rustle of wind, a lone branch scraping a window. She wished she weren't alone. Wished that Anna were asleep down the hall. Wished, these years later, that Tom were in bed beside her. Her mind returned again to spring, four years ago, 2012. The spring her marriage ended, the spring she and her husband drove back and forth to a therapist's office in Augusta. The spring there was a monster sitting in her classroom. The spring her child began to fall apart. *It'll be okay*, Maggie had reassured her daughter, as panic had consumed her. She'd always been intent on making Anna feel safe, but maybe this determined optimism had bled into her own field of vision, made her blind to the actual danger that had been sitting in front of her.

Daylight was sidling up the bedroom wall. It was pointless to try to sleep again, so she pulled an old wool sweater over her T-shirt and sweatpants and made her way to her office at the other end of the hall. Her canvas bag was still on the chair where she'd left it weeks before. She withdrew the essay, still seamed faintly with squares, then refolded it carefully, almost tenderly, slid it in her pocket, and made her way downstairs.

Outside, the backyard looked white, slightly misty, like the surface of the moon. In the kitchen, Maggie brewed a pot of coffee, drank two cups, and ate the stiff end of a loaf of bread. When she opened the back door, the air felt like winter. A Sunday, the first day of November, the sunrise a slow orange stain across the sky. Frost crunched beneath her boots. When she opened the barn door and stepped inside, the air was stale and dry and only slightly warmer than the air outside. She climbed the ladder to the loft, and at the top, confronted what looked like the scene of a crime: pools of ransacked papers, upended boxes. She allowed herself one pointless flare of regret—*if only she'd never*—then knelt amid the mess.

It took several minutes to locate the right box, the one containing Nathan's classmates' papers, but there it was. Maggie unfolded his essay and added it to the pile, tucked it beneath the roll book, and replaced the lid. Her eyes welled briefly. Then she turned to face the rest of the strewn pages and dusty folders. She began returning them to boxes, thoughtfully at first, then haphazardly, without regard for logic or organization. She paused sometimes to give one an extra-long look, but she knew that she would never see them again. This, she thought, was the sadness of teachers. Each semester is a contained little life—a relationship that begins, peaks, but always ends. They cycle in, cycle out, but you stay in one place. The teacher grows older, but the students never age. They are perpetually eighteen, twenty-one, lives always just on the cusp of beginning. You watch them walk off into the world, knowing you helped them become what they're becoming. You suffer the same ending again and again.

By the time Maggie made her way back to the house, the sky was woolly, sunless and lightly snowing. The smell of a neighbor's burn pile seeped into the late-morning air. She was tired and hungry. Fresh paper cuts on her fingers stung in the cold. As she neared the back door, she stopped—her garden had been destroyed. The fence was ripped down completely on one side, a trail of sharp deer tracks visible in the snow. Broad daylight, Maggie thought—the audacity—before she was overcome with rage. She strode to the garden, kicking hard at what remained of the fence posts. Her foot rang with pain. Then, from the front of the house, she heard a car rolling up the driveway. She paused, breathing hard, and listened: This time she was not mistaking the sound for something else. The car radio was blaring. It wouldn't be Robert, that music. Too loud, too young. Her first thought was Gavin Newland—how many nights had she sat up marking papers, alert to the rumble of his truck as she waited for Anna to come home? Now, though, the engine shut off, music stopped. When she heard the car door slam, fear kicked in. Yesterday, she'd heard a car pull up and discovered four kids standing on her porch in costume—"Trick or treat!" they yelled as their parents sat idling in the drive. Maggie had forgotten Halloween, had had to quickly scan her cabinets and offer them oranges, face their disappointment, then shut off her lights and spent the rest of the night in the dark. But now it was Sunday morning. An ordinary Sunday, the first of November. There was no reason for anyone to be there. As she stepped into the kitchen, she heard an insistent knocking, and her mind raced with fresh and frightening possibilities—a reporter, an angry Internet commenter, a young man with a gun. Nothing seemed impossible. As she closed her hand around the knob, she considered the distance to her nearest neighbor, whether if she shouted they would hear her.

"Maggie?"

It took her a moment to register the girl on the porch, but when she did, she reached out and hugged her. "Kim," she said. "It's so good to see you." She stepped back to get a look at her, saying, "You know you don't need to knock." In fact, Kim and Janie had been walking in and out of Maggie's house for years, but she supposed it didn't feel the same without Anna there. "You look terrific," Maggie told her, and Kim did—slightly older, more confident, with different-colored hair. Maggie knew this shift well. She smiled. "College suits you."

"Thanks," Kim replied, but tentatively, and Maggie was suddenly aware of her own appearance, the dirt under her fingernails and the misshapen sweater, the dust on the knees of the sweatpants she'd slept in the night before. "Sorry to just stop by like this."

"Oh, it's fine. You know that. Anytime."

"I knew I couldn't find you on campus."

Of course: Kim would know she was no longer teaching this semester. Maybe this was the reason for her visit, for the hesitation in her voice.

"Right," Maggie said brightly. "Well, come in, come in. I was just doing some work outside." She widened the door and began switching on lamps in the dim living room. "How's your first semester going?"

"I'm liking it," Kim said, but by the sudden light, Maggie fully registered the emotion on her face. She looked pale, almost frightened, and Maggie felt the air leave her.

"Kim," she said. "What is it?"

Kim's eyes grew abruptly teary. "I tried calling but no one answered," she said. "But I know I should have called you sooner," she told her, and suddenly it was three years ago, and Maggie was back in her office on campus, Kim and Janie telling her they were worried about Anna, that she would kill them, but they didn't know what else to do.

Maggie made the four-hour drive in three hours and fifteen minutes. She didn't listen to the radio and didn't stop. When she'd spoken briefly on the phone to Anna, her daughter immediately started crying. "I'm coming," Maggie said. "Right now." Then she made her put Alexis on the line, and instructed: "Do not leave her side."

As she drove, Maggie replayed the story Kim had told her, over and over. How, when she'd called Anna at eleven that morning, it was Alexis who picked up the phone. She'd said Anna was still sleeping, then started telling Kim how strangely she'd been acting lately—the dieting, the swimming—and Kim had made her wake Anna up and check that she was okay. Half an hour later, she'd shown up at Maggie's front door.

Now, as Maggie sped past Portland, she thought of calling Tom and telling him to meet her at Anna's dorm, but she was too upset, too angry. He'd seen Anna only a few weeks ago. He'd gone to check on her—it was the very *reason* he'd gone. He'd actually said she looked healthy. How had he not seen it? How hadn't Alexis? Because she was spoiled, self-centered—Maggie had disliked her from the start. What about that teacher, then, the grad student Anna loved so much? She felt like weeping and like kicking something at the same time. Blame splayed in all directions, like a brushfire, but when she arrived at the dorm and saw her daughter, it narrowed onto Maggie in a point of almost unbearable pain.

Anna had slipped backward three years. Sitting on the bed, knees drawn, she was a history of moments collapsed into one. She had lost weight, Maggie thought, fifteen pounds at least. But it was the look in her eyes that alarmed her. Maggie could see how distracted she was, how removed from herself, her mind a buzzing hive. "I'm sorry, Mom," she said, and started crying, a flat, defeated sound.

Maggie sat beside her, put her arms around her, and stayed there. "Are you okay?"

Anna nodded, a rustle against her shoulder.

"Did you take them on purpose?"

A nod again.

Maggie pulled back, heart thumping, and looked at her daughter. "Were you trying to commit suicide?" she said, and though it felt impossible to even ask the question, the directness of it kept her afloat.

Anna whispered, "I don't think so."

"Okay," Maggie said. "Okay." She felt like she might collapse but told Anna to call Theresa and leave a message. Tell her it was an emergency. Anna brushed at her eyes and reached for her phone. It was only then that Maggie registered Alexis's presence. She was sitting cross-legged at her desk. At first, the very sight of her made Maggie want to boil over, but she could see that the girl was scared. It was she, after all, who had finally tracked down the RA on duty, gotten Anna to the health center. She glanced at Maggie, sensing her attention. "Thank you," Maggie said. "For helping her."

Alexis shook her head. "Honestly, I didn't know it was this bad."

Anna was saying, "I'm sorry to call you like this but—"

"I mean, I knew something was wrong," Alexis continued. "I told her she should talk to someone a while ago."

"How long has this been going on?"

"A month?" she said, and Maggie felt a flash of despair. "There was this guy she was seeing. I think it all started around then."

"Guy? What guy?"

Anna had hung up the phone. "He was older," Alexis was saying. "He was intense." Her eyes moved to Anna. "He was kind of political, right?"

"He's the one who made that YouTube video," Anna said.

She was looking only at Maggie, as Maggie said, confused, "What YouTube video?" Her first thought was of the video Nathan Dugan had posted on that horrible morning, the morning that started it all. But Anna kept her gaze level, waiting for her to piece it together, and Maggie paused, and suddenly realized: the YouTube interview. The male voice asking questions offscreen.

"I told him about you, and Nathan Dugan," Anna said. "And that paper. I know you asked me not to." Then she started to cry again, tears dripping without sound. "Then I broke up with him," she said. Maggie was stunned—not that Anna had confided in this person, but that she'd been involved with someone who had gone and done this. She was struck by all she didn't know about her daughter; she had a life that was entirely her own.

"I didn't know anything about it," Anna was saying. She'd started picking her lip. "But I shouldn't have talked to him about it in the first place. I shouldn't have—"

"Listen to me," Maggie told her, firmly. "Look at me." She waited until Anna had lowered her hands, focused on her face. "You were right," she said. "I found that paper. In the barn that morning." She was aware of Alexis listening, and was tempted for a moment to stop talking, but she owed it to her daughter to admit it all. "And I lied about not having it," she continued. "Which I never should have done. The anonymous person who sent it to the press, that was the wife of a man I was involved with—that I was having an affair with," she confessed, watching as these truths moved slowly across her daughter's face. "This is my fault," Maggie told her. "No one else's." Then she stood up, retrieved Anna's old pink duffel from beneath the bed, and started packing her things.

Part Four

Twenty-One

There was a period of time, the summer after his mother died, when Luke couldn't leave the house. Not just that he didn't want to, he couldn't. Matt came by and sometimes they ventured across the street to mess around by the river and pretend they were explorers, but that was as far as it went. Mostly, Luke stayed inside, though he didn't remember much of what he did there. Watched TV? Drew? He didn't have a computer. Aunt Millie lived with them for part of that summer, and she'd frequently ask him to run errands with her—the supermarket or the shoe store, even tried to bait him with a stop at the Dairy Queen—but Luke didn't respond, didn't even look at her. His stomach seized at the prospect of deciding to go with her, and again at the prospect of deciding not to. The grocery store—was she insane? Either way, something terrible might happen. Eventually he said, *Please stop asking me*, and she'd looked surprised, but done as he asked. She resorted to giving him long worried looks. She made him drink Metamucil. Before she left, she bought him a computer, a gift from her and Uncle Dean.

By August, Luke lived mostly in his room. Brent must have been around, though he had no real memory of it, except for the time he discovered him in the bathroom flooding his eyes with a little dropper and threatening to kill Luke if he told. Told what? And who would he tell? His father wasn't there—at least, he couldn't have been there too often. Later, all Luke remembered of him was the feeling of his absence, his silence. The deep groove, like a quarter slot, that sank between his eyes.

Luke's need to stay inside just grew bigger. His stomach started hurting all the time. By the end of summer, he could barely bring himself to leave his room, until the morning of the first day of sixth grade, when his father walked in and said: *Get up.* Luke was still in bed, covers pulled to his chin. He shook his head. *Get dressed*, his father said, yanking the covers off. Luke closed his eyes as his father started pulling clothes from his dresser and tossing them on the bed. *Mom wouldn't make me*, he said, crying quietly. His father said, *Oh yes she would*, and it felt, impossibly, like he'd lost her even more. His father just looked at him until finally Luke wiped his nose and stood up. Fifteen minutes later, when he appeared in the kitchen, his father handed him a peanut butter sandwich and a limp backpack and walked him out to the truck. Luke saw his brother watching from his bedroom window; he would be taking the bus to the high school. As Luke's father drove him to the junior high, he steered with one hand and pinched Luke's elbow with the other, as if he might otherwise jump from the car. When they pulled up by the entrance, his father sat there waiting until Luke was on the other side of the door.

Ten years later, lying in April Peale's bed, drunk after a party, Luke had told her a little about the summer he didn't leave the house. *Aw, Luke*, she said, and Luke wondered if this would be the default thing girls would say about him for the rest of his life. April's expression was sorry but also, he thought, sort of captivated, as if there was something about this tragic story that made him more valuable to her. *You were just missing your mom*, she said. *You were grieving.* But Luke knew that it was more than this. It wasn't that he was just too sad to go outside; he was paralyzed. He literally couldn't open the door. Then April told him about a reality show she'd seen where a person afraid of spiders was cured by having to sit in a bathtub full of spiders. Luke thought it sounded incredibly stupid, though he didn't say so. *Then the thing lost its power over them*. April smiled. *It was really pretty incredible*, she said.

Luke heard through the online grapevine that Maggie had taken a leave of absence. He didn't know if this meant quit or was fired, but it didn't matter. She was gone. A few days earlier a video had appeared on YouTube, an interview with Nathan's mother, who said Maggie had shown up at her house apologizing. It seemed, to Luke, like a nice thing to do—the kind of thing he should have done too—but it set off a fresh round of Internet blame. That Maggie should be fired. That Maggie could have stopped him, had obviously known about him. Even Nathan's mother seemed angry that she'd come. *I told you this wasn't all my fault*, she said.

Over the next week, Luke stopped going to work. A few times, he called to say he was still sick; then he didn't bother calling. He woke up and acted like he was getting ready, said he was scheduled a little later or felt like riding his bike, then waited until his father's truck had pulled off and returned to his room. He tried to stay off the computer—instead of bringing him relief, it was beginning to make him feel sicker— but he couldn't resist for long. He left the house only to let the dogs out. The air smelled spicy. Late October—his favorite part of the year, maybe even his favorite week—but he couldn't bring himself to venture more than ten feet from his back door. Back upstairs, back online. He stared through the window of the computer. Instagram, Snapchat, Twitter, YouTube. He felt edgy, lonely. He'd deleted his original post— *hey, where'd you go?!* Katie had messaged him. He hadn't replied, but still roamed constantly on Facebook. There was a picture of the fountain at the mall, normally filled with pennies but now choked with white flowers. There was Meredith Kenney, posting that today was her dead brother's birthday; he would have been twenty-eight. *I think about you every day*, she wrote. A chorus of sympathy. *Sending hugs Mer!!! <3 <3 <3* Occasionally he heard Brent and Mike and Layton come banging through the back door. He stayed in his room, drifting, unseen. Through the thin carpet, he smelled weed, heard the loose spills of laughter and slamming cabinets as they raided the kitchen, then the sound of tires tearing up gravel as they left. Silence again. Meredith Kenney's brother. Nathan Dugan's mother. It was hard to picture Nathan Dugan having a mother, but everyone did. *I loved my son.* She was crying. *I just wanted to be close to him.* Luke watched it again and again.

Saturday, Halloween, was the first day of hunting season. His father had taken the day off from work. He always did. The night before, he'd asked Luke if he wanted to come, which caught him off-guard. His father had taken him out hunting lots of times, but it had been a few years since he'd asked; usually he went with Brent, or Ray from work. Luke understood that he wasn't a good partner. He was a lousy shot, and worse, he was a wimp. *They're more afraid of you,* his father used to say. This time Luke shook his head without even thinking about it, but his dad pressed the point. *Why not?* Luke had no good excuse. What came to mind was Nathan Dugan's essay about going hunting with his own father—even though, in that interview, his mother said they never actually went. *I just don't feel like it,* he managed, and his dad gave him a searching look. Luke waited, wanting his father to see what bad shape he was in, to call him on it. But he didn't. Saturday morning, Luke stayed in bed until the truck roared off. He heard the engine dissolving, the faint clack of leaves still clinging to their branches, and closed his eyes. There was the world outside, an outdoors filled with woods and rivers and clouds, but visible, and vulnerable, and there was the world online, which was its own kind of landscape, edgeless and endless, where no one could stare back. He got out of bed, sat down at his computer and disappeared.

That night, Luke was in his room, the dogs asleep at his feet. Brent had left an hour earlier, headed to a party at Layton's, and the house was silent, a silence so complete it almost hurt. When his father knocked, Luke jumped. "Yeah?"

His father opened the door. Luke couldn't remember the last time his father had stepped foot into his room. He stood just inside the doorway and for a minute said nothing, simply scanning the room like a search-light, rubbing at his jaw. "What are you up to?" he asked finally.

"Nothing."

"Did you eat?"

"I wasn't hungry."

His father just kept looking around, and Luke felt a small, hopeful movement in his chest. Then he said, "I hear you stopped showing up for work."

Luke had known, in theory, this conversation would be coming, but he hadn't done anything to prepare for it, and now he had nothing to say.

"Brent told me you quit," his dad said, and Luke felt a flash of hatred for his brother. There were a thousand things Luke might have ratted him out about and never had. "Then I talked to Ray," his father went on, "and he said he heard you stopped going. Which one is it?"

"Stopped going."

His father frowned. "And you think that's the right way to treat an employer?"

"No," he admitted.

"Then what? You just don't need a job all of a sudden?"

"No. I just don't need that job."

"Oh?" He raised his eyebrows. "You have a side career I don't know about?"

Luke shrugged. "I have some money saved."

"I guess you would," his father said, with a chuckle. "Seeing as you live here rent-free."

"Actually," Luke said, gathering his nerve. "I'm going to move soon. To Portland." But just saying the words out loud made him go rigid, spine tightening like a row of screws—he wasn't at all sure it was true, that he could do it even if he wanted to.

"What are you going to do there?"

"I'm figuring that out," he said. "Matt's there. He has an apartment. I can crash with him while I find something."

"And how are you getting there?"

"I'm looking for a car."

His father didn't forbid it, didn't laugh. He looked like he didn't believe it, which was worse. "You know I see used cars come through the shop, right?"

Luke nodded, barely.

"So if you were really serious about it, you'd let me know."

Luke didn't reply. He felt chastised, the flimsiness of his plan exposed. But his father looked uncomfortable, hands sunk in his pockets, gaze roving around the room. "What do you do in here all the time, anyway?"

"What do you mean?"

"Brent says you stay in here all day—"

"Brent said?" Luke replied, with a sudden burst of indignation. "Did he ever think maybe that's just so I don't have to be around him and his asshole friends?" He met his father's eyes. "You do know Brent's a total fuckup, right? He's a slacker. He's a pothead. And he's an asshole. And his friends are all assholes."

He was faintly trembling with anger. He could see, though, this had made a small impact on his father, the slash mark deepening between his eyes. Then his father seemed to reset himself by inches. His jaw loosened, nostrils expelled a stream of air. The groove between his eyes disappeared, like a dent banged smooth.

"But at least he has friends," his father said calmly, and Luke felt dread, like a thick oil, filling his limbs. His father had hit him only a few times in his life, and each time Luke felt that same slow-filling sense of fear, but he reminded himself that this was different. He was almost as big as his father now.

"At least he leaves the house," his father said. "At least he's normal." He paused then, mouth twisting. His words were hurtful but they didn't sound angry; they sounded regretful, resigned. "This thing on the Internet you got caught up in—I don't get it. I don't get any of it. And I don't know what you get up to in here, by yourself day after day, on the computer. But I know it isn't good, Luke."

His father's eyes held steady on his face, and Luke could see then that he wasn't going to hit him. His father looked worried about him, which made Luke feel like he might cry. "That kid you went to school with," he said. "That shooter. His mother didn't have a clue what he was up to." He paused. "I'm not saying— You're a good kid. I know that. But from now on, I want you to stay off the computer."

Luke let out a short, high-pitched laugh. "How are you going to make me do that?"

His father looked at him, then at the computer, as if sizing up a big fish he might try to catch.

"It's mine," Luke said, panicky. "It belongs to me. You can't just take it. And it wouldn't matter anyway. I could get online on my phone—I could get online anywhere."

Luke saw something pass, unguarded, across his father's face, like a ripple in still water—helplessness, or fear. "I just don't want you turning into one of those kids," he said.

"What kids?"

"You know what I mean," his father said. "Those kids. Weird kids."

An hour later, Luke was driving. He hadn't asked his dad if he could borrow the truck though no doubt he'd heard him leave. He'd probably be in trouble later. Or maybe his father would be glad that his son—*a loner, weird, not normal*—had finally left the house. Luke felt raw shame, and anger, but underneath those things, the fear that his father might be right.

He rambled over the bridge, pointed toward the center of town. The road was dark, shadowy and tree-covered, and he narrowly missed a bunch of kids spilling along the shoulder. A few looked like they were wearing masks—costumes, he realized. Halloween. A night when other people, normal people, dressed up and went to parties. *Sorry*, he said out loud, though of course they didn't hear.

As he approached a red light, the truck swerved slightly. Luke pulled to a stop, wiped hard at his face. The light turned, but still he sat there, engine chugging. A block ahead was the town center: auto body,

Dunkin' Donuts, Hannaford—the sadness that rose into his throat was so thick he thought he'd choke. He turned left, toward Layton's. It was only three blocks away, in a shitty row of apartments next to the fire station, a little grassy lot behind it surrounded by a metal fence. As Luke pulled in, he saw a bunch of cars parked haphazardly under some trees. He shut the engine off, facing the backs of the houses. At one of them, a few girls were smoking on the steps under a weak yellow porch light. A cowgirl, a cheerleader. Costumes—this was a fucking costume party. For a minute, Luke sat there, trapped. He didn't want to wear a costume, didn't have a costume, but he couldn't be the guy without a costume because then he'd have to hear about it all night. He flicked the overhead light on and rummaged in the backseat. It was all hunting stuff from that afternoon. Balled-up tinfoil, thermos, shirt, vest, hat, guns. He threw on the camouflage shirt, the orange vest. They almost fit. They smelled like his dad. He pulled the hat down to his ears. Then he climbed out of the truck and stumbled toward the porch, the ground carpeted with dead blue-black leaves.

"Luke?"

It was one of the girls. The cowgirl. Limp blond pigtails, brown hat, bad skin. Heather, from Dunkin' Donuts.

"I didn't recognize you," she said.

"Oh. Hey."

"I didn't expect to see you here." She sounded confused, though not particularly disappointed; there was a jump in her voice, like she was glad he'd come.

"Yeah. Well, me neither." Luke stepped up to the porch, maybe a little too close. He felt out of practice being in the world, around actual people, gauging where to sit and stand.

"What happened to you?" Heather asked, and Luke felt alarmed— what had?—then refocused. She was asking him about work.

"Oh, right," he said. "I quit." His head felt hot. "Can I have one of those?" he asked, reaching down to grab a can of beer from a bucket of melting ice.

"You quit?" Heather asked, watching as he snapped the can open. She seemed to be studying him closely—did she not believe him? Had she heard a different version?

"Basically," he said, drinking fast.

"Where are you working now?"

"I'm not," he said. "I'm moving. To Portland." Every time he said this it felt a little more true.

"Oh, really?" Heather replied, and this time he thought she did sound a little disappointed, but Luke felt encouraged that she believed he was really moving. The truth was, it wasn't that big a deal. People moved all the time.

"Hey," the cheerleader spoke up. "I know you." She had small, pinched eyes and a raspy voice, long purple nails. Luke had seen her before, waiting to pick up Heather when her shift ended, smoking out front or picking at a doughnut in the corner of the store.

"Yeah, I've seen you at work, I think," he said, wiping his mouth with the back of his hand. He chucked his empty can on the grass.

"No, not that," she said, eyes narrowed to dimes. "Weren't you all over the Internet or something?"

"Nope," he said, and fished out another can.

"Yes, you were, Luke," Heather said, turning to her friend. "He was. He's being modest."

"Yes," the girl said, nodding slowly. "You wrote that thing on Facebook. I read it. I think we're friends." Which made Luke laugh out loud—the sound was like a pinball dislodged in his chest, a rolling, careening ache.

"You knew that kid, didn't you?" she continued, sucking air against her teeth. "That's right. You did. You were friends with him or something."

"No!" Luke said, practically shouting. The cheerleader raised her eyebrows. "I wasn't friends with him. I had one class with him. But I barely knew him. He was fucking crazy," he added, and at this she smiled a little. Luke suddenly imagined kissing her, pressing her back into the side of the house and sticking his tongue down her throat.

Then the back door swung open and Luke heard, "Hey! Is that my little brother?" He looked up to find Brent standing in the doorway. He sounded unusually friendly, but Luke realized this was because he was extremely stoned. He was smiling loosely, holding a giant Big Gulp cup of what appeared to be water. Layton was beside him. Neither of them was wearing a costume; apparently it was optional after all.

Luke shrugged. "I just had to get out of the house."

"Since when?" Brent said, and Layton burst out in a laugh. "I'm kidding," Brent said. "Here." He chucked another beer toward Luke. It landed on the dirt, missing him. "Drink that. You need that more than anyone I've ever known."

"Be nice," said the cheerleader, swatting Brent's ankle.

"What? He does," Brent said. Luke concentrated on draining the beer in his hand. "I *am* being nice. He never leaves his room."

"Maybe that's because he's busy writing important things," she said. "He was just telling me about his Facebook post."

No, Luke thought, he wasn't.

"I totally remember it," she said, and Brent snorted, "Congratulations."

"It was really popular," Heather added.

"Yeah," Brent said. "I'm aware."

Luke's face, his whole body, was growing hot. He watched as the cheerleader pressed the tip of her purple nail into the toe of Brent's shoe. "Did *you* ever write anything that anyone bothered reading?" she asked.

"Nope," Brent said. He sounded proud, but with an edge. "Can't say that I have. That's because I have a life."

Layton laughed again, a high-pitched laugh, and Heather flashed Luke a *sorry* look. Brent took a gulp of the water and spilled a little, came up crunching ice cubes, addressed the group. "You want to know what he does all day?" he announced, and Luke's stomach twisted. "Sits in his room. Reading about sick shit on the Internet."

Luke shook his head quickly. "No I don't," he said. "That's not true."

Layton was still laughing, just a stream of giggles, not connected to anything.

"You read about that guy all the time," Brent said. "The lunatic who shot up a mall."

"The one he went to school with," said the cheerleader.

"He was a psycho. He went hunting with a fucking semiauto—"

"You don't know what you're talking about," Luke said. He stared at his brother, jaw clenched, unable to look anywhere else. "And what, are you, like, spying on me or something? Are you reading my search history?"

"See?" Brent cracked, triumphant. "What did I tell you."

"Why do you even give a shit? Why'd you have to rat me out to Dad?"

His brother frowned. "About what?"

"About *work*," Luke said. He didn't look at Heather or her friend; he didn't care anymore. "You act like you have some great life or something and you just lie around. You're a loser. You don't actually do *anything*."

Brent looked at him in surprise, stopped crunching. He seemed to sober up a little. "You better shut the fuck up," he said.

Even Layton finally stopped laughing. "What's your problem?"

"I don't know," Luke said. "What's yours?"

"This is my house, you know," Layton said. "You're on my property."

"Property?" Luke laughed shrilly. It was a chain-link fence, surrounding the saddest yard in the world.

"Hey," Brent said, and his face was hardening. "You showed up here, remember? I didn't invite you. Maybe you followed me here or something—I don't know. I don't know what you get up to. Maybe you're a stalker now. Maybe all that time in your room made you a little nuts." His brother's frown deepened, eyes squinting as if into sudden sunlight. "And what the fuck are you wearing?"

Luke glanced down at himself. "I thought it was a—"

"Are you *dressed* like him or something?"

For a minute, Luke thought he was talking about their father; then he realized he was talking about Nathan. Nathan Dugan. The possibility— even untrue, even accidental—was so horrifying it made Luke's insides turn to liquid.

"Oh God," the cheerleader said. "Is he?"

"It's just a costume," Luke fumbled. "I thought—"

Brent breathed, "What the *fuck*."

"Shut up," Luke said. His stomach was pulsing. "Shut up. Just do your dumb shit with your dumb friends." Then he turned and started back to the truck. He wished he could melt into the ground. But he could hear Brent following, trampling through the sodden leaves.

"So you're a tough guy now, all of a sudden?" his brother said.

Luke kept walking but Brent was gaining on him, breathing roughly. He had just opened the truck door when he was shoved hard on the shoulder and fell against the dashboard. "Get off," he mumbled.

"Dad said you were too scared to come hunting."

"I wasn't scared," Luke said, scrambling into the driver's seat.

But Brent reached in and grabbed the rifle from the back. "I bet you can't even hit that tree," he said, and stepped back, taking aim. It was a skinny birch, branches nearly bare. Still, the shot caused a rattle in the leaves.

From the porch, Layton started laughing again. Luke shut the truck door, groping in his pocket for the keys. His palms were sweating, face prickling. Brent was turning in slow circles, looking for a target—the wretched apartments, barren field. "Hey, put it down," Heather said, as Brent shot at another tree, a screeching flurry. Layton shouted: "Ten points!"

Luke started the engine and turned on the high beams, flooding the yard, bleaching the sky. As the truck lurched forward, his brother aimed the gun at the windshield, laughing, and in a panic, Luke cut the wheel hard. He heard the scrape and crunch of metal as he sideswiped another parked car, and then his father's truck was hurtling toward the trees, and for a moment he felt light, weightless, he felt nothing, until he heard the shattering of glass, and the branch came crashing through the window and into the front seat.

Twenty-Two

When Anna stepped inside the house, the first thing she noticed was the smell of cleanser. Fake pine—it filled her nose as sharply as chlorine. Her head hurt on contact, a small flowering of pain in her temple. As she returned the car keys to the hook by the front door, she grew abruptly teary-eyed, from the smell or the appointment she'd just left or both.

"How did it go?" her mother said.

She was in the kitchen, standing in the middle of the room, dishes and dry goods piled on the counter. She appeared to be scrubbing the cabinets, something Anna could not recall ever having seen her do. This, though, was the new version of her mother, the one who wasn't teaching. She was constantly at home. It was November, the heart of the fall semester, when she was usually dashing back and forth to campus, marking papers and meeting students, and now she was so available, so visible somehow—the rigid squares of her shoulders, twin blades jutting through the back of her shapeless sweater, constant worry on her face.

"It was fine," Anna clipped, and pulled out a chair at the kitchen table. Over the week and a half she'd been home, Anna had met with Theresa four times, and her mother had asked about each appointment, something she hadn't done since Anna started going sophomore year. She'd always assumed this lack of inquiry was out of respect for her privacy, but also because, deep down, her mother didn't really want to know. Now, though, Maggie was constantly watching her, questioning her, as if searching for symptoms. In the absence of students, all her mother's attention was finally focused on her.

That's quite a reversal, Theresa had observed not an hour ago. *You always described her as so distracted by her students. The night she took Alison Bower to get help, you've said how much it hurt that she didn't notice the pain you—*

Yeah, Anna had said, cutting her off. *And without them, she's, like, aimless. She has nothing else to do.*

"Well, what did she say?" Her mother was still looking at her, still waiting, a sponge clutched in her hand.

"I mean, I'm not secretly starving myself, if that's what you're implying," Anna said. "I'm stable." It was technically true. She was back on Lexapro and steadily adding more calories, more and different foods, soft foods, foods she could handle—she'd been through this process before and fell back into it with a combination of shame and deep relief. But the food, the meds—that was the easier part. Or, at least, the more tangible. Beneath it lurked the real problem—abstract, seemingly insurmountable—which was that Anna was so paralyzingly afraid. Gavin used to joke about his neighbors, the old Abbotts, who had exiled themselves after their son died, but Anna thought she understood the impulse completely. She was still avoiding the Internet because she couldn't risk running into any more horrible stories, shootings or dead bodies. The one time she drove past the mall she'd had to pull over and breathe into her knees.

I know it's scary, Anna, Theresa had said. *And it's true. Things will happen. Things that are not in your control. But you do have choices.* Anna hadn't replied, tearing at the hole in the knee of her jeans.

Now she said, "We talked about me going to this party. With Kim."

"And she thought that was a good idea?" her mother asked—hopefully, it seemed. Her hope was unbearable.

"I mean, it would involve being around other people, so that's probably a step in the right direction," Anna said, then glanced away. Theresa had stressed this point: that by exposing herself to the things that made her anxious, Anna would realize those things couldn't hurt her. But she felt bad, seeing the sadness on her mother's face. She wondered about who, besides herself, her mother even talked to. Without her students, it was striking how unpeopled her life was. The affair she'd had was over; Anna had asked, and she believed her. Her mother seemed so unmoored she couldn't possibly be involved with someone right now. Initially, Anna had found the news of the affair upsetting—the fact that it had happened, the difficulty of aligning this version of her mother, of the world, with the one she thought she knew—but she could no longer summon any anger. Last week, when Maggie had appeared at Anna's dorm, she'd been steely and determined, single-minded, but now her mother had collapsed, insides showing, like a house with its walls stripped away.

Then Maggie asked, "Is it on campus?"

Anna paused. "What?"

"The party. Kim's party."

"Yeah. In her dorm." Anna really didn't want to go; she was only considering it because Kim had asked her. *You owe me*, she'd said. Then Anna hesitated. "Oh," she said, and looked up at her mother. "Is that not okay or something?"

Her mother looked back. "Why wouldn't it be?"

"I mean—should I not go to campus?"

"I'm not banned from setting foot on campus," she said, with a weak laugh. "And neither are you, certainly." But she looked pained. Anna had always resented her mother's love for her students but was beginning to comprehend how truly outsized it had been, how small and shrunken the life that was left. "It was my decision," she added, and Anna nodded. Then her mother pulled out a chair and sat across from her, shifting a stack of plates to one side. "So Dad's coming," she said. "Next week."

"Really?" Anna replied, caught off-guard. "Coming where? Here?"

"He wants to spend some time with you. And we thought—we both agreed—given everything, your appointments with Theresa—and, just, everything—it might be best that way."

Anna pinched a fingernail into her exposed knee. "Felicia's not coming, is she?"

"I offered," she said. "But no. Just him."

"Thank God," Anna said, and her mother cracked a small smile. "Still. Will that be weird?"

"Yes," her mother admitted. "Probably." She shrugged, an unconvincing twitch of one shoulder, and Anna felt a swell of sympathy for her. For what she'd put her through, and what she'd lost. It would be hard for her, Anna realized, to have her dad there. It was the reason she was cleaning. It used to be that her mother barely seemed to register the dust and the mess, but now everything was more exposed.

The next morning, Anna woke at eight thirty, and the house was silent. For a moment, she tried to enjoy the peace and quiet—had she experienced a moment of true peace since she'd left for school?—but as she lay there listening, the quiet stole inside her brain. Her mother was always up early, by five thirty usually, but there was no trace of her. Anna was reminded of that morning in August, returning from Gavin's, hungover. She'd searched the empty house, roaming through room after room and feeling more and more disoriented, like being inside a bad dream, until eventually she'd checked the barn.

This time, when she got out of bed and looked out the window at the driveway, the car was gone. There was a note on the kitchen counter: *at store.* Anna sat at the table and ate her cereal and milk and apple. She felt agitated, her edges ragged. Maybe it was yesterday's appointment with Theresa, or the prospect of Kim's party that night, which she now felt pressured to attend. When she caught herself crunching her stomach in/out, she said out loud: "Stop it, Anna. Stop." She pressed her palms against her eyes and inhaled as deeply as she could. Then she stood and pulled on her coat and grabbed her backpack from the hall closet, checking that her laptop was still inside. When she stepped out the back door, the smack of cold made her teeth ache. She headed toward the barn—*dilapidated*, she'd once described it, which James had applauded as authentic, but the reality of it was just sad. She steered her bike through the rusty door, wheeled it across the yard, and then took off down the driveway, spackled with flat wet pinecones and fallen leaves.

The chill was bracing, the sky an alert white, so white it looked almost pink. Bare maples stood along the side of the road. They looked like naked lungs. Anna's cheeks were quickly numb, but it felt good to be moving. It was six miles to the town library, and by the time the white clapboard house came into view, she felt calmer, her edges smooth. But as she pulled into the parking lot, Anna realized her mistake: On Saturdays, the library didn't open until noon. For a minute she just sat there, staring at the pearl-colored sky. In the past, she would have taken her laptop to the mall— there was Wi-Fi in the food court—but that wasn't an option anymore. The only other possibility was one of the coffee shops on campus. She entertained the idea of biking past the mall to get there, but only for an instant. She couldn't unsee the sign by the road, the one that had always advertised sales or photos with the Easter Bunny but now said only RIP NEVER FORGET.

Ten miles of back roads later, Anna parked her bike outside a coffee shop. It was still relatively early, uncrowded. Inside, a few people worked on laptops, flanked by mugs of coffee. A group of runners sat together in their school-branded windbreakers. All of them were Central Maine students, surely. Strange to think Anna would be assumed to be one too. Since coming home, she'd received two texts from Alexis—*doing ok, roomie?*—and one from Isabel. For the most part, though, she hadn't had, or wanted, any contact with school (in that regard, her mother's canceled Wi-Fi had been a perfect excuse). Now she ordered coffee and found a table by the window, plugged in her laptop. After so much neglect, it seemed to wake up slowly. She picked up her mug and took a sip. Outside, a few snowflakes drifted slowly toward the sidewalk. Apprehensively, she opened up her school email, but there wasn't much

there. Missed announcements about advising for next semester, an an-
thropology lecture, a Halloween party in the student union. She deleted
as she went. Then, bracing herself, she clicked on Facebook—but there
were no longer any comments about the shooting. No comments about
her mother, or the YouTube video. It was back to the usual dumb stuff.
It was both soothing and depressing. Drunken posts from the night before, selfies from college parties. A Groupon deal, an ad for the Gap. *Get
to know your new favorite pair of boots!* She clicked her notifications: *New
Message from Luke Finch.*

Anna knew the name, though it took her a few seconds to search
her brain and retrieve it. When she did, panic tunneled through her—
her mother's old student. The one who wrote that thing. Why, possibly,
would he be writing to her? She checked the date on the email: It had
been sent over a month ago, early October. There were needles in her
palms. What did he have to say to her? Was he going to attack her, or her
mother? Her finger hovered over the DELETE button, ready to make the
message vanish, but then she took a breath and looked around the room.
She reminded herself that she was here, in this coffee shop, and this message was online, it couldn't hurt her. It was scarcely real. If she chose to
read it, then she couldn't torture herself with thoughts of all the terrible
things it might have said. She could read it once and make it disappear.

*Hi my name is Luke Finch. I was your mother's student and I'm sorry about
everything. I'd take it all back if I could. I never thought your mother was a bad
teacher and I never wanted to get anyone in trouble and actually I'm a hypocrite
because I'm the one who screwed up. I was a jerk to Nathan when he was maybe
asking me for help one time and there was a moment when maybe if he'd connected with somebody things could have ended up different. Or not. Maybe he
was just really screwed up more than I thought but if anyone should be getting
blamed it should be me.*

For a minute, Anna stared at the screen. Her mouth was dry. She'd
been prepared to be indignant and now she didn't know what to feel.
She read the message twice more; it sounded sincere. She pulled up
Luke's Facebook page and, channeling Alexis, picked through it. Home-

town: Paxton, Maine. Birthday: March 29, 1993. A profile picture of two dogs, identical golden retrievers. Recent albums he'd been tagged in—*Spring Break, Graduation, Senior Week*. He had a nice smile, though he was rarely looking at the camera. In most of the pictures, he was with the same girl, tagged April Peale. After *Senior Week*, she disappeared. There were no more recent photos, hardly any recent anything. Ironically, it didn't seem that Luke Finch was too active on Facebook. His long, sprawling post from August was no longer there.

The only recent post was this: *The reason I wrote about Nathan Dugan in the first place is because one time he asked me to hang out with him and I said no and I felt bad about it.* It had attracted only a few vapid responses, stupid smiley faces. They were missing the point. He wasn't asking to be reassured; he felt guilty. It was an apology. *I dare you,* Anna thought, and before she could talk herself out of it, she had opened up his message and written: *hi thanks for sending.*

As soon as she hit RETURN, she felt a whorl of panic—that her message was out there, loosed in space. She watched the laptop for a minute, willing the words back, then stared out the window. The snow had started coming down more quickly. She went back to the counter for a refill and by the time she sat down again, there was a reply on the screen.

Luke: *hey*

Luke: *thanks for writing back*

She surveyed the coffee shop, as if he might be sitting there undercover, but there were only the students with their laptops and their coffees. A barista was crouched next to the display case, arranging muffins behind the glass. She returned to the empty box.

Me: *sorry it took so long*

Me: *i just saw your message*

Me: *been avoiding the internet lately*

SEND, SEND, SEND. She waited, heartbeat ticking. It was a strange thing to put out there, she thought, about the Internet. She took a long swallow of coffee, preparing for his response, but he wrote only: *thats probably a good thing*

Luke: *the internet i mean*

Anna set her coffee down. Outside, the snow was starting to stick.

You think? she typed. *I thought you were some kind of online sensation.*

Luke: *hahaha*

Luke: *i hope not*

She smiled a little.

Luke: *hows your mom?*

Anna considered the screen.

Me: *fine*

Me: *not teaching right now*

Me: *but you probably knew that*

Luke: *is she going back next semester?*

Me: *she says she isnt sure*

Me: *but its literally impossible to imagine her doing anything else*

Me: *im living with her actually*

Me: *temporarily*

Me: *im on a break from school*

It was another bizarre thing to admit to a stranger. He'd probably judge her for it, think she was needy and screwed up, but did it matter? The whole exchange was real and not-real at the same time. Her pulse beat quickly as she watched the dots that meant Luke Finch was typing. Worst-case scenario, he asked her questions she didn't want to answer, and she logged off, never wrote to him again.

Luke: *i get it*

Luke: *im actually living with my dad*

At his kindness, her entire body relaxed a notch. They went on like that for a while, trading messages, like raindrops falling into the ocean, one and then the next.

Twenty-Three

As Maggie watched Tom's car pull up to the house, headlights beaming in the falling late afternoon light, she remembered the day he left. It was the last time he'd been there: a bitterly cold Saturday in March, patches of black ice on the driveway, the sky a leaden gray. To Maggie's dismay, Anna had skipped swim practice, wanting to be there to say good-bye. She'd stood on the porch steps, crying as Tom's truck rolled away, dragging the slippery U-Haul behind it, and by the time he was turning onto the main road—excruciatingly slowly, the patient blinking of the turn signal almost an insult—Anna was folded over her knees, sobbing. Maggie remembered observing her from a distance, as if her own daughter were a wild animal she had no idea how to appease or to approach.

Now, Tom was driving a hatchback and carrying a single duffel. Anna greeted him with a long hug, and the sight of them together made Maggie's eyes stir with feeling. He was older, Maggie thought. Thicker around the middle, and his hair was gray all over. It shouldn't have surprised her. She made herself smile, like a host, and showed him to the office-turned-guest-room. Offered him a cup of coffee the way he always took it, no sugar, a touch of cream.

That first night, they ordered pizza from Mario's. Tom didn't say much.

He was still angry, Maggie knew, that she hadn't called him the day she went to pick up Anna. Perhaps sensing her parents' discomfort, Anna did most of the talking. She told Tom she was doing a little better, mentioned the party she'd gone to with Kim the weekend before. She was starting to think about going back next semester, she told them. She could take extra credits and still graduate on time. She and Theresa had discussed holding weekly Skype appointments. Maggie watched as she ate two slices, and without leaving a pile of oily napkins beside her plate.

After dinner, Anna went upstairs, and Tom said he had to make a phone call. Maggie offered the land line, reminding him about the cell reception, but he said he'd try his luck with his phone outside. As she washed the dinner dishes, Maggie watched him swivel like a weathervane, attempting to pick up a tendril of reception. She heard him cursing. It had never frustrated him much before, she thought, but of course now he was accustomed to a more efficient sort of life. He was heading back toward the house just as Anna skipped downstairs, saying, "I'm going out."

"You are?"

"Just to the coffee shop," she said, as Tom stepped through the back door.

"Now?" Maggie said. "It's late."

"It's seven forty-five," Anna said. "It's only late here. Everywhere else in the world it's early."

"She's right," Tom said.

"I need Wi-Fi," Anna said. Maggie had told herself that, for Anna, the canceled Internet had been a good thing: It had led her to this coffee shop she liked, motivated her to leave the house.

"That makes two of us," Tom said, and Maggie felt an old twinge of annoyance—his easy attitude toward Anna, their old alliance. But Anna looked at her and said, "I won't be late."

After she was gone, Maggie gestured again to the old phone on the kitchen wall. "Help yourself," she said, then retreated to the living room couch. She tried to focus on the book in her lap while Tom made his call.

He spoke quietly and quickly, with urgency, though Maggie couldn't make out any words. After Tom hung up, there was silence. Maggie watched the dark television screen, breathing as quietly as she could. She pictured Tom standing in the kitchen, which had once been his kitchen, noticing the grime between the floor tiles or the way the wallpaper they'd chosen together years ago had started curling at the seams. Then she heard him clanking in a cabinet, and he appeared in the living room with a bottle of wine clamped under his elbow, two glasses in his hand. "Porch?"

"Where did you find that?" she replied, but he was already heading across the room. She peeled the afghan off the couch and followed, turned off the porch light to keep moths from flocking the bulb. Outside, they each assumed one of the white wooden rockers. It was something they had never done before; maybe that was why Tom had suggested it. The chairs should already have been brought inside for winter—their wood was chipping, cushions caked with dirt—but the sky, she thought, was luminous. A waste that they hadn't sat there years ago.

Tom wrenched the cork off the bottle and picked up a glass. Maggie drew the afghan around her shoulders. "I can't believe we're back here again," she said.

Tom said nothing, focused on pouring.

"It was visible," she added.

"You should have called me, Maggie."

"You had lunch with her in—what? October? And you didn't see it? You actually said she looked good," Maggie snapped, but her anger dried in her throat. She didn't have any right to it. She too had missed it. "Sorry," she apologized, before he could speak. Tom handed her a glass, set the bottle by his feet.

"What can I say. I saw her. I spent two hours with her," he said. "I thought she was doing well."

He was always more forgiving of them as parents than Maggie had been, more generous, and this had once annoyed her too. Now she was grateful. Maggie took a sip. Despite everything, it was comfortable, talking to Tom: the familiarity of him, their long shared history. To really know a person—how much work it was, how much effort.

"So, how is she?" he asked, settling back in his chair, holding his glass by the stem.

"She seems better," Maggie said. "She says she is. But who knows. I don't know." She shook her head. "It's not as if I exactly trust myself these days."

"Well," Tom said. "It can be easy to miss things."

"I seem to be making a career of it."

Maggie took another sip. She rarely drank, and already a pleasant lightness had settled in her fingers and toes. Then Tom said, "I don't know. It didn't seem all that clear-cut to me."

It took her a moment to realize he wasn't talking about Anna, but the essay. Nathan's essay. When she did, her heart pitched toward him. "It didn't?"

"I mean, it was strange, sure. But was it a definite call to action? I thought it was hard to say." He looked at her. "You saw the kid every week. If there was a real emergency, you would have known it."

"I don't know about that." She spread her hands. "Look at us now."

She took another swallow, and Tom did the same. The night was quiet, filled with the clicking and rustling of invisible creatures.

"So what happens next semester?" he asked her.

"I'm not sure," she said. "But I can't go back. My decision," she clarified, when she saw his eyebrows rise.

"Maggie," Tom said. "Don't let this thing scare you off. You're a good teacher."

"Says the man who resented me for it for seventeen years."

But it was light, it was teasing; it was the past.

"You were right about that, by the way," she told him. "It got too big. It took over."

"Still," Tom said, though he didn't argue the point. He was looking at her with concern. "Don't leave because of pride."

"It's not that," Maggie said. "I'm just not sure I'm cut out for it anymore. Too much responsibility."

"You love responsibility," he said. "Your best self," he reminded her, and lifted the empty glass from her hand. "Besides, what would you do instead?"

"I don't know. Maybe I'll finally get back to working on my book," she said, but sheepishly, for they both knew how the book had stagnated over the years, more symbolic than real. "Or—you'll laugh, but—a colleague offered to put me in touch with a friend of his who's looking to hire writing instructors online."

Tom smiled a little. "You're kidding."

"I know." She hated it—in theory, objected to it—but it had certain advantages: the flexibility to keep teaching but stay at home. Robert had texted to say he'd talked to this old friend, unprompted, and recommended her. Perhaps he felt he owed her; if so, so be it.

"I miss this," Tom said, and there was an uneasy lurch in her gut. Then he gestured around them. "All this space. This quiet."

"Oh," Maggie said. They sat in silence. Warmth was coursing through her limbs. The trees shone black, the sky a deep blue. "I think that's why I was afraid of elevators," she said.

Tom chuckled. "Come again?"

"Growing up in a place like this. Surrounded by so much space."

"I don't remember that," he said. "You and elevators."

Maggie turned on him, incredulous. "You must be kidding. If I went anywhere more than one floor, I had to take the stairs because I was afraid of being trapped in that little metal coffin. Even if I had Anna, I dragged her along. Come to think of it, that was probably the root of all her problems," she said, with a strained laugh. For surely this was the worry of every parent, that you've passed on your own greatest fears, your deepest weaknesses. "It was probably the exact wrong thing to do," she said. "I didn't want her to know I was afraid of them. Now she's so afraid of everything that she can't function in the world."

"Come on, Mag," Tom said. "That's not true."

"Isn't it?" Maggie said. She drew a breath. "But how are you supposed to know? Do you expose your kids to all the things that might upset them, so they get used to it, or do you protect them?"

"You do your best," Tom said, and this was what she missed: the simplicity with which he saw the world, the inclination to give people passes, let things slide. He looked into his glass, then said, "Felicia wants to have a baby."

"Oh?" Maggie said. She was startled. "I had no idea it was that serious."

"She's thirty-eight," Tom replied, flexing his empty hand. "I'm not sure I can do it. She keeps telling me I'm not too old. But it's not my age. It's just—the world," he said. "Where will it all be three decades from now? One decade? Is it even fair to bring a kid into a world like this?"

Maggie didn't know the answer, was glad that she didn't have to. Because she understood. The future had never felt so perilous, so unreliable, the world a dangerous and often frightening place.

"She doesn't get it," Tom said.

He looked up then, peering at the vast and darkening sky, as if at a vision of what was coming. Maggie saw the old worry lines on his face. Instinctively, she reached out and touched his leg, and when he looked at her, she leaned over and kissed him. He pulled back in surprise. "Maggie," he said, gently, pressing his hand over hers.

She took her hand back. She was ashamed, humiliated, and at the same time amazed a person could still feel such things so deeply around someone they'd been married to for seventeen years. She set her glass on the porch floor. "I'm sorry," she said. "I don't know what I'm doing. I never drink."

"It's okay."

"I'm not myself," she said.

They sat under the empty sky, neither of them speaking. The night was dark and it was quiet, except for the occasional passing car. It would start as a faint sound, as a brightness gathering, growing louder as the car drew closer and its headlights flickered madly between the bare trees, then continued by.

Twenty-Four

11/15/2015 9:55AM

Luke: *hello?*

11/15/2015 12:58PM

Luke: *trying this again...*

11/15/2015 4:02PM

Anna: *hi*

Anna: *still there?*

11/15/2015 4:14PM

Luke: *im here*

Anna: *hi sorry i havent been online since yesterday*

Luke: *avoiding the internet right?*

Anna: *partly*

Anna: *also theres no service at my moms*

Luke: *your mom has no internet?*
Luke: *is she a pioneer?*

Anna: *essentially yes* ☺
Anna: *she canceled it a couple weeks ago*
Anna: *which is bizarre i know but at least makes me leave the house*

Luke: *maybe i should cancel the internet too*
Luke: *ive been trying to cut back*

Anna: *to be honest i recommend it*
Anna: *although then we wouldnt be talking . . .*

Luke: *thats true*
Luke: *. . .*
Luke: *so where are you?*

Anna: *coffee shop on campus*

Luke: *which?*

Anna: *oh right you went here*
Anna: *thats kind of hard to picture actually*
Anna: *i barely know you and this is a gross generalization but i was at a party here last night and it was packed w bros*

Luke: *how do you know im not a bro?*

Anna: *haha true*
Anna: *wait- are you?*

Luke: *definitely not*

If We Had Known

Anna: ☺☺☺

Luke: *where was the party?*

Anna: *woodside*
Anna: *one of my best friends lives there*

Luke: *was it fun?*

Anna: *not even a little*

Luke: *haha yeah i can see that*
Luke: *i bet i can top it though*
Luke: *at the last party i went to my brother was waving a gun around*

Anna: *what??*

Luke: *and i freaked out*

Anna: *understandable!!*

Luke: *and then i crashed my car into a tree*

Anna: *omg*
Anna: *are you ok?!*

Luke: *i broke my leg*
Luke: *and my face is kind of scratched up*
Luke: *but basically yeah*
Luke: *at least now my brother leaves me alone haha*

Anna: *thats a relief*

Anna: *and also terrible*
Anna: *and yes you definitely win*

11/19/2015 1:02PM

Anna: *hi?*

11/19/2015 1:06PM

Luke: *hey what are you up to?*

Anna: *i just left my therapist*
Anna: *tmi?*

Luke: *no thats cool*
Luke: *why do you see a therapist?*

Anna: *um*
Anna: *. . .*

Luke: *that was dumb you dont have to answer*

Anna: *no its ok*
Anna: *i had some issues in high school*
Anna: *food and anxiety basically*
Anna: *thats actually why im taking time off from school*
Anna: *please respond quickly to minimize mortification . . .*

Luke: *ok*

Anna: *ok?*

Luke: *im sorry im an idiot*
Luke: *i meant are you ok now?*

Anna: *getting there i guess*
Anna: *except for the fact that i cant drive past the mall*
w/o having a panic attack

Luke: *im sorry*

Anna: *and im living back at home*

Luke: *well at least youre not alone* ☺

11/20/2015 4:24PM

Anna: *so . . .*
Anna: *my dads coming to the house tonight*
for the first time since the divorce

Luke: *whoa*
Luke: *i guess that will be weird?*

Anna: *yes and no*
Anna: *for a while i wanted them to get back together but now they seem so*
wrong for each other its sort of hard to believe they were ever married
Anna: *plus he has a whole other life in portland with his gf*

Luke: *portlands cool at least*

Anna: *yeah i spent a lot of weekends there*

Luke: *i want to live there someday*

Anna: *you should!*

Luke: *my dad thinks so too*

Anna: *are your parents still together?*

Luke: *no*
Luke: ...
Luke: *actually my mom died*

Anna: *oh my god luke*
Anna: *i am so sorry*
Anna: ...
Anna: *when?*

Luke: *i was ten*
Luke: *a car accident*

Anna: *i dont know what to say*
Anna: *except that fb is totally inadequate for replying to something like that*
Anna: *and this is terrible timing but i have to get back home before my dad gets there...*
Anna: *but do you want to talk later?*

Luke: *sure*

Anna: *8?*

Luke: *its a date*

11/28/2015 7:12PM

Anna: *do you ever wonder what a loser sitting in a coffee shop in her hometown thinks about on a saturday night?*

Luke: *haha yes definitely*

If We Had Known

Anna: *if you want to live in portland why dont you just move?*

Luke: *i mean*
Luke: *...*
Luke: *i cant go anywhere until my leg heals*

Anna: *i know*

Luke: *and i need to get a car*

Anna: *yeah but those arent real reasons*
Anna: *i mean right?*
Anna: *plus doesnt the cast come off next week...?*

Luke: *ok ok*
Luke: *you really want to know?*

Anna: *yes*
Anna: *if you want to tell me*

Luke: *i was having a hard time leaving*
Luke: *like actually leaving my house*

Anna: *ok*
Anna: *like an anxiety thing?*

Luke: *its never been diagnosed or anything but yeah i guess*

Anna: *i get it*
Anna: *seriously i do*

Luke: *well thats good*

Luke: *i dont mean good*

                                                 Anna: *i know what you mean*

Luke: *its just that most people dont*

                                                 Anna: *right*

Luke: *but whats weird is now that im stuck here i actually want to go*

12/12/2015 3:05PM

                                                Anna: *NEWS FLASH*
               Anna: *kim is co-hosting a big party with high school people the weekend after christmas and im dreading it*

Luke: *how come?*

                                  Anna: *too many people i dont feel like seeing*

Luke: *so dont go*

                                                 Anna: *have to go*
                              Anna: *kim and janie would kill me*
                                      Anna: *and i owe them*

Luke: *well at least you have them there*

                                                 Anna: *true*
                         Anna: *i sort of wish you could be there honestly…*
                              Anna: *is that a weird thing to say?*

Luke: *no*

Luke: . . .
Luke: *actually i had an idea*

                                            Anna: . . .

Luke: *it might be really dumb*
Luke: *but what if i got a car and drove to portland*

                                            Anna: *not dumb . . .*

Luke: *and i could make a stop along the way*

                                Anna: *i know a coffee shop thats not horrible*

Luke: *or i was thinking*
Luke: *what if you go to the mall and i meet you there?*

Twenty-Five

T he Saturday after Christmas, the party was at Brian Tucker's house but it could have been anywhere. The details were all familiar: the sleeve of red plastic cups in the kitchen, keg on the back porch, coat pile in the corner. It was freezing, which meant there was an attempt at a bonfire in the backyard, spitting sparks into the night sky. Anna had been to this party a thousand times.

Though, in fact, she had actually never been to Brian Tucker's. He lived in one of the ranch houses in the neighborhood behind the mall. His parents had gone to visit friends in Vermont for the weekend. Since Brian and Kim were now a couple, they were sort of joint-hosting. Kim had dressed up a little, wearing more makeup, jeans with a blouse tucked in. She looked less quirky, Anna thought, less Kim-like. More like someone who went to Central Maine.

"Good to see you, D–B," Brian said when she arrived, kissing her cheek. Anna found his new maturity disconcerting. The entire party felt a few degrees more sophisticated. Kim had put out plastic bowls of chips and pretzels, and claimed Brian had run a vacuum that afternoon.

It was a cold night, true cold, predicted to drop below zero. Except for the people stepping onto the porch to get refills or grab a smoke by the fire, the party stayed mostly indoors. The living room was quickly filling, everybody dressed for the weather. Even Claudia and Tara, the notoriously underclad, were wearing turtlenecks and big furry boots. There was lots of hugging as people entered, as if it had been years since they'd seen each other instead of less than four months. Most of them were from Anna's class, though there were some juniors and seniors. Maybe they'd been invited; maybe they'd heard the rumor of a proper party, of the extra alcohol Brian had bought with his newly passable fake ID. As Anna watched Kim and Brian greet people by the front door, her arm tucked around his waist, she realized that Kim might well marry Brian Tucker, settle down in Stafford and never leave.

"Anna!"

She scanned the room to find Claudia Jones smiling, heading toward her. The smile was disorienting. Their last contact had been on Facebook, when Claudia had posted a link to the article about her mom, the essay, and Anna had never replied. Now, though, Claudia hugged her. "How *are* you?" she said.

It wasn't clear what exactly Claudia was referring to: Obviously she'd heard about Anna's mother, but did she know that Anna had been living back at home? She smiled noncommittally. "I'm okay."

"I'm so glad you came," Claudia said, squeezing her arm.

It sounded sincere, but before Anna could respond the front door flew open and a group of guys arrived together, provoking a boisterous round of back slaps and hugs. There was Leo, and Gavin. Anna saw Kim quickly scour the room for her, eyebrows raised. Anna gave her a nod. She watched as Gavin was met with more slaps and handshakes, handed one drink and then another. He looked a little like a hipster, Anna thought, as he threaded his way across the room. He was wearing a checkered button-down, red-and-white and fitted across his chest.

"Well, hi," she said, when he was standing in front of her.

Gavin didn't even bother speaking before he folded her into a hug. She could smell the cold on his shirt. He held her tightly, and it occurred to her that he would have heard everything from Brian.

"How are you?"

"I'm good."

He stepped back, holding her loosely by the shoulders. "Really?"

"Really."

"You look good," he said, and she resisted dwelling on what this meant—good as in thin? Good as in healthy? The truth was, it probably meant nothing.

"You do too," she said. "You look different."

He laughed. "Thanks?" he said, but his expression was concerned. "So you've been home now for a while, right?"

"I was," she said. "But I'm going back next semester. It was a rough beginning, but now I'm doing better—"

"Hey, Newland!" someone shouted over his shoulder, followed by a hard clap on the back. Then Gavin was swept up in another round of greetings, ushered toward the round of shots someone had lined up on the dining room table. Anna watched as Mindy Reddy ran over to kiss him on the cheek. Then Brian and Leo emerged from the kitchen, snow dusting their hair and shoulders. They had each packed a few weak snowballs, which they pelted at Mindy and Tara, who obligingly shrieked.

This, Anna thought, was a detail she would file away to tell Luke tomorrow. All night, she'd been collecting little stories she wanted to remember. She realized this was slightly unorthodox, seeing that they hadn't even met yet in person—in truth, she didn't really know him, though he was so easy to be herself around, it felt like she did. *What if I have nothing to say to you in real life?* she'd asked him in the coffee shop that afternoon. *It's true, I'm pretty intimidating*, he'd replied.

About their plans to meet, she had told only Kim and Janie. Tomorrow Luke was driving down to Portland in the used truck his dad had tipped him off to buying. On the way, he would stop in Stafford and meet her at the mall. When he'd first suggested it, the very concept had been unimaginable, but she also knew that Luke, leaving home, was facing his own hard thing. *Inside or outside?* she'd asked, and he'd answered, *Your call.* Her first instinct had been the parking lot, as far from the building as possible, but she reconsidered. *Fountain by the escalators*, she told him. If she was doing this, it seemed important that she walk through the door herself.

At first, hearing about this plan, Kim and Janie were incredulous, and appropriately wary. *You mean the Facebook guy?* Anna had given them access to transcripts of their conversations, and they'd conceded that he seemed sweet. She hadn't told anyone else. Not Theresa, and not her mother, though Anna had managed to awkwardly ask her impression of her old student—*the one who wrote that thing online*, she'd said. *Luke Finch?* her mother had replied. She'd been reading but looked up, and her face took on a faraway look. *He was quiet. Observant, obviously. Though at the time I didn't appreciate it.* Then she paused, and looked so troubled and regretful that Anna wished she hadn't asked.

Janie and Kim appeared by her side with shots of Kahlúa. "One, two, three," Kim said, and they swallowed them. Anna's insides glowed.

"I miss you guys," Kim said, resting her head on Anna's shoulder. "How was it with Gavin?"

"Fine," she said. "Nice, actually."

"She's impervious to Gavin," Janie said. "She's thinking about her new boyfriend." But Anna wasn't. She was watching as someone stepped through the front door. Anna had pictured her so often, staring back from that dressing room mirror, felt trapped alongside her so many times she seemed more imaginary than real. Yet there she was: Laura Mack. Her face was less round than Anna had remembered, less freckled. Her skin was blotchy from the cold. She wore striped mittens, a matching hat. Anna was struck by the actuality of her, the immediacy of her presence. It was both ordinary and surprising. In Anna's mind, Laura Mack's life had paused in that dressing room: been rendered paralyzed, stuck. Yet here she was at a party, the most normal of parties. She was shrugging off her parka and tossing it on the coat pile. She was pressing both palms to her cold cheeks. In one hand, she took the plastic cup that someone offered. With the other, she brushed snow from the ends of her hair. Her knuckles were red, her fingernails tipped with silver sparkles. It was December, and it was snowing. She was smiling. She was making her way into the room.

Acknowledgments

As a teacher, I have the good fortune of working with the tremendously talented students at the University of the Arts. Their creativity, drive, and generosity—including thoughtful feedback on these pages—have kept me motivated and inspired throughout the writing of this book. Thank you to my students in the Creative Writing program and to my colleagues Rahul Mehta and Zach Savich.

Thank you to the brilliant women who have helped see this novel to completion. Katherine Fausset has believed in this book since it was a different book entirely and guided it steadfastly into being ever since. Emily Griffin embraced the original idea and gave wise advice on the early chapters. Millicent Bennett's amazingly scrupulous edits, countless readings and rereadings—not to mention unfailing good cheer—helped this book immeasurably in finding its final form. From the beginning, everyone at Grand Central has treated this book with enthusiasm and care, and I am grateful.

Thanks to Krissy Clark, Bill Gillespie, Maureen Gillespie, Chris Villere, Brian Sung, Sarah Bernstein, Brian Gallagher, and Phil Juska for fact-checking and quick, smart input.

To Betty Bonshoff, Mike and Jil Hollenbach, Susie Hollenbach, and Emily and Shaun O'Connor for letting me borrow their quiet houses to write in.

To my mother, Dolores Juska, without whose help babysitting and on-call editing I would not have finished this book until 2025.

To my husband, Jake, who made it possible for me to write this book and did so steadily, patiently, and gladly. It was a gift.

And to Theo, who was born the day after I received the book contract. You tell the very best stories.

About the Author

Elise Juska is the author of four previous novels, including *The Blessings*, a Barnes & Noble Discover Great New Writers selection and one of the *Philadelphia Inquirer*'s Best Books of 2014. Her fiction and nonfiction have appeared in *Ploughshares*, the *Gettysburg Review*, the *Missouri Review*, *Good Housekeeping*, the *Hudson Review*, *Prairie Schooner*, and many other publications. She is the recipient of the Alice Hoffman Prize for Fiction from *Ploughshares* and her work has been cited in *The Best American Short Stories*. She lives outside Philadelphia and directs the undergraduate Creative Writing program at the University of the Arts, where she received the 2014 Lindback Award for Distinguished Teaching.

B²